THE ALIAS AGENDA

Also by Holly James

The Big Fix

HOLLY
JAMES

kensingtonbooks.com

This book is a work of fiction. Names, characters, businesses, organizations, places, events, and incidents either are the product of the author's imagination or are used fictitiously. Any resemblance to actual persons, living or dead, events, or locales is entirely coincidental.

To the extent that the image or images on the cover of this book depict a person or persons, such person or persons are merely models, and are not intended to portray any character or characters featured in the book.

KENSINGTON BOOKS are published by

Kensington Publishing Corp.
900 Third Avenue
New York, NY 10022

All Kensington titles, imprints, and distributed lines are available at special quantity discounts for bulk purchases for sales promotion, premiums, fund-raising, educational, or institutional use. Special book excerpts or customized printings can also be created to fit specific needs. For details, write or phone the office of the Kensington Special Sales Manager: Attn. Special Sales Department, Kensington Publishing Corp., 900 Third Avenue, New York, NY 10018. Phone: 1-800-221-2647.

ISBN: 978-1-4967-5259-8

First Kensington Trade Edition: May 2026

ISBN: 978-1-4967-5177-5 (ebook)

10 9 8 7 6 5 4 3 2 1

Printed in the United States of America

The authorized representative in the EU for product safety and compliance
is eucomply OU, Parnu mnt 139b-14, Apt 123
Tallinn, Berlin 11317, hello@eucompliancepartner.com

For my little one, who was along for the ride.

CHAPTER 1

Vivian Martel's phone woke me with a start. I would have been annoyed with her if I hadn't been pretending to *be* her. And if I'd actually been asleep.

Peaceful rest evaded someone with my lifestyle. Too much time away from consciousness was dangerous. It took no more than a voice, a car door, a heavy footstep—things often signifying *run*—to snap me awake. Or the case that rarely signified good news—the one happening at the moment—a phone call in the dark pit of night.

I slithered a bare arm from beneath the sheets soft as butter and snatched the phone off the nightstand, not daring to wake the man in an enviable state of oblivion beside me. I knew he was out, *really* out, thanks to the pill I had slipped in his drink, and I was hoping to catch a little shut-eye for myself in the cocoon of his high-rise bedroom before I had to finish the job and make my escape. But still, I needed to be quiet.

His blood was as blue as it came, and his hands were filthy. A Wall Street stereotype so deep into insider trading, he was lucky they'd sent me to extract the incriminating evidence and not someone with a tire iron.

Unknown flashed on the phone's screen, and as soon as I saw it, I wanted to go back to sleep even if it was restless and fleeting.

I knew who was calling. There was nothing unknown about it. Every time I got a new phone, I saved his contact information under *Unknown* because it was safer that way. And on the rare occasion it truly was an unknown number calling to offer me a free estimate on refinancing the auto loan I didn't have, it made for a pleasant surprise.

I blinked a dry eye at the time and was not amused. The contact lenses I'd been wearing to turn my blue eyes brown scratched like sandpaper. The same as the brunette wig squeezing my scalp, I couldn't wait to throw them in the trash.

"It's three a.m., Wallace," I hissed when I answered the phone.

"We're moving you."

The gruff voice came down the line with the same detached authority I had known since I was eighteen. I had heard that phrase more times than I could count, and every time, it upended and replanted my life somewhere new. Perhaps it was my semiconscious state, or maybe the city lights staring in the cold window at me, but the phrase sent a tingle down my spine. Something ominous flickered inside it.

"What? The job's not done. I'm still—"

"Then finish it. *Now.* You'll be in California by morning on the West Coast."

I glanced over my shoulder at the sleeping man beside me. The sharp nose, the pale flesh of his throat. He looked stuck-up even passed out. He had gone to schools I had only seen in movies and was driven around in cars my dad had taught me how to hotwire before I hit puberty. He had *snob* written all over him, and having spent my life in the shadow of privilege, I didn't mind slipping that pill in his pinot and hacking his laptop while he slept.

But I wasn't finished.

The computer had bio security, and I needed his fingerprint. I could get it easy enough once he was passed out—and I knew he'd be passed out for a solid four hours given the dose of that pill. But I was tired from the weeks of earning his trust that had led to this night and had planned to spend three and a half of those four hours curled into his luxury linens before I swiped the files the man on the phone needed and disappeared from his life as easily as I had come.

"What's in California?" I whispered.

I heard wind through the phone, sounds of walking, perhaps at a hurried pace. Wallace was outside somewhere.

"Your next job," he said. "Travel arrangements are at the usual drop. Your flight leaves at six a.m. Don't miss it."

I glanced at the time and considered whining about it, but that had gotten me nowhere as a smart-mouthed teenager and no further as an adult. After ten years together, I knew Wallace's boundaries like guardrails on a cliff. He was quick to remind me of why he owned me. Of why I wasn't in prison and how he could put me there faster than I could even consider running.

I swallowed my complaint and slipped from the bed, my bare feet pressing into the chilled hardwood floor. I straightened the little black dress I'd worn to dinner from where it had twisted around my hips. "What do I do with the files?"

"Leave the drive at the drop. It'll be collected."

The wind whistled again. I thought I heard something catch in Wallace's throat, a scrape of a shoe on pavement. I glanced out the yawning bedroom window at an American flag hanging perfectly limp on the rooftop across the street. The spring evening stood quiet and calm. Wherever Wallace was, it wasn't the Upper East Side.

"Where are you?"

I listened to his footsteps as his breathing grew heavier. Even nearing retirement, Wallace was in excellent shape. The tremor in his breath reminded me not of someone sucking air for being unfit but of someone breathing at a rate related to emotion, namely an emotion I had felt many times over the years thanks to positions he had put me in.

Fear.

"Are you all right?" I asked him as I tiptoed from the bedroom toward the office. I had to collect the laptop and return for a fingerprint.

Wallace ignored my question and asked his own. "Can you finish the job before you go?"

I rolled my eyes as I passed a towering vase in the entryway crawling with ornate, hand-painted roses, which looked like it should have been on display in a museum. It was hideous, and probably priceless, and I considered pushing it over on my way out.

"I'm working on it."

I rounded into the office and caught a glimpse of the man's safe mounted low in the glossy floor-to-ceiling bookshelf. The thought of cracking it flirted with my focus, trying to lure me away from the job I had to do. The chance it held what I needed—the thing I'd spent ten years searching for—was impossible, as was the case with every home safe I saw. I might find a Rolex in there, some heirloom jewelry, maybe a gun—helpful things, but not what I needed. But still, every locked door signaling *keep out* made me wonder.

I shook off the thought and continued around to the desk. I jumped, but not at my ghostly reflection hovering in the black windows. A loud crack rang through the phone, and Wallace sucked in a breath. I couldn't place the sound. A breaking branch? Something clattering onto concrete? Something . . . worse?

"Get the job done and get to the airport," he demanded.

The dark edge in his voice put a skip in my step. I hurried back to the bedroom and crawled up onto the bed. The man still wore what he'd worn to dinner too, minus his shoes and the tie I'd seductively unwound from his neck as I pulled him into his bedroom. He lay flat on his back, one arm curled above his head and gentle snores coming from his parted lips. I had kissed his lips once, and it had been a good kiss as far as deceitful kisses went. He had already swallowed the pill at that point, and the kiss would be the last thing he remembered before waking to the authorities pounding on his door later that morning.

A pang of regret snapped through me that on the rare occasions I got a kiss, it was never real. There'd been a few between-job hookups, sure, but nothing lasting because that was impossible for me. I tried not to dwell on it as I pressed the sleeping man's index finger into the pad on his laptop. The lock screen dissolved into the password prompt, and I tapped in the code I had recovered with some covert spying.

Alas, access.

I pulled a flash drive from my clutch on the nightstand and shoved it into the laptop.

The man grumbled in his sleep, and I froze, my hands splayed across the keyboard. I knew he was knocked out, but perhaps he could sense his secrets being extracted like gold from a digital mine. I felt a moment of pity for him, then took one glance around the ostentatious room: the sleek flat-screen TV, the marble-top furniture, the original art—all things he'd procured by stealing other people's money—and changed my mind.

"Got it," I told Wallace and shut the laptop with a soft click.

I stood from the bed and searched for my shoes. The night that had led to drugging the man in his own home began with a five-star dinner, in heels and a dress he would want to peel off of me, and if Wallace wanted me to get to the airport on time, I hoped he had stashed a change of clothes at the drop because an extra pit stop was not in the cards. No way was I flying across the country in stilettos and a cocktail dress, though it wouldn't have been the most inconvenient thing I had done in the name of staying out of prison.

"Good girl," Wallace said, and I gnashed my teeth at the phrase.

He had been saying it like I was a trained poodle since I was a teenager, back when I first became his pawn. I hated it, and he knew I hated it. And we both knew it served as a reminder of who was in charge.

I left the laptop on the bed. It would be a dead giveaway something was off when the man woke to his computer in my place, but it didn't matter. I would be in the wind. A ghost. A sweet memory turning sour as the gravity of what I had done to him took hold.

With a final look at him, I tiptoed from the room. I sighed. "See you in California, I guess," I told Wallace.

A long pause filled the line. The wind kept whistling until a car door sharply cut it off. Wallace's voice came back with the rounded resonance of someone speaking inside a small space. He took a deep, wavering breath. "Don't miss your flight, Erin."

He hung up, and I froze by the hideous vase in the entryway. I stared at my phone, shocked by what I had just heard.

No one had called me by my real name in ten years.

CHAPTER 2

Wallace had in fact left a change of clothes at the drop, and by the time I landed in California, my gratitude for the yoga pants, hoodie, and sneakers was overwhelming. My head ached; my body craved sleep. Or caffeine. Whichever I could get my hands on first.

The DSA didn't fly anyone first class unless the covert occasion called for it. I had spent the past six hours wedged in a middle seat, head bobbing between a guy with a man bun who smelled like patchouli and a woman who somehow managed to read a book with her whole body. She sighed, gasped, jerked in surprise, bent the poor spine until it broke, and laughed out loud more than once. Great to know it was such a good book, but did it need to be read at the crack of dawn on a cross-country flight beside someone who hadn't had a decent night's sleep in a decade?

No. No, it did not.

The full-body read-a-thon paired with the patchouli-scented hippie who had to be returning to his yurt in the weed-growing California redwoods left me in a spectacularly foul mood.

You pulled out all the stops for this one, I planned to tell Wallace as soon as I saw him.

I did my best. It was last minute, he would say and maybe

mean it but probably not because he would have flown in on something chartered. Or maybe he had already been here when he called me last night, I couldn't say.

I also intended to ask him the reason for the last-minute move, and fully expected him to grumble something about urgency and DSA priority, which I knew was less the reason and more a reminder, again, that I was at his mercy.

That day ten years ago when my father had gotten arrested by the FBI and I, his accomplice, had been intercepted by an agency so off-the-books no one knew about it, I had no idea what I was walking into. I had fled the hotel room where our job had gone terribly wrong and ended up on a stormy street in the pouring rain with blood on my adolescent hands and a gun pointed at me. I may well have made a deal with the devil. Desperate and completely alone, I'd handed over my life to the government rather than follow my father to prison.

Sometimes, I wondered if prison would have been the better option.

No one even knew the DSA existed. I certainly hadn't until working for it became my life. The Directorate of Secret Affairs was the interstitial tissue between organizations the likes of the FBI and CIA but with fewer rules and more secrets. It filled gaps the others couldn't. Sidestepped funding pipelines and operated invisibly other than to those in the know. I was more in the know than I ever wanted to be but still often in the dark. Wallace doled out only the necessary information to me, which was why I had to trust he knew what was going on when he told me what to do.

I usually got a break between jobs. A spell of reprieve to get out of Dodge after whatever hammer I'd been helping to lower dropped. I'd ditch the disguise—wigs, contacts, whatever wardrobe fit the role I'd been playing—and go back to being me, Erin, whoever that was. Wallace would set me up in a small apartment or house with some flat-box furniture and the occasional bloodstain under the rug from whatever DSA purpose it had previously served, but never for long enough to feel like home.

I hadn't had one of those since my mother died when I was twelve.

I really wasn't sure what the rush was all about this time, but ever faithful, I made the drop and caught my flight.

Once I deplaned, I exited the airport like every other wearied traveler. I toted only the backpack Wallace had stuffed with the essentials: ID, new phone preloaded with accounts in my new name, address, the key to whatever new set of four walls would serve as my living quarters.

Would it kill him to pack me a snack?

The coffee cart near the exit caught my eye, and seeing I had no idea how far a drive it was to the rendezvous point, I decided to fuel up.

"Name?" the bouncy barista asked from behind the counter, pen hovering and ready to ink.

A tangle of identities pulsed and retracted inside my mind. My trained tongue patiently waited for permission to shape around the correct choice. I had gone to bed in New York as Vivian and arrived in California as someone else.

The fleeting moment in between I had spent as myself, when Wallace uttered my real name before ending our call, had stuck like a seed in my teeth. I wasn't sure why he'd done it; maybe another reminder of the girl I once was, that day in the hotel and the choice I made. I couldn't be sure, but hearing it was a haul back to memories that haunted my plane ride as I slipped in and out of consciousness. Promises, lies. The sweet smile my father trained me to wield as a weapon, which would ultimately lead to my downfall.

I shook the thoughts away and gave the barista a smile.

"Lauren," I said, using the name on my new fake ID stuffed in the bag.

The double espresso scorched my tongue when I impatiently sipped it. I waited at the curb for my rideshare as a never-ending stream of cars passed like different shaped beads on a string. Wallace sent me to Silicon Valley, where the ratio of electric vehicles to standards was truly something to behold.

My own driver pulled up to collect me in a nondescript gray Prius and returned to the stream of curbside traffic as smoothly as a raindrop into a river. I gazed out the window as we navigated a complicated knot of freeways and exits. My knowledge of the local geography was basic at best, but I knew I was at the bottom of the bay, and San Francisco waited somewhere to the north with its foggy shores and impossible hills.

And just north of that, clung to a picturesque shoreline, was the prison housing my father. I hadn't seen him since that hotel room ten years ago and had no intention of getting near, regardless of whatever reason Wallace had brought me to the area. Still, I could feel his presence pulsing like a wound in the distance.

Thankfully, we weren't heading up the peninsula, but rather across the lower belly, down by where its appendix would be. After nearly an hour, my driver stopped on a street lined with more electric cars, hedgerows, and giant oaks swaying in the breeze. The trim lawns shone a deep shade of emerald and the flower borders popped like colorful confetti. We'd pulled up outside a small apartment complex sitting at the top of a T intersection, and diagonally across the street from some of the most beautiful houses I'd ever seen.

"Ma'am?" the driver awkwardly asked. "This the right spot?"

I caught myself gaping in a daze. I had no idea how long we had been idling at the curb.

"Yes, it is," I said, trying to sound like Lauren, the woman who had been driven home from the airport and not like the informant in a hoodie who had landed in Pleasantville with a fake name. "Thank you," I told the driver. I climbed out into the air, which smelled like freshly clipped lawn and baking bread.

The driver pulled away as I spun in a slow circle, taking it all in.

It was a street from a storybook. Charming homes, each similar but unique, as if they came from the same cookie factory but had been stamped with a different cutter. Shiny cars, dogs on leashes, strollers, children's laughter on the air. The apartments were spitting distance from the mansions, and yet seamlessly blended into the neighborhood.

It was a far cry from the places Wallace had sent me before. I'd seen dumps, hovels, crack houses with bullet-riddled walls. My last job landed me in the lap of Manhattan luxury, and I had been a few similar places before, but this place, this street, was like nowhere I had ever been. Standing on the sidewalk beneath a mighty oak felt like a warm, protected embrace, and I couldn't imagine what lurked beneath that warranted Wallace sending me here.

I stopped spinning and matched the address in my file to the apartments. The boxy beige building was U-shaped with two stories, outdoor staircases, and front doors that opened to outside. Based on the apartment number in the file, I'd be living in the first-floor corner space. It was nothing like the Manhattan apartment I'd spent last night in, but it still looked upscale and welcoming.

The espresso in my veins and my lack of sleep had me jittery—more jittery than usual when I began a new job. I never knew what Wallace had in store for me, what file he would slap down on the table to lay out the plan: the targets, the stakes, the goal. It was my job to get information he couldn't. I slipped into cracks where he didn't fit.

We could help each other, he'd said to me that night so many years ago.

At the time, it sounded like a good deal: Go undercover or risk going to prison until I was forty. If only I had known how imbalanced the *each other* part of that deal was. If only I had known how much more help I would be providing than receiving. Although Wallace had kept his word. I hadn't ever seen the inside of a cell. But in exchange, I had become a nomad informant. A true specter in the wind.

The truth was, when he'd looked at me that night my father and I got caught, he not only saw someone desperate, but he also saw someone useful. A blond, doll-eyed key with a sweet smile who could fit into locks a middle-aged man with a mustache that screamed *Authority* couldn't.

Exploited, would be a proper description.

I followed the little sidewalk bisecting a trim green lawn and leading to the building, and pulled out my key. Right as I reached for the door to my new place, the neighboring door swung open.

A young woman stepped out backward, humming a soft tune and bouncing. She pulled her door shut, and turned to reveal a baby attached to her chest by a complicated tangle of fabric. Two pudgy brown legs sprouted from the bottom of the little sack, softly kicking against her abdomen.

"Oh!" She stopped short but instantly smiled a row of shockingly white teeth. "You must be the new neighbor!" Her cheeks pulled like rounded plums toward her dark eyes, setting her whole face aglow with welcome. She wore running leggings and a bright yellow band in her hair, which matched her sneakers. She marched over, managing not to break stride with the bouncing, and held out a determined hand. "I'm Alisha. I'm so happy to meet you!"

I spent enough time lying to know when people were telling the truth, and Alisha's welcome was nothing but genuine.

"Hi. I'm . . . Lauren."

The name took a moment to recover, perhaps because of the

disorienting kindness radiating off my new neighbor, or perhaps due to my lack of sleep and the espresso drilling a raw hole in the pit of my stomach. I hoped Wallace stocked the fridge.

"It's *so* nice to meet you!" Alisha squeaked. "And this is Jeffrey!" She leaned forward, holding her hand to the back of the tiny head bobbling inside her harness. From inside her pouch, enormous brown eyes blinked up. A tiny bubble popped from Jeffrey's bow lips.

I had precisely zero experience with babies, and very little interest to be honest, but even I couldn't deny Jeffrey was cute.

"He's sweet." I dutifully smiled.

"Yes, we just *eat him up!*" Alisha's voice turned into something between a dog's squeaky chew toy and a feral animal in heat. "Anyway, we saw them bringing in new furniture the other day, so the girls and I assumed we'd have a new neighbor soon." She paused to look up and down the street for signs of a moving van as I made note of the *new furniture* comment and sent a silent thanks to Wallace.

I gave her a tight smile. "The girls? Do you have more than just Jeffrey?"

She tilted her head in confusion before nodding in understanding. "Oh, Jeffrey is not mine. I'm his nanny," she said, still bouncing, and waved one hand over her head in a loop. "I meant the other girls in the complex. This is basically nanny central."

I blankly stared at her, unsure how to respond. Luckily, she kept the conversation flowing. "I work for the Wilson family." She pointed over my shoulder, back down the storybook street. "Jeffrey and I were out for a walk, and I remembered I'd left something at home, so we stopped by. I'm glad I ran into you! Welcome to the neighborhood!"

"Thank you," I said, hoping she wasn't about to ask me more about my reason for being here.

I could lie, sure I could—and I was really good at it—but I usually never had to until after Wallace briefed me on my new identity. All I knew about Lauren was her address and that she had a very friendly neighbor named Alisha.

Alisha kept smiling at me. "I'm sure you're excited to get started with—"

"Ms. Thomas?" someone said from the sidewalk.

We both turned to see a tall man in a suit with a leather messenger bag looped over his shoulder. I immediately clocked the telltale but discreet bulge at his hip.

"Lauren Thomas?" the man said as if it were a statement and a question at once.

"Yes," I said, recognizing my new name and feeling more certain this man had arrived to help me.

"Hi. I'm Age—*nt*." He caught himself with a deep blush, glancing at Alisha. "*The* agent. I'm the real estate agent." He recovered with a smile that wobbled at the edges and gave him a boyish look. The sun glossed his wavy brown hair into a shine. An eagerness rolled off him, which I could feel from a distance.

Alisha looked between the two of us, confused, and I silently begged her to go away.

"Right, yes. I forgot we had a meeting this morning. Please, won't you come in," I said to the man on the sidewalk.

Alisha, mercifully, took her cue to leave. "I'll see you later, Lauren. It was so nice to meet you."

I gave her a small wave as the man in the suit approached with wide steps in shiny shoes, which softly clicked on the pavement. When he arrived on my doorstep, I smelled soap and mint and realized he was a lot taller than I had thought.

My key was suddenly sweaty in my hand, and I hoped I was right about the man with a gun I was about to let into my new apartment.

CHAPTER 3

The door opened to a small entryway. A sunny living room sat to the right, furnished with a suede couch, pale wood end tables, and a pile of cream-colored throws and pillows, which looked like clouds.

I took it in with an approving nod, noting Wallace had taken care to supply the caliber of furniture fit for the neighborhood. No flat-box anything in Lauren Thomas's place.

I turned to my left and saw a kitchen with a high-top dining table, a hutch hanging with colorful coffee mugs, stainless steel appliances, and a fridge I hoped contained food.

I dropped my backpack and turned to my guest.

He closed the front door behind him and gave me a stiff smile. I had taken in his height on the doorstep, but up close and inside, the size of his body beneath his suit became apparent. His shoulders strained the slim lines; the fabric left little mystery about the shape of his biceps. He was large and strong and probably looked fantastic in a tight T-shirt. The angles of his face, though sharp, landed easy on the eyes: knives for cheekbones, ski-slope nose, eyes the color of a foggy day at the beach. And lips. Lips that made me wonder what one kiss would feel like, real or not. The only break from the symmetry was a small scar near his jaw. A jagged slash that looked like it had been deep once upon a time.

As I stared at him with curiosity blossoming somewhere deep in my belly, I noted he was not gazing around the space like someone would upon visiting another's home, which more likely than not meant he had visited this home before.

He took a step toward me, and I held my ground though reflex told me to step back. I wanted the upper hand.

"Hi," he said, sounding more uncertain than I expected for a man of his size. "Sorry about that out there. I didn't mean to slip in front of your neighbor. I'm not your real estate agent. I'm—"

"I know who you are."

He paused and tilted his head like he really wasn't sure. "How?" His jacket gently flapped when he adjusted his bag, and I saw my chance to really take the upper hand.

I stepped forward, reducing the space between us and feeling the warmth of his body. Another whiff of his clean scent hit me, and I wondered what I smelled like after donning clothes stuffed in a backpack and taking a cross-country flight.

"Well, first, you called me by a name that until eight hours ago was hidden in a locker only two people know the combination to. So, you either intercepted some highly classified information, or you're already privy to said information."

He blinked long lashes at me, looking legitimately surprised, and I felt a pang of tenderness at his innocence.

And then I dove on my opportunity.

Without dropping his eyes, I reached my hand out to his hip. Quicker than a lightning crack, I breached the warm pocket of air stuck between his jacket and torso. My fingers tingled when they brushed the smooth fabric of his shirt then closed around cold metal. My heart hit my ribcage in a thrilling surge both at what I was doing and at the fact I was so close to him. Before he knew what had hit him, I pulled his gun from its holster and held it between us, pointed at the ceiling.

"And then there's your gun." I gave him a sly grin. "Standard DSA issue," I said, glancing at the markings and happy to see I was right. In truth, I hadn't been one-hundred percent sure until that moment.

He sucked in a breath and reached for it like a kid grasping at a loose balloon string.

I yanked it away and handily released the clip with a few clicks. I knew how to handle a gun long before I became the DSA's errand girl. I held the disassembled parts in each hand with a smug grin. "What, did you graduate the Academy last week? Gotta be quicker than that, ace."

His dagger cheekbones spotted red, and the soft curve of his lips went thin and colorless.

My smile grew bigger. "And I also know you're left-handed, but now I'm just showing off." I nodded at the holster on his left hip and handed him the pieces of his weapon. I brushed my hands together and pivoted toward the kitchen.

The sharp click of a firearm being reloaded rang out behind me. His footsteps quickly followed.

"You can't tamper with DSA equipment," he said, flustered.

I swung open the fridge and found a modest offering: milk, butter, something green and leafy in the crisper, apples, a brick of cheese, and a dozen eggs. I reached for the cheese and an apple, then started opening cabinets, looking for the pantry.

"If that *is* actually a crime, I suggest you keep a closer eye on your equipment, so you don't get us both in trouble."

I caught his frown from across the room. He holstered his gun and placed his messenger bag on the table. In the third cabinet I tried, I found some pantry staples: rice, beans, canned soup, cooking oil, and what I had come for: a box of crackers. I dumped a pile on a plate, found a knife, and carried the first meal I had had since New York to my new dining table.

The man in the suit, who still didn't have a name, cautiously watched me slice the cheese. The pointy little paring knife was hardly longer than my finger, but I enjoyed the look on his face at the sight of it in my hand. Just for fun, I deftly twirled it like a small propeller and then sliced the apple with five quick cuts in as many seconds, and let it fall open like a star on the plate. I picked up a wedge and bit it with a chunk of cheese. "Want some?" I asked, pushing the plate toward him.

He stared at me both like I was the most interesting thing he'd ever seen and like he was a little afraid.

"When is Wallace getting here?" I asked around a slice of apple.

The pause was not long, but it was palpable, and it shot a bolt of concern straight up my spine. Wallace always met me at a new job. Every time. Landing in the gorgeous neighborhood already felt off, and now his absence had me feeling like I was standing on a tilted floor.

The man stuck out his hand. "I think we got off on the wrong foot."

I chewed and swallowed my apple slice. "By *foot* do you mean that I disarmed you in under ten seconds and then made you a snack?"

His frustration was obvious and damn it, if it wasn't charming. I sensed a balance in him, a softness and a strength, and I hazarded a guess based on his size and shape coupled with the way he was trying to look authoritative but coming off endearing instead that he struggled to keep that balance from tipping too far in one direction.

"I'm Agent Bray. Calvin Bray."

"Nice to meet you, Cal," I said, trying to keep my cool over the strange situation. "I assume you know my real name, but you'll be calling me Lauren for the duration of this flight, wherever it is we are headed." I plopped another chunk of cheese in my mouth. "And again, I ask, where's Wallace?"

My feigned indifference to a new identity bounced off him

like a rubber ball. His eyes softened. "This must be hard for you. Moving around all the time."

A fiery lump lodged in my throat and almost made me choke. He held my gaze with a look I never once saw in Wallace's eyes—in anyone's, really, perhaps save my mother, but those memories were distant and clouded at best. No one ever took the time to care. And now this agent fresh from the Academy with bottomless eyes and kiss-me lips was staring at me like he wanted to read my diary.

I forced the cheese down with a painful swallow and smiled. "This must be your first time working with a CI. We can't afford to have feelings." I took the knife to the cheese block with an aggressive whack, which made him lean back. "Speaking of business, are you going to tell me why I'm here? And where Wallace is?"

Memory of my phone call in the small hours of the night came back to me. The whistling wind, that cracking sound, the hitch in Wallace's breath. The way he'd called me Erin. All of it was off, and pairing it with his absence had me fighting to hide my nerves.

"You have been passed to me," Bray said.

A rustle called my attention to the files he had spread on the table. I had drifted off thinking about my phone call. I watched his long fingers separate sheets of paper with an elegance that made me wonder if he played an instrument. Probably something classy like the piano or violin. Try as I might, I could not picture Calvin Bray holding a guitar or drumsticks.

"I've been *passed* to you? I've been with Wallace for ten years; I don't get passed to anyone, especially not some rookie."

Bray bristled, then flipped through his papers like he was searching for patience. "I got word yesterday you would be arriving here, and I was to meet you. Please, if you have a seat, I'll fill you in on this case."

I arched a brow at him and pointedly did not sit.

"Fine," he said with a matching arched brow. He spread the files to show a smattering of DMV records photocopied above bullet point lists: occupation, income, known medical conditions. I had seen it all before; the *CliffsNotes* summary of people's lives. The DSA could get its hands on pretty much anything.

"This is one of the most exclusive neighborhoods in this area. The families are like local royalty," Bray continued. "They sit on boards, work for the major tech companies, lead community groups." He placed the photo of a gorgeous woman below a photo of an equally attractive man and pointed at them. "Melanie and Scott Browning. He's a lead software engineer; she's a stay-at-home mom."

The couple glorified suburban chic, even in their driver's license photos. Melanie smiled like a beauty queen, her hair rolling in golden waves. Scott looked like a prom king.

"Jana and Paolo Russo." He placed another set of photos beside them, again with the husband on top and the wife below. These ones showed a couple with matching dark hair. Paolo had thick brows and olive skin, Jana had delicate facial bones and sharp eyes. "He's a venture capitalist, and she's a stay-at-home mom."

He produced two more photos and laid them out in the same order.

"And Sandra Whitley and Michael Vassar. He's a web designer, and she's a—"

"Stay-at-home mom?" I finished for him, sensing a trend.

He smiled sideways at me, a hint of smugness shading his eyes. "Actually, no. She's a freelance writer."

I picked up Sandra's photo with a curious frown. The woman coyly smiled back like she guarded a secret. Something in her eyes put an uneasy prickle in my belly. I set the photo down. "So, what are they up to?"

Bray straightened Sandra Whitley's photo so it lined up perfectly with Melanie's beside it. I wondered if it was a nervous habit. Or maybe he was just a control freak. "We have reason to believe Melanie, Sandra, and Jana are key players in a smuggling operation."

I balked and managed to keep a quiet *whoa* from slipping out. I had seen many things over my years aiding the DSA, but I never would have guessed the Stepford Wives would be up to no good. I fully expected Bray to point to the husbands, or perhaps suggest the whole set was involved in some underground sex cult.

I traced a fingertip over Sandra's photo again since it was closest, my mind running wild with potential. "What's their operation?"

Bray reached out and straightened the photo again. "Baby products," he said with such sincerity, I thought it had to be a joke.

"Are you serious?"

His face said he was completely serious. "The baby goods market is a nearly seventy-billion-dollar-a-year industry. Do you know how much a quality stroller costs? The BuggyBaby X3 is the hottest status symbol on the market right now and retails for almost nine hundred dollars. These women are running some backdoor scheme getting goods imported illegally and reselling them to turn a profit. The problem is, I can't find their supplier or where they keep their merchandise. They have to have a warehouse somewhere with the numbers they're turning over."

The sudden image of Sandra Whitley hawking a stroller in an alley almost made me laugh. I bit my lips because Bray was not laughing. "What evidence do you have?"

He slipped a new photo from his file, this one of a shiny black SUV. "Well, for one thing, Ms. Whitley recently got a new Porsche, and the financials don't add up."

A spark of irritation sizzled at the back of my throat, and I couldn't stop it coming out my mouth. "Because a woman couldn't afford that car? You said she's a freelance writer."

Bray frowned. "That's a ninety-thousand-dollar car. Unless she's ghostwriting for the president, she's not making that kind of money."

I silently and reluctantly agreed with him.

"But the real red flag is her husband. Michael Vassar recently got laid off, and she somehow pulls this beauty into the driveway a few weeks later?"

He made a good point, but I felt the need to play devil's advocate. It was something I did with Wallace all the time. Poke holes in the story, find the weak spots. It only served my benefit to know all the vulnerabilities.

"Maybe they are saving face. Husband gets fired, they don't want anyone to know, so they buy a status car."

He pursed his lips like he was considering it, and I watched the line of his jaw lift. The tiny scar stretched. "Maybe so, but even then, where did the money come from? I checked with the dealer: paid for in full on purchase. Cash."

I involuntarily scoffed. The rules for who could and couldn't run around with bags of money were drawn nearly parallel with those marking social class divisions. With the right skin color, outfit, and name, I could walk into a car dealership with ninety grand in my purse and drive off the lot, no problem. But someone else would be questioned as to how they came into the money in the first place. In some cases, they would probably be accused of stealing it. Sandra Whitley, blonde, brown eyes, five foot five, one-hundred-twenty pounds according to her driver's license, fell into the former camp, and the thought made me realize, with the right clothes on, so did I.

Well, so did Lauren Thomas.

And it was that moment I understood why I had been flown across the country to suburbia.

I looked up at Bray, who had stood beside me to lean over the photos. "So, you want me to infiltrate their operation. Their baby operation."

"Baby *products*," he corrected with a nod. "Don't say baby operation; it gives the wrong idea."

He made a good point. *Baby operation* could mean something else entirely.

"And yes. I can't crack them, so that's where you come in." He placed a hand on the table and angled his body toward me.

I eyed the length of his arm, the curve of his thumb where it rested atop the photos. His hands were clean, soft. I guessed he did a lot of desk work. "How exactly do I *come in* to this case, Agent Bray?"

His lips split into a grin, and he picked up the center photo. "Lucky for us, Melanie Browning needs a new nanny."

A laugh burst from my mouth. I had posed as many things over the years: a student, an art gallerist, an insurance agent, a cult member, a drug smuggler, a radicalized nutjob on the verge of domestic terrorism, but this . . . This might have been my hard limit.

"A *nanny?* I don't know anything about kids."

Bray gave a pleasant chuckle. "Come on, you have to have nieces and nephews or something. Friends with kids?"

I gave him a stare so flat it could have penetrated lead. "Have you read my file?"

His smile dropped, and I saw his Adam's apple bob when he gulped. "I read what I could. Parts of it are classified." His voice hitched with interest, but now was not the time to get into that element of my past.

"Then you know I have no siblings and had no childhood because my mom died when I was twelve and my father was a career criminal who used me as bait. Then when I was eighteen, he got himself sent to prison and almost took me with him. Lucky for me, the DSA was there to prey on a vulnerable young woman who bargained immunity in exchange for a life of servitude. Or is that last part not in my file?" I gave him an artificially sweet smile.

He looked mortified.

"So, in case it's not clear, no, I don't have any nieces or nephews. And you have to have friends in order to have friends with kids. Kind of a prerequisite, no? Hard to keep any gal pals around when you're constantly lying about your identity and moving cities all the time." My tone dripped with sarcasm, and a look of genuine remorse smoothed over his face.

"Look, Lauren, I'm sorry. I didn't mean anything by it. I just thought . . ."

I waited for him to finish his thought, but he didn't. He left the sting of my new name lodged in my chest like a thorn.

"It's fine. All part of the job." I gave him a tight smile, which didn't reach my eyes.

Bray tried to smile back, and most of it ended up in his eyes. The bottomless blue-gray swam with sympathy. It turned that thorn into something soft and warm. He released a tight breath and picked up Melanie's photo. Back to business. "She's kind of the queen bee of the neighborhood. I figure you get close to her, and we get close to the whole operation from the inside."

I took the photo and studied it. Melanie Browning's shiny smile reminded me of a tiger. I got the sense she knew how to hunt and enjoyed the thrill of toying with her prey. "What happened to her old nanny?"

"She fired her."

I had a feeling I knew the answer to my next question—or at least I knew what the answer would *not* be—but I asked anyway. "How many nannies has Melanie Browning fired?"

A telling beat of silence passed.

"Four."

I scoffed, hard, just as the doorbell rang.

Bray's hand snapped out and gripped my arm. Not forcefully, but protectively, and I put a little more faith in his reflexes. I felt the warmth of his curled fingers through my hoodie and decided not to shake him off. When his other hand moved to his holster, a nervous tingle started at the base of my spine.

"Who's that?" he whispered.

"Hopefully Wallace coming to save me from this," I muttered. "Why are you whispering and reaching for your gun?"

He looked down as if he suddenly realized he was holding on to me and his weapon. He dropped his grip from both and began shuffling all the photos back into a folder. "Sorry. Just . . . be careful."

I wasn't sure what I needed to be careful about in a place where contraband baby products were enough to call in one of the most secret off-the-record branches of the government, but still, I set off to answer the door with caution.

CHAPTER 4

It was not Wallace on the other side of the door, but a different familiar face, and it was only familiar because I had been looking at a photo of it moments before.

"Hey, neighbor!" Jana Russo greeted with a megawatt smile from behind a three-wheeled stroller she rolled back and forth like she was revving up to shove in the door. The front tire looked fit for off-roading. "I'm Jana. We've been watching to see when you would show up, and you're finally here!" She sang the final word like it had multiple syllables and tilted her body back and forth in rhythm to her song. Her dark hair lay in a heavy braid over her shoulder left bare by a drooping tunic top. A hot-pink flash of spandex painted her bronzed skin where her sports bra held up her chest swollen with motherhood. She expectantly smiled, as if waiting for me to ask her inside.

From the corner of my eye, I saw Bray take a step closer. Even if I wanted to, which I didn't, I couldn't very well invite Jana Russo in to meet the agent laying a trap for her as we spoke. And my brief interaction with him was enough to ensure me Bray couldn't convincingly pull off pretending to be a real estate agent for more than a few seconds. He would blow both of our covers.

I angled the door to shield my arm and discreetly waved him deeper into the kitchen and out of sight.

He shook his head in refusal.

Jana was still beaming, rolling her stroller. I managed to hold my own smile while clenching my jaw. Behind the open door, I pointed a stern finger at Bray, telling him to *back up*.

I heard him quietly huff before he sealed himself to the fridge, still in earshot and only inches out of sight.

"Hi there," I greeted. "I'm Lauren."

The name already fit like a well-worn glove.

"Lauren," Jana said as if she were rolling the word around her mouth, testing it out. She managed to keep smiling while she did it. A disarming energy pulsed off her, one perhaps planted in my mind thanks to the records tucked in Bray's file and everything he'd accused her of, but perhaps it was more than that. Perhaps it had to do with the way she said *we've been watching*. Also, they'd been waiting for me?

I scanned the street as if it might reveal which house Jana hailed from: the Tudor with paned windows and rose border, the Colonial with manicured hedges, the Craftsman with a porch swing and pull-through driveway. She had to have been watching from one of them if she managed to ring the doorbell so soon after my arrival.

I eyed the stroller and reconsidered. Perhaps she had been passing by on a walk and saw activity at the door.

But still. *We've been watching* was an odd thing to say.

"That's me," I said. "I've only just arrived. I'd invite you in, but the place is a mess." I stepped forward and pulled the door further closed, shielding any view of my neatly kempt new home and the lie I'd just told.

Jana's smile drooped for the slightest second as if disappointed she wouldn't get to scope out her new neighbor's place. "Oh, that's completely fine," she recovered. "I was just dropping by to say hi and invite you to movie night tonight. I know Melanie and the kids can't *wait* to meet you in person! They are so desperate for help. She'd be here saying hi too, but she's tied up right now." Her expectant smile returned as my brain spun and tried to keep up.

Usually, my assignments took weeks of careful infiltration. I would circle a target until I got close enough, until stepping inside came naturally. I was used to a considerable amount of patience and perseverance, and it appeared I'd already been shoved headfirst into this world.

I was too shocked to say anything.

"*Nanny*," Bray quietly coughed from around the corner, but not quietly enough.

Jana leaned to peek, and I mirrored her movement to block her view. "Is someone else here?" she asked, a smile returning to her face as if she were ready to make another acquaintance.

"No." I nervously laughed. "It's only me!"

"Huh. I thought I saw you walk in with a man. I assumed it was your husband."

I heard Bray shuffle. I waved my hand behind the door again, urging him to hold still. "Oh! No, that was my real estate agent stopping by, but he left."

Jana studied me with skepticism written all over her face. Thick tension hung between us, and I hoped Bray wasn't going to cough some other cryptic message and ruin it all. I was an excellent liar, but someone actively sabotaging me made for a different story.

Another smile crept over Jana's face, and, in the same way I knew my neighbor Alisha's was sincere, I could tell this one wasn't. "Well, I hope you can join us tonight!" she sang, back on point. "It would be a great way to meet everyone before you start your new position with the Brownings." She pointed over her shoulder at the Tudor on the corner, and I found it fitting the severely angled house, which looked like it would cut me if I touched it, belonged to the woman who had fired four nannies.

The last thing I wanted to do was socialize after my impromptu cross-country trip and identity change. I needed a moment to adjust.

"Oh, that's nice of you, but I can't—"

Bray loudly cleared his throat.

I decided to put an end to the standoff before he unintentionally did it for me.

"You know what? I'll think about it." I smiled at Jana. "I have to go right now." I shut the door and pivoted to glare at Bray. I held a finger to my mouth to silence him as I crossed toward the window to watch which way Jana went.

Jana waited on the doorstep for a moment, looking baffled for having had a door slammed in her face, before she did a three-point turn to move her stroller. She cast a curious look over her shoulder before turning left at the end of the walkway.

Satisfied to be rid of her, I turned around to deal with the agent in my kitchen and found myself face-first into his chest.

"*Jesus.* Do you have to stand so close?" I bounced backward, and his fresh smell tempered with the slightest bite of nervous perspiration lingered in my nose.

"Sorry," he muttered and released the two slats he had pinched open to see out the window. His arm remained hovering over my shoulder.

I looked up at him, and a charge passed between us. Something unnamed I felt crackling all the way to my fingertips.

I quickly sidestepped and moved away from the window. "So, I get that you're invested, but that's not how this is going to work, okay? I don't need you trying to intervene and screwing things up."

A look of surprise crossed Bray's face, as if he may have expected me to say something else. He cleared his throat. "Sorry. I just know you haven't been fully briefed yet, and she showed up out of nowhere. I didn't want you caught off guard."

I rounded the table and snatched another apple slice. His

apology seemed sincere. "Well, then why don't you finish briefing me, Agent Bray."

A tiny smile tugged at the corner of his mouth. He pulled a binder from his bag. "Everything you need to know is in here, but basically, you're lined up to start as Melanie Browning's new nanny ASAP. You've got an airtight background and references, come highly recommended, and aced your online interview. All that's left is a trial run."

I took the binder and skeptically frowned at him. "I *aced* my interview? I've never met this woman in my life, let alone interviewed with her. What are you talking about?"

He whipped out his phone and tapped at the screen before flipping it around to show me. "We generated your image and voice with AI from digital records we have at the DSA. Pretty cool, right?"

I gaped at the sight of myself on the screen. The fake was alarmingly convincing, right down to my mannerisms. I was not the least bit surprised the DSA had resources for such forgery. "Uh, cool is one word for it, I guess," I muttered.

"*I* think it's cool," he said and shoved his phone back in his pocket. "But the point is, you've already wowed them, so all that's left is to do it in person. You're set up to start working with them this week."

The sense I was being dragged by a moving train had me off-balance again. I set the file back on the table and held up my hands. "Wait. Let's just take a step back here. You still haven't told me where Agent Wallace is. Why isn't he here?" The answer to that question still had my nerves jumping.

Bray took a breath like he had to stop himself from barreling on with my brief. His face flattened. "I can't share that information."

I frowned at the non-answer. "Can't or won't?"

He stroked his hand over his jaw, and a wave of frustration pulsed off him. "Can't because I don't have it. Some of my clearance has been revoked due to a recent . . . *incident*, and the higher-ups don't feel I need to know that detail. All I know is you've been transferred to me, and I was supposed to meet you here."

The sense of being dragged by a train suddenly morphed into a stomach-dropping free fall. I struggled to process everything he'd said. Not only was he a rookie, but something had recently gone wrong enough to revoke his security clearance, and I was supposed to trust him?

"No," I said flatly.

He cocked a brow at me. "No, what?"

My heart had kicked up a gear. The implications of this new setup were too many to articulate, especially to someone as junior as him. "No, I'm not doing this. Not without talking to Agent Wallace."

He stubbornly stared back at me. "Like I said, I can't help you with that."

"Then find me someone who can."

He huffed an annoyed breath and put a hand on his hip. "What's the big deal? I always heard that guy was kind of an asshole. I thought you'd be happy to be free of him."

Again, another statement too loaded to unpack. "*Asshole*, yes, but my relationship with Wallace is . . . important."

It was perhaps the biggest understatement I'd ever made.

Bray looked at me with a purse of his lips, interest clearly piqued again. "Does the importance have to do with the classified parts of your file?"

"My security clearance to answer that has been revoked," I said with a smirk.

He narrowed his eyes to study me, apparently realizing I wasn't the pliable puppet he expected. After a few beats of silence, he put his hands on his hips again and nodded. "How about this: You do this nanny job for me, and I'll do what I can to get information on Wallace for you. Sound good?"

I mulled his offer. In truth, I didn't have much leverage to work with, other than being stubborn. That never got me anywhere with Wallace. Wallace had never even offered me a quid pro quo. The fact Bray was offering anything at all was a welcome change. And he was softly smiling at me, which I had to admit was hard to resist.

"Fine, but like I said: I don't know anything about kids."

His smile grew. "Better start reading then," he said, and handed me the binder.

I glared at him and felt the heft of it like a death sentence between my fingers.

"Plenty of time before movie night tonight." The smile on his handsome face had only grown, and I wished in that moment for the burly grouch I was used to dealing with.

"You better find out what happened to Wallace," I said.

"You'll know as soon as I know." He began gathering the papers on the dining table as if for distraction and like he didn't want to talk about it. "I need you prepared for this, Lauren. You're my only hope for cracking them at this point."

I flipped open the binder in my hands and skimmed the first page: the bullet-point life history of Lauren Thomas. "Well, then maybe you should have picked someone who knows how to be a nanny."

He slung his satchel over his shoulder. "Based on your case history, I know you'll figure it out. You're the best."

The compliment landed oddly because Wallace had never said such a thing. He just handed me case after case, each one increasing in difficulty and danger to the point I had to adapt or die. There'd never been praise or any feedback, really. Just the occasional *good girl* and maybe an extended stay in a tropical or otherwise vacation-destination-worthy locale as a bit of a treat.

"Thanks," I said to Bray as I soaked in the knowledge that I apparently had a reputation within the DSA. Or at least in his eyes. His gorgeous gray eyes, which hooked mine every time they met.

"You bet." He grinned and I felt that spark in my fingertips again. "See you at movie night."

I went to tell him I'd better not see him there, because it would risk our cover, but he was already making his way toward the door.

Bray left me in peace to wander about my new home. The self-guided tour took all of sixty seconds, seeing the one-bedroom apartment was maybe eight hundred square feet. But it was still very nice. The DSA had to be shelling out a chunk of change for rent, given the location. The bedroom was decorated in soft, earthy tones like the living room. The bathroom had a soaking tub, which I promptly decided I needed to test out.

I sunk into bubbles up to my chin and tried to let New York, the red-eye flight, and the encounters with my new neighbors melt away, but my worry over where Wallace was kept me from fully relaxing. I was exposed without him. As naked and vulnerable as I was sitting in this bathtub. I reached for my phone on the tub's ledge and decided to look for answers myself.

I pulled up *Unknown* and sent him a text.

I'm here. Where are you?

Nothing indicated he received the message: no read receipt, no bouncing ellipses. He rarely ignored me.

The place is cute, by the way.
But your stand-in is a little . . . green.

The thought of Bray made me consider texting him—he had given me his number—but what would I say other than ask him where Wallace was again?

I convinced myself Wallace would respond soon and climbed

out of the tub. I settled on my fluffy bed in an equally fluffy robe and flipped through the file Wallace had prepared. If I was going to do this, I needed to be ready.

Lauren Thomas was twenty-five, born in Sacramento, previously employed as a nanny by a family in Marin County, and had a degree in early childhood education.

A pang of resentment always fizzled behind my breastbone whenever Wallace gave me an identity who had gone to college. Other than the handful of classes I had slipped into under the radar on an assignment, I had never had the privilege.

I flipped a few pages to find reference information for my previous employer, someone I was sure was entirely fictional but would answer the phone should anyone call and ask about Lauren Thomas. I assumed it would be "Sue" from some department deep in the bowels of a DSA building somewhere, the same woman who had played the part of my mother, my teacher, and even my parole officer when needed. I had never actually met her, but she faithfully picked up the phone when Wallace deemed it necessary to the case.

Turned out Lauren Thomas used to work for the Van Sant family of Tiburon. She tended to their twin children, Milly and Taylor, from the time they were two until their fifth birthday a month before when the family moved to Amsterdam. Lauren had then been paired with the Browning family through a nanny-finder website and had relocated to the Del Rio neighborhood in the South Bay to begin working with them.

I knew the Brownings simply did not *find* Lauren Thomas on a website. She'd been planted and their paths purposely crossed by Wallace.

I lay back on the pillows, wondering what someone with a degree in early childhood education knew that I didn't. Children were little lumps of clay, I knew that much. Easily molded and carved by their surroundings and the adults in their lives.

My own childhood had begun in the warmth of my mother's

embrace. Deep in the hidden layers of my memory lived the quiet murmurs of a hummed lullaby, the scent of skin fresh with soap and powder. A laugh like sunlight on a spring day. The gentle hands that had shaped my early years abruptly turned to a merciless chisel, which gouged away everything soft and supple. As a young teen, my mind had still been pliable enough to be formed into an accomplice.

Father knows best. It was the two of us against the world, he had convinced me, and I had to listen, I had to follow. I had to learn how to pick locks, slit window screens, lie without blinking. To slip my fingers into handbags, pockets. To nimbly strip a wristwatch by simply bumping into someone. He'd weaned me on petty theft: wallets, jewelry, pocket change. Then my body blossomed, and I became useful in a different way. No longer the child no one noticed stealing into the coat closet, but the young woman flirting as a distraction while my father rewired someone's security cameras, stole their car, or siphoned their offshore bank account.

You're my beautiful flower, baby, he used to say. *Everyone's looking at you and won't even notice me.* He'd cast himself as Robin Hood, preying on the rich to redistribute wealth, but he was a common con artist—a good one until he got caught. His hubris was his downfall, and he had his claws in deep enough to nearly drag me down with him.

Memory of our last job seeped into my tired mind like a shadow.

The deal, the hotel. The room the FBI had wired without us knowing.

The blood. The body.

I woke with a start, the sharp crack of a gunshot echoing across a decade. My heart thudded in my chest, sweat dampened my brow. I didn't remember falling asleep, but the murky blue haze of twilight blanketed the bedroom.

I sat up and reached for my phone, shaking my head to chase away thought of the night that had changed everything.

A new text message waited for me, not from Wallace, as I hoped, but from Bray.

Don't miss movie night! ☺

He honest to God used a smiley face.

His jolly though annoying message, my surroundings, and the prompt about my evening plans reminded me I was far from crime scenes and gunshots. I was Lauren Thomas, neighborhood nanny extraordinaire, and I had to mingle with the local moms.

I thought of texting Bray something snarky back but didn't want to encourage the micromanaging. Instead, I climbed from my bed and headed to the closet to find something appropriate to wear for a night out in suburbia.

CHAPTER 5

In all honesty, I was not sure what movie night would entail. As it turned out, it involved a spread of lawn chairs and blankets filling Melanie Browning's driveway and a projector casting a singing snowman and two princesses on the garage door. Someone had rolled out a popcorn cart worthy of a carnival and filled the night air with the smell of kernels and butter. Children bobbled and crawled, dangling from their parents like jungle animals. A string of lights swung from the oak tree in the lawn's center to the picket fence at the end of the drive. The whole scene emanated a warm, wholesome glow.

I lingered on the edge, assessing how best to insert myself. I didn't have to wait long before someone made the move for me.

"Hey, neighbor!" Alisha sang as she approached. Jeffrey was not strapped to her chest this time but bundled in a stroller even more impressive than the one Jana had nearly pushed in my front door earlier.

"Hey! Still on the clock?" I said and wondered what kind of hours being a nanny entailed if she was still on duty at this time of night.

"Yes. The Wilsons asked me to come help with the baby since they have the other two watching the movie." She pointed at the crowd filling the driveway.

I observed the crowd for a moment. My best guess was five families in attendance: the three women I knew from Bray's photos, a pair of dads, and one other couple who were likely Jeffrey's parents. They sat together like a little tribe, their offspring sharing toys and babbling at each other. The barrier between them and me and Alisha was almost physical.

"Is that the new BuggyBaby X3?" I asked with a nod at her stroller, and remembering what Bray had said about the hottest stroller on the market.

Alisha rolled it back and forth. "Sure is. You could break down a door with it. The titanium rods are triple reinforced but light as a feather." She lifted its back wheels off the pavement to demonstrate.

I tried not to gape, not being well-versed in stroller features, but needing to keep up my front. "So I've heard. My old family had the X2," I said, only guessing the X3 had a predecessor.

"We had that one for Kendra, but upgraded for Jeffrey," she said like thousand-dollar strollers were a dime a dozen. "So, are you getting settled okay?"

"Sure am, thanks!" I smiled to match her enthusiasm. "Jana stopped by earlier and invited me to this. I figured it would be a great way to get to know people."

"Oh, how nice of her. Melanie hosts movie night once a month, so it's perfect timing for you to move in!" Jeffrey started to fuss. I studied how Alisha carefully lifted him from the stroller and patted his bottom like a sack of sugar as she bounced.

I didn't get the chance to covertly ask her for any tips because Jana came over, excitedly waving both hands like plane propellers. "Lauren! I'm so glad you made it!" She pulled me into a hug, which felt overly intimate for only our second meeting. Over her shoulder, I recognized both Sandra and the hostess herself, Melanie.

I snapped to, realizing I needed to be on point.

"Here she is," Melanie all but purred at me with a feline smile. "I'm so glad you could join us tonight for this informal kickoff."

A little boy, maybe five or so with a slash of sticky blue painting the side of his mouth, swung from Melanie's arm. He chattered at her and bounced from the concrete like he'd had too much sugar. Fear pummeled my heart that this was my future.

"Kaden, Mommy is talking right now. I need you to go watch the movie," Melanie said.

"But *Mom*, the swing broke again!" he whined and thrust an arm toward the oak tree where I saw a plank dangling from a long rope while the rope that was supposed to hold up its other side pooled on the lawn, having come loose from the branch.

Melanie sighed in exhaustion, and I wondered if the firing of four nannies had more to do with an inability to handle the child rather than the mother, as I had assumed. "Damn swing," she muttered. Then she turned her head and shouted toward the crowd watching the movie. "Scott! The swing!"

A blond man glanced over his shoulder from his camp chair and waved a casual hand. "I'll get it in a minute, honey," he called back but made no effort to get up.

"*Mom!*" Kaden whined again and danced around her in a circle.

The other moms must have been immune to it because they didn't look bothered at all. Jana was still smiling, Sandra was gently stroking her belly, which was rounded into a telltale bump. Alisha had retreated further into the dark to shush Jeffrey.

As much as I wanted to walk away from the whole thing and go back to my quiet, empty apartment, I saw a golden opportunity.

"I can fix it," I said. "Be right back." I jogged over to the lawn and gazed up at the tree. The ropes had been tied to a thick branch a good fifteen feet off the ground. A walk in the park compared to some other things I'd climbed.

I grabbed the end of the rope on the ground and looped it around my waist to secure it and carry it with me. Then I got a running start at the tree and launched myself up into it. I climbed branches until I got to the big one and straddled the top of it. Then I resecured the loose rope into position with a tight knot and climbed back down. I landed on the ground to gaping faces.

"Whoa, how did you do that?" Kaden said, eyes wide and glowing.

His mother and the rest of my audience had the same question on their faces.

I casually brushed the stray bits of bark off my hands. "Lots of CrossFit. Should be good to go," I said and patted the plank. I sat on the swing myself to make sure.

"Mom, she's *so* cool," Kaden said with a look up at Melanie, and then he came running over to me.

The look on Melanie's face was at once impressed, thankful, and skeptical. I didn't have time to worry I'd shown too much of myself because Kaden bounced around asking if he could have a turn on the swing. I surrendered it to him and gave him a good push before rejoining the moms.

Melanie gave me a beguiling smile. "I was already impressed from our interview but had no idea you'd be this impressive in person," she said and stuck out her hand. "Pleasure to meet you, Lauren."

I pleasantly laughed. "It's so nice to finally meet you in person, Melanie. I can't wait to start my position with your family." Years of training was the only thing that kept me from flinching at the blatant lie. But I had to do it if I wanted to find out information on Wallace.

"We are thrilled to have you. Welcome to the neighborhood."

As she smiled at me, I ran my customary assessment when meeting a target for the first time. Melanie Browning was as pretty in person as in Bray's photo, though perhaps a bit more tired looking. She was the kind of woman you would notice in a crowded room. Her hair captured the light even in the dark, the blond waves pulling in every nearby source. Her smile was bright and her eyes sharp. She had the look of someone calculating something at all times. Sandra Whitley stood at her left side, Jana at her right, putting the queen bee description Bray used on full display.

"Thank you," I said warmly, though I felt like a small fish in a tank of sharks.

"Sure," Melanie said. "Why don't you come over tomorrow morning and we can give things a test run before you fully start on Monday? That way you can meet Kaden and Karli one-on-one before we go to the park."

With all my might, I forced the smile on my face to stay put. My new life was sucking me in at record speed. I could already feel the squirming kids tugging on my limbs and sapping my energy. The laughter and shrieking put my nerves on edge, and I wondered if I could abort the mission. If I could tell Bray to forget our deal and that I wanted out. Maybe I'd ask to go to prison instead. Despite it all, I found myself saying, "Sure! That would be great. What time?"

"On Saturdays, we usually head over to the park around nine, between breakfast and naptime, so how about you come over to the house at eight?"

I balked at nine being *between* breakfast and naptime. On a Saturday, I wasn't even out of bed by nine, and I had to be up and ready to take care of two kids by eight a.m.? There wasn't enough caffeine in the world. "Sounds great," I said through another forced smile.

"Lauren! I need another push!" Kaden hollered from the swing.

Melanie gave an adoring laugh and expectantly looked at

me as if I were already in charge of caring for her child. In fact, everyone expectantly looked at me.

I put on my best Lauren Thomas face and cheerily skipped off to the lawn. I felt the moms watching as I greeted Kaden with all the enthusiasm I could muster. His *push* turned into demands for more, and then leaping from the swing to do midair acrobatics.

While we played, I saw a car drive slowly in front of the house as if it were looking for parking. I paid no mind to it until I saw it a second time, five minutes later.

Kaden eventually tired of swinging and ran back to the driveway for more popcorn. The moms had dispersed to their lawn chairs a while before, apparently trusting Lauren the supernanny could manage on her own.

I returned to the end of the driveway where Alisha still lingered, with Jeffrey now back in his stroller. Alisha leaned on the handlebar and nibbled popcorn from a large plastic cup. "Damn, girl. Be careful climbing trees like that, or the kids are going to ask you to do it all the time." She held out the cup with a smile.

"Noted," I said and accepted a handful of popcorn. From the corner of my eye, I noticed the same car I had seen before slowly pass a third time, and this time, it turned the corner and parked.

"I think I'm going to call it a night. It's been a long day with all the moving," I told Alisha. "Will you be at the park tomorrow?"

"Not tomorrow. We're heading up to the city to see the grandparents. But have fun, and good luck."

"Thank you!" I said, thinking I honestly needed it.

I stepped onto the sidewalk and did my best to keep out of the pools of light cast by the streetlamps, not wanting the not-so-mysterious parked car to get away. I stayed to one side of the street, moving two houses down before I crossed and swung the corner wide to approach the car from the passenger's side. The driver had eyes on the sideview mirror, effectively looking over his shoulder in the other direction, so he didn't see me coming when I bent down and knocked on the passenger window.

Bray jumped so hard, he nearly hit his head on the ceiling. His hand shot down to his holster, but he caught my grin in time not to draw his weapon.

I pointed to the door handle when it didn't lift and gave him credit for at least locking the doors.

"You know, it's generally a good idea during a stakeout to make sure the person you're spying on doesn't see you. I made your car out like an hour ago," I greeted as I climbed in the car.

The standard sedan was unmarked and utilitarian. Given the size of it, I'd bet it had enough power to go fast if needed. Even so, Bray's bulky frame took up his side of the front seat. The warmth of his body filled the stuffy air as if he hadn't cracked a window while waiting. He still smelled like a hint of mint.

"Yeah, it's generally a good idea not to sneak up on people with guns too." He scowled at me.

Being in an enclosed space with him, I felt the same crackling energy from earlier but at a higher intensity. I leaned back against the window. "What are you doing here?"

He fished his phone out of the cupholder and waved it at me. "You didn't answer me earlier, so I wanted to make sure you showed up."

I frowned at him. "I said I would come, and I'm here. I don't need you checking in on me."

He held up his hands and hunched his shoulders. "Sorry. I wasn't sure."

"Well, you can be sure."

Silence settled between us. We both looked out the windshield. A cat licked its paw in a ring of light on the sidewalk.

Bray lasted ten whole seconds before he said, "So, did you learn anything?"

I turned my head so he could see me roll my eyes. "Yes. I asked them straight-up if they are smuggling baby products, and they detailed their whole operation without hesitation."

He blinked, looking like he might actually believe me for half a second.

"Really, Bray? No. It doesn't work like that. I know nothing other than Melanie Browning has a hyperactive five-year-old kid, and Jana Russo and Sandra Whitley stick to her like glue."

He sat silently beside me, brooding. The snap in my voice was sharper than normal, perhaps due to the complete one-eighty my life had taken in the past twenty-four hours, which wasn't his fault. He was just trying to do his job, though he wasn't very good at it.

"Well, Melanie did invite me over tomorrow to go to the park with them before I fully start on Monday, so I guess that's something."

He turned to me quickly enough to rock the car. "Really?"

A smile bent my lips. His excitement pulled it from me almost on reflex. "Yes, really. I'm going over to her house at eight, then to the park at nine."

Bray held up his hands like he might reach for me with a smile parting his lips. Instead, he closed both his fists and pointed at me. "Good job."

"Thank you. In exchange, did you learn anything about Wallace?"

His face twisted into a frown. "It's only been a few hours."

I shrugged. "I managed to learn how to be a nanny in a few hours."

At this, he sighed. "Give me more time."

Time. It was one thing I didn't have. Every minute Wallace was off the grid left me exposed to dangers Bray didn't even know about. The classified parts of my file were monsters waiting in the shadows for their moment to leap out of the dark. I *needed* to know where Wallace was, not just to get me out of this absurd nannying gig, but also to protect me from the monsters. Bray didn't need to know more of the story, but every minute I didn't know where Wallace was, was a minute too long.

"Well, I'd appreciate it if you could fast-track your part of the deal. Also, try to blend in a little better. Or better yet, stay away and let me handle my part of the deal."

He gripped the steering wheel and let out a breath. "Sorry. I'll . . . back off."

"Thank you."

I reached for the handle to leave.

"But let me know how tomorrow goes?"

"Good night, Agent Bray," I muttered and climbed back onto the sidewalk.

The warm night air hugged close. I crossed the street to my apartment, ready to get to bed despite sleeping all afternoon. The day had taken a toll, and I had to be up with my nanny face, whatever that was, on by eight a.m. I locked the door behind me and dialed a familiar number, hoping I could take matters into my own hands.

Unknown showed on my screen as the call went out.

It went straight to voicemail.

"Wallace. Leave a message."

I ended the call with a frown and another jump in my nerves, never having left my handler a voicemail, and sincerely worrying about why I hadn't heard from him.

CHAPTER 6

I still had no word from Wallace by the time I left for the Brownings' the next morning, but I did have a text from Bray.

Good luck with your first day! ☺

I rolled my eyes at the smiley face and considered sending a middle-finger emoji back. I'd had three cups of coffee, and my hands had almost stopped shaking by the time I stepped onto the stone pathway bisecting the Brownings' front lawn and leading to the door like a scene from a storybook. Evidence of movie night had been cleaned up and tucked back into wherever it had come from. This morning, the front yard was all bird chirps, soft sunlight, and a rose border prim enough to look like each bud had its own butler.

I didn't even get a chance to knock before the front door swung open and Melanie and Scott Browning were beaming at me like Barbie and Ken.

"Good morning!" Melanie cheered.

I put on my best nanny smile. "Hi!"

"This is my husband, Scott," she said and gestured to the handsome blond man beside her. The prom-king aesthetic was even more pronounced in person. Tan, gleaming smile, and a distant look in his bright blue eyes, which said he mentally spent most of his time someplace far from wherever he was physically.

"Pleasure to meet you, Laura," he said and extended his hand. His palm was soft and a tad clammy.

"It's *Lauren*, sweetheart," Melanie said and pecked his cheek. She brushed the smudge of gloss her shiny lips left behind.

"Ah, forgive me," Scott said with a demure smile. "Pleasure to meet you, Lauren."

"No problem. Nice to meet you, Mr. Browning," I said.

"You can call me Scott. Please, won't you come in." He pressed an unnecessary hand to my lower back as I stepped across the threshold.

The thought of how quickly I could reach back and break his fingers flitted through my mind, but sending my new employer to the hospital two minutes into my first day was not likely to get me invited back for a second day.

I discreetly stepped out of his reach and gazed up into their entryway.

It opened into an airy space with a skylight at its summit, showering down natural light like it was hooked up to the sun itself. A dark wood banister shiny enough that it must have been someone's full-time job to clean it of fingerprints curved the eastern wall in a dramatic sweep fit for Scarlett O'Hara. An enormous vase spilling orchids like a white volcano perched atop a round table in the center of the room. At first glance, it didn't look like any children lived in the house. In fact, it didn't look like *anyone* lived in the house. It was too perfect. There wasn't even a dust mote floating in the high-beam sunlight.

"I'll leave you two to it," Scott said and returned Melanie's earlier peck on her cheek. "I've got to meet the guys at the country club for a morning nine in a few anyway." I noted the tight smile Melanie shot him as he stepped away. I also noted his attempt at discreetly squeezing Melanie's taut rear end on display in her spandex pants. I'd known him all of five minutes but got the sense he was a handsy guy.

"So," Melanie began once he walked off into the far reaches of the house. "This is the foyer, obviously. Formal living and dining rooms to the left, family room to the right. Kitchen is in the back of the house along with Scott's office, the playroom, and two bathrooms." She pointed her toned arms in each direction like a windmill as she spoke.

I logged the information that she'd called the entryway the *foyer*, which, given its grandeur, was fitting in addition to pretentious.

Melanie headed for the stairs. She placed her left hand on the pristine railing, and I wondered if Melanie Browning's hands didn't produce oil. Perhaps she had no fingerprints. "The kids spend most of the day downstairs; you'll be in the playroom if you're not outside. Kaden went through an awful sleep regression, and our pediatrician recommended we reserve their bedrooms for sleep only, so they don't spend much time up here during the day."

I made a mental note to google *sleep regression* when I had time later.

"Kaden, Karli, bathroom," Melanie said and pointed to the first three doors to the right of the landing. One was decorated with a pink K, the other with a green K, and the third door was nondescript but partially open to view a shower curtain with rubber ducks on it.

"Scott's and my bedroom is back there, and the laundry room is behind those doors." She pointed at the suite at the end of the hall and the accordion doors shoved shut over the sound of a churning washing machine.

She very pointedly did not mention the sixth door opposite the bathroom and to the right of the suite.

"What's that one?" I said. It had a brass knob on it, which

did not match any of the others in the hall, and I would bet good money it required a key.

Melanie gave me a tight smile. "My office. You won't need to go in there at all." She said it with an innocence holding an underlying threat, and I knew of every room in the house, that was the one I needed to get into most. She waved her hand in a big scooping motion and turned around. "Let's go back downstairs."

As we walked, she began rattling off the kids' schedule. I did not hesitate to pull out my phone and take notes because there was no way I'd remember they had apples for snack on Mondays, and dance class on Tuesdays, and playtime at the park every afternoon except Friday, and Kaden went to preschool three half days a week, and Karli was allergic to strawberries, and Kaden hated broccoli but he had to eat it due to an iron deficiency . . .

"Honey, are you writing this down?" Melanie asked when we arrived in the kitchen, which seemed to be one continuous expanse of granite and stainless steel.

"Oh, um, it's just a lot to remember, so I thought—"

She cut me off with a charming laugh. To my profound relief, and slight terror, she reached for a binder on the countertop. "It's all in here, don't worry."

"Oh good," I said and took it.

She eyed me with another smile. "Though, I doubt you need an instruction manual with your experience and credentials." She left the words expectantly hanging in the air as if they were a challenge.

Feeling called out, I disguised the nervous gulp I took.

I'd played many parts in my life; I'd fooled many marks. Hell, I'd had guns pointed at me and been forced to snort illegal substances so no one pulled the trigger. But somehow none of that measured up to Melanie Browning. The intimidation I felt standing inside her palatial home looking at her beguiling smile, which I could not determine the sincerity of, knocked me on my undercover ass.

"Juice?" she sweetly said, and I didn't dare refuse.

"Yes, please."

She went to the fridge, a double-paneled behemoth camouflaged to look like the cabinets, and yanked open a door. "I have a few things to take care of before we head to the park. The kids are in the playroom." She tossed me a bottle of organic apple juice like it was a live grenade and gave me another cryptic smile. "Good luck!"

I stared after her as she crossed to the wall of French doors leading out to the pool deck. Through the paned glass, I saw what had to be their pool house or gym or yoga studio or maybe all three sitting like a cute little sidekick cottage in the backyard.

I snapped the seal on the juice and drank it like it was booze.

Elite suburbia was a trip, that much was clear.

I clutched the binder and tried to remember which direction it was to the playroom. I backtracked into the hall and found it by way of a loud shriek. My instinct was someone was injured, perhaps gravely, but then I remembered children were prone to screeching for no good reason at all. Still, I hurried to the room opposite the kitchen at the back of the house.

Upon entry, I noted the kid stuff was most definitely concentrated to one part of the house.

A toy store had exploded inside. An expensive one. A rainbow of toys, puzzles, books, balls, mats, costumes—literally everything a kid could want—littered the space. Shelves lined the walls in a nod to organization, but most of the stock was on the floor. Karli and Kaden sat in the midst of it, and, thank God, they were laughing.

The screech appeared to have been in response to a game they were playing with a tower of blocks and a set of stuffed animals. I exhaled in relief that I didn't walk in on a full-blown tantrum minutes into my first day.

The kids stopped what they were doing and looked at me. Kaden's face split into a grin, and he held up a stuffed penguin. "Want to be Flips?" My tree acrobatics last night appeared to have been enough to impress him into welcoming me.

I smiled. If they were not screaming or crying or touching me with sticky hands, I would be anyone they wanted me to be.

"I would love to be Flips," I said and entered their space. I set the binder on a miniature, color-blocked wooden table and knelt with them.

"Flips lives here," Karli instructed and pointed to a ring of wooden blocks someone had constructed in a wobbly circle. She was younger than Kaden, with blond braids dangling at her shoulders.

"Oh, is this his iceberg?" I asked and made him dance side to side.

Karli giggled.

"Here comes Willy!" Kaden bellowed and brought a stuffed orca crashing down onto Flips's iceberg.

I jumped at the sudden violence.

Kaden made war sounds as he smashed the whale into the blocks over and over, and I had to admit, the kid wasn't wrong about the animal's natural demeanor.

We played with the stuffed animals until they tired of them, and we moved on to a complicated board game, which I was pretty sure they were making up new rules for on every turn. But it passed the time, and soon I needed to excuse myself to the bathroom. The organic apple juice had run straight through me. Or maybe it was the three cups of coffee I'd had.

"Be right back," I told them and climbed from sitting cross-legged on the floor. I hoped leaving two small children to play while I went for a bathroom break was permitted, but I figured I would find out if I came back and someone's hair was on fire.

I tried to remember the floorplan Melanie had rattled off and backtracked to a bathroom down the hall. On the way there, I stopped at the sound of voices.

"Scott, we can't take a trip to Tahoe that weekend, I'm busy. And is there even any snow left? It's almost May." Melanie's voice carried out from a doorway with an annoyed pinch. It must have been coming from Scott's office.

I sealed myself to the hallway wall next to a large oil painting, which could have either been priceless or original Browning children art, I couldn't tell. The white canvas was splashed with hues of green and blue in messy streaks.

"Thanks to a couple of late-season storms, there *is* snow left, so the timing is perfect," Scott said. "Come on, you could use a break. Let's get away for the weekend." His voice turned syrupy and warm, and the sucking sound of lips meeting skin popped out from the doorway. Perhaps he'd kissed her neck or her cheek.

"I told you, I can't that weekend. I'm busy. And besides, a ski getaway for *me* is nothing like a ski getaway for *you*. You go running off on the mountain all day, and I'm left stuffing the kids into snowsuits and getting them in ski school, and there is sunscreen and snacks and ten meltdowns because they are cold and wet."

The muffled sound of Scott chuckling echoed out from the room, followed by more sounds of kissing. "Isn't that what what's-her-name is for? The new nanny? Just bring her and make her do it."

There was a *thunk* like something got knocked over atop a desk, then the sound of papers scattering. I couldn't see, but I imagined him leaning her back onto his desk, kissing her neck.

"Her name is Lauren, and the point still stands I can't go that weekend. I'm busy. You should go by yourself. *You* could use a getaway too."

"Busy doing what?"

"I have plans. With the girls."

At this, the sounds of kissing and mussing of desktop items stopped. Scott sighed, but a hint of levity hid in it.

"If I didn't know any better, I would think you were having an affair. All these busy weekends, late nights, mysterious last-minute out-of-town errands. The way you sometimes come home smelling like a body shop. And always with *the girls.* What are you up to, Mrs. Browning?" The playful purr found its way back into his voice, and the kissing sounds resumed. They carried on for several seconds, long enough to sound like she was kissing him back and make me consider ending my eavesdropping before I overheard something I wouldn't be able to forget.

Smelling like a body shop. The phrase clung to the web of my mind. Bray had said he hadn't been able to figure out where they were hiding their goods. Maybe it was someplace less obvious than a warehouse. Maybe it was a business fronting as something else.

"Scott, I have to go soon. We're going to the park," Melanie said. Her voice was hot and breathy, and she didn't exactly sound like she wanted to leave.

"Mmm, five more minutes," he hummed as she softly moaned.

They continued kissing, and I wondered how far things would escalate with the door open and their children right down the hall. But in their defense, they believed their nanny had the kids occupied.

"Three minutes, if you agree to take that trip by yourself," Melanie said over the sound of a zipper.

"*Oh my God,*" I managed to whisper and threw a hand over my mouth. My whole body flushed with embarrassment.

"Deal," Scott said, and I couldn't take anymore.

I beelined for the bathroom and shook the image of Melanie sinking to her knees, because I knew without a doubt that was what was happening inside the office. I shut the door as quietly as I could and turned on the sink to drown out any sounds that might carry down the hall. This guest bathroom was painted a deep shade of navy blue with white accents. Towels, orchids, a tile shower stall, and fluffy rugs. My hands were shaking as I pulled out my phone to text Bray.

A body shop might be a front for their operation. Also, pretty sure Melanie uses sex to control her husband.

My heart was still pounding when I set my phone on the sink. I somehow managed to pee while doing my best not to imagine what was going on a few yards away. When I finished washing my hands, my phone buzzed on the glossy white countertop. My screen showed Bray was calling rather than texting me back.

I declined the call and wrote him another message.

Can't talk. Hiding in bathroom.

I need to talk to you.

Later. We're going to the park soon.

I shoved my phone in my pocket and figured I had better get back to the kids before one of them went wandering and walked in on something that would scar them for life. When I stepped into the hall, Scott was exiting his office. Even if I hadn't overheard what they'd been up to, the flush in his cheeks and pleasantly dazed look on his face were telling enough. He was too sated to notice me standing there and instead adjusted his pants and walked off in the other direction.

"Gross," I whispered and headed down the hall back toward the playroom. I had to pass the office to do so and stopped once again at the sound of Melanie's voice quietly tinkling out.

"Hey. We're good for the weekend after next. Scott is going to be out of town."

I strained to make out any clue as to who she was talking to, though I had a good idea.

"Don't worry about it. I convinced him," she continued. Another pause passed while she listened. "How do you think? The most surefire way to convince a man to do anything."

I silently confirmed my suspicion as to how Melanie wielded control over her husband.

"Yeah, well, three minutes on my knees is well worth fifty thousand in profits."

I managed to throw my hand over my mouth before I gasped. I fully expected Bray to have been mistaken about the whole situation, but here I was overhearing proof he wasn't.

Melanie clucked her tongue, suddenly sounding annoyed. "I know it's not enough, but what else are we supposed to do? It's been three weeks already. If Scott finds out I put a lien on the house, there's no amount of time on my knees or in any other position that could fix it."

Thankfully, my hand was still over my mouth because I gasped again. *A lien on the house?* I took quick inventory of my surroundings—the polished floors, the high ceilings, the fact this house had four bedrooms and two offices *and* a guesthouse—and estimated in this part of California, it would go for *at least* four million.

If Melanie put a lien on something as valuable as her house, that meant she was desperate. Really, *really* desperate.

I whipped out my phone again to text Bray.

I think our girls are in some bad debt.

Melanie sighed, and I shoved my phone back in my pocket. "I'll see you at the park in fifteen or so," she said. "I've got to help the new nanny wrangle the kids." I gathered she was talking to either Sandra or Jana, but I didn't stick around to find out since she was going to come looking for me any second.

* * *

The Del Rio neighborhood park was something to behold. A rolling green lawn, pristine playground equipment, sparkling drinking fountains, a cluster of picnic tables without a spec of graffiti on them, and public bathrooms I was pretty sure had floors clean enough to sleep on.

And it wasn't only the amenities. The people occupying the park on a sunny Saturday morning were even more impressive.

The moms and dads, and a few nannies I presumed, basked in the morning glow and their children's laughter like a commercial for parenthood. They made it look like an elite club of smiles and unbridled joy that wasn't just hours of screaming and sticky hands. I wondered if it was in fact some kind of performative exhibition. Showing off their mastery of childrearing to the other locals like it was a competition. Who could make it look easiest? I noted how happy everyone appeared: the moms laughing together in little groups, the dads pushing strollers in T-shirts and baseball caps—a sight that stirred something primitive inside me I did not know existed.

Back at the house, Melanie had led me to the garage and instructed me to load a large wagon with toys and snacks and a picnic blanket—truly, enough to survive in the wilderness for days. I'd towed it three blocks to the community park while she walked in front of me, her children's hands in each of hers, and now, we were setting up camp on a shady lawn along with Sandra and Jana and their respective broods.

Sandra leaned back on her arms, making it look like her pregnant belly was a ball pinning her down. Jana held a tiny little girl with a shock of dark hair sticking straight up in a pink bow, and Melanie gazed out at the playground, watching the kids before, I presumed, she passed the task to me. All around us stood an assortment of baby gear: Jana's off-roading stroller; another just like it but bigger that belonged to Sandra; tote bags sprouting spit rags, teething rings, toys that looked like they made obnoxious sounds; our wagon with toys for older kids: balls, buckets, plastic shovels. We even had a platter with strawberries; something Sandra brought, which looked home baked and crumbly; and little juice boxes.

Once the camp was set, Melanie looked at me expectantly. She nodded at the playground where her children had already tangled themselves on the jungle gym, as if dismissing me to chat with her accomplices.

I would have given anything to dive behind a tree to stay and listen.

I dutifully returned her smile and headed off toward the woodchipped play area where a dozen or so kids flung their bodies at play equipment. Kaden and Karli both hung upside down from their knees on a metal bar, their faces tomato red and giggling. I wasn't sure what to do but followed an instinct and tickled Karli. She sent a shrill shriek of laughter into the air when I caught sight of a familiar figure in the distance.

Agent Bray stood under a tree next to the playground. In an effort to blend in, he had worn a hat and sunglasses, and I had been right: He looked fantastic in a tight T-shirt.

But still.

"You've got to be kidding me," I muttered.

"What?" Karli asked, her voice wobbly and hoarse from being upside down.

Bray caught my eye and nodded his head like he wanted to talk.

I shook mine as discreetly as I could and turned my smile back to the kids. "I said you're like a monkey in a tree." I attacked her with more tickles and sent her into a giggling tizzy.

"I'm a monkey too!" Kaden bellowed, and I moved my tickling fingers to him.

I spent the next ten minutes climbing in and out of the jungle gym with them, pretending to be a jaguar, because Kaden declared it so. I felt my phone intermittently buzzing in my pocket throughout those ten minutes and knew Bray was texting me because I could see him tapping his phone across the park.

I was about to grab my phone and text him *STOP IT* or maybe a string of middle-finger emojis, when my phone began buzzing with the sustained cadence of an incoming call. I internally rolled my eyes that Bray had graduated from texting to calling—Wallace never would have done either with my targets so close by. When I looked to the tree to silently scold Bray, he wasn't there. Wherever he was, he desperately wanted my attention, and he wasn't going to stop.

"Be right back, guys," I said to the kids as I climbed out of the jungle gym and pulled my phone from my pocket. To my shock, it wasn't Bray calling but *Unknown.*

Without even waiting for the kids to respond, I strode away from the playground and hid behind a tree to answer the call.

"*There* you are. What the hell, Wallace? You snatch me out of the middle of a job in New York and send me across the country to *this*? I know you were born without a sense of humor, but is this some kind of joke? You've got me out here playing nanny with the Real Housewives of Del Rio and Agent Paw Patrol trying to micromanage me. I swear to God, if I have to change one dirty diaper, I'm—"

The call dropped with a telltale *boop boop.*

"Wallace? Hello?" I frowned at my screen. "Damn it."

A sharp whistle caught my attention. I looked up to see Bray waving at me from over by the bathrooms. I glanced at the kids to see they had returned to the picnic blanket for snacks. I gave Melanie a wave and gestured toward the bathrooms. She nodded back.

"What are you doing?" I whispered at Bray as I took in the sight of him. Up close, the T-shirt looked even better. I saw the vague outline of toned muscles beneath it, and those biceps were on partial display. I also saw my angry scowl reflected in his aviators, and I gave him an ounce of credit that at least he didn't have SPECIAL AGENT branded across the front of his hat.

"I'm blending in, like you said."

"Yes, I see that. But you're still *here.* What happened to backing off and letting me handle this? And what the hell are you thinking being a dude in a hat and sunglasses *alone* in a park full of kids?"

"I—" His face paled and he pulled off the shades. His gray eyes were sharp in the morning light. "You're right, I totally see that now. But I really need to tell you something."

"Then tell me, Agent Bray, before someone calls the cops, and we find ourselves in a very complicated situation."

"Wallace is dead."

And just like that, the world as I knew it stopped spinning.

"What?"

"I found out this morning. He was found . . ."

His voice turned into the white noise of a TV with no signal. I didn't hear anything else he said.

My whole adult life, I had never known a world without Wallace instructing me what to do next. He was the only real relationship I had, the only person who really knew me. I couldn't imagine my life without him in it.

The disbelief suddenly sent me hurtling back to earth like an asteroid as a thought struck me.

"Wait." I cut off Bray. "That's impossible. He called me a minute ago."

Bray stopped talking and gaped at me. "He—he called you?"

"Yes."

"That doesn't make any sense. When I finally was able to track down the information this morning, I found out he died two days ago. I have a guy on the inside who was able to confirm. There's no way he just called you."

A chill hit me like the sunny day turned to a blizzard. "Two days ago?" My mind scrambled to piece together a timeline as Bray nodded.

"Yes. I'm sorry, but I knew you'd want to know."

The earth seemed to crumble beneath my feet. Two days ago lined up with the night I had left New York. That phone call. Was I the last person he spoke to? An uncomfortable warmth pushed its way up into my eyes and blurred my vision.

"How did he die?"

Bray searched my face, looking pained and like he didn't want to answer.

"Bray, how did he die?"

"They're saying heart attack."

I pictured the man I knew to be in good health. It wouldn't register. A heart attack? None of it made sense.

I looked down at my phone, confused. "If he's dead, then who called me?"

We didn't get the chance to discuss because Sandra Whitley came around the corner holding her little boy by the hand. His face was screwed up like he badly needed the bathroom. "Lauren?"

Bray peeled off around the other corner out of sight. I tried to compose myself, and in failing, slipped into the first lie that came to mind and let myself cry.

"Oh, honey, are you okay?" Sandra asked, her face folding with concern.

I held up my phone and sniffled. "Yeah, sorry. I just got news my uncle passed away."

"Oh! I'm so sorry to hear that." Her son danced at her feet, looking like the bathroom was higher priority than his mother's condolences.

"Thank you. I think I need to head home for the rest of the day. Would you please tell Melanie and Jana I had to run?"

"Of course. Don't you worry. And again, I'm so sorry for your loss." Her son pulled her into the bathroom so she couldn't have said more even if she wanted to.

I wiped my eyes and turned the corner to run straight into

Bray's chest again. This time, he gripped my upper arms so I didn't lose my balance.

"Whoa there," he said. "You know, you're a really good liar." When I kept my eyes down instead of returning some sass, his voice softened with concern. "Hey, are you okay?"

I looked up at him and fought the tears burning my eyes. We stood under the overhang outside the bathroom, half shielded in shade. Still, the sunny day framed his handsome face and his look of honest sympathy.

"Do you want to, um . . . Do you want to go get some coffee or something?" he asked.

I had never socially hung out with my handler; it was a surefire way to blow my cover. But I had just lost one of the only people in the world who knew who I really was, and I had never felt so impossibly alone.

"Yeah," I told Bray. "That would be nice."

CHAPTER 7

Ten years ago

I'd had dreams about getting caught. Nightmares, really. My father had promised me it would never happen. *We're too good for that, baby. Trust me.* I had trusted him, mainly because I'd had no choice. Nor did I have any other adults around to intervene if they noticed little whatever-my-fake-name-was being forced to play along with a con. And that really was a testament to how good my father was. No one ever knew what we were up to until it was too late, and we had vanished into new identities.

I was alone in so many ways.

And here I was, alone in the worst possible way.

Save for the ones where we died, the darkest versions of my nightmares about getting caught culminated in the scene I was currently sitting amid. Me, alone in an interrogation room with no idea what was happening or who to call for help. On top of the sheer terror tightening my veins with adrenaline, I was soaking wet with someone else's blood staining my hands. My feet had begun to regain feeling after having gone numb from running in the rain in strappy heels, but I was still freezing. I shivered in the small, ugly room with concrete walls and a bald floor the color of pea soup.

Hours had passed since everything had gone sideways in the hotel room and I'd fled down the service stairs into a back alley. Lucky me, I'd run straight into an FBI agent ready to arrest me. I had no idea where my father was nor if one of the gunshots I fled had hit him. I'd been sitting in this cold, empty room with no answers and only my spiraling thoughts for company.

I jerked in surprise when someone opened the door. *Finally.*

A man with dark hair beginning to hint at gray, a mustache, and crow's feet at his eyes from squinting at criminals like he was squinting at me, stepped inside. He wore a jacket and slacks and a neutral face other than the squinting. He wasn't the man from the alley who'd cuffed me, and he hadn't been in the hotel room, but an intimidating authoritative energy pulsed off him, filling the small room and making me stiffen.

My father had trained me on what to do should I ever find myself in this exact situation, but his lessons expired with my childhood. Refusing to talk without a parent present no longer held water since I was one week past my eighteenth birthday. I had to assume the man now sitting across from me at least knew my age, if not many more troubling details based on the textbook-thick folder he set on the table.

"So, Erin Daniels . . ." he said, flipping the file's cover.

My stomach sunk through the pea-soup floor. I nearly dissolved in terror. If he knew my real name, I was beyond trouble.

"You were a tough one to track down. Lots of different names in your past, aren't there," he said.

It wasn't a question, so he didn't phrase it like one. Instead, he began pulling photocopied images of me from the stack. School photos, still surveillance footage, an old library card. The artifacts dated back to the time I was twelve. I recognized my class photo from the school in the new town we moved to soon after my mom died. It was the first time my name had changed.

"Looks like you've been all over the place for the past six years."

Visual evidence of my nomadic life put a bitter taste in my mouth. We never stayed anywhere for more than a year. As soon as we finished a job, we were in the wind. I had half a mind to shove all the photos off the table and erase the reminder, but I was still shaking too hard. My teeth had begun to chatter.

He laid the most current of my fake IDs on the table: the driver's license for Ana Prescott. "Tell me about her."

I stared at the photo I had posed for in a motel bathroom before my father sent it off to his favorite counterfeiter. Ana Prescott looked just like me, of course, but she came from a world of privilege. Her father bought her jewels for her birthday and sent her on vacations to Aruba. On paper, she went to a private school and ran in elite social circles. In reality, she was a con artist's daughter being dragged to another job with a promise it would be the last.

It was the last, but not for the reason we had planned.

"Who is she?" he prompted when I didn't say anything.

I braved meeting his eyes. He stared at me with an honest curiosity accompanying the penetrating inquiry.

I knew how to dance verbally and mentally. To outwit and outmaneuver; I'd been trained by an expert. If I hadn't been so terrified, perhaps I could have summoned some of my skills and talked my way out of the situation. But the way he was staring at me, *watching* me, had me too afraid to make a move. Not to mention, he literally held all the cards what with my life's fabricated history belly-up on the table.

"Who are *you*?" I asked, realizing he hadn't introduced himself, nor was he wearing a badge visibly displaying his name.

His mustache twitched at the corner with what might have been a small smile. "We'll get to that. First, I want you to tell me about Ana Prescott."

The name ground against my ears like sandpaper. I *hated* all my fake names. Hated them. They served as a constant reminder that my identity did not belong to me. A burst of anger gave me the guts to sass.

"Looks like you already know all about her," I said, and nodded at the photo and folder.

He pursed his lips, undeterred by my attitude. "I know some, but not enough. I'd really like to know what she—*you*—were doing in that hotel room tonight with your father."

A hard shiver shook me at the mention of my father. The memory was still solidifying in my reeling brain, but it came rushing back. The gunshots, the panic.

"Where is he?" I said.

He looked up at the raw scrape in my voice and the sound of my teeth chattering.

I stared back at him, trying to muster whatever nerve I had left and fight the tears burning the backs of my eyes.

He watched me wring my bloodstained hands and involuntarily shudder from cold, from fear. From everything. As he took in the thin straps of my dress, my stringy hair, my makeup, which had run with rain and tears, his face softened. He looked like he was seeing a person sitting across from him and not just a crime.

When he stood from his chair, the metal legs scraping the floor, I cautiously leaned back, not sure what he was doing. He removed his jacket, exposing the gun holstered to his hip, and I flinched at the sight of it. The sound of the shots in the hotel room rang out in my memory again, forcing my eyes closed in fear. I could see it all again, feel it all again.

I jumped when I felt something warm and soft land on my shoulders.

He draped his jacket around me and moved back to the other side of the table. He gave me the slightest sympathetic smile, and the tears almost boiled over.

"Now," he said, pulling out a paper pad and pen, "why don't you tell me what you and your father were doing in that hotel room tonight."

Chapter 8

Present Day

Because we had walked to the park, Bray gave me a ride to the coffee shop.

I sat at a small table and stared out the window while he ordered. Wallace's death hadn't fully registered, but the consequences of it were starting to set in like a million little teeth. If he really was gone, that meant I had no one watching out for me.

Bray returned to the table with a mug embellished with a heart drawn on the liquid's surface. He set it down with a faint flush to his cheeks.

I arched a brow at him. He shrugged and set an enormous blueberry muffin sparkling with sugar crystals beside it. His knees bumped mine beneath the table when he folded himself into his chair.

"Sorry," we said at the same time.

I shifted sideways and reached for the fancy drink. The gorgeous muffin would go to waste because I had lost my appetite with the news about Wallace.

Bray leaned forward on his elbows. He picked up his mug with one hand and blew on his drink. The rounded shape of his lips and the soft *whoosh* that came out of them made me sit up straighter.

"*So!*" I said for distraction without anything to follow it up.

He watched me with his bottomless gray eyes, expectant.

I couldn't think of any words, so I lifted my drink and promptly burnt my tongue. "Shit," I hissed and reached for the dribble on my lip.

"Oh, careful. Here." He quickly grabbed a napkin and extended it. The table was so tiny, and he was so big he all but pressed it to my lips.

"Thank you."

"I should have warned you; they tend to make things extra hot here."

I looked around at the quaint shop's deep brown walls, overstuffed furniture, locally sourced abstract art. The barista was doing a poor job of pretending not to stare at us. I caught a coy grin on her lips.

"Do you live around here?" I took a stab in the not-so-very dark.

"Am I that obvious?" He quietly laughed.

"Yes, Bray. Everything you do is obvious."

His face fell. "Sorry, I thought it would be good to go somewhere familiar, given the circumstances."

"Yes, and the issue with that is people *know* you here—like that barista who's watching us like we're on a date—and now they've seen you with *me* when I'm supposed to be undercover."

His eyes widened the same way they had in the park when I pointed out his error in lurking in sunglasses and a hat. "You're right. Sorry. I'm sorry." He looked over his shoulder like he wanted to hide under the table. Despite yet another faux pas, his fluster came off charming. "Then maybe we should?"

"Should what?"

"Act like we're on a date."

The idea struck me as so absurd, I laughed out loud, which I realized a second too late only played into his ridiculous plan. "What will that fix?"

He glanced at the counter where the barista was still watching. He lowered his voice and spoke through a smile. "That's Amber." He nodded at her. "She and her wife own this place, and they've taken a, let's say, *keen interest* in my social life. That's why she's staring at us. And that's why she put a heart in your drink," he said like it just dawned on him. He closed his eyes and shook his head. "I'd rather she thinks I'm here on a date than here with a CI."

I glanced at the woman behind the counter. She was petite with, appropriately, amber-colored curls piled on her head. She wiped down the espresso machine with one eye still on us.

"Does she know what you do?"

"More or less."

"Of course she does."

"What does that mean?"

"It means you suck at this!" I blurted in a harsh whisper.

He flinched, looking hurt.

"Sorry."

I glanced around the shop at the other patrons, noting there were at least two other couples dressed similarly to me and Bray: T-shirts, yoga pants, hoodies. A Saturday morning coffee date was apparently a viable con.

"Give me your hat," I demanded and held out my hand.

"My hat?"

"Yes. We can at least hope Amber forgets what I look like."

He removed it and ran a hand through his mashed hair, leaving it ruffled and all sorts of perfectly messy. There was also the bicep popping out to say hello when he lifted his arm.

His hat sat low around my head, being at least a size too big. His scent lingered on it, a hint of scalp and citrusy shampoo. I took care to pull my hair forward to further shield my face. I had to look up from under the brim to see him.

"Thanks."

He smiled at me, and the color of his eyes made me forget we were in fact a government agent and a career criminal meeting to discuss someone's death rather than a couple enjoying coffee.

I gathered my mug with both hands and blew on it, hiding under the hat's bill.

After a few quiet moments, Bray broke the silence. "You know, if we're on a date, we should probably be talking to each other."

My face warmed. I was embarrassed to tell him I had never been on a coffee date, and I didn't know what to do. I discreetly eyed the other couples and noted one pair was holding hands on top of the table and the other was sharing a laugh.

Both options made me wildly uncomfortable.

"Maybe the date isn't going well," I said into my latte, which was nearing a drinkable temperature.

"Well, you're already wearing an article of my clothing, so I have to assume it's going at least somewhat well."

I fought the smile tugging at my lips. He may have been a crap agent, but damn it, was he a charming fake date.

"I'm really sorry about Agent Wallace," he said, and brought the mood crashing right back down. "Were you two close?"

There were much more important matters at stake than my emotional relationship with Wallace, what with him being dead, but opening up *that* box was not something I was prepared to do on a fake coffee date.

I glanced out the window and reminded myself Del Rio was ridiculously safe. The chances of being found here were slim to none. Not to mention, I had a big, strong secret agent sitting across from me with a gun attached to his hip, though my confidence in his skill with it was lacking.

I staved off the worry rising inside me with a sip of my latte. Bray's question, *were we close,* felt intrusive. I had never talked about Wallace with anyone because I couldn't. Exposing our relationship was a death wish. More than a few of my targets would have put a bullet in my head if they found out I was a rat. Wallace had been the only consistent thread in my life for a decade. He was all I knew, and the only one who truly knew me.

But were we close?

"Our relationship was . . . complicated."

"How so?"

I huffed a dark laugh. "In pretty much every way you can think of. He saved me, in a sense. But he also controlled me—literally—for ten years. I couldn't do anything without his permission or without him knowing about it."

Bray nodded with a look on his face I couldn't read. Something between pity and understanding.

"He was also the only person I really knew, but to say I even knew him is a stretch, which speaks volumes about my tragic social life. We were more like employee and boss, except one of us held the power to send the other to prison for life if he felt like it." My attempted laugh fell flat.

Sympathy colored Bray's face, and I realized something I couldn't believe I had only just thought of.

"Wait, if Wallace is dead, does that mean I'm free?"

He turned to look out the window and stroked his chin, his thumb catching the scar on his jaw. Anyone watching would have assumed our date had hit an awkward speed bump. He looked back at me and pressed his lips together. "Not exactly. With Wallace gone, and as of this morning, I've been reassigned as your interim handler."

The news hit me like a brick I saw coming a mile off. Of course I wasn't free. I would never be free.

"Until when?"

"Until we figure out what to do with you."

"I'm not a commodity."

"No, but you are an asset. One with a decade of DSA knowledge, which needs to be carefully monitored."

His sudden shift into dehumanizing me—so much for whatever butterflies our fake date had been giving me—made me bristle.

"You really do suck at this if you think I'm foolish enough to consider ever sharing any of the information I have."

He sighed a tense breath. "Look, I don't think you're foolish. It's . . . complicated."

"It always seems to be with you agents." I frowned and looked out the window. The sunny morning was in full swing. People pushed strollers down the sidewalk, walked dogs, stopped for a chat on the corner. It all looked so normal, a normal I had never known as an adult. A longing for it ached inside me.

I turned back to Bray and found him studying my face. It made me blush. "What if I decide to run?"

"Then I'll have to chase you."

As tempting as it sounded, there were multiple reasons I couldn't run. The truth was, I was safer imprisoned in my agreement with the DSA than I would be out on my own—or in actual prison. There was only one scenario where I could ever safely escape, and it was beyond a longshot because it required finding something that had gone missing the night my father got arrested. Something no one had seen in a decade.

The thought chilled my mood and reminded me what was at stake. "How do we find out what really happened to Wallace, because I don't believe he had a heart attack."

Bray started to say something and then stopped. "I told you, I only have so much clearance. I'm doing the best I can, but I can only ask so many questions, and I don't have access to his files."

I tapped my fingers on the table, wondering if I should just spill the whole truth about me and Wallace right here, right now. "Then you owe me some other information. That's what we're doing here, remember? Information for information."

His eyes hardened. "What do you want to know?"

"Why was your clearance revoked? What did you do?"

He gave me a hard stare like he didn't like the implication. "I didn't *do* anything. I—" He cut himself off mid-breath and sighed again. "I'd rather not talk about it."

So, I wasn't the only one keeping secrets.

"Fine. Is our deal still on, then? Because I am not spending another day with Melanie's kids until you tell me something useful about Wallace."

He gave me a stiff nod. "Yes, it's still on. I will continue to find out what I can if you keep up with the Del Rio moms."

"Is that what we're calling them now?"

"Seems to be a good description. I saw your texts. Did you get anything more out of them at the park?"

I sighed, feeling the familiar routine of reporting to my handler slide into place like a hand into a worn glove. Though, this handler was a lot easier on the eyes and didn't have the personality of a cactus. I found Bray studying me again.

"Not really. I was too busy with the kids—which might be a flaw in your little plan here, by the way. I don't know what I'm doing with them in the first place, and I don't know how I'm supposed to get close to the moms if I'm on kid duty twenty-four seven."

"You managed to gather some intel at the house this morning, didn't you?" he said as if to justify his plan.

"Yes, but only because I got lucky and overheard something on the way to the bathroom between rounds of stuffed animal make-believe and a board game with very subjective rules."

He looked at me like he was trying to fight a smile. "The kids like you. I saw them playing with you at the park."

"A credit to my winning personality, no doubt," I said flatly and pinched a blueberry off the top of my muffin.

Bray sat forward and folded his hands. "Tell me more about what happened at the house."

I ate the blueberry and pretended to gaze off in thought. "Well, first we played a game where I was a penguin named Flips, and then—"

"Not with the kids. With Melanie."

I smirked at him, knowing this was what he wanted but unable to resist reminding him what position he'd put me in. "She gave me a tour when I got there. Her office is the only room in the house with a lock on the door, so I'm sure that's where anything useful will be. I would bet good money the whole house is decked out in nanny cams too. She'll probably find out I overheard her *negotiating* with her husband in his office, but hey, maybe they're into exhibitionism. Rich people do weird shit."

Bray arched a brow like he wanted to know more but was shy to ask.

"Her husband wanted to plan a ski trip for the family the weekend after next, and she *convinced* him to go alone." I drew out the word with an unsubtle implication. His face flushed a knowing shade of pink. "She said she was busy with the girls, which prompted him to get suspicious, but not really. I get the sense as long as she keeps him distracted and satisfied, he doesn't ask too many questions."

He nodded like this made sense. "And the body shop thing? Where did that come from?"

"When her husband was asking what she was always so busy with—late nights, last-minute plans, those types of things—he mentioned she sometimes comes home smelling like a body shop."

"Interesting," he said, and stroked his chin. "Did she say anything else?"

"No. She unzipped his pants and got busy convincing him to stay out of her business."

He awkwardly cleared his throat and sat up straighter. He was flustered, and *God damn it* why was it so charming?

"When I came out of the bathroom, because no *way* was I sticking around for that, I heard her on the phone, I assume talking to Sandra or Jana. She quipped that three minutes on her knees was worth fifty thousand in profits."

His flush burned away to pure interest. Both of his thick brows lifted, and his lips bent with curiosity.

"I know, right?" I said. "I'll be honest with you, I thought you might be wrong about the whole thing, because a baby-product smuggling ring sounds ridiculous, but they are definitely up to something."

An undeniable bloom of pride filled his face. "I know they are. And what about the bad debt thing? Where did that come from?"

"From Melanie telling whoever she was talking to on the phone that she knew fifty K wasn't enough to cover it, and her husband would freak out if he found out she put a lien on their house."

"Oh shit," he said with wide eyes.

"Yeah."

He thoughtfully stroked his jaw again, drawing my attention to his scar. "That would explain a few things, like why their operation seems to have slowed down lately."

"It has?"

"Yes. Maybe they're trying to lay low because they are in trouble. I wonder how they got into debt in the first place though . . ." He trailed off in thought and then shook his head. "Anyway, this is further than I've gotten on my own, so thank you. Great work."

I nearly flinched. Wallace had never thanked me for anything. Ever. "You're welcome," I said with an unfamiliar but pleasant warmth in my cheeks.

He nodded with a smile, and for the first time, I felt like he might not be completely hopeless at his job.

"What else do you know about them?" I asked, leaning in, and pinching another chunk of muffin to pop in my mouth.

"I've got files on all of them: employment history, education, social affiliations. The usual. I've got several photos indicating foul play, but nothing solid enough to make an arrest. Yet. I've also managed to track down all of Melanie's previous employees."

"And?" I asked, eager to learn about the predecessors who'd filled my new position. Namely, why they had gotten fired.

Bray squared himself as if bracing to deliver the news. "The first worked for the family when the kids were really young. Apparently, Kaden was a colicky baby, and she couldn't handle the crying to Melanie's preference. The second got a little too close to Mr. Browning, if you know what I'm saying. And the third stormed out when Melanie went off on her for buying a pack of plastic straws instead of the requested paper. Apparently, it was literally the final straw that did it."

I groaned. "You've been hanging around these families too much because that was a grade-A Dad Joke."

He chuckled a warm sound, and I had a sudden vision of him pushing a stroller.

"What about the fourth one?"

His face turned serious. "I haven't been able to get ahold of Brittany. She hasn't returned my calls."

A thrilling rush filled my chest. I'd been covertly trying to penetrate restricted zones for long enough to recognize what this meant. A break, an opportunity. A way in.

"That's perfect."

Bray arched a brow. "How is that perfect?"

"Because usually when someone doesn't want to talk to you, it's because they're hiding something."

"What would Brittany Condor have to hide?"

I shrugged, pinching another chunk of muffin and noting the ex-nanny's full name. "Maybe she saw something she wasn't supposed to see. Like something worth getting fired over that would be useful for a new nanny to know." I chewed the bite and reached for the rest of the muffin, having gotten some of my appetite back. A clue made me feel useful. I couldn't decide what to do with my feelings about Wallace's death, and I didn't want to think about it. I wanted to sink my teeth into the muffin and the case for distraction.

Bray watched me take a full bite, his eyes widening as he realized what I was implying. "You have to talk to Brittany."

I nodded at him with a smile.

CHAPTER 9

Despite not wanting to think about Wallace, I found myself unable to avoid it once I got home, thanks in no small part to the billowing vase of white roses and lilies on my doorstep. I plucked the card from the prongs buried between the blossoms and got a face full of floral fragrance.

We are so sorry for your loss. Our thoughts are with you—Melanie, Jana, & Sandra

I looked over my shoulder as if the moms might have been watching, but only saw the quiet street. It was early afternoon by now, and most everyone must have been inside for nap time.

My fake date with Bray lasted another round of coffee while we discussed our plan to approach Brittany Condor. Since her break with the Browning family, Brittany had taken a position at a local bookstore. I would stop in for a visit the next day during Brittany's shift. A simple phone call to the store, Sweet Briar Books, asking for Brittany was enough to learn her schedule. I took the easy win and chalked it up to people being either way too friendly or way too trusting in Del Rio, and decided it was likely both.

The flower vase was not light when I lifted it, and it hardly fit through my doorway. The moms must have spent a fortune to have something so extravagant delivered on short notice. I nearly sneezed from the dusting of lily pollen, which brushed my nose as I squeezed inside with it. I set it on the dining table and gave it a quick once-over, looking between the blooms for any hidden cameras or listening devices. A hazard of the job, surely, but also, knowing we were dealing with actual criminals and not some figment of Bray's imagination, the chance was not zero the gesture held an ulterior motive. When I didn't find anything nefarious, I chalked the delivery up to the moms simply being thoughtful.

I stepped back from the table and removed the envelope protruding from my hoodie's pocket.

Before we had left the café and I called a rideshare to get home, Bray handed me an envelope of cash.

"Your allowance," he'd said as awkwardly as he possibly could. He had blushed like he was paying me for sex, and I almost laughed at his embarrassment.

Wallace had been handing me envelopes, bags, cases, sometimes straight wads of cash as payment over the years. I needed money to live, and that was part of our deal: I did their dirty work, and they paid me a modest living stipend. Whether the money was tax dollars, skimmed funds, or perhaps reappropriated evidence, I never knew. I did know it was never enough to skip town though. Wallace doled it out in carefully measured amounts and at specific times to keep me dependent. I tried saving it up once, back in my early twenties when I thought escape was possible, but Wallace kept close enough tabs to notice.

I didn't have a personal bank account, obviously, and usually kept my allowance split between my person, my sock drawer, and a plastic bag in the toilet tank, just in case. For the time being, I left it on the table and untucked from under my arm the folder Bray had given me.

I needed to do my homework if I was fully diving into the case, first by getting to know everything I could about the moms, and then by talking to Brittany. Bray had handed over copies of his files on the moms and everything he knew about their operation, which he admitted wasn't much.

I sat at the dining table and started with Melanie.

Melanie had a business degree from an elite school, which made sense if she was running a covert smuggling operation—especially one which the DSA couldn't trace; she was good enough not to get caught. She had married Scott Browning eight years ago, and their two children were born within the past five years. Scott worked for a tech giant, and Melanie stayed home with the kids. She had held a job outside of the house before the kids were born, working for a wholesale shipping company. Again, something I noted made sense.

Melanie had the necessary experience and connections, and she knew how to run a business.

I flipped next to a series of photos obviously shot with a telephoto lens, and pictured Bray leaning out of his sedan's window, clicking a shutter. My lips involuntarily moved into a smile at the thought of him, and how he probably took several shots with the lens cap on before he noticed. In the photos, Melanie stood behind her SUV with the back hatch open and the inside filled to the brim with rows of identical boxes. I pulled the photo closer to see the boxes were holding those rainbow-colored stackable rings for babies. I counted a dozen versions of the same thing—and that was only what I could see in the photo. Given the size of the SUV, there had to be upward of fifty boxes inside.

I flipped to the next photo. This one showed Melanie outside of her SUV again, this time with a pile of collapsed strollers jammed into the back. *Do you know how much a quality stroller costs?* Bray had said when he first told me about the case. I didn't know, but just like the rainbow rings, I doubted anyone needed, from what I could tell, eight identical strollers.

I placed the two photos side by side to study the background in each, and recognized the driveway where I had stood the night before. The photos were of the front of Melanie's house, and given the angle, I had a strong suspicion I knew where they had been taken from.

Wanting to confirm, and feeling a little creeped out, I carried the photos and my phone with me into my bedroom. I marched to the window facing the street and held up each print. My stomach dropped in realization when the angle matched perfectly.

I pulled out my phone and texted Bray.

Have you been in my bedroom?

His bouncing dots appeared right away.

I assume you're looking at the photos in the file?

Yes. You didn't answer my question.

I looked at the area where I stood while I waited for his response, checking for evidence someone had been in the exact spot to spy on the neighbors: a footprint in the carpet, a smudge on the window. I saw nothing of the sort.

Yes, I have. But it wasn't your bedroom at the time.

The thought of him in my space filled me with a strange but pleasant warmth and also a feeling of vulnerability. I quickly scanned the room looking for any blinking red lights I may have missed as discomfort washed over me.

There's not surveillance equipment in here or anything, is there?

No, but that's an excellent idea to keep watch on the street. Would you mind if we put some up?

I'm pretty sure you don't have to ask my permission.

You're right, I don't. But I am ☺

His damn smiley face threatened to put a smile on my own face. I fought it with a twist of my lips and barely succeeded.

Fine. But don't be obvious when you get here.

10-4.

While I waited, I flipped through files on the other two moms.

Jana held a degree in communications and had done a brief stint at a PR firm before she married Paolo. As a teenager, he'd moved to the U.S. from Italy with his parents. The two met at an event Jana's company had been promoting. They had a three-year-old son and an infant daughter.

Sandra had attended journalism school and had bylines in several major outlets. In recent years, her work appeared mostly in parenting and family lifestyle outlets. She had a four-year-old son—who must have been the little boy needing the bathroom at the park—and her second child was due in the fall.

Nothing about any of the moms screamed *criminal.* On paper, they all looked normal. Harmless. The photos Bray had of them—in the park with their kids, having coffee at a sidewalk café, dressed up and glamorous for black-tie fundraisers—looked nothing but ordinary. I knew, though, the best criminals hid in plain sight. They blended into the scenery so no one saw the misconduct going on right under their nose.

I flipped next to a file of bank records.

"Whoa." The word slipped from my lips. I figured they had to be loaded, given the neighborhood but, *whoa.*

Scott Browning's income was exorbitant. Same for Paolo Russo, and Michael Vassar's was too before he got laid off. Despite Bray's comments about Sandra's new car being out of budget—which it was, based on their family income records—she still did plenty well for herself. These were the types of families to use "summer" as a verb, to have hired help for everything, to never have to think about the price tag before purchasing, whether it be a gourmet cheese at the grocery store or a house.

On paper, none of the families *needed* money. Whatever bad debt the moms had, there was no paper trail. I wondered if it had come as a *result* of their operation somehow, rather than them starting a smuggling ring to clear an existing debt. But still, why would a group of neighborhood moms be running an underground smuggling ring for baby products? What was their motivation?

I spread out the files around me, looking for an answer and making a nest of papers on the bed. The title of one of Sandra's written pieces caught my eye. The printout poked from underneath Sandra's photo. "The 21st Century American Mom." I pushed it sideways to find several more beneath it: "The Silent Struggles of Motherhood." "Seven Natural Solutions for Diaper Rash." "What to Do When None of Your Friends Have Kids."

I read what was available. Sandra was an excellent writer, her tone adapting to the variety of topics ranging from the mundane to the profound. Her commentary was searing in pieces about the brunt of labor many moms bore and lighthearted in others, like the pieces suggesting honey for an angry baby bottom. I was midway through a piece on breastfeeding in public when my phone rang.

My heart seized when I looked at the screen and saw *Unknown.* My reflex was to answer—I still hadn't fully accepted Wallace was dead. But I hesitated due to the fact he was supposed to be.

Curiosity won out and I picked it up.

"Hello?"

Silence.

"Hello?" I tried again.

Over the sound of my own heart beating in my ears, I thought I heard a soft exhale.

"Who is this?" I asked, at the same moment I heard activity at the front of the apartment. I gasped as the call dropped and left me staring at the empty bedroom doorframe in fright.

I knew how to defend myself; I'd insisted on lessons years before when Wallace kept putting me in increasingly dangerous situations. But I had not had time to outfit my new home with anything resembling a weapon.

I quietly slid from the bed, aware of every breath, and moved to the closet. I hoped for a bat or maybe even a shoehorn but only found an umbrella. It wouldn't do much, but it was better than nothing.

I did not know who had just called, but I assumed it was the same person who'd called at the park, and any option of someone mysteriously calling me was not good. Paired with someone sneaking into my apartment—the sounds coming from down the hall were obvious—I'd gone nearly rigid with fear.

My heart beat in my throat. My sweaty hands gripped the umbrella. I'd done plenty of creeping in my time, but most of it involved the protection of a real weapon and shoes to run away, not socks and a parasol.

I crept into the hallway on silent feet and saw a large figure coming in the front door. The afternoon light blazing in the front windows backlit the figure to the point I couldn't make it out.

I raised the umbrella, ready to strike, and let out a shout that was half scream and half battle cry.

"Whoa!" Bray said and threw up his arms. I came inches from hitting him with the umbrella. "It's me!"

My heart nearly punched a hole right through me. I took a heavy breath and searched for my bearings. "What are you doing here, Bray?"

He wore a duffel bag looped over his shoulder. He held a set of keys in the hand he had raised like he was telling me not to shoot. "You told me to come over."

Memory of our texting conversation fought its way back through the adrenaline screaming in my veins. "You could have knocked! You're lucky I didn't hit you!"

He quietly laughed and eyed the collapsed stick of black nylon in my hand. "With all due respect, that's an umbrella."

I shot a glare at him. "Do you want to see what kind of damage I can do with an umbrella?"

He visibly swallowed at the threat in my voice.

"Why do you even have a key?"

He paused and frowned. "Who do you think stocked your house?"

The realization landed like a stone on my head. Thought of Bray picking out groceries for me and changing my linens struck me as odd. It also put a curious warmth in my chest; he had obviously done it with great care.

"Oh," I said, and tossed the umbrella on the coffee table, still a little rattled.

A few beats of silence passed between us.

He adjusted the strap on his shoulder. "So," he eventually said, "it would be good to set these up facing the street. I was thinking one in the dining room and one in the bedroom."

I thought of making a snarky comment about one at the front door to catch intruders too, but I kept quiet. Instead, I gestured to the dining room. "Be my guest."

He still wore the T-shirt and jeans he'd worn to the park and on our fake date. I watched the muscles in his back move when he walked past me and lifted the duffel bag from his shoulder.

"Do you want something to drink?" I asked him, the words tumbling from my mouth.

He cast a look back at me. "Sure."

I entered the kitchen and opened the fridge.

"I'll take a seltzer," he said before I even asked.

I smiled to myself at the thought that he knew what was in the fridge because he had put it there. I grabbed a silver can and tapped the top of it with my nails.

"So, did they, like, give you a budget and send you to Pottery Barn?"

He set the duffel bag on the dining table and unzipped it. "Something like that," he said with a smile. He began pulling out a tangle of electronics: small circular cameras with little pedestal feet and dotted lights on their faces for night vision.

"Well, you did a good job," I conceded and snapped open the can. I found a glass in the cabinet and poured it in.

"Thanks," he said and took it when I offered. "For the drink and the compliment."

"Mm-hmm."

Something, perhaps his bulky frame in Saturday casual clothing standing in my dining room looking like a handyman come to fix my router, compelled me to keep probing.

"Is your house this nicely decorated?"

He pulled up the blinds a few inches to balance the small

camera on the windowsill. Then he bent over so he was eye-level with it and left me staring at his back pockets. "I mean, I try, so I'd like to think so."

I tore my eyes away and retrieved myself a seltzer. I snapped it open and took a sip of crisp bubbles. "Do you live by yourself?"

He stood up and turned around to face me. His eyes said he knew what I was implying with my question, and sharing might not have been appropriate, but he was going to tell me anyway. "Yes."

The sense of relief I felt made me bite my lip. I turned back to the fridge to find a snack.

When he finished with the dining room camera, I followed him to the bedroom.

"I see you've been studying," he said, and nodded at the files I'd left spread out over the bed.

"I have, yes. And I have to say, given their backgrounds, the moms, I'm not surprised they know how to run a smuggling ring."

He dropped the duffel bag beneath the window and squatted to reach into it. "Well, yes. You don't run an operation like theirs without background experience first. Mistakes are a surefire way to get caught."

I sat on the foot of the bed and leaned back on my arms, watching him work. "What I can't figure out is if they are in trouble *because* of the operation, or they started the operation to get *out* of trouble."

"I would guess the former. You saw their files; it's not like any of them were hard up for money," he said, and lifted the blinds.

"So then what's the motivation? Why would a group of moms break bad?"

"*That* is what I'm hoping you can tell me. It's a piece I'm missing, and I think it will tie things together and hopefully give us a way in. Can I get a hand?" He was using his elbow to hold the curtains back while he tried to mount the camera in the window, but they kept falling forward.

I climbed off the bed and moved to join him.

"I want this one higher to get a wider angle on the street," he said as he reached over his head. He'd attached an adhesive strip to the little pedestal foot and pressed it into the belt of wall bordering the window frame.

I stood beside him holding the curtains, a wispy drape of beige linen, off to the side. The angle put me beneath his raised right arm. I felt the heat coming off him and could smell the same minty spice I'd smelled when he first stepped onto my doorstep days before.

"Got it," he declared with a final press into the wall. He lowered his arm in a way that brought it down as if he were looping me inside. "Sorry," he said with a shy smile.

My face flushed and I slipped away from him. "What are these connected to?" I pointed at the newly mounted eye in my window.

Bray went back to his duffel bag and pulled out a tablet. "Me. We can keep an eye on anything suspicious."

"What do you expect to see?"

"More of what's in the photos. Maybe another person not yet on our radar. Speaking of, what time are we going to see Brittany tomorrow?"

I narrowed my eyes at him. "*We* aren't going to do anything tomorrow. *I'm* going to see Brittany on my own."

He looked up from poking his tablet, about to argue, and I silenced him with a stern look.

"You can't keep popping up everywhere I am, Bray. They're going to catch on, if they haven't already. Jana thought you were my husband the other day when I arrived. Clearly, they're watching. They had flowers delivered before I even got home from coffee today, for God's sake."

"Flowers?"

"Yes. At the park, I told them my uncle died, remember?"

"Right. That." He paused. "Well, that was nice of them."

"It was," I agreed, though the swiftness of their intervention still unnerved me. "And in my experience, they are sucking me into their world with record speed, which is all the more reason for you to keep clear. If you want this to work"—I waved my hands around at the apartment, the cameras, the two of us standing in what was essentially a stakeout room—"then I need you to let me handle it."

To my surprise, he nodded with a purse of his lips. "I understand."

"Good."

We stared at each other, and I was acutely aware there was a bed between us.

Bray's eyes flashed back down to his tablet. "I'll be ready to hear what you learn from Brittany ASAP though."

I rolled my eyes. "I *know,* Agent Bray. Now, I'd like to enjoy the rest of my afternoon, if you don't mind." I held my arm toward the door.

"Yes, of course," he said, looking disappointed as if perhaps I was going to invite him to hang out. "I'll get out of your way. Let me know if you see anything in the street."

"Won't you be watching the camera feed?"

His face reddened. "Yes. Right. Okay then. I'll let myself out."

I smiled at his fluster as he zipped up his bag and slung it back over his shoulder. "Bye, Agent Bray. Lock the door behind you, please."

"Of course. Have a good afternoon."

He left me alone in the bedroom, and I realized I hadn't told him about the mysterious phone call.

Chapter 10

Ten years ago

I told the man interrogating me the truth about what my father and I had been doing in the hotel room. I figured I had no choice since he had the chronicle of my whole life laid out in front of him. He knew every identity I'd ever had; I had no room left to lie.

When I finished, he gazed at me with a look hinting at pity.

"When can I see my father?" I asked. My teeth had stopped chattering. The jacket he'd draped over my shoulders had taken off the chill. I'd finally stopped shaking.

He stroked his mustache with his long fingers and rested his hand on top of my open file. "Probably never."

The answer hit me like a blow to the chest. At the same time, a sense of freedom buoyed my spirit.

Despite my father's promises that the hotel was going to be our last job, I'd had my own plans. I was finally eighteen and ready to be free of his lifestyle. Our life—all the lies—was all I'd ever known, but I was ready to break away. To live on my own. I was nothing if not independent. I'd hoped to escape and find my own apartment, maybe sign up for community college courses and be a normal young adult.

But all that had changed when his gun went off in the hotel room.

Someone else's gun had been held to my head moments before, and I had not yet processed how lucky I was that my father's gun had gone off instead. I had come close enough to death not to feel it yet. The terror of the cold metal barrel against my temple, that man's merciless arms around me, would set in later, I was sure.

"Where is he?" I asked.

The man casually flipped my file closed and rested his hand atop it. He looked like he was silently considering something and didn't answer my question.

"I just told you everything," I said through gritted teeth. I did not want to beg, but I did not like the game he was playing. "Can you at least tell me if he's okay? Please?"

He looked up at the shaking plea in my final word. His eyes softened with sympathy. "He's fine. Recovering from a gunshot wound to the leg, but he's in custody."

I sagged with relief. I may have wanted to be free of him, but that didn't mean I wanted him dead. "What's going to happen to him?"

At this, he let out a small, dark laugh. He straightened and tented his fingers over the closed file. He leaned forward. "Erin, if I have this much on *you,* just imagine what I've got on him."

My throat went dry and stiff. I quietly coughed and hoped he'd offer me some water, but instead, he leaned back in his chair.

"And that actually leaves us in an interesting position."

The dark note in his voice set my hair on end. I tried not to look nervous.

"Look, I know you've been through hell tonight—and for a good portion of your life—and most of it wasn't your fault. But there are many judges who'd try you as an adult for many of the things you've done. You're eighteen now, and there's enough in here to put you away for decades." He picked up his pen and tapped the file. He remained silent and gazed at me until I met his eyes. "Including accessory to the murder your father just committed."

My heart surged up into my mouth and brought the taste of bile with it. "I didn't do—"

He shook his head. "You were in the room, Erin. Your father had a gun. You were a coconspirator in an attempted robbery. No one is going to let you off that hook."

My heart was pounding. I knew we were in trouble, but *murder* wasn't on my radar. My father had never killed anyone before to my knowledge. Until that moment, I hadn't known the man from the hotel room had died.

I shook my head in a grip of panic. Perhaps it was the shock from the night, but all my training had left me. "Please, I wasn't—We weren't going to—"

He calmed me with a raised hand. "I imagine you weren't, Erin. I think you were just going along with what your father told you to do, and things didn't go according to plan. That's not your fault." He leaned in and lowered his voice. His gaze grew deadly serious. "But I can tell you, with a record like yours, no one's going to believe that."

I felt like I was drowning right there in the interrogation room. All the air had turned to murky, cold water filling my lungs like cement. I was terrified and alone.

He sat back and released a breath. "But," he said, and my head jerked up, "maybe we can work something out."

A sick feeling swirled in the pit of my stomach at the thought that he was suggesting an exchange of services I did not want to provide. I became intensely aware we were alone, locked in a room together. I broke out in a cold sweat.

When he opened my file again, I relaxed a fraction. "You have a very impressive skill set, Erin. One that takes most people many years to master. Someone so young being so talented at assuming identities could prove to be a valuable asset." He paused and looked up at me.

The layers of shock and nerves still clouding my consciousness made me slow to understand. "What do you mean?"

A slow smile spread his lips, lifting his mustache. "I mean we could help each other."

"We could?"

He quietly laughed, seeming to find my innocence amusing. "Yes. Do you know what a confidential informant is, Erin?"

I'd heard the words before but only in movies and on TV. "Like a spy?"

He laughed again. "Sure. Like a spy."

I didn't find any of it funny. "What does that mean? You want me to like, go undercover?"

He stopped smiling and looked at me straight on. "I want you to think carefully about what you want, Erin. Do you want to go to prison for most of the rest of your life? Or do you want to stay out of prison by working for us?"

It might have been the shock of the whole night, but it wasn't until he said *us* in an unusual tone that I realized I wasn't even sure who he was referring to. I thought I had been talking to an FBI agent the whole time, seeing as that was who'd busted into the hotel room, but on closer inspection, I didn't see a badge or any of the storied letters I'd grown to fear shouting in block letters from his clothing: FBI, CIA. He was entirely nondescript. I wondered fleetingly if I'd somehow been kidnapped on the way to being interrogated.

"Who are you?" I asked, unable to keep a note of fear from cutting into my voice.

His mustache twitched when he gave me a soft smile. "I can only tell you if you agree to take the deal."

I knew then I was right. I had been intercepted. I steadily held his gaze, finding whatever nerve I had left. "Why would I take the deal if I don't know what I'm agreeing to?"

He leaned forward on his elbows and looked impressed.

"Fair point. Let's just say I work for an organization within the government that is very interested in acquiring your skill set."

The government. So, he wasn't a criminal who'd kidnapped me on my way to getting arrested. He was a legal authority figure, though apparently some secret, covert off-radar kind.

"Can you at least tell me your name?" I asked. "Seems only fair since you know all of mine," I said with a sweep of my hand over the table.

He seemed to consider with another amused twitch of his mustache. "My name is Joseph. Joseph Wallace."

I nodded, happy to have even that bit of information.

"Take the deal, Erin," he said after I sat in silence for several moments. "I promise you, whatever horror you are imagining trusting me might lead to, prison would be a thousand times worse."

A shiver shook me, but the choice seemed obvious. I was alone and drowning, and when the man sitting across from me threw me a lifeline, I saw no choice but to grab it.

Chapter 11

Present Day

I woke with a start. I sat up, rigid in the warmth of my new bed, the soft linens bunched around me. My heart raced. Something had summoned me, a sound like a crack against the window. Despite my experience with weapons over the years, any such unexpected noise reminded me of the gunshot that had changed my life a decade before. I shook away the images that so willingly swam to my mind's forefront at any opportunity.

The blood. The faces. The fear.

I blinked in the darkness of my silent bedroom. I'd fallen asleep at a reasonable hour and saw it was well into early morning now. Close to two a.m. I held perfectly still, waiting for any follow-up to the sound that had called me from sleep.

When I heard nothing—no footsteps, no creaking doors, nothing louder than my own heart pulsing in my ears—I slipped from bed. The plush carpet greeted my bare feet. I considered flipping on my bedside light to chase away shadows but instead crept to the windowsill to peek out into the dark. I pulled back the curtain slowly, with my pulse in my throat, ready to duck or call the police.

I let out an exasperated sigh when I located the source of the sound.

Bray's camera had come unstuck from the wall and landed with an innocent *thunk* on the windowsill.

"Seriously?" I muttered and picked it up. I pointed it at myself and gave it the finger with a frown for good measure, just in case he was watching. Then I pressed its sticky little pedestal to the sill and reached for my phone on the nightstand.

When I went to text him something rude for rudely waking me in the middle of the night, my phone slipped from my hand. I sucked in a sharp breath.

A man stood in the street outside my window, gazing in at me.

The streetlight bathed him in a ghoulish pale glow. His short hair was fair enough to look like he didn't have any at all.

I stumbled backward and smashed into the bed. My knees buckled. I fell to the floor and scrambled for my phone. My breath came hard and fast.

I'd just seen a ghost.

My fingers trembled as I brought up Bray's number. Without hesitation or consideration that it was two a.m., I hit dial. As the call went out, I cursed under my speeding breath and crawled toward the window, keeping myself hidden.

"Hello?" he answered after several rings. His voice was thick with sleep.

"Bray! There's someone outside my window. I need you to check the camera feed." I spewed commands at him, only halfway realizing what I'd seen was impossible. The fear in my gut and shooting through my every nerve blinded me to that fact.

"What? What time is it?" He was groggy and clearly, I'd woken him.

"It doesn't matter!" I snapped. "Wake up and look at the feed from my bedroom! Now!"

"Okay! Stop yelling! Just . . ." He trailed off. I heard rustling sounds and wondered what he slept in; maybe pajama pants, maybe boxers, maybe nothing at all. He came back after what sounded like a yawn. "Give me a second."

I rolled my eyes even though he couldn't see. "For the record, *you* woke *me* up, and that's why I'm calling right now."

"What are you talking about?"

"Your camera came unstuck and fell. The sound woke me up, and when I got up to fix it, I saw someone in the street. He was staring at my window."

He paused and then sounded much more awake. "Oh shit. Seriously?"

"Yes, seriously!" I hissed. "I don't know if he's still out there, but I need you to look at the feed from the last few minutes."

"Yeah, yeah for sure. Hang on a sec."

I heard him rustling around. The thought of him in pajamas put an odd warmth in my belly despite being on the edge of panic. I inched my way closer to the window but could not bring myself to peek over the sill. I did not want to see him again.

"Bedroom camera?" Bray asked.

"Yes. Go back like five minutes and watch."

I heard a keyboard tapping in the background and imagined him propping his laptop up in bed.

He stayed silent for long enough to put me on an even sharper edge.

"Do you see anything?"

"So far, just the street."

I ground my teeth to dust while I waited.

"Oh!" he said, and I gasped. "Oh, that's just when it fell down." He paused again, and I imagined the image having turned to black, since I'd found the camera face down against the sill. "Oh, that's cute," he said sourly.

"What is?"

"You, flipping me off. Thanks for that."

I cringed, having already forgotten about my message. I glanced down at my braless chest in the tank top I wore to bed and knew he'd gotten a glimpse of that too. Heat filled my cheeks. I quickly changed the subject. "Do you see anything now? He was there when I put the camera back up. I saw him like ten seconds later."

He let out a quiet hum, and I held my breath. "*No*," he said, drawing it out like he was watching and waiting to change his answer. "The angle is lower than it was, but I don't see anyone."

An exhale left my lungs with a painful sharpness. "Are you sure? I saw him standing there. Right outside my window."

"There's no one there."

I blinked and worked up the nerve to lift my eyes over the sill's edge.

The street was empty.

"Well, can you check the kitchen feed? Maybe that picked something up, because I swear, he was there."

"Sure. Give me a second."

I waited again, chewing my thumbnail, and scanning the empty street. Melanie's house sat tucked in and sleeping across the way. The rest of the storybook street was quiet and dark as well.

"I don't see anything here either," Bray said.

My heart sank at the same time I grew dizzy with relief. "How is that possible?"

He audibly yawned. "Dunno. Maybe it was a shadow or trick of light. Sorry the camera fell and woke you. I'm going to go back to bed."

"Bray, I know what I saw."

He paused at the edge in my voice, perhaps sensing that my fear stemmed from more than a neighborhood smuggling ring. "Well, there's nothing on the feed, so I think it's fine, but do you want me to come over just in case?"

His offer caught me off guard. If it was a chivalrous act or perhaps a job duty he felt obliged to perform, I wasn't sure. Either way, it felt excessive in the middle of the night.

"No," I told him. "I'll be fine."

I convinced myself it was the truth because, after all, the man I had seen standing in the street was dead.

Chapter 12

Sweet Briar Books stood in the middle of a strip of local businesses fit for Del Rio: an upscale clothing boutique, a hair salon, a baby store, and a vegan café. Each had an awning, hand-painted sandwich signs luring customers, and dog bowls full of slobbery water outside the door.

It was way too cute and welcoming for the fear fizzling in my veins from last night. Even though I'd told him to stay out of my way, I half wished I'd taken Bray up on his offer to accompany me in talking to Brittany the ex-nanny, because at least then I'd have someone with a gun nearby. The only reason I hadn't skipped town after seeing the ghost in the street was because of our deal. Finding out what happened to Wallace was even more pressing now. If I'd called *him* at two a.m. to tell him what I'd seen—*who* I'd seen—he'd have pulled me off the case right then. But Bray didn't have the clearance to know why, and I wasn't sure I was ready to tell him.

A happy little bell jingled when I pushed open the bookstore's bright red door. The signature smell of bound paper and book jackets hit me like a salty breeze at the beach. I may not have had as much formal education as most, but reading was one thing I held sacred. I escaped into stories of other people's lives whenever I could, whenever the web of lies of my own life got to be too much. Which was often. Unfortunately, I hadn't come to browse the adult fiction. I'd come to glean information from the young woman behind the counter.

Brittany Condor looked friendly enough from a distance. She was younger than me, mid-twenties, I knew from Bray's file on her, and was a graduate student at one of the local universities. She wore her blond hair in a thick French braid, and hoop earrings, which glinted as bright as her smile when she moved. She rang up an old man buying a gardening book who looked like he might have come in only for her company.

The store was a long, narrow galley with the register on the north wall, floor-to-ceiling shelves lining everything but the front window, and parallel rows of free-standing shelves like giant equal signs down the center.

I casually wandered past the short shelves of adult fiction toward the wall of children's books at the back. I knew the Browning children had mountains of books already, but I needed an excuse to visit Brittany and figured showing up for work with gifts after my abrupt departure from the park would only earn me favor.

Plus, it wasn't my money I was spending.

I eyed the old man at the counter still chatting up Brittany, who was being nothing but polite in return. Another woman wandered the romance section with a stack of pastel-colored paperbacks in hand. A teenager in a hoodie scoped the young adult section while tapping his phone at the same time.

I squatted in front of a children's rack and randomly pulled out one of the thin spines. An illustrated unicorn stared back at me, and I imagined Karli Browning would appreciate the attention to detail in its sparkly tail. I kept one ear on Brittany's conversation while I searched for something for Kaden. The old man was telling her about his garden and offering to drop off some carrots next time he came in. When Brittany politely thanked him and said goodbye, I dove on an opportunity to beat anyone else to the register. I hastily chose a book with a smiling dragon on the front and moved for the counter. Thankfully, the other customers appeared to be wrapped up in shopping.

"Hi there," Brittany greeted me with a warm smile. "Find everything you were looking for today?"

"I did, thank you," I said and placed my books on the counter. Little racks of bookmarks and pens and book-y trinkets lined the wooden slab. "I'm new in town and just started a nannying position. I figured I'd bring bribes."

Brittany's lips pulled up into a tight smile, which looked forced. "That's a good idea, though a gift for the parents will probably serve you better in this town."

"Good tip. Got any recs?"

She pointed her scanner at the barcode on the back of the unicorn book. She shrugged. "Oh, you know, just the standard: booze, your undying allegiance. Maybe a blood sacrifice."

A genuine laugh bubbled from my lips. I did not expect to find Brittany Condor entertaining. "Do you speak from experience?"

She sighed a long breath as she scanned the dragon book with a beep. "Unfortunately." She slipped a Sweet Briar Books bookmark into each book and neatly stacked them. I sensed she was closing off and not going to say more, so I pushed an obvious button.

I leaned in and lowered my voice like we were sisters-in-arms. "Listen, I'm totally new here, but I get the sense this is a tight community. I just started with the Browning family, and I—"

Brittany's eyes shot up at the name in a way too obvious to cover up.

"Do you know them?" I asked.

She swallowed. The bell jingled and her eyes darted to the

front door before she looked back at me. Realization settled into her gaze as she put the pieces together to understand I had taken over her old job. "They moved quickly, didn't they."

Of course I had to play ignorant. "Sorry?"

Brittany sighed again. "Your total is $36.30. Would you like a bag?"

She closed off. The conversation was falling off track and I needed to get it back. I spotted a solution on the shelf behind her. "Actually, I was hoping you would gift wrap these? Separately?"

Brittany looked down at the books and forced another smile. "Sure." She turned and tore off two sheets of wrapping paper from the roll behind her and got to work.

I tapped my nails on the countertop while I waited. "So, do you know the Browning family?"

Brittany neatly placed the unicorn book in the center of the sheet of shiny red paper. "Everyone knows the Browning family."

I tapped my nails again and tried to ignore the ominous note in her voice. I laughed with a not-so-forced dash of nerves in it. "So, should I like, be afraid of them or something?"

She folded the paper and carefully taped it down against the book. "Just don't piss off Melanie and you'll be fine."

I laughed again, desperately wanting to know what more there was to the story and finding it hard to pretend I knew nothing to begin with. "What does that mean?"

She finished with the first book and tied a white ribbon around it. She reached for the dragon book and started the process over. She glanced side to side. "Look, I'm not really comfortable talking about this, but I used to work for the Browning family. We didn't part on good terms, so just . . . be careful, I guess."

I gripped the countertop so I didn't lunge across the counter and grip Brittany and demand more information. "Can you be more specific?"

A flush curled up her neck. She looked up with only her eyes. "Not really, no."

I feigned another nervous laugh and leaned into the counter. "Come on, help a girl out. I'm new here, and I want to know what I'm getting into. I mean, do I need to quit before I even start?"

Brittany shook her head and finished the dragon book. She tied it with a gold ribbon, and I was certain I would forget which was which the second I left the store. "No, the kids are actually great. I mean, Kaden has tons of energy, but what five-year-old boy doesn't?"

I shriveled at the comment.

"But Melanie," Brittany went on, lowering her voice so much I had to nearly climb on the counter to hear her, "Melanie is pretty intense. She likes things certain ways, and she has a lot of boundaries."

"Boundaries like what?"

She snorted. "Well, don't overhear her phone calls, either on purpose *or* accident."

I cringed, thinking of how I already had, and wondering if Brittany heard something even more incriminating than I had. "Why, is she like, a secret criminal or something?" I went for broke and made another joke.

Brittany's eyes jumped to my face once more. "I can't believe I'm telling you this, but maybe it'll spare you some trouble. If you ever hear her mention someone or something named Montrose, ignore it. Don't ask any questions. Pretend it never happened, just trust me."

I stored the name in my memory and wondered what it referred to. Their supplier? A shipping company? A location?

"Did *you* ask?"

Her face burned again. "Yes, and it cost me my job. I still have no idea what it refers to, so I can't tell you anything else anyway. Just know once you're on Melanie Browning's bad side, you're pretty much exiled in this town. I'm lucky I got this job. Your total is $36.30."

That was all I was going to get, I knew it. And it wasn't nothing.

I reached in my wallet for forty dollars just as the doorbell jingled again. "Thanks for the info, and sorry things didn't work out for you."

Brittany took the money and made my change with a shrug. "It's fine. I just need something to help cover rent for the rest of this semester, and I've always loved books, so it all works out. Good luck." She handed me a handful of loose bills and coins, then pushed the wrapped books at me.

"Thank you," I said as I stepped away, juggling the change, to make room for the woman shopping for romance novels who had queued up behind me. I took two steps into the young adult shelves when I stopped dead in my tracks. My change fell from my hand, the bills fluttering to the floor and the coins dropping like heavy rain on the carpet.

The man who had been outside my window the night before stood in the middle of the aisle, staring right at me.

The ghost.

My brain could not make sense of it. I hadn't seen him for a decade, and he was dead.

But there he was.

My body went rigid with fright. An icy-hot blast of adrenaline hit me so hard, my fight-or-flight response turned into freeze-and-gape.

I had to be dreaming. I *knew* I was dreaming. It was impossible.

The man who'd held a gun to my head that night in the hotel room a decade before—the man my father had shot and killed—was standing right in front of me. He had the same nearly invisible blond hair cut close to his scalp. His face was pocked with more signs of age, but the unmistakable scar that slashed across his right eye in an angry, puckered welt was as prominent as ever.

"Hello, princess," he said in the voice that had haunted my dreams since that night. The way my body began trembling at the sound, a reflex as if no time had passed and we were back in the hotel room, told me I was not dreaming. His thin lips turned up into a sinister grin and he stepped toward me. "I believe you have something of ours."

At those words, my insides liquified. I shoved my wallet in my pocket and turned to run. He was blocking my path, so I peeled back around the end of the aisle and headed up its other side. He was halfway to the other end of it already and stepped out to grab me as I dashed for the front door.

He lunged and got a grip on my left arm, knocking the books loose. I let them fall and let my instincts kick in.

In a blink, I whirled on him and drove the heel of my palm into his nose with a sharp uppercut. He never saw it coming. When his head snapped back, I swung the side of my rigid hand into his exposed throat. I could have cracked his windpipe with the right pressure, but the thickness of his meaty neck spared him. Still, he stumbled and gasped, clutching at his face and now struggling to breathe. It allowed me to free my other arm from his grip. The woman shopping for romance novels screamed and threw her hands over her mouth. Brittany ducked behind the counter. I'd lost sight of the teen shopping for YA books and prayed he wasn't live streaming the whole scene from his phone. I threw myself out the shop's door without a glance back and ran like all get-out up the sidewalk.

My mind was near blank with panic. How he'd finally found me, I didn't know—how he was *alive*, I didn't know. All I knew was I had to get away.

I flew past all the fancy shops, turning heads and forcing myself not to look back. Turning to look would only slow me down, I knew from experience. I also knew from experience he was following me. The bad guys always followed unless you knocked them down. All I'd succeeded in doing was pissing him off and giving him watery eyes and maybe a nosebleed. I might as well have poked a grizzly bear with a sharp stick.

I heard gasps behind me as I sprinted past the hair salon, and knew he was following. A woman with a dog on a leash appeared in my way, and I leapt over the goldendoodle like a hurdle.

I'd stayed in shape for a decade for this precise reason: escape.

The loud scrape of a café table being thrown aside and dishes shattering on the pavement followed by shocked screams *almost* made me turn around to look, but not quite. I kept sprinting, my pounding heart pumping blood to my limbs, and lungs pulling air. He was gaining on me; I could sense it. He was much larger and swallowed up huge sections of the sidewalk with each step. Thought of his size took me back to the hotel room when he'd grabbed me and held the gun to my head. He had felt like a brick wall with arms behind me, towering over my teenaged body, which hadn't been much smaller than my adult body was now.

The row of buildings ended up ahead, with a gap before another row started.

An alley.

Short of diving into one of the shops, it was my best bet.

I turned the corner wide, my feet smashing the concrete as the smell of trash bins and damp pavement hit my nose. A fence blocked the alley at the other end, of course it did.

I began breathing deeper, prepping my legs to launch me up over the fence in a climb for my life because I knew if he caught me, he would kill me.

The end of the alley felt miles away with every step closer he came. I heard him gaining on me, his breath heavy and thick.

I'd hopped many fences in my life, so I knew exactly where to aim. I assessed the chain-link screen coming closer by the second and knew to get one foot above the crossbar and reach for the top. It was all in the jump. Stick that, and everything else was easy.

My feet scraped the pavement, and I took a breath like I was diving into the sea. My thighs burned as I propelled myself off the ground without stopping and threw my right knee as high as it could go to come down with my foot on the crossbar. I felt the horizontal piping solid beneath the sole of my shoe and jammed my fingers between the metal diamond cutouts. The fence swayed and bucked under my weight as I scrambled for the top. Thank God there was no barbed wire waiting for me.

I hadn't stopped to think, hadn't taken a breath that wasn't desperate air flowing into my lungs, and I could do neither until I was on the other side and out of his reach. I crested the top and threw one leg over. The other suddenly felt like I was wearing a lead boot when the man caught up and reached for my ankle. He gripped my bones hard enough to crush, and I screamed. I kicked and thrashed, high-centered on the fence and trying to get loose. He was pulling me down with ten times my weight. I got one solid kick to his face, loosening his grip, before his hands slipped and peeled off my shoe. I hurled my free leg over the fence and jumped down the other side.

We stood with the fence between us, me rigid with nerves and ready to bolt, and him holding my shoe in one hand and his injured face in the other. His paw of a hand covered the side of his face without the scar, leaving him glaring at me through the angry pink worm of a welt. We stared at each other, heaving breath, until a car came to a screeching stop behind me.

I turned, expecting to see a windowless van, which would be my demise, but instead saw a familiar cruiser with a very welcome face behind the wheel.

"Get in!" Bray shouted through the lowered window. He reached across the front seat and threw open the passenger door.

I had never been so happy to see anyone in my life.

I looked back at the alley before I turned to run, and the man was gone.

My ankle screamed in protest when I dashed for the car. The hard concrete pushed gritty rocks into my sock, and I tried not to limp. I threw myself onto the front seat, and Bray hit the gas before my door was even closed.

"What the hell was that? Who was that guy?" he shouted as he sped off. We were still in quaint downtown Del Rio and attracting attention in his loud, powerful vehicle.

I pulled my injured ankle up on the dash. "Just drive," I told him with a wince.

"Oh, shit. Are you okay?" he asked when he saw it.

I'd pulled my sock down to reveal mottled purple in the shape of a handprint circling my ankle. It was already starting to swell.

"I'm fine."

Bray took a quick left turn, which rocked me against the door. "That doesn't look fine. Let me take you home so you can ice it."

"I'm not going home," I said, my heart finally starting to calm.

"What? Why not?"

I replayed the past five minutes in my head to make sure I wasn't hallucinating. All of it had actually happened. Which meant they'd found me. They knew where I was. Finally.

I sucked in a breath and winced at the pain throbbing in my ankle. "You know that classified part in my file? Well, it has to do with him. He knows where I live. He was outside my window last night, and he wants to kill me."

CHAPTER 13

Bray drove us to his place, an apartment complex across town by where we'd had coffee the day before. He parked outside a building with an outdoor staircase, and I hoped he lived on the first floor. We climbed out of the car.

"Let me help you," he said when I took a painful step toward the stucco building hedged with greenery and pink flowers. The property was beautiful; even nicer than mine. I assumed a good chunk of his rent went to landscaping.

"I'm fine," I said through gritted teeth. My ankle felt both like it was on fire and like it was full of shards of glass grinding against each other with each step. I wondered if the man had pulled and twisted it hard enough to effectively sprain it.

"No, you're not," Bray said and rounded the car's hood toward me. "You can barely walk, and we have to go upstairs."

I closed my eyes and sighed. "Of course we do," I muttered.

"What?"

I would have let it slide, but the cooling adrenaline in my blood and everything that had just happened had my mood sharper than normal. "I said, *of course we do*. Of course you live on the second floor of this building where I need to go hide so some whack job from ten years ago doesn't find me and try to kill me! *Of course!*" I whirled on him, arms out and balancing on one foot, and glared. "What were you even doing there, Bray? I told you I was going to handle Brittany on my own."

He recoiled like I'd slapped him, looking incredulous. "Uh, don't you mean *thank you*?" His face pinched into an affronted scowl. "I'm pretty sure I just *saved you* from some guy—who apparently wants to kill you—trying to snatch you off the street!"

He was completely right, but admitting it felt like treason.

I glared at him and turned for the stairs. "I didn't need to be saved."

He pressed his fob and the car chirped behind us. "That's not what it looked like. You still haven't told me who that guy was."

I sucked in a breath and put my foot on the first step, preparing to bear my weight. Memory of the man chasing me crawled through my veins like an army of ants. I didn't want to think about it until I was safely behind a locked door, preferably one where the owner inside had a gun. Too bad there was a switchback staircase in my way. "I'll tell you inside." I took one aching step and winced.

"Here." Bray reached out for me, and I swatted him away.

"I don't need your help!"

No one ever offered to help me. I did everything on my own. I'd had plenty of injuries before, but this one felt like it topped the list. I wasn't sure my ankle wasn't broken. Perhaps it was because of the fear coupled with the pain and the knowledge they'd found me, and nothing would ever be the same. Or perhaps it was the humiliation of Bray watching me struggle up the stairs. Either way, every step made me want to cry.

I made it to the fourth step with a biting wince when Bray stepped in.

"Okay, this is going to take forever." He came up behind me and looped my arm over his shoulders.

"Bray, what are you—?"

"Up we go, tiger," he said and effortlessly scooped me into his arms.

Almost effortlessly.

"*Ouch!*" I cried when my injured ankle banged into the wall in the narrow space.

"Sorry!" he said and pulled me closer to his chest. "Tuck in your legs."

"Put me down!" I fought the tight grip of his arms but couldn't get anywhere against his strength.

"No. You said that guy chasing you wants to kill you, and I'm not about to die waiting for you to climb these stairs."

He walked up them as if the inconvenience of my weight was a bag of groceries rather than an adult body. My feet bobbed with each step. I felt his arms behind my back and knees, his hard chest pressed into my ribs. He cradled me against him like I was precious cargo, and it sent an embarrassing wave of warmth from my head to my toes.

"This is mortifying. I feel pathetic."

We rounded the switchback, Bray moving slowly so as not to smash my foot again, and started up the second half of the stairs.

"Are you kidding?" he said. "I saw you scale that fence. You're a badass."

I blushed again.

"Where did you learn to do that?"

"You don't want to know."

"Actually." He paused to carefully set me down at the top of the stairs. His warm hand lingered on my hip as I found my footing on one leg. "I do. That's why I asked." I gripped the short wall for balance both from being set down and the feel of his touch. He fished his keys out of his pocket.

Memories of all the times I'd scaled fences played through my mind like a highlight reel of a delinquent youth. In truth, I couldn't even remember the first time; I'd probably been thirteen years old. No one had taught me how to do it. I'd learned out of necessity, either because I was running from bad guys, or I *was* the bad guy making a getaway. None of it was charming or *badass* as Bray implied. It was mostly terrifying.

"I'm not sure it's in my best interest to confess all my crimes to a government agent," I told him.

He shoved his keys into the lock and shot a grin over his shoulder. "Well, it's not like you can run away from me, so." He glanced down at my swollen ankle, and I knew he'd meant it as a joke, but it served as a reminder that I was trapped. Always trapped.

We entered his apartment to a spacious and tidy living room. He tossed his keys into a bowl on a small table and turned to throw the dead bolt behind us. "Let me get you some ice," he said and pointed at his couch.

I took in the room, and it was indeed decorated much like my own apartment: soothing neutrals and cozy furniture. The only splashes of color lighting up the walls were a painting and a bookshelf stuffed to the gills.

I pictured him lounging on his couch and turning pages of a book with his long fingers. Perhaps he wore reading glasses. I bit my lip at the thought.

I hobbled over and lowered myself into the plush cushions. I considered putting my foot up on his stone coffee table but thought that might be rude. Instead, I lay back and tried not to think about the fact I'd just been chased by a ghost and what it all meant. I focused on Bray's living room and not the pain in my leg or the fear in my mind. He had nice furniture and a big, but not obnoxiously big, TV mounted on the wall. Given the tidiness of the space, I wondered if I'd been right about him being a control freak that day we'd first met.

"Here you go," he said and returned from the kitchen I could partially see through a cutout wall. He passed through the small dining room and crossed the room to the couch with a bag of ice wrapped in a tea towel. I silently watched him reach for a pillow and gently place it under my injured ankle. He used another pillow to prop against the ice bag and hold it in place. Then he leaned over me, his chest coming close to my face and the smell of him hitting me like a gust of wind, and adjusted the pillows behind my back.

"Comfy?" he asked with a smile. He'd created a little nest, which supported my body in all the right places to make me feel weightless.

"Yes, thank you."

He sat atop the coffee table, directly facing me and rubbed his palms on his knees.

"Where did you learn to do that?" I repeated his question from the stairs. "Do they teach pillow fluffing at the Academy?"

He laughed. "No." His face flushed, and he ran a hand through his hair. "No. I spent some time recovering from an injury and learned a lot about the proper placement of a pillow."

The statement felt miles deep, and I wondered if it had to do with his security clearance being revoked. His face held a secret. I couldn't help but probe. "What happened?"

He looked at me with his lips softly pressed together and shook his head. "Doesn't matter."

Something about the way he said it told me it *did* matter. A lot. Apparently, we were still keeping secrets from each other. I wanted to know his, but the look on his face told me not to ask.

"Do you want anything for the pain?" he asked and nodded at my foot.

The throbbing had stopped now that I wasn't standing on it, and the ice was helping, but something to take the edge off sounded great.

"Yes. Got anything good? Any repo'ed narcotics? I could go for a line of Percocet," I said with a suggestive bounce of my brows.

His face fell and his eyes widened in horror.

"Bray, I'm kidding. Jesus. I'm not a junkie. I'll take some ibuprofen."

He released a breath and stood from his table. He headed down the hall this time, and I wondered what Agent Calvin Bray's bathroom looked like.

"You know, I *have* sampled my share of drugs though." I found myself disclosing more information, and I wasn't sure why. Perhaps it was being in his personal space and the fact that he was taking care of me, but I felt closer to him.

"Oh?" he said from down the hall.

"Yeah, unfortunately. I've been in a few situations where I couldn't blow my cover and passing up on an offering would have done just that."

He returned and placed two blue gel pills in my hand. "That sounds . . . awful."

A laugh, of all things, burst from my throat. Most people asked which was my favorite when I talked about drugs, and then reliably launched into their own anecdotes of wild nights and hazy memories. In truth, I'd hated every last second of it. But if the alternative was a bullet in my head—or something worse—I'd take a line of coke any day.

Bray walked to the kitchen to get me a glass of water.

"It was awful. I hated when Wallace put me on drug cases. They were always the most dangerous and usually required me to *do* drugs at some point." I rolled my eyes and accepted the glass of water.

Bray stared at me in awe while I sipped and swallowed the pills.

"What?" I asked him.

He shook his head like he was snapping out of a daze. "Nothing. You just talk about it like it was a bad day at the office, and not a threat to your life."

A sad laugh shook my shoulders. "Well, I kind of have to think of it that way, you know? Don't have much choice."

He sat back down on the coffee table and leaned his elbows

on his knees. He was only a foot away from me. "I'm sorry, Erin." The sincere furrow in his brow and the sound of my real name put a hard lump in my throat. I had to take another sip of water.

Uncomfortable, I sat back against the pillows and sighed. "Well, at least the Del Rio moms aren't into *that* kind of smuggling—unless, are we sure they aren't?"

Bray held my gaze, seeing through my attempt to joke and not bending. "They aren't. I've checked."

The heat of his eyes pushed a flush into my cheeks. I tried to fight it off with another quip. "Good. I'd hate to discover diapers full of heroin or something."

"You don't have to do that," he said, his eyes still on me.

I swallowed another gulp of water, emptying the glass. "Do what?"

He reached for the glass and set it behind him on the table. He pressed the tips of his fingers together and leaned his elbows on his knees. "Act like this is all normal and not very hard for you."

I suddenly felt like I was naked. Like he'd been stripping layer after layer from me and finally gotten to the bare skin beneath, where he could see all my scars and secrets. The urge to cry swelled up in my throat, my eyes. I blinked away a wash of moisture and deflected.

"Thanks, but I don't need a therapist, Bray."

The look of disappointed hurt on his face immediately made me regret saying it. He stood from the table and turned away.

"I'm sorry!" I blurted, my face hot with embarrassment. I searched for the right words to salvage the situation. So rarely had I been close enough to someone to hurt their feelings, I didn't know what to do. "I'm sorry," I said again. "I know you're only trying to help—and thank you, really. It's just . . ." My throat tightened again, and I spilled the truth. "No one ever offers to help me, so I'm not used to it."

He stilled before turning back to me. When he sat on the coffee table again, a wave of relief washed over me. "That's really sad."

I scoffed and rolled my eyes, wondering if he matched me in lack of interpersonal social skills. "Thanks."

He blushed and waved his hands. "Sorry, that sounded rude. I didn't mean to—" He cut himself off and took a breath. He looked up at me. "You know what? Maybe we should just get back to the case."

A pang of disappointment struck me in the chest, but I agreed. Keeping our relationship professional was in everyone's best interest.

"Good idea."

Bray nodded and smoothed his palms over his knees again. "So, what happened back there?"

I knew he wasn't asking me to report on my conversation with Brittany, although there was valuable information to be shared there. He wanted to know about the man who'd chased me down the alley and nearly broken my leg. I leaned back into the pillows, wishing I could sink into them and disappear along with the day. I didn't want to speak the words aloud for fear of making it all real.

"Something very, very bad," I finally said.

He studied me with narrowed eyes. "What does that mean?"

I sat up and adjusted the bag of ice. The chill on my fingertips even through the towel was shocking. Part of me didn't want to say anything more. Part of me, perhaps the part that had looked in his eyes in the coffeeshop and momentarily imagined we were on a date, wanted to go back to that moment and stay there pretending it was real. The same part of me wanted to go back to the moment we'd just had, where he was sincerely kind to me, sympathetic, and wrap myself in someone else's care. If I told him the truth, he'd never look at me the same. It would change everything. I would go from whatever he thought of me now to a true criminal.

But, in the end, that's who I really was.

I took a big, heavy breath and got straight to the point. "The classified part of my file fills in the gap between my father and I arriving at that hotel room in Houston and me becoming a CI. That guy from the alley was there too."

Bray slowly nodded with a purse of his lips, making his scar jump. "I figured."

Only a handful of people knew what happened in that missing space. Two were in prison, one—I thought—died that night, one had died just a few days ago, and the other was me.

I didn't want to tell Bray for a host of reasons, but I knew on some instinctual level I could trust him. I took a breath and told him a story I'd never shared with another living soul.

Chapter 14

Ten Years Ago

What I had been doing in that hotel room with my father that night was a long story. Sometimes, I liked to pretend it was just that: a story. Something that happened to someone else and not the reason I'd spent the next decade changing names and hiding. After all, everything I had done with my father, every job, was rooted in fiction.

I'd played the part of a debutant that night. A spoiled rich girl whose daddy had promised her an extravagant birthday gift. One we'd had to fly all the way to Houston to meet a jewel dealer in a private hotel room to obtain.

It had all gone according to plan. Until it hadn't.

"I was hoping for something bigger," I'd said, pouting, and playing the part of Ana Prescott when the woman with the jewels presented a dazzling tennis bracelet worth a year's college tuition. We sat at the dining table in a lavish suite, the pendant lamp hanging above us casting glittering rainbows. I'd been instructed to do whatever it took to make them bring out *the big one.*

My father had it on good authority, thanks to the circles he ran in, the dealer had traveled to the jewel expo in town with a diamond of life-changing proportions. He'd arranged a private meeting with them in a hotel room. Little did they know, the briefcase of cash we'd arrived with was completely fake—a *good* fake, thanks to my father's favorite counterfeiter, but still fake. Contrary to pop culture lore, five million dollars is way too heavy to haul around in any kind of case; it would weigh over one hundred pounds if it was made up of hundred-dollar bills. That night, we'd brought a million (fake) dollars as a show of good faith, and my father was going to wire the rest of the money from a bank account that didn't exist, but we would be long gone before they figured out none of the money was real. The plan was to make a deal for the diamond in the hotel room and then disappear. We'd be in the wind, old identities burned, before they realized. We had another dealer lined up to sell it to in Peru. Javi, a man my father had known for years, was waiting for our call. It was supposed to be our ticket out. The final job to set us free.

They'd laid out their best to impress us that night: necklaces, earrings, rings. But what we were after wasn't mounted or strung. It was loose and the size of an acorn, if the rumors were to be believed.

"Olena, please," my father cooed from where he casually leaned back in his leather dining chair beside me. "I want only the best for my princess's birthday. You only turn eighteen once." He turned and winked at me. "We didn't come all this way for trinkets we could buy at home. Impress us."

I sweetly smiled with all the entitlement I could muster. As much belief that I *deserved* the biggest and best.

Olena, a stunning woman with ice blue eyes and birdlike features, considered us with a purse of her painted lips. She herself dripped in glittering jewels and looked both like she could readily serve us tea or kill us, depending on her mood.

My hands were slicked with sweat beneath the table. I held them in my lap to keep them from shaking. It wasn't so much the hot lamp overhead or the performance or the terrifying woman sitting across from me. It was the man standing behind Olena with a gun in his belt.

He had a mean scar like someone had tried to gouge out his eye with a knife and missed. He stared at me with a hunger that reminded me of a shark, watching my every move. His lips peeled into a sinister grin when my father called me *princess*.

Olena partially turned her head and spoke to him in a language I didn't understand.

The man nodded once and took a step closer to the table. A beam of light glinted off his gun when he folded his arms over his chest. I gulped at the sight of it.

Olena rose from her chair like an elegant bird taking flight. She slipped away toward the bedroom to get the diamond and left me and my father sitting at the table with the bodyguard watching over us like a gargoyle.

My father casually lifted the glass of brown liquor Olena had poured him and sipped. I fought to steady my heart, knowing the moment we'd been working toward was almost upon us.

Just then, the suite's doorbell rang.

The man with the gun swiveled his thick head and reached for his hip. I sat up straighter when I noticed my father do the same in a motion almost too slight to detect.

We weren't expecting anyone else.

The man with the gun eyed us before throwing a glance toward the bedroom where Olena had gone. He hesitated. I could see his jaw muscles working as he thought, perhaps about how much trouble he'd get in if something went wrong while his boss was in the other room.

"Who is it?" he eventually called in a thick accent.

"Room service," a muffled voice said through the door.

The thought of food tempted me since we hadn't eaten before arriving at the hotel. My father said we couldn't be late, and with having to put on a dress and heels and the identity of a spoiled rich girl, I hadn't had time for a bite.

The man with the gun threw another glance toward the bedroom and must have decided he was hungry too, or that Olena would be upset if he turned away her dinner, because he stalked off to answer the door.

My father and I were left alone.

It was in those moments I longed for some kind of encouragement from him. A pat on the back, a wink. *Something* to indicate I was doing well. But he never broke character. It was a surefire way to get caught, he'd told me. *Never* let on to your true identity.

He took another sip of his drink, and I forced myself not to fidget.

Olena returned carrying a small jewelry box at the same time the man with the gun came back with a hotel employee on his heels pushing a cart. Olena and the man with the gun exchanged words in the language I did not know, but I could tell she was not happy based on her tone. They seemed to argue, the man shrugging and holding out his arms. Olena eventually grumbled and pointed across the room.

"Over there," the man instructed and shepherded the waiter toward the living room.

I wondered if the waiter thought it odd since we were sitting at the dining table, the obvious place to deposit food, and he was being guided elsewhere, but he didn't object and instead pushed his cart toward the couch.

"Now," Olena said. She turned her terrifying smile on me and my father. She pried open the jewelry box, and inside was the biggest diamond I had ever seen in my life.

My mask slipped for a second—and I let it. Even Ana Prescott would be impressed by the glinting meteor before her.

My father sucked air between his teeth and chuckled. "Now we're talking. Look at that thing, princess. Do you like it?"

It was undeniably beautiful. A diamond so pure it was white and every color of the rainbow at the same time. I felt its reflection shining in my eyes like I was a cartoon character. I nodded and remembered what I was supposed to do.

"Can I hold it?" I asked.

Olena's painted lips peeled into a grin. She pulled a small cloth from the box and used it to pluck the stone from its cushion. She placed the diamond in my outstretched hand. It felt like a piece of ice on my skin. A hard, heavy piece of glinting ice.

My heart lifted with relief. I'd done my part. My father had been planning for months to get that rock in my hand, and there it was.

I turned to him with a proud smile. "I love it, Daddy. Can I keep it?"

He smiled back at me, pride in his eyes, and one of the last times I'd ever look at him up close, but I didn't know that. "Yes, princess. It's yours."

Olena tutted. "Let's not get ahead of ourselves here. I trust you brought payment?"

My father gave her a feline smile and reached for the briefcase near his feet. "Of course."

"Open it," she demanded when he lifted the case.

He did as he was told and set the case on the table. I'd seen the money myself earlier. It looked completely real—and this would not have been the first time we'd used counterfeit cash for a deal. The bills could stand up to scrutiny. They had all the proper watermarks and security threads. There was only one way to prove they were fake. If lit on fire, the ink burned bright green rather than black. Lucky for us, not many people were in the habit of lighting their payment on fire.

Olena's eyes widened at sight of the neatly stacked bills lining the case. Image after image of Benjamin Franklin's apathetic smirk stared up at us. "I have heard rumor," she said in her icy, lyrical tone, "of a clever man and his clever daughter moving around this country taking advantage of hardworking people." She pinched a stack of bills between her needle fingers and lifted it from the case.

My heart kicked up a gear and sent blood rushing through my veins. I fought to keep calm and hold still. I noted my father's jaw twitch from the corner of my eye. But ever the con man, he played it cool. "I've heard that rumor too. That's why I've taken measures to protect my family and my assets against any danger." He nodded over at me still holding the diamond in my hand.

"Hmm," Olena purred and freed the top bill from the stack. "Smart of you to protect the things you hold valuable. I do the same." She jerked her head toward her henchman and said something in their language.

He approached her, and when he pulled a shiny silver lighter out of his pocket, I nearly fainted.

I glanced at my father, knowing it was all over if they lit that bill on fire. We'd be exposed. Caught.

He didn't even blink, and I hated him. Hated how calm he was in the face of imminent danger. Hated how I couldn't reach out for his hand and tell him I was scared. Hated that he'd trained me to put on the same façade and keep it together no matter what.

I let my training take over and dampened the emotions slicing me raw inside. "If you burn that, we won't replace it," I said coolly.

My father tittered a laugh and placed his hand on my arm. "Let her do what she wants, princess. She needs to know she can trust us."

I felt my pulse leaping in my wrist where his hand lay. I tried to read his face, to know what he was thinking, and, more importantly, what his plan was for escaping this room when the bill burst into green light like a firecracker.

Olena only continued to smile at us, giving nothing away. "Sweet girl. Thinks I care about a hundred dollars when there are millions more." She brusquely said something to her henchman, and he flicked open the lighter. The flame sparked to life and licked the edge of the bill before I could take my next breath.

I continued not breathing because I was too shocked when the bill burned like a real one. The edge of it caught fire and curled with a wisp of black smoke.

The room was tense enough to explode.

My father calmly held up his hands. "There, see? All this fuss for nothing. Now—"

Olena narrowed her eyes and barked something at her henchman. He dropped the bill and stomped out the flame while she reached for the stack she'd pulled it from and took another one from the center. "Again," she demanded and held up another crisp bill.

"Olena, please—" my father said with a weary sigh, and I heard it in his voice. The tiniest tell only I could make out. We were about to get caught.

I glanced at the case and realized he'd lined the stacks with real bills, but their insides were made up of the fakes for this exact reason. My father expected a test; he knew she was going to take a bill from the top of a stack and burn it to make sure it was real. His error was assuming one bill would satisfy her.

Olena muttered something in the other language, and her henchman flicked the lighter again. When this bill caught, it burned emerald like a radioactive orb.

I didn't have time to panic because a hell we weren't even expecting broke loose.

A loud clang called our attention to the living room. The waiter dropped the silver dome, which had been covering one of the plates. I'd honestly thought he'd left, and Olena must have too, based on the startled look on her face. The dome clattered on the floor, and when the waiter bent as if he were going to pick it up, he reached for his ankle and retrieved a gun. He stood back up with it aimed right at us.

"FBI, nobody move. This room is surrounded."

Nobody listened, and everybody moved.

Olena's henchman reached for his own gun at the same time my father leapt out of his chair. I knew he was armed, and it would be a matter of seconds before someone pulled a trigger.

I tried to dive under the table, but Olena grabbed me. Her bonelike fingers dug into my upper arm hard enough to bruise. "Where do you think you're going, princess?" she snarled.

I shot her a terrified glance and prayed she didn't pull out a gun too. Though, Olena probably knew how to kill me with one hand if she wanted, no weapon needed.

A gunshot rang out, and we both flinched. Someone cried out in pain, and I was too terrified to figure out who it was.

"Get out of here!" I heard my father shout. If he had been the one shot, he at least had enough life left to instruct me to run.

My heart pounded in my chest, my ears, my eyes, it felt. I scrambled to get away from Olena's death grip. I yanked my arm free and threw it back to slam my elbow into her beak of a nose. I felt the bone crack against the hard point of my bent arm. She screamed and threw her hands over a sudden gush of blood. I sucked in a breath, ready to escape, and made it half a step before I slammed into a brick wall of a body.

The henchman hooked an arm around me, and before I could blink, he was squeezing the air from my throat and jamming his gun into my temple.

The entire room froze, and my life teetered on the brink.

I blinked, already getting dizzy from lack of oxygen, and saw the waiter, who was apparently an FBI agent, on the floor. A wave of relief hit me because the gunshot from earlier had not struck my father. I wondered if the man was dead.

"Don't move," the henchman pointing the gun to my head said.

My father aimed his weapon at us. His jaw clenched and his eyes were black pits. I saw a slight twitch in his lip and a fraction of a shake in his hands. To anyone else, it would have been invisible, but I knew all his tells. He was nervous, and it terrified me.

"Dad," I whispered.

"Shut up!" the henchman barked and tightened his grip on my throat. The gun pushed into my temple like a screwdriver. I squeezed my eyes shut in terror.

Olena croaked something from the floor, her bloody hand muffling the sound of her voice. The man gripping me glanced down at her, and another gunshot rang out. It split my hearing in half, deafening me to everything but a mind-shattering ringing.

I screamed and it took a few seconds to realize my ability to scream was a result of the vise around my neck having gone slack.

The enormous henchman swayed against me, his weight threatening to collapse and take me down with him.

I spun in his arm still loosely hooked around me and found myself face first into his bloody chest.

Another scream ripped from my mouth as I shoved him away. My palms were blood soaked and my legs like rubber. Before I could gather my thoughts, another gunshot tore through the room.

I heard my father cry out in pain, and I feared the worst.

"Dad!"

He'd been shot in the leg and had fallen to one knee. His face twisted in pain. He gripped the dining table with a sweaty hand and used his other to wave me away. The FBI agent in the living room was not dead. He'd sat up and landed a successful shot. He was preparing to take another.

"Get out of here!" my father screamed at me. The pain from

the gunshot looked excruciating, but not as painful as the fear in his eyes that something would happen to me.

"Dad, I can't!" I cried. I couldn't leave him. A warped sense of loyalty wouldn't let me.

The henchman was dead from the bullet my father had fired, I knew it. Olena was nursing her broken nose, swearing in another language and spitting blood, and the agent was preparing to do more damage.

I rounded the table to get to my father. His leg was pouring blood. He'd been hit in his left calf. The wounded limb lay out behind him like a useless log. I knew I couldn't lift him, especially not with someone actively shooting at us. The best I could do would be to drag him to the door.

He held out a hand to stop me approaching and gave me a look that was at once pleading and a command. "Stop. You have to get out of here."

"Dad, I'm not—"

"Erin, *go*!"

The sound of my name stopped me in my tracks. He never broke character. Ever. The significance of it was too much to ignore.

"Go," he said again, and I had no choice but to obey.

I pivoted on my toe before the agent rose and got off another shot. I hurtled myself toward the door, not knowing what to expect on the other side. It wasn't until I was in the hall eyeing the glowing green EXIT sign that I heard a voice command me to stop. I threw myself into the stairwell and ran down as fast as I could. My lungs were on fire and my heart about to beat out of my chest when I reached the ground floor and yanked open a service door. I found myself on a side street in the pouring rain.

I ran into the night, getting soaked, until a sturdy voice commanded me to stop, this time from in front of me and with a gun barrel aimed at me for emphasis.

Cornered, I splashed to a stop, my body drenched, and my toes numb in my strappy shoes. I hadn't noticed the blood on my hands until I raised them, and it began to wash off in the rain.

The man pointing his gun at me had FBI in block letters on his coat slicked with rain.

I knew it was all over.

Chapter 15

Present Day

I finished my story and watched Bray for a reaction. He hadn't expressed much as he listened. I'd been looking for cues he might have been forming an unfavorable opinion about me, but he hadn't given anything away.

"The man who chased me today, it was the man from that night," I said. "The man who held a gun to my head and who my father shot so I could get away. The man my father went to prison for *murdering*. That's who that was."

Saying it out loud even though I'd just relived the story sent shivers all over my body.

The ghost.

"How is that possible?" Bray asked.

"Excellent question. My guess is he wasn't dead, and he escaped, but they wanted to pin my father with something on top of the counterfeit money, so they overlooked that minor detail and framed him for murder."

"Wouldn't they need a body for that?"

I arched a brow at him. "You work for the DSA. You think the FBI can't get their hands on a spare corpse?"

He held up a hand like he couldn't argue. "And how did he find out where you are?"

I lifted my shoulders in a shrug. "Hell if I know. I've been on the run for ten years with no contact from anyone from that night."

"Not even your father?"

"Not even him." I swallowed the complicated emotion that always rose at the rare mention of him.

Bray frowned. "And what about Olena? What happened to her?"

"Prison. Almost the same sentence as my father. The FBI was there for her that night; diamonds weren't the only thing she trafficked in. We just happened to be in the wrong place at the wrong time, and they got a two-for-one deal when we all got caught. As soon as my father handed over the counterfeit money for the diamond, they knew they had busted something bigger than just a trafficker. I've only learned about this from Wallace over the years. He'd feed me updates because I obviously couldn't go around asking since I had disappeared."

"Disappeared?"

I pursed my lips and nodded. "This is the part that's above your security clearance. I'm not only undercover to stay out of prison, Bray."

I watched him to see if he would put the pieces together on his own. If he could reason out why I had willingly changed my identity over and over since that night in the hotel room.

"No one knows I'm alive." I filled in the blank. "Not as the real me, anyway. Wallace made sure of that by redacting parts of my file and keeping me mobile every few months. He did that in exchange for helping him on cases, because he knew Olena would have killed me if she found me."

Bray intently studied me. "Why?"

"Because of that night. Olena ended up in prison and, I thought, the other guy had died. My father obviously didn't get away with anything, so that only left me." I paused and held his eyes. "And the diamond. It was in my hand when everything happened."

Realization dawned on his face, lighting his eyes. The pieces came together, and it all made sense. The reason I had no name and no home. The reason I had remained a puppet for my own safety.

When he finally spoke, it was the last thing I expected him to say. "Do you have it?"

I gaped at him. "Seriously? *No!* You think I've been running around for a decade with a five-million-dollar diamond in my pocket? You think I wouldn't have cashed in on that the second I could have and *really* disappeared forever?"

Just the thought made my head spin with joy. And relief. To be gone for real. To be free. What a dream. I still had Javi's contact info in Peru. He'd been waiting for a call for ten years, and I'd been waiting to give him one. The good thing about diamonds was they never went out of style. All I'd have to do was get the diamond, get it to him, and vanish with my newly found wealth—which I had been trying to do for the past decade.

Too bad that rock was still missing, and freedom was an impossible pipe dream.

I sighed. "I have no idea what happened to it; that night was pure chaos. But you're not the only one to think I have it."

Bray looked up at me.

"Olena thinks I disappeared with it. She probably thinks I am off living my best life while she's been in prison for ten years, plotting my death for having a hand in getting her sent there. That's why I've been looking over my shoulder. Her network is wide. The DSA knows all this. Part of our arrangement is basically witness protection. Wallace classified the details about the diamond in my file to keep me safe. It has worked until now." I swallowed a hard lump in my throat. The threat had finally come to fruition.

He studied me for a moment. "Wow. That's . . . a lot."

I snorted. "You're telling me. Now do you see why I was so freaked out when Wallace wasn't here? He's been protecting me this whole time."

"I can protect you," he said without a beat of hesitation.

The offer filled my face with a warm rush. "Great. You can start by getting me off the Del Rio case and finding me a new place to live."

"Well . . . I can't exactly do that," he half muttered, looking like his offer might have been more reflex than reality.

"Why not?"

"It's . . . complicated."

"Bray, these are the people who were going to kill me when I was a teenager, and they know where I *live*. I don't see what's complicated about that."

"Yes, I get that, but I don't have authority to pull you from the case."

"Well, then call someone who does."

"That's . . . even more complicated."

I growled in frustration and whacked my hands on my pillow nest.

Bray looked pained. He sighed a tight breath and stood. "Just give me some time, okay? I'll report what happened today and have a patrol unit put outside your apartment. And anyway, Del Rio is probably the safest place you can be. With all the helicopter parents in that neighborhood, someone will probably call the cops on my patrol unit."

"That's reassuring," I grumbled.

He squatted down so we were eye level. He spoke with a determined sincerity. "Erin, I won't let anything happen to you." The earnestness in his voice, the promise in his eyes—even when he'd been irritating me moments before—put a lump in my throat. He held my gaze, waiting for me to acknowledge.

I considered it, wondering how much he could do against

the people who were after me. *Not much*, I thought. But at the same time, no one had ever really offered to protect me. Wallace hadn't even gone this far. No one had ever treated me like I was a person and not an expendable object. Even if he was bossing me around and reminding me how short my leash was, he was doing it with a level of humanity I'd never been afforded.

And he called me by my real name.

"Fine. I'll stay, but I want a gun."

He gave his head one firm shake. "No."

"Yes."

"*No*," he said with a commanding authority. It stirred something inside me.

"Bray, I have nothing to defend myself with, unless you count the umbrella. And besides, I'm injured now. I can't even run away if I have to."

He looked at my ankle buried under the bag of ice. "I somehow doubt a sprained ankle would slow you down."

"Then you are overestimating your skills as a nurse."

He shook his head with a quiet laugh. "I have some bandages you can use to wrap your ankle for support. I'll show you how and then call you a ride home." He stood and left me stewing in worry about going *home*, and wondering how I was supposed to keep up with my cover, and with two kids, with only one foot.

"Speaking of Del Rio, I got some intel out of Brittany today," I called down the hall where he'd disappeared.

"Oh?" he called back.

"Yeah. Apparently, she overheard Melanie on the phone one day saying the word *Montrose*. When Brittany asked Melanie what it meant, she fired her."

"Yikes," Bray said when he returned with a beige spool of stretchy fabric. "That's a red flag reaction."

"Definitely. Brittany said she had no idea what it meant, but I would guess it has to do with their operation, maybe their supplier or a location. I got the sense she was worried. Whatever trouble they are in must be serious." *Which I can relate to*, I thought but didn't say. Bray wanted me to crack their case but part of me wanted to . . . help them.

"I'll look into it," he said. "May I?" he asked, and pointed at my feet.

I nodded and scooted up the couch to make room for him. I wasn't sure what he planned to do, but it certainly wasn't that he'd gently lift my legs and sit with my feet in his lap.

A warmth filled my face at the feel of my calves pressed into his firm thigh. It grew hotter when he rested one hand on my shin. He tossed the bag of ice onto the coffee table and gently pulled off my dirty sock.

"Oof," he said at the blotchy combo of purple from the bruises and pink from the ice having chilled my skin.

I winced at it myself. It was not pretty. "And you're going to make me go to work in this condition."

He gently cupped my heel in his hand and began wrapping the bandage. "Hopefully it's just for a day."

I watched him gingerly wrap my ankle a few times. He pulled the bandage taut but did so gently enough not to hurt.

"How am I supposed to go to work? I don't even have a shoe, Bray," I said when I remembered the ghost had pulled it off in the alley.

"I'll get you a new pair."

"How do you know what size I wear?"

"It's in your file."

My face warmed again just as he looped the bandage under the sole of my foot. I squirmed and tried to keep still.

"Are you ticklish?" he asked. I did not miss the hint of levity in his voice.

"What, that's not in my file alongside my favorite color and list of known allergies?" I fought to keep a smile out of my voice and off my face.

"Do you have allergies?"

"Cats, actually. My mom brought one home when I was six, and I broke out in hives. We had to take it back to the shelter." The memory rolled off my tongue before I even knew I'd released it from my keep. I never talked about my mother. And instead of feeling like I'd exposed some sacred, protected truth to someone unworthy, I felt a warmth at the sympathetic look on Bray's face.

"No cats. Noted. That must have been tough as a kid, to get a pet and have it taken away."

In truth, I didn't remember it as being sad. I just remembered cuddling the kitten and becoming incredibly itchy and struggling to breathe. My mother had hugged me and kissed me and apologized for things I hadn't understood at the time. The whole ordeal had upset her much more than anyone else.

"It worked out," I told Bray. "We went back and got a dog the next day."

He laughed. "You seem like much more of a dog person."

"I would love to have a dog," I said with a smile, which quickly fell.

The reason for my being unable to own a pet settled between us like a cold front.

Bray cleared his throat and finished wrapping my ankle. The end of the spool was Velcro, which he tightly fastened to hold it in place. "There," he said. "Take it off when you shower, obviously, but otherwise, wearing it should help support it."

I examined his handiwork and decided not to tell him I already knew how to wrap an ankle and was perfectly capable of doing it myself, because doing that would have denied me the opportunity to feel his hands touching me, something I enjoyed more than I wanted to admit.

"Thanks."

"You bet."

We sat there, me lounged back with my feet in his lap, and I briefly imagined we were the couple we'd pretended to be in the coffeeshop, enjoying our Sunday afternoon at home together. Perhaps we were watching a football game or a movie or simply basking in each other's company.

The fantasy snapped when he lifted my feet and stood. "Okay. Time to get you home."

He left me sitting there, sadly wondering if I would ever have a life with that kind of Sunday in it.

Chapter 16

When I arrived home, I decided the best way to avoid (a) my still conflicted feelings about losing Wallace, and (b) dissolving into a puddle of fear the ghost would come knocking, was to keep digging into the moms. But only after I'd closed all the curtains, triple-checked the door was locked, and stationed the baseball bat I'd insisted on taking from Bray's closet near me on the couch. My rideshare driver surely had questions as to why a hobbling, one-shoed woman with a tattered wooden bat had climbed into his car, but he had the decency not to ask.

I propped up my foot with more ice and stationed my loaner laptop on a pillow on my lap. The DSA always gave me one when a case called for it. Same as my loaner phone, it was equipped with basic accounts, apps, a Wi-Fi connection. All the things one would need for run-of-the-mill internet use. Plus a little back door I'd learned how to engineer that granted me access to off-limits places on the web.

I started with a generic search for *Montrose*, hoping I might get lucky. It yielded listings for local apartment complexes with the name, a residential street, and flights to the local area from a city in Colorado called Montrose. They could all have been leads or all been nothing. Without breaking into Melanie's office to look for more information, it would be hard to say.

After a few hours of rabbit holes, I decided to take a more direct approach.

I'd worked a case several years ago with a fellow CI who lived in the darkest corners of the web. She'd since paid her dues to the DSA and rejoined civilian life but had told me where to find her if I ever needed a hand. A dog-grooming message board was about the most innocuous place I could think of, I had to give her that.

I logged into perfectpaws.com and searched for @yorkiedork123. I didn't even know her real name, but I knew I could trust the person behind the cute little Yorkie profile picture. I'd chosen the name @muttmama because, should the day ever come when I could own a dog, I wasn't about to pay for a fancy breed when there were plenty of rescues out there in need of adoption.

I opened the General Tips message board and typed.

@muttmama: **My pooch stepped in a mysterious sticky substance, and I can't get it off his paws. Any tips? I feel like @yorkiedork123 always knows what to do. Thanks!**

I waited approximately two minutes before she responded. I could only imagine what kind of notification system she had set up to keep her looped into all the corners where she hid.

@yorkiedork123: I have the perfect solution! I will DM you the recipe.

"Perfect," I said aloud. Surely someone somewhere could access every DM sent on the platform, so it didn't matter if we kept sensitive information off the main threads. But the only way to get into a DM conversation was to invite someone from a main thread. Alas, I had to come up with a believable story about dog grooming every time I wanted to talk to @yorkiedork123 privately.

A little window popped up in the corner of my screen.

@yorkiedork123: Muttmama! It's been a while. What's up?

@muttmama: Hey. Do you know anything about a company or person named Montrose that might be tied to a smuggling operation?

@yorkiedork123: Hmm. Location?

@muttmama: Bay Area, California. Specifically a neighborhood called Del Rio, in the South Bay.

@yorkiedork123: Hold please.

I held, by staring at the TV, where I'd left a series of rom-com movies quietly playing while I searched the web. After the scene in the alley, I'd been grinding my teeth and couldn't bear to watch anything with even a hint of tension or a jump scare in sight.

My laptop pinged with a new message.

@yorkiedork123: Looks like the name of a black-market supplier. They run all sorts of things: arms, drugs, counterfeit designer goods.

@muttmama: Baby products?

@yorkiedork123: Weirdly, yes.

"Shit," I said out loud, still a little stunned any of this was real. I did quick math to think back to what I'd overheard Melanie say on the phone that day. Whatever had happened to get them in trouble happened three weeks ago.

@muttmama: Any chance you see record of a deal or delivery from three weeks ago?

She disappeared for a few minutes again, and I imagined her clacking away at a keyboard in front of a wall of computer screens. I had no idea what information she was accessing or who she might be talking to.

@yorkiedork123: Nothing specific, but apparently there's been chatter about a seized shipment.

My mind kicked into high gear, thinking of other smuggling cases I'd worked. A seized shipment of smuggled goods usually meant someone didn't get paid because the goods were never sold. If whatever was in that shipment was valuable enough for Melanie to put a lien on her house, whoever they owed money to was probably pretty upset.

But if a shipment of baby goods had been seized in one of the local ports, wouldn't it have crossed Bray's radar? At least I *hoped* he'd set up alerts for such a thing.

Something was still missing. But this was way more to go off than I expected.

@muttmama: Thank you. This is very helpful.

@yorkiedork123: Sure thing. Anything else?

@muttmama: Any hits on Dwayne Johnson?

@yorkiedork123: Still MIA. You'll be the first to know if I hear anything.

I sighed in completely expected disappointment. I'd asked her to keep her ear to the digital dark web ground, in case any chatter about the diamond cropped up; maybe it had been found, maybe it had been sold. So far, no luck. We'd dubbed it Dwayne Johnson in a stealth nod to the Rock. The nickname used to make me smile, back when I had hope of her helping to find it, but now it fell flat.

@yorkiedork123: Anything else? Need any actual dog grooming tips?

@muttmama: Ha, if only. Still flying sans canine, unfortunately.
@yorkiedork123: Your day will come, girl.

The reality that having a dog was a remote chance, if not impossibility, slapped me in the face once more, but I didn't feel the need to darken her day with my sorrow.

@muttmama: ☺ See you next time, Yorkiedork.
@yorkiedork123: Happy trails, Muttmama.

I closed my laptop and sighed. I lifted my phone to text Bray an update right when the doorbell rang.

Evening had fallen, and I couldn't imagine who was calling.

I instantly tensed and reached for the bat. My heart rate shot through the roof as I paused the movie still playing on TV. With one hand on my phone and one on my makeshift weapon, I rose to stand and managed to remind myself the people wanting to kill me would not ring the doorbell. They would bust down the door or shatter a window.

I hobbled across the living room using the bat as a small crutch. I held my breath as I leaned close to the slit in my curtains to peek out the window. Bray's patrol still sat down the street in an unmarked car, which miraculously blended in. I'd half expected him to send a black van with DSA blazing in yellow print. Instead, he'd sent a man in a nondescript SUV. I could see him in the driver's seat sitting up and looking my way with interest. Given he hadn't left the vehicle or otherwise flipped on a siren and floored it to my driveway to intervene, I had to assume whoever was on the porch didn't look like a threat from his vantage point.

I angled my body for as good a look as I could get of my doorstep, and saw a pale blue skirt fluttering in the breeze.

I exhaled with an ounce of relief.

When I worked up the courage to look out the peephole, I saw none other than Melanie Browning holding a casserole.

I quickly recomposed myself and leaned the bat out of sight. I opened the door with a smile. "Melanie! What a surprise," I greeted.

Melanie's pretty face froze on a discerning expression I couldn't identify before it split into a warm smile. She wore an effortless A-line dress, which looked right for skipping through the countryside and braiding bracelets out of wildflowers with her children. The golden-hour light seemed to set her aglow from within. She was the perfect picture of domestic tranquility.

The urge to blurt *How much money do you owe Montrose and why?* danced on my tongue.

"Lauren, honey, how are you doing?" she asked with a sympathetic lilt.

I mentally stumbled over how Melanie could know about my injury. I'd slipped inside as quickly as I could when my rideshare dropped me off, and even if she had been watching, was baking a casserole over a twisted ankle really the going rate in Del Rio?

She clucked her tongue and softly shook her head. "I'm sorry. Of course this is hard on you. I trust you got our flowers yesterday?"

And then it clicked.

"Oh!" I said, suddenly remembering the moms thought my uncle had passed away and I was holed up in my apartment mourning. The casserole—which smelled delicious—made sense. Flowers, food: things people gave to other people when someone died. Our house had been buried in both when my mother died.

I gave my head a small, discreet shake to bring my senses back online. I was off my game to have forgotten my cover story. What had done it? The blast from the past, surely. But also, maybe . . .

I shook away the mental image of Bray carrying me up the stairs, the way he'd laid me on the couch and taken care of me. For every on-screen kiss I'd watched that afternoon, I'd wondered anew what his lips felt like.

I had to stop thinking about him because, obviously, it was messing with my mind.

"Right, thank you," I told Melanie. "This is so kind of you."

"Oh, don't worry about it," she said and handed over the casserole. "I know cooking is the last thing anyone wants to think about at times like these. This is my famous enchilada casserole," she said and peeled back a corner of the foil layering the top. A waft of spicy, saucy cheese hit my nose, and I realized I'd made no plans for dinner. "Neighborhood favorite!" Melanie gushed. She said it like the dish had won a prize, and I would not have been surprised to learn there was in fact a Del Rio casserole cook-off.

"Well, it smells delicious. Thank you so much."

"Of course. And if you need tomorrow off, don't even worry about it. We can have you continue another day when you're ready."

I internally scoffed. My fake dead uncle could get me a day off from work, but my very real injury couldn't. The offer was tempting, I had to admit. But what was I going to do? Hide in my house all day wondering when the man with the scar would come calling? At least at the Brownings' house I'd have the protection of other people around, even if two of them were small children.

"No, it's fine," I told Melanie. "I'll be there."

Melanie gave me a curious look, and I felt like I'd said the wrong thing. I'd been young when my mother died and didn't remember the etiquette of death, but I knew people expected certain behaviors.

I forced my face to look desolate and exhausted, the look I

remembered most from my father's face back then. "It happened so quickly and unexpectedly; it's going to take a few days for the family to get things in order. I'll just be in the way right now."

Melanie gave me another sympathetic nod. She reached out and gently squeezed my arm in a move so tender, it made me feel guilty for lying to her. "Well, you take your time when you need it, honey. In the meantime, enjoy that casserole and we'll see you in the morning." She waved by way of wiggling her manicured fingers and sending her rock of a ring glinting.

"Thanks, Melanie. See you tomorrow."

She turned and stepped off the porch. Behind her back, I made eye contact with the agent in the SUV. I held up the casserole in a half shrug as if offering it to him. He nodded his head once and didn't get out of the car, so I assumed he wasn't coming in for dinner.

As with the flowers, which turned out to be innocuous, I gave the casserole a once-over. Melanie had no motive for poisoning her new nanny, and chances were she was simply being kind again. But still. I used a fork to poke at its edge, and when I sniffed, I only got a whiff of mouthwatering temptation. It was, of course, delicious. I gorged myself on it, having hardly eaten in the drama of the day, and found myself pleasantly sleepy by the time night had fallen. The feeling evaporated when I peeked out my bedroom drapes to see the SUV was gone.

In a grip of nerves, I pulled out my phone and texted Bray.

Patrol is gone.???

I chewed my lip and eyed the street end-to-end while I waited for him to respond. He took more than his standard ten seconds, and I began to worry.

The door was locked. I *knew* the door was locked; I'd

checked three times and hadn't opened it except to greet Melanie. The bat was still by the couch. I'd never played baseball other than in gym class, but I was sure I could do some damage if I had to. But I really hoped I wouldn't have to.

A familiar car turned the street corner and pulled to a stop in the same place the SUV had been. An involuntary smile teased my mouth at the same time my phone buzzed with a text from Bray.

Shift change. Don't worry.

My smile widened when I noted the telltale glow of a phone in the driver's seat.

I'm definitely worried if
it's you out there, Agent Bray.

I slipped out of sight so he wouldn't see me spying on him from the curtains.

Hard to get someone to cover
the nightshift on short notice.
You'll take what I can give you.

Just don't fall asleep on me.

Keep me awake then.

The thought of keeping Agent Bray awake all night made me clutch the windowsill. I walked to my bathroom to wash my face with cool water and brush my teeth. I texted him again once I was under the covers.

With what, a bedtime story?

Sure. Got any good ones?

None that I'm at liberty to share. Confidential, sorry.

I knew I could trust you with secrets ☺

That damn smiley face again. I rolled my eyes but couldn't help smiling to myself.

How about you tell me one instead.

I mean, kind of in the same boat with the confidentiality thing . . .

I'm a vault, remember?

True.

I waited through a long pause. When his bouncing dots didn't appear after a solid minute, I decided to give him a prompt.

I know where you can start. Tell me about the injury you recovered from that turned you into an expert pillow fluffer.

Another long pause passed, and I wondered if I'd crossed a line. Or perhaps he'd nodded off.

Bray? You fall asleep out there?

Of course not.
That's just . . . a long story.

Isn't the goal to stay awake all night? I'm all ears.

He paused again, and his reluctance only stirred my already deep curiosity.

Fine. You want to go 20 questions about it?

LOL. No.

Did you just LOL? What is it, 2012?

You know, you're funny when you're not being mean.

I scoffed out loud, and before I knew what I was doing, I pressed the icon to call him.

"I'm not *mean*," I scolded as soon as he answered.

He quietly laughed. The enclosed space of his car dampened the sound into a warm rumble. "Calling to yell at me for calling you mean isn't mean?"

"I'm not yelling!" I shouted.

Bray only laughed harder.

"You know what? Forget it. I don't need this from you." I'd tried for sharp, but my tone came out snappy and playful.

"Oh, *okay*," Bray said. "Like you haven't been giving me shit since the moment we met."

"What are you talking about?"

"Uh, how about telling me I suck at my job every step of the way?"

"Well, you—"

"If you're about to tell me I suck again, I'm hanging up."

The exact words caught in my throat. I sheepishly cut myself off. "Sorry. I guess I have been a little harsh."

"Uh-huh. Understated, too."

I rolled my eyes again and wished he could see it.

A pause passed. I let the comfort of being on the phone with him settle over me like a blanket.

"How's your ankle?" he asked.

I flexed my foot. "You know, it's feeling a lot better."

"Good. I'm glad some rest helped."

"Yes, but it might also have been Melanie Browning's award-winning enchilada casserole that did the trick."

"Oh? And how did you come by that?"

"She hand-delivered it to my door as part of my condolence package for losing my fake uncle."

He paused, and I assumed we were sharing the same thoughts. "Ah, right. That."

"Yeah. What are we going to do about that, by the way?"

"I guess roll with it for now."

"Okay. I actually have an update for you."

"Oh?"

"Yes, I didn't know what to do with myself when I got home, so I went down a rabbit hole on Montrose, and found out it's the name of a black-market supplier."

"How did you come by that information?" he asked, sounding impressed and surprised.

"Doesn't matter. But they run all sorts of things: guns, drugs, *baby products*." I let the words linger. "And apparently there's chatter over a seized shipment. I'm thinking this has to be what's got our girls in trouble."

Bray stayed quiet for a minute. "Interesting. I've got eyes at all the local ports, and no one has reported a seized shipment of baby products."

A tiny wave of relief swelled inside me. At least he'd done that right.

"Yes, obviously there's still a missing piece here," I said. "But it's more than we had, so thank you."

The praise fizzled through me. I was so unused to the feeling, it made me a little dizzy. "You're welcome. Were you able to find out anything today? About my case?"

Bray sighed a weary breath, which set my nerves on edge. "Not really; I'm still battling security clearance. But the timing of Wallace's death and the reappearance of your ghost seems awfully coincidental. I mean, the only person who knew where you were—and *who* you are—dies, and then a henchman from your past shows up a few days later?"

The exact thoughts had been milling around my mind, but I'd refused to grant them purchase for fear it was all connected. And hearing Bray say it made me realize, how could it *not* all be connected?

"That's a great thing to tell me when I'm home alone and already freaked out," I said flatly.

"You're not alone. I'm right here."

The blanket-like, warm sensation I'd gotten earlier came back, and the comfort of it pulled words from my mouth. "Do you want to come inside?"

A pause passed.

"Um . . ."

I recognized how my question had sounded and quickly clarified. "I mean come inside to keep watch. Since all you gave me was this old bat, I'd really rather have your gun in the house than out there on the street. And besides, I can make you coffee to help keep you up." It all came spilling out, and I flushed at how clumsy I'd sounded.

Bray seemed to consider it. I heard a shuffling from inside the car. "Sure," he said. "I can come inside. I have something for you anyway."

My interest was piqued. "Okay. Use your key so I know it's you."

He quietly laughed. “You’re not going to hit me with an umbrella again, are you?”

“No. I have a bat now, remember?”

“See you in a minute.”

In that minute, I put my bra back on and swept my messy hair up into a ponytail. I gingerly walked down the hall and heard his key in the lock. I reached the door at the same time he opened it. He stepped inside carrying a bag from a sporting goods store along with his messenger bag and wearing a collared shirt under a windbreaker. His hair looked damp, and he smelled like a fresh shower.

“Hi,” he said, and quickly stepped out of the way to close the door behind him. Doing so brought him closer to where I stood. We bumped into each other for a split second.

“Sorry,” I said.

He shot me a smile and locked the door. I watched him throw the dead bolt so I knew it was locked, and then I clocked his gun holstered on his hip.

I let out a breath of relief at both things.

We stood together in the small entryway, his size taking up most of it, and I couldn’t help but feel safer with him close by.

“Thanks for coming in.”

He softly smiled down at me and didn’t move. The air between us grew heavy. “Of course.”

Tearing myself from his gaze felt like a physical effort. “Do you want some coffee?” I asked, and turned toward the kitchen.

“Sure.” He followed, his footsteps louder and heavier than mine in my socks with only one good foot. “You seem to be walking better,” he said when we made it to the kitchen. He lifted the bag onto the dining table.

I reached for one of the colorful mugs hanging from the hutch. “Yes, well I had my ankle expertly wrapped earlier, and it helped a lot. What’s in the bag?”

The rustle of a shopping bag filled the air behind me when I turned around to make the coffee.

"Your new shoes." He pulled one out and modeled it like a Home Shopping Network product. A ribbon of hot pink ran down each side of the sleek black sneaker. It looked fast sitting still.

"Running shoes," I said with a nod. "Is that so I can faster escape bad guys chasing me down alleys?"

"That, and so you are comfortable on your feet with two small children all day," he said with a grin.

I rolled my eyes, which I'd done more in the past few days since I'd met him than I probably had in the past ten years combined.

His K-Cup finished brewing, and I handed him the steaming mug. I grabbed one for myself and set it under the machine.

"What are you doing?" he asked.

"Mak-ing coff-ee . . ." I said, splitting up all the syllables to make it more obvious.

He reached out and took the mug from me. "You can't have coffee now. You have to sleep because you have to work tomorrow."

I scoffed and reached for the mug back. "And you don't?"

He grabbed the mug again like we were kids fighting over a toy. "I'm at work right now, and believe it or not, sleep deprivation is part of training at the DSA Academy." He said it with the same authority as when he'd earlier told me I couldn't have a gun. It stirred that feeling inside me again, and I backed off.

"Fine. But I can't promise you I'll fall asleep. Not with ghosts outside and you making no progress on my case."

He set both mugs down and stepped toward me. I followed his eyes with mine as he drew closer, having to look up from my sock-footed stature far below his. He placed the hand that had been holding the coffee on my shoulder, and I felt the warmth through my T-shirt. "Erin, I'm doing the best I can, I promise." His thumb took a brief but thrilling journey over my collarbone and back. It lodged my breath in my throat. "And you can go to sleep. Don't worry. I'll be here all night."

My voice was raspy and thick when it came out. "Okay."

"Okay." He slipped off his windbreaker and hung it on a dining chair. Then he unbuttoned his shirtsleeves and began rolling them up, making himself comfortable.

"Um. Good night then," I said awkwardly.

He shot me another smile. "Good night."

I returned to my bedroom and climbed into bed, acutely aware he was moving about my apartment. I heard the TV turn on and thought of texting him something snippy about slacking off on the job, but I remembered his comment about being mean. And anyway, I'd rather him be sitting inside my apartment with a gun and all the doors locked watching TV than have him fall asleep outside in his car.

I sighed and rolled over to face the window, hoping there was no one out there watching.

The room was still pitch-black when I felt the mattress dip beside me. I'd fallen asleep on my side, and his weight pressed the bed down enough I slightly rolled back into him. His solid body caught me like a warm, hard wall. The smell of his shower still lingered. He stretched out behind me and leaned over to whisper my name into my ear—my real name.

A little moan escaped my mouth at the sound and a deep breath filled my lungs. He pushed up against me, and my body responded on reflex. I rolled my hips into him, arching my back and feeling what I'd been imagining for the past few days press into me. I heard him suck in a sharp breath. He flipped his hand beneath the sheet and pressed his palm to my bare thigh, dragging it higher and squeezing as he went. The stirring I'd felt deep inside earlier bloomed out into a dizzying heat.

He whispered my name again, and my breath came faster. I was suddenly too hot for the covers, so I kicked them down. He hooked his leg over mine and dragged it back to open my hips. I was all but gasping, on the verge of a climax sneaking up on me too fast to keep at bay, when his fingers traced the elastic band on my underwear. He snapped it against my skin, and by the time he slipped his hand beneath, greedily palming me, I woke to a pounding rush of blood receding like the tide and my sweaty fists strangling my pillow.

I sat up in bed, alone, panting, and fought to hold on to the best dream I'd ever had. I blinked in the dark and caught my breath.

"Shit," I said, afraid of what it meant.

I couldn't fall for my handler. I couldn't ever sleep with my handler even if I—apparently, if the dream were any indication—really wanted to. It was all too complicated. It might even have been illegal, I didn't know.

But I knew I needed a glass of water and a fresh shirt because mine was damp with sweat.

I climbed out of bed and pulled on a stretchy camisole and replaced my sweatpants. It was after three a.m. according to my bedside clock.

I quietly made my way toward the kitchen, my foot sore and stiff from a few hours of sleep. The living room glowed a milky blue in the light of the TV. The volume was way down low, and to my pleasant but slightly annoyed surprise, Bray was asleep on the couch. I wasn't sure I would have been able to face him after the dream I'd just had if I'd found him awake.

The sight of his bulky body curled onto my couch sent a wave of warmth washing over me like an aftershock. I couldn't even remember the last sex dream I'd had—or sex, for that matter—and whenever and wherever it had been, I certainly hadn't had the star of the dream under my roof when I woke.

Bray had removed his collared shirt and shoes. He lay on his side with his arms crossed, in a tank top undershirt that put his biceps on full display. I bit my lip at the sight. His gun sat on the coffee table next to his phone, and I thought of stealing both just to teach him a lesson.

Instead, I rolled my eyes again and reached for the blanket folded up on the armchair. "So much for that sleep deprivation training, huh?" I muttered as I draped the soft cotton throw over his long body. I leaned down to secure it behind his back, and the dim light from the TV caught a patch of shiny skin on his left shoulder. Two patches, in fact.

I angled my body to allow for more light and squinted at the strange patterns just below his collarbone like two nickel-sized, misshapen stars I suddenly realized were scars. Big scars that looked a lot like . . . bullet holes.

I sucked in a tight breath and stood back, alarmed.

Bray had been shot?

I suddenly ached to know the story at the same time a visceral rage at whoever had shot him boiled up inside me. I wanted to tear their head off or maybe shoot them back. I was no doctor, but the location of the wounds had to have been life-threatening; they were inches from his heart.

A pain filled my chest, and I felt an involuntary warmth wash my eyes. I pressed a hand to my mouth. This had to be the injury he didn't want to talk about—and I couldn't blame him.

The urge to wrap my arms around him, to protect him from the horror of the past, hit me so hard, I had to move away before I did.

But I couldn't completely resist touching him.

I reached out and smoothed my thumb over the furrow in his brow. I wondered if he was having a bad dream or could perhaps sense me standing there and was unconsciously scolding me for being out of bed. Either way, his face relaxed into a serene calm at my touch.

I jerked back when a car door closing outside caught my attention. It was after three a.m. If anyone was out and about at this hour, they were up to something they didn't want anyone else to know about.

Like coming to tie up the loose end from a decade-old crime.

I forced a deep breath to fill my lungs and glanced at Bray's gun on the coffee table. He'd kill me if I grabbed it, but I wasn't about to die while he dozed on my couch. I left it for the time being and crept to the living room window. The apartment was silent other than the dull hum of the TV and my thudding heart. I was hardly breathing.

When I peeled back the curtain, I didn't see an enraged henchman coming to collect. I saw Jana Russo having climbed out of a luxury EV parked in front of Melanie's house. She wore all black like a cat burglar and glanced down the street as Sandra Whitley climbed out of the passenger side, also in all black.

I blinked a few times and flinched when headlights turned the corner and flashed across their bodies. Within a few seconds, Melanie's SUV was pulling into her driveway.

"Bray!" I called in a whisper like they might hear. "Bray, come here and look at this!"

He stirred with a grumble but didn't wake.

"Oh, for the love of—" I snapped and hurried back to the couch, worried I'd miss something if I was gone from the window for too long. I gripped his beefy shoulder and shook it. His skin was hot and smooth under my hand. "Calvin Bray, wake up. I need your assistance, please."

His eyes fluttered open, and he blinked up at me a few times. Embarrassment filled his face when he saw me glaring down at him. "Did I—?"

"Fall asleep on the job? Yes. But we can worry about that later. Come here and look." I tugged on his arm. He was still sleepy enough his arm stretched all the way out while my hand slid down until our palms touched.

"What's going on?" he said groggily.

I squeezed his wide palm and yanked him off the couch, sending the throw blanket to the floor. "You know, you really need to work on your nocturnal endurance since half the shady shit you need to see seems to go down at night. Come to the window. The moms are up to something."

At this, he snapped to attention. His hand tightened around mine, and he let me pull him to the window. "What are they doing?"

"I don't know. I heard a car door outside, so I looked out the window. I just saw Jana and Sandra pull up in that car, and then Melanie came home." I pointed at the scene still playing out across the street. Melanie had opened the garage and pulled the SUV inside. Light poured out from the open garage, casting the driveway in a golden pool. Melanie climbed out of the driver's door and closed it. She too wore head-to-toe black.

"I know I'm only one day into nannying, but I don't think you go on three a.m. diaper runs with your gal pals dressed like that," I whispered.

"Definitely not," Bray said. "They are coming home from a job."

Right as he said it, Melanie came to the edge of the garage and swept the street with her gaze. When her eyes landed on my apartment, both Bray and I gasped. We ducked at the same time, landing crouched shoulder-to-shoulder on the carpet below the window.

"Do you think she saw us?" I asked, heart hammering.

"Let's hope not. Shit, we need to see what they are doing though."

We stared at each other from inches apart. Our breath mingled. I could still smell his shower somehow. His eyes shone in the dim TV light.

"What were you doing out of bed?" he whispered, like the thought had only now occurred to him.

A heat wave instantly burned my body. I felt like I had *A sweaty sex dream about you woke me up* written on my forehead. "I, um . . . woke up and needed something to drink."

I couldn't tell if the answer satisfied him, because he was suddenly distracted by a thought. His eyes lit. "The cameras."

"What?" I asked, still reeling from thoughts of my dream.

He spun away from me, still in a crouched position, and crawled to his bag by the couch. The curtains were closed, but we still needed to stay low, just in case. "The security cameras are recording right now. We just need to look at the live feed and we can see what they are doing in the street." He dug in his bag and pulled out his tablet.

"Good idea," I said, and moved to join him.

He'd sat with his back to the couch's end and glanced up to see me crawling. The color spotting his cheeks made me realize he had a view straight down my camisole. He quickly looked away as I scrambled to sit next to him.

"Do you see anything?" I asked as if my heart wasn't pounding.

He tapped at the screen to bring up the app. Soon, we were staring at a black and white live stream of the street. I leaned in to see the small screen, and neither of us made an effort to move when our bare arms pressed together. He was hot and solid, and the feel of his skin touching mine quelled the nerves coursing through me over what we might witness. He used his thumbs to pinch the screen to zoom in.

Jana had returned to the sedan parked at the street to open the trunk. From it, she pulled a duffel bag, which looked heavy by the way she hoisted it.

"I thought their operation had slowed down. What do you think is in there?" I whispered.

Bray shook his head. "Hard to say."

She carried it up the driveway to where Melanie stood at her SUV's open back. She slung it into the back of the SUV alongside another duffel bag already sitting there.

"Money?" I hazarded a guess. "Black market binkies?"

Bray shot me a look.

I playfully grimaced.

"Whatever it is, we need to find out," he said. "Maybe they are into other things to compensate for their slow business."

"And to pay back their pissed-off supplier," I added.

We watched as on-screen Melanie shut the SUV's back hatch. She then pecked Sandra and Jana each on the cheek before they parted ways. Melanie's garage door slid closed, sealing off the light and view of her with it. The other two made their way back to Jana's car where they climbed in and drove off screen. We continued watching Melanie's house. Not a single light flicked on, as if she was used to prowling around in the middle of the night.

"Do you think you can get into their garage tomorrow?" Bray asked.

I considered. Though we'd popped in there to gather the wagon to head to the park that day, the garage hadn't been part of the tour, and maybe for a reason. Maybe the incriminating evidence wasn't only stashed in Melanie's office like I had thought. Maybe she kept it locked up in her car too.

"I can probably come up with an excuse," I offered. "If nothing else, I can pretend I got lost in that house looking for something."

He nodded in approval.

"I still can't believe you're going to make me go to work tomorrow when there's a hitman out there looking for me."

"I promise you the Brownings' house is the safest place you can be right now," he defended.

"You say this after we literally just witnessed Melanie Browning engage in criminal activity."

"If that were the case, I'd cross the street and arrest her right now. We need more evidence still."

I growled at him, and he had the gall to smile. "You are unbelievable."

His eyes softened and he gave me a steady look. "Erin, I'm doing everything I can to keep you safe, okay?"

The sound of my name on his lips called me back to my dream. To when he'd whispered it in my ear as he'd touched me in a way I hadn't been touched in far too long.

I was suddenly too hot and bothered to be sitting in the dark and whispering secrets with our bodies pressed together. I wanted too much more.

"I'm going to go back to bed," I announced and pushed myself to stand.

He looked up at me with a pang of regret, as if he wanted me to stay up with him all night. "Okay. I'll stay out here and watch for anything else." He nodded at his tablet.

"Good night, Agent Bray," I said and headed for my room.

"Good night, Erin."

The sound of my name followed me like a lonely shadow full of longing.

Chapter 17

I found my house empty the next morning and the SUV patrol car back in its position. Bray had neatly folded the blanket on the couch and left before I woke. He'd left a note on the dining table.

Nothing new to report overnight. Good luck today! ☺

That damn smiley face again.

Despite myself, I smiled at it. I pressed the note to my nose as if I might smell him on it, but all I smelled was paper.

I braced myself for another day at the Browning house. Not only did I have to take care of two kids all day, but now I also had to figure out how to get into the garage and find out what was in those duffel bags. At least that would serve as distraction from thinking about Wallace and the ghost.

I rewrapped my ankle and stepped into my new running shoes. I took a picture of my feet and sent it to Bray with a little thumbs-up emoji.

I nearly rolled my eyes at myself.

When I left the house, I subtly nodded at the agent in the SUV. I locked the front door and then tried to open it against the lock just to make sure. It didn't yield.

I took one step off my porch when I heard a friendly voice from the sidewalk.

"Hey, neighbor!" Alisha said. Jeffrey dangled from her chest in his complicated harness. "I'm so sorry to hear about your uncle."

News travels fast, I thought.

"Thanks," I said without much else to add.

Luckily, she kept the conversation moving. "Things are working out with the Brownings, I assume?" she asked, and nodded across the street where I was clearly headed.

I cast my gaze in the same direction and tried not to wilt. My eyes dragged over the SUV, and I had a thought. "They sure are!" I cheerily said before changing topic. "Hey, Alisha, have you seen anyone strange around the neighborhood lately?"

Her face fell. She patted Jeffrey's bottom and bounced. "Strange? What do you mean?"

I tried for a casual shrug. "I thought I saw someone in the street the other night. He didn't look familiar to me, but I'm so new here, I probably just didn't recognize him."

I hadn't expected Alisha to know anything; she had been gone the night the ghost appeared in the street. My intent in asking was to put her on the lookout. More eyes on the ghost meant more chance of staying safe.

"Huh," Alisha said. "Well, I doubt it was anything to be concerned about; it's so safe around here. I'll keep my eyes peeled though!"

"Thank you," I said sincerely. "I've got to get to work. Have a good day!"

"Bye!" Alisha matched the singsong I hadn't even noticed I'd performed.

Between Bray's smiley faces and everyone's friendly greetings, the neighborhood was really getting to me.

I marched across the street with a determined step, ready to face the Browning family and praying Bray hurried the hell up with whatever he was doing to get me out of here as soon as possible.

The thought of leaving suddenly struck me as sad as I passed through Melanie's rose border. No one had been anything but nice and welcoming since I'd arrived, despite the mild criminal activity. My apartment was beautiful, the neighborhood was one of the best in the country—literally, according to a ranking. Sure, I'd lied to everyone I'd met from the second I got here, but of all the places I could be, Del Rio seemed perfect, despite my limited tenure.

Not to mention, if I left, what did that mean for Bray? Would he stay my handler? Would our relationship become primarily phone calls, brief rendezvous, and shadowy drops in the middle of the night, as it had been with Wallace?

But if I stayed, was I going to end up in a body bag?

I hadn't even noticed I'd made it to the Brownings' front door until it was swinging open in front of me.

"Good morning!" Melanie sang with the pep of someone who hadn't been up doing illegal things in her driveway at three in the morning. She glowed in welcome, and I wondered if I'd dreamed the whole thing the night before.

"Hi!" I said, trying to match her energy.

She waved me in, and I followed. If she'd seen me and Bray spying on her last night, she didn't let on. She wore an outfit similar to last night's, but instead of the sleek spandex being black, it was a shade of rosy pink. It made her look like Workout Barbie. "I'm so glad you're able to continue today; I have a busy morning."

"Oh?" I casually asked, hoping she wasn't about to jump in the car and speed off with the evidence in the trunk.

"Yes. I'll be out back on the Peloton for the next hour." She pointed out the back doors at the guesthouse. I must have been right about it being their home gym, especially given her outfit. "And then I'll be in my office for most of the morning after. The kids are in their playroom." She hardly took a breath, and I decided she compensated for her late-night activity with copious amounts of caffeine. "You all set?" she asked me with nothing but sweetness. It set me on edge.

"Yep!" I lied.

"Great. Remember the instruction binder is in the kitchen. Shout if you need anything." She pivoted and glided off toward the back of the house.

I wondered if right then was the optimal time to dash to the garage, but I decided I needed to get set up with the kids first.

I found them in the playroom among another explosion of toys. Karli had built herself a fort of blocks and a few pillows, and Kaden was driving toy cars around an elaborate plastic racetrack and making motor sounds.

My ankle gave a pang of protest when I squatted to join them. "Hey, guys. What are you doing today?"

They each took a turn explaining their respective games to me and invited me to play. I casually folded myself into their little imaginary world and realized infiltrating playtime was just like infiltrating any other job I'd had, albeit a lot cuter and less dangerous.

"Did your mom tuck you in last night?" I nonchalantly asked while I looped a neon-orange racecar through Kaden's track. I figured I'd see if I could get any useful information out of them.

"No. Dad puts us to bed when Mom is busy," Kaden innocently reported.

"Was Mom busy last night?"

"She had a party!" Karli sang and made a stuffed dolphin dive off the top of her fort.

"A *party*?" I said gleefully. "That sounds fun. Do you know where it was?"

"Somewhere fancy. She dressed like a princess," Kaden reported.

I silently considered. A fancy party could be many things. Maybe a fundraiser, a gala, a banquet. But why leave the house for that and come home at three a.m. dressed like a bank robber?

"I have to go potty," Karli suddenly announced and stood up. Flips the penguin fell to her side. She stared at me expectantly, and I realized I was supposed to help.

"Oh!" I said, trying not to sound nervous. "Okay." I stood as well, and she slipped her little hand in mine. She led me back into the hallway and to the bathroom I'd hid in the other day after I overheard her parents' tryst. "Do you need me to come in with you?" I asked and held my breath, praying she'd say no.

"No. You can wait here," she announced and marched inside and shut the door.

"Okay. I'll be right here," I said with full intention to use the excuse to find the garage. I heard the toilet lid lift and clank against the tank and wondered how much time I had before she came back out. When she started singing to herself, I figured it would be a while.

I closed my eyes and drew a mental map of the house, remembering where Melanie had led me that day we gathered the wagon to go to the park.

I paused to make sure I could still hear Karli singing. When her tiny voice carried down the hall, I dashed for what I was pretty sure was the right door.

It opened with the suction of a door sealed off to the outside, and in an instant, I was standing in front of Melanie's SUV.

I whipped out my phone to text Bray.

Made it to the garage. Kids said mom was out at a party last night, dressed up.

I shoved my phone in my pocket before he could answer. The hulking SUV flashed its lights at me when I reached for the door handle, and I thanked my lucky stars it was unlocked. It seemed like Melanie was the scariest thing in this neighborhood, other than my roving henchman, so why would she need to lock her car inside her garage anyway?

When I leaned inside to look for the back hatch release, the smell of expensive leather and perfume hit me. The car was spotless. Regularly detailed, surely. Perhaps to keep up with Melanie's standards or to erase evidence.

"Got you," I said when I found the hatch release.

The back of the car opened with a soft ding. I winced at the sound as I hurried around to look inside.

The duffel bags were still there.

Relief washed over me at the same time adrenaline pumped into my veins. For the first time in this case, I was getting my hands dirty. The rush of breaking rules was still tied to some hardwired need for it.

My trained fingers were lightning fast with the first bag. I ripped open the zipper and found . . . computers. Two laptops, a mobile router, a tangle of what looked like microphones and discreet earpieces.

"Surveillance equipment," I muttered at the telltale package. I pried the bag open as wide as it would go and snapped a few pictures for Bray.

I moved to the other one, not sure what to expect, and found a burst of colorful, expensive fabrics.

Gowns.

Kaden had said his mom was dressed like a princess last night. I pawed around at the silky fabrics, thinking of all the times I'd donned a dress from a duffel bag. I almost laughed when I felt another object I was very familiar with. I pulled out a long red wig and wondered which one of them dressed up as the Little Mermaid last night.

"What were you ladies up to?" I murmured as I snapped

pictures of the bag's contents. I texted images of both bags to Bray with another message.

I think our girls pulled off a heist last night.

"Lauren?" someone called from the garage door.

I swallowed the shriek in my throat and zipped both bags shut.

"Lauren, are you out here?"

My heart nearly rocketed through my chest, but it calmed a few beats when I recognized the voice as Kaden's and not his mother's.

"Yeah! I'm right here," I said and swung the SUV's hatch shut.

His little footsteps sounded on the paved floor. "What are you doing?"

"Just looking for something for your mom, bud." I ruffled his hair with a friendly smile.

He looked up at me like he wasn't quite sure I was telling the truth. "Someone is at the door," he said, and caught me totally off guard.

"What?"

"The door. Someone rang the doorbell."

I stared back, waiting for instruction and suddenly on edge. I reminded myself the patrol car was still parked outside. And besides, the Browning house was a fortress. They probably had an armed guard hiding in the hedges.

"Should I get it?" I asked his expectant stare.

Kaden shrugged. "Mom's busy, and we're not allowed to answer the door."

Not allowed to answer the door felt like a significant statement. Sure, they were small children, but perhaps their mother didn't want them answering the door for . . . other reasons?

"Why not?" I innocently asked.

Kaden shrugged his slight shoulders again. "Mom says so."

I logged the information and headed for the garage door. "Well, we better do what Mom says, then. Come on."

When we made it back inside, Karli had emerged from the bathroom and was wiping her wet hands on her pants. "All done!" she announced.

"Good for you!" I sang, thankful she'd managed on her own because I had zero idea how to help in any bathroom situation.

I wound my way back to the foyer and looked through the paned glass on either side of the front door as I approached. All I saw was slices of emerald lawn and rose border. I took a breath and told myself to relax, reasoning it was probably one of the other moms dropping by to chat.

"Stay here," I told the kids and left them at the back of the foyer.

I made it to the front door and turned the knob. It opened to a shocking surprise.

"Brittany!" I blurted.

The young woman from the bookstore and the last person to hold my job stood on the porch with a stack of gifts in her hands. She quickly looked over her shoulder and adjusted her purse's strap.

"Hi. I know I shouldn't be here, but I know Melanie is on her bike for the next hour, so I thought now would be safe." She glanced over her shoulder again.

I noted the patrol SUV had inched forward enough for me to see the nose of it. I had to assume the agent inside had full view of the Brownings' and my front doors now. I also noted Brittany appeared to have memorized Melanie's schedule.

Brittany extended the gifts, and I recognized them as the books I had purchased the day before. "I just wanted to drop these off and check you were okay. You dropped them yesterday when that man . . ." She trailed off and her eyes moved over my shoulder.

"Brittany!" the kids called in unison.

I turned to see the two of them galloping across the foyer with huge smiles on their faces, clearly not having listened to me.

"Hi, you guys!" Brittany sang and crouched with her arms out.

Karli blew straight past me and launched herself at her old nanny. Brittany wrapped her in a hug. "*Oh,* I miss you already!"

I knew in that moment, which I really had known all along but had never seen it on full display, there were people on the earth who were meant to work with children, and I was not one of them.

Kaden danced around them in a circle, bouncing on his toes like he was waiting his turn for a hug too. Brittany beamed at them both and squeezed them tight. The sight actually made me smile.

My smile snapped out like a light when I heard a voice behind me.

"What's going on?" Melanie asked.

"Mom! Brittany came back!" Kaden shouted.

Melanie approached with a towel hung around her neck. A light sheen of sweat glistened her brow. She dabbed at it as a tight smile stretched her lips.

"I see that, sweetie, and what a . . . surprise!" Her laugh was a few degrees above frigid.

I stepped back on reflex.

Brittany set Karli on the ground and smoothed her shirt. "Hi, Melanie. I'm not staying. I just came by to drop something off." She extended the books. We had crossed into very hot water very quickly.

Any explanation would circle back to a lie I had told to one or the other of them. Plus, I didn't want to get into the details of why I'd fled the bookstore and left the books behind.

"Oh?" Melanie said with a tilt of her head like she couldn't wait for the explanation I was rapidly forming in my head.

For a moment, I considered if feigning ignorance was a viable option. Perhaps I could claim I had no idea who Brittany was, and it was all a mistake.

I decided a version of the truth was the safest route.

"Yes," I said. "I got a gift for the kids yesterday, and I met Brittany. We got to talking and found out we have a lot in common." I chose my words carefully so as not to call their mother out for firing their nanny in front of her kids. Although, perhaps they already knew.

Melanie eyed the wrapped books, clearly distilling there was more to the story. "And Brittany is . . . delivering them for you?"

I was skating on a frozen lake, which could crack at any second. I would plunge into the icy black water and drown. I was usually so quick on my feet; lies were second nature. But something about Melanie had me scrambling for the correct thing to say.

Or maybe it wasn't completely Melanie. Maybe it was because the truth about the day before and the books I had left behind was still too terrifying to fully think about.

"I am," Brittany chimed in. "We were out of wrapping paper at the store, so I told her I'd bring them over this morning once we got more and I had the chance to wrap them."

I threw her the sincerest look of gratitude to ever fill my face. I couldn't say why she'd covered for me, but I took the pass, and assumed Brittany knew how to behave around Melanie better than I did. The lie had to be better than explaining I had abandoned the books when I'd been chased out the door.

Melanie's face held a forced grin as her eyes narrowed. "That's right, you work at Sweet Briar now, don't you?" The words *because I fired you* somehow managed to be silent and deafening at the same time.

"I do," Brittany said with a tight smile. "Well, I need to get going. It was great to see you guys!" She ruffled Karli's and Kaden's hair with each of her hands and turned off the porch.

Luckily, I had the distraction of the gifts to give the kids to avoid the pending awkward confrontation with their mother. I squatted down in front of them and tucked the books behind my back. "Guess what? I got you guys something."

They both bounced up and down in excitement.

I whipped them out and saw Brittany, bless her, had put a sticker with the right name on the right book. I handed them over to delighted squeals.

"Kids, why don't you go open your gifts in the playroom," Melanie said. "Mommy needs to talk to Lauren for a minute." The tone of her voice sent a chill up my spine. I almost opted to throw myself in the children's way to stop them from leaving me alone with their mother.

They ran off with their shiny packages like little traitors.

Melanie turned her smile on me. "Can I see you in the kitchen, please?"

I dutifully nodded and followed. The temperature in the granite room seemed to drop when Melanie rounded the massive island to face me. I stood on the other side, marking the distance to the back doors and wondering how well I could scale a fence with my sore ankle if I needed to make a quick escape.

My mind always prepared for the worst because most of the time, the worst was what I ended up facing. I reminded myself Melanie didn't know who I was or anything about the man in the bookstore. She probably only wanted to tell me not to talk to Brittany anymore.

"Are you a danger to my family?" she said and caught me completely off guard. She was in her right to question if I was qualified for childcare, but the way she'd said it, the threat in her question, told me she was asking about something else.

"Excuse me?"

Melanie leveled a steady gaze at me and had a look in her eyes I had not seen before. "Listen. I know you aren't who you say you are. I knew you were a plant before I hired you. I need a new nanny, and a perfect one just drops into my lap at the same time a secret agent starts sniffing around? I know you are working with him. This welcome wagon bit has only served to reel you in. Keep your enemies closer, right? I also know you don't have enough to arrest me, or you would have done it by now. If I thought you or that agent was a real threat, I wouldn't have let you in my house."

I fought to keep my mouth from falling open and barely succeeded. "Um, I don't know what you're—"

Melanie's lips thinned into a flat line. "I'm not a fool, Lauren. And I know that's not your name, but I haven't been able to find your real one. Whatever you've got going on, that part is tight."

I felt as if I'd been punched. I gripped the island so I didn't fall over and took a step back to steady myself.

"What I don't know," Melanie went on, "is if there's more going on than you trying to infiltrate my life. You're here for two days and your uncle suddenly dies, you've got some kind of secret relationship with my old nanny, you obviously have no experience with children—"

"Hey—" I began to protest, thinking I'd been doing a decent job.

She held up a hand. "I wasn't finished. There's also an unmarked car surveilling our street, and you show up to work limping today. It all makes me wonder just what side of the law you are on. Are they forcing you to do this?"

I continued gaping. In all the times I'd had my cover blown, it had never happened so calmly and to my face. The standard—though rare—scenarios usually involved shouting and threats, guns and escape. Never had I been quietly standing in someone's immaculate kitchen next to a fruit bowl while my fabricated world unraveled around me. I could not comprehend what was happening. Who had slipped? Me? Bray? Wallace? Or perhaps Melanie was just that good.

I thought for a moment of denying everything. Of asking if she were feeling all right for having come up with such a wild story about her perfectly innocent new nanny. Perhaps she bumped her head on the Peloton or was fever dreaming. But given the obvious depth of her research—to infiltrate a cover story miles deep—and the very real threat on my life, *and*, not to mention the fact that Melanie would probably kill me with a serving spoon for putting her family in harm's way, I decided to go with a version of the truth.

"You're right. I'm not here entirely willfully, and you don't know who I really am. And for everyone's best interest, it needs to stay that way."

She stared at me so intently, I felt like I was being X-rayed. Her eyebrow twitched and her jaw clenched. What she was considering, I could only imagine: calling the police; where she would dump my body when she killed me. With all the hardened criminals I'd dealt with, never would I have thought the Queen of Suburbia would be my demise.

To my surprise, her rigid gaze softened around the edges. A moment passed between us, something unspoken but profound, where I got the sudden sense we were equals.

"How much trouble are you in?" She said it less as an accusation and more like a concern she could relate to.

Knowing she *could* relate to it, and looking for any way to keep the upper hand in this conversation before it completely derailed, I countered with, "Probably as much as you are in. I know about Montrose."

Her face morphed into shock before settling into a clearly feigned calmness. She roughly cleared her throat. "And what exactly do you know?"

"That you're in enough debt to have put a lien on your house. What was in that seized shipment?"

At this, her face completely drained of color.

"Did you trust the wrong guy? Because I sure as hell know what that's like." I kept pushing, thinking of my father, and to some extent, Wallace.

Melanie looked like the truth was ready to leap from her tongue, but she wouldn't let it. I was apparently more of a threat than she'd realized. But perhaps not entirely a threat, based on the look on her face. Maybe more of an equal, and from what I could tell, that scared her even more.

"Look, I know you don't trust me, but maybe there's a way we could—"

"You need to leave." She cut off my offer.

"But I—"

"Get out!" she snapped. The threat in her voice was ice-cold, and I knew if I stayed, things would get ugly. She knew we didn't have enough to arrest her, otherwise DSA agents would have been swarming the place. And given her knife block full of stainless-steel blades sitting about a foot away, the Brownings' house was no longer a safe harbor for me.

Out of options, I turned to leave. In a state of shock that my cover had been blown, I headed for the front door. The ache in my ankle throbbed with each step and I had the sudden and embarrassing urge to cry.

It had all been fake. As someone who lied for a living, it shouldn't have hurt at all, but I'd thought the moms had actually liked me. That they'd genuinely been welcoming me into their world, but it had all been a scheme to keep tabs on me. They had known from the very start I wasn't who I said I was. And that was mostly Bray's fault for being so obvious.

I grumbled in frustration as I opened the front door, ready to call Bray and yell at him for blowing my cover. To my surprise, a man in a suit stood there waiting for me.

"Ms. Daniels," he said.

I startled at the sound of my real name. A few seconds passed as I tried to assess the threat this stranger posed. He had a familiar air about him, but I couldn't place it. He was stocky and solidly built. Like the kind of guy who threw heavy weights around a gym and could kick down a door. In truth, he was the same shape as Bray only shorter and more compact. I eyed his hip and noted the telltale bulge of a weapon. Then I saw the discreet coil of an earpiece disappearing down his collar and understood he was not here to harm me.

I closed the front door and stepped out onto the porch with him. "Yes?"

"I need you to come with me," he said and pointed at the SUV.

I noted it was empty, and realized he was the driver I'd been seeing through the window for the past few days.

I took a step back, alarmed. "Why?"

"Because Agent Bray said so."

The sound of his name reminded me I was annoyed with him. Even so, I wasn't about to pass up an opportunity for a free ride away from here. "What's going on?" I said and started down the front path alongside him.

Instead of answering, he pulled his phone from his jacket pocket. I watched him dial it and press it to his ear. It rang only once before someone answered.

"Do you have her?" Bray's voice came through the other end. My heart stuttered at the urgency it carried.

"Yes, sir," the other agent said.

"Let me talk to her."

He held the phone out to me.

I took it. "What's going on, Bray?"

"I need you to go with Agent Simmons," he said. The note of alarm in his voice made my stomach clench with worry.

"I am, but why?"

"I'll tell you when you get here."

"Get where?"

"We don't have time for questions right now. Just *please*, get in the car with Agent Simmons."

I glanced up and down the street and saw nothing out of place. No immediate threat other than a gardener buzzing a Weedwacker over the neighbor's lawn. Still, my curiosity was too strong.

"Okay, but I'd like to know—"

"Wallace was murdered!" he blurted.

I stopped in my tracks. The air in my lungs became solid.

Bray continued, his voice strained with fear and urgency. "I just obtained information Agent Wallace was murdered, Olena Nova's prison sentence was shortened, and she is being released *today*, and there's a hit out on you, so *get in the fucking car, Erin*!"

A loud ringing filled my head as if a gunshot had gone off nearby. I wasn't sure if it was memory, a premonition, or just plain fear, but I handed the phone to Agent Simmons and walked straight for the SUV.

Chapter 18

Agent Simmons drove me to the local station in Oakland. The long ride around the bottom of the bay gave me plenty of time to think about what Bray had told me.

Wallace had been murdered.

Olena was getting out of prison early—*today*.

There was a hit out on me.

Not to mention, my cover had been compromised.

The dark thoughts swirling in my head had me terrified and sick to the point I nearly hugged Bray when I saw him.

He wore a black T-shirt and slacks and looked like he hadn't slept—which I knew he had to some extent since I'd found him that way on my couch. But still, the shadows beneath his eyes said he hadn't gotten much. He greeted me and Agent Simmons in the station's lobby, a completely and intentionally nondescript building on the outside, and guided me into an elevator, which delivered us to an underground floor of busy cubicles and open office doors. Phones rang from every direction, and people walked around holding stacks of papers looking frazzled. It was a run-of-the-mill office, just one buried under so much security clearance no one knew about it. Similar stations were hidden all over the country. I'd been to plenty of faceless concrete buildings, old dry cleaners, empty restaurants. Fronts for an underground organization—literally—that policed crime off the radar.

Bray led me to a small office at the end of the room. He glanced over his shoulder before he guided me in the door and closed it behind us.

I took in the small space stacked with papers, a whiteboard covered in scribbles, a small potted plant by a box light emulating an external window. An internal window faced the cubicles in the busy office belly.

"Is this your desk?" I asked and welcomed myself into the chair. My ankle was not as recovered as I'd thought.

"No. That's my desk," Bray said and pointed through the internal window at one of the cubicles. "I just wanted some privacy; Jeremy won't mind." As he said it, I noted a framed photo of two men and a little boy smiling from the desk's corner.

Bray leaned on the desk with his arms spread. The T-shirt strained to accommodate the position. "Are you okay?"

I looked up at him, chasing away thoughts of his arms and how they'd held me in my dream. "Of course not. Will you please tell me what's going on?"

He stood up with a heavy breath. "I finally got clearance to get the information we need, not exactly legitimately, but that's beside the point. We were right: It's all connected, and you are in danger."

"Clearly," I said. "What did you learn about Wallace's death?"

"It *was* a heart attack, but the autopsy showed a high dose of potassium chloride in his blood, which can trigger a cardiac event, and found evidence of an injection site on his neck."

"Oh shit. He was poisoned?"

"It appears so, yes."

I shook my head, trying to keep at bay the complicated wave of pain lapping at me. "I knew he wouldn't just drop dead. He was too healthy."

"Well, you were right. I want to have us moved, but I need sign-off first. I'm waiting on a meeting with the director in a few minutes, and I wanted to get you safe in the meantime."

I was used to my life taking sharp, unexpected turns; the thought of disappearing was not new to me. But my brain snagged on one word he'd said.

"Us?"

Bray nodded. "Yes. With Olena Nova out of prison, I don't want them shipping you off to another case who-knows-where with a new handler, and have all your classified files go back underground. I want you with me until this is over."

His declaration nearly knocked the wind out of me. He wanted to stay with me. To keep me safe. Any annoyance I'd had with him over blowing my cover fizzled out and was replaced by a feeling deep in my chest that I'd never felt before. Something warm and curious and a little disarming.

"Okay," I said. "Before you talk to the director, you should probably know my cover is blown, so I can't go back to Del Rio anyway."

He looked up in surprise. "What?"

"Yeah," I said and stood up. I rounded the desk to his side of it. "Right before you sent Agent Simmons to the door, Melanie told me they'd been on to you, and they knew I was a setup from the moment I got here. She said it was all an act, welcoming me and hiring me, so they could keep tabs on both of us."

Bray's mouth fell open. I could see him reliving the whole case like a highlight reel of his mistakes. "Shit, Erin. I'm so sorry."

I reeled, not expecting him to apologize. "Well, I was right: Melanie is scared as hell of Montrose. When she called my bluff, I confronted her with what we know, and she told me to leave. But maybe it doesn't matter anymore if someone is coming to kill me anyway."

Bray opened his mouth to respond, frustrated, when someone knocked on the door. He spun to open it.

"The director is ready," a young woman in neat pants and a blue blouse said.

"Thanks," Bray told her. He shut the door and turned back to me. "Look, I'm going to fix this. Just come with me and don't say anything." The determined, apologetic look on his face told me not to argue.

I nodded and followed him.

We traveled back through the belly of the office to a hallway of closed doors. Bray stopped at the farthest one with two uncomfortable-looking chairs sitting outside it and knocked. He tilted his head at the chairs. "Sit here."

I did as I was told, wondering if I was going to be paraded in front of the director in an attempt to plea for my protection.

"Come in," someone said from inside the office, and I was surprised to hear it was a woman.

Bray slipped inside and left the door open a crack. "Thanks for making time for me," he said.

"For you, Agent Bray, always," the director said. I imagined a woman in a prim pantsuit with a sharp bob, though I couldn't see her at all. "What can I help you with?"

He got straight to the point. "I have reason to believe our asset in Del Rio is in danger."

The director paused. Her voice took on a serious tone. "What kind of danger?"

"It's related to the case that brought her on as a CI years ago. The parties involved in that night have discovered her location, and I have reason to believe they are actively trying to intercept her. I would like to have the both of us reassigned from the Del Rio case."

The director paused, and the air grew tense. "You don't have security clearance to look into those matters from the past, Agent Bray. In fact, I personally told you not to."

"Yes, but that was before—"

"Before what? Before you decided to break protocol and risk the progress you've made in recovering? You had strict instruction: Del Rio *only*."

I reeled at the tone of her voice and imagined Bray blushing in shame. Further thoughts of what had happened to him spun in my mind: What had he recovered from that had resulted in being assigned Del Rio with me, but also revoked his clearance?

"Yes, but there are bigger things at stake now," Bray said.

"Maybe so, but they are *things* you don't need to concern yourself with."

A long pause passed. I heard what sounded like a stack of papers being tapped on a desktop to straighten it. "You both stay, Agent Bray. If you'd like to request an increase to her protection detail, fine, but no one is being reassigned."

He paused again, and I imagined him chewing his bottom lip in distress. "With all due respect, you denied the request for overnight protection last night."

I blinked in surprise. That was why he'd shown up at my apartment the night before; his request got rejected so he'd had to do it himself.

The papers tapped again. The director's voice came back with a slight bite to it. "Then ask again, Agent Bray."

A tense silence passed.

"I think it would just be easier if we were reassigned."

I was waiting for him to confess my cover had been blown, but he didn't. He was dancing around the detail and instead using Olena as an excuse to have us moved.

The papers landed on the desk with a smack and a chair audibly rolled back. "*No one* is getting reassigned, Agent Bray. The both of you are staying on the Del Rio case until it's finished. Is that clear?"

I flinched at her tone and wondered if Bray had done the same at closer range.

"Yes, ma'am," he eventually said, defeated.

I let out a heavy sigh in the next pause. When the director's voice came back, it had softened enough to sound as if someone else was speaking.

"Cal, darling, you look exhausted. Why don't you come for dinner on Sunday? Your father would love to see you."

I startled, unsure I'd heard correctly.

Bray sighed. "I can't, Mom. I'm busy."

"All right, sweetheart. But please take care of yourself."

Bray mumbled something unintelligible before returning to open the door. My jaw was on the floor when he stepped back into the hall and closed it behind him.

I immediately stood from the chair and gaped at him. "I'm sorry, did you say *mom*?"

He glanced over his shoulder toward the door with a dark furrow to his brow. "We're not talking about this," he muttered and began walking away.

I hurried after him, a smile stretching my face. "Oh, but we definitely are! The director is your *mom*?!"

In the quickest motion I'd ever seen him make, he gripped my arm and yanked me toward the door at the end of the hall. He pushed our way through it, and before I had time to react, he had me up against the wall in a drafty stairwell with bare pipes and concrete floors. He leaned in so close, his nose almost touched mine.

"Yes, okay? The director is my mother, and she's a little overprotective. See this?" He spoke through tight lips and pointed at the scar on his jaw, the only imperfection on his otherwise handsome face, which was inches from mine. "Well, it has a pair of siblings that didn't miss," he said. He yanked his T-shirt's collar aside and exposed the star-shaped scars I'd seen the night before while he slept. His eyes searched mine for understanding, and I was too shocked to do anything but stare back. "I spent eighteen hours in surgery, ten weeks in physical rehab, and then six months at a desk. Ever since I've been back in the field, she's got me working mommy crimes over in Del Rio. I'm doing the best with what I've got, and I would appreciate it if you would cut me some fucking slack."

The air between us crackled. I was holding my breath.

Bray exhaled and let go of me. He hung his head and leaned a hand against the wall. "I'm sorry."

I was at a loss, reeling, and wanting to take back everything bad I'd said about him. The scar on his jaw was from a third bullet, which had nearly hit him in the face. My knees went weak at the thought. "I saw your scars last night," I managed, unsure why I chose that as my response. "When you were sleeping. What happened?" My words came out in fragments as I tried to recover.

Bray let go of a long breath. He spoke to the stairs beside us instead of facing me. I watched the scar on his jaw move with every word. "Child abduction case. The abductors didn't want to hand him over. The kid lived. I almost didn't."

He'd saved a kid? *God*, I felt terrible for every quip.

"I've been so unfair to you. I'm sorry."

He shook his head and met my gaze. "No, you're right. I've made mistakes. This is just my first case since then and it's taking me a while to get back in the swing of things. And my mom—" He cut himself off and closed his eyes to take a breath. "The director seems to have lost a little faith in my abilities too, so it's been a rough ride." He sighed and sat down on the top step of the nearest flight.

I was tempted to reach out and touch him. To somehow encourage him and apologize for how I'd treated him when he was doing his best. But I thought it best to keep my hands to myself.

I crossed the small landing and sat beside him. "Is that why your security clearance was revoked?"

He snorted. "Yeah. She used agency bureaucracy to keep me *safe* in her eyes." He made air quotes around the word with his fingers. "I guess she thought me knowing anything about your past would have been too stressful. *'Low stress cases only, Cal,'* " he said, mimicking her voice.

"Damn. She pulled your clearance because she thought information might give you an ulcer?"

"Something like that. Little did she know *you'd* be the most stressful thing I've encountered in months."

I scoffed in offense, but it melted into a smile. "I won't apologize. But I do have a question. Why didn't you tell her my cover is blown with the moms? I can't go back to Del Rio anyway."

"Because I don't want her to know I blew it. She'll never trust me with another case again." The defeated ache in his voice stopped me from questioning if that was a wise decision.

"So, then, what are we going to do? I can't go back there with Melanie *and* the ghost out to get me."

He sighed. "I'll think of something, don't worry."

I honestly didn't know what the options were, given our restraints. "Thanks for trying with your mom—I mean, the director, at least," I offered.

He tugged at his pant leg and huffed. "Sure. Unfortunately, she can tell me what to do both because she's my mom *and* my superior officer."

I snorted. "I get that. I've been told what to do for the past ten years. 'Go here, be this person, say this, do that,'" I said, mimicking Wallace. "I think Wallace got off on it, honestly. Being bossed around is all I've ever known. I can't tell you how many times I've wished I could just . . . take matters into my own hands."

Bray looked at me with a knowing honesty in his eyes. "Probably as many times as I have," he said with a soft smile.

We gazed at each other, connected in our desire to have control over our own lives but also treading water in the depths of being unable to.

"At least you've seen some action," he said, breaking the

spell. "Well, before Del Rio, I mean. My mom put me on this case because it's minimal risk."

"Ha. Tell that to the terrified look on Melanie's face when I said *Montrose* earlier."

He half shrugged, like it was something to consider. "After what happened," Bray went on, "she just wants me to be safe."

I thought about how Del Rio stacked up against other cases I'd been on. Despite what I now knew about the moms, I had to agree with its smiling neighbors, playdates, and snack times, it was, by far, the friendliest case I'd ever worked. Even though I wasn't one myself, I couldn't blame a mother for wanting to protect her child, even if he was a grown man. I had so few people protecting me in my life, I wondered what it might feel like—

"Oh, my God," I said aloud as a thought suddenly struck me.

"What?" Bray asked.

I stared at my feet and blinked a few times while I fit the pieces together in my mind. I hadn't thought of it until that moment, but what Bray had said about his mother keeping him safe suddenly took root in a way that made a new kind of sense.

I looked up at him. "Bray, do you think he did the same thing to me?"

"What thing? And who?"

I stood so the thoughts in my head would fall into place with the help of gravity. "Wallace. Do you think he sent me here, to Del Rio, because he was thinking just like your mom, that it would be safe?"

Bray pushed himself to stand on the step where his feet had been planted. He stood two below me and met me at eye level. The gray of his eyes narrowed into focus. "Where were you before here?"

"New York, and the move was really sudden. He called me in the middle of the night and said I had to catch a plane to

California." I sucked in a gasp and slapped a hand over my mouth, thinking back to the sounds I heard through the phone that night. "It was that night! He died that night! I heard weird sounds through the phone, and he wouldn't tell me where he was. He just told me to finish the job I was on and get to the airport. Bray, he'd planned it." I looked at him with wild, searching eyes. "He's known for the past decade Olena is after me. He must have known she was close to finding me, so he relocated me."

I thought back to more details about that night: the wind, the car door, the fact Wallace had told me the data drive *would be collected*, not that *he'd* collect it. The sound I was pretty sure had been a gunshot in the distance. How he'd called me by my real name.

"Shit," I said out loud, understanding there was much more to the story than I'd thought. "Where was he when he died?"

A spark danced in Bray's eyes as he too put pieces together. He climbed up to the landing where I was, resuming his standard stature of a head taller than me. "I don't know. That's what I was looking into right when I found out Olena was being released from prison today and there's a threat on your life. I got a little distracted."

I didn't have time to fawn over him dropping everything to tend to my safety. I needed answers.

"Well, please, let's continue looking into it."

Chapter 19

5 years ago

The harsh bite of burnt hair still hovered around me as I all but kicked down the cabin door. Inside the authentically rustic space, Wallace sat at the small, wooden dining table, right where I'd left him.

"I quit," I spat and yanked off my wig, the source of the burning smell. Luckily, I'd been able to smash out all the embers before they sparked and set my whole head on fire. The wig was synthetic—a *good* synthetic—but still, I didn't know how flammable it was. I'd run from the burning barn without looking back. My throat still felt charred from the black smoke, and I could only hope whatever chemical castoff I'd inhaled wasn't burrowing into my lungs to put down cancerous roots.

Wallace calmly looked up at me, unbothered by my dramatic entrance or appearance. I hadn't had time to glance in a mirror while running for my life, but I could feel the ash on my face, the heat from the fire still keeping my cheeks flushed. I threw the burnt wig on the table, where it landed sprawled like a dead brown animal. Wallace glanced at it, and then looked back to me.

"Did you get it?" he asked in that steady tone of his. No matter that my heart was still pounding, my ears still ringing from the explosion, the fear of death still speeding through my veins. The job always came first.

His apathy crashed into my anger like gasoline into flame—or like ammonium nitrate into fuel oil, as I'd learned from this very job—and caused me to combust.

I crossed the small room to the table and gripped the back of the chair across from him. My heavy boots clomped against the cabin floor. "Did you not hear what I said? I *quit*. I want out." I unzipped my thick jacket, thinking some ventilation would help me breathe easier. I was dressed for the location: deep in the Pacific Northwest woods, fifty miles outside of Portland, where a domestic terrorist group was building chemical bombs to further their cause. One of those bombs had gone off by accident tonight. I'd fled the hidden compound with everyone else lucky enough to escape, but I knew when the flames went out and the ash settled, there'd be bodies inside that barn. I was still reeling over the fact I could have been one of them.

"Did you not hear *me*?" Wallace repeated my question back to me. "I asked if you got it." His cold indifference straightened my spine into further defiance.

"Doesn't matter. The Department of Forestry is going to be all over that place soon, or a wildfire is going to burn down half the forest. You can almost see the flames from here." I pointed over my shoulder with my thumb. My cabin was a solid ten miles from the barn, which was testament to the size of the blaze. "They're going to know it was chemical and arrest anyone who made it out alive—which I almost didn't, by the way," I bitterly added.

Wallace smoothed his fingers over his mustache and sat forward in his chair. "And you think any of those zealots are going to confess? You've gotten to know them."

He was right. I'd infiltrated their little cult over the past months; I knew them well. At face value, they didn't fit the mold. Young women my age with names like Skye, Lily, and Willow, who wore their hair in blond braids with wildflower crowns. And their counterparts, the men of the group like Asher, Clark, and Xavier, who built weapons in the name of environmental conservation and plotted to use them against logging companies and GMO testing labs. To anyone looking, they were a group of passionate college kids who held protests on weekends trying to save the environment, not a hive of ecoterrorists playing chemist deep in the woods.

When I hesitated to answer Wallace, he knew it was because my answer was *no.* They would not turn on one another and confess. They might even get the fire out before any authorities noticed and bury their dead on their own, and it would all remain secret.

Wallace gave me a stern look. "Did you get it?" he asked, again, with a note of finality like his patience had expired.

The child in me wanted to throw a tantrum. I wanted to refuse and pout and tell him to do his own dirty work. But I had almost just died completing the job and wasn't about to admit I'd failed when I hadn't.

I shoved my hand in my coat pocket and yanked out my phone. I tossed it on the table atop my singed wig and glared at him. "Of course I got it. And now I quit."

He leaned forward to grab the phone and unlocked it with the passcode he'd supplied it with. I winced when the incriminating video began to play. Sounds of the minutes leading up to the accidental explosion were already looping through my mind; I didn't need to hear the recorded version too. I'd walked through the barn and filmed footage of the gallons of explosives sitting in jugs, the powder kegs, the tubing, and igniters. I'd been discreet in capturing shots of most everyone there: Willow and Skye packing nails into bins, Xavier and Asher lugging crates from a truck. Clark in a pair of goggles stirring the mixture that would blow up in his face minutes later. *I* was the one who was going to turn on them. They would have died for one another and their cause, but little did they know that Rain from Seattle was an undercover informant plotting their demise from day one.

Wallace's mustache twitched up at the corner as the video finished. "Good girl," he said with a soft smile.

I gnashed my teeth at the phrase. It grated on my nerves and put me in my place every time he said it. But I was done. No more putting myself in danger's way when it so easily crossed paths with death.

"Okay, job's done. I want out," I said and folded my arms over my chest. My heart rate had finally recovered, but I could tell by the look on Wallace's face, it was about to speed up again.

"Out of what?" he asked.

"*This!*" I cried and flung out my arms. "Being undercover. Being sent into the woods where idiotic kids blow themselves up by trying to make bombs, or shipyards where drug deals go down at gunpoint, or back alleys were people get stabbed and left to bleed out because they can't pay a gambling debt. I don't want to do this anymore!"

Wallace finally stood from his chair. He rounded to my side of the table and leaned back against it with his arms folded. "The work you are doing is important."

"Says the guy who gets to sit behind a desk and boss me around," I angrily spat. "You're not the one out here trying not to get shot and running away from barn fires."

His face softened with the slightest bit of sympathy. I wouldn't have caught it if I hadn't been looking at his hardened features for the past half decade. "You're right, but you know the agreement."

"Fuck the agreement. I almost died tonight."

He flinched at my outburst but quickly recovered. "And what do you think is going to happen to you if we stop protecting you? You know this isn't just about staying out of prison. As long as Olena Nova doesn't know where that diamond is, you are not safe, remember? She's going to keep searching for you until it turns up, or until you turn up dead, so she doesn't have to kill you herself for sending her to prison."

That Goddamned diamond. I wanted it and hated it in equal measure. *It* was holding me prisoner more than any person. Finding it before anyone else did would solve everything. I'd steal it, sell it, and disappear. Away from the DSA, away from Olena. Poof. Gone.

"Well, where the hell is it? *Something* had to happen to it that night," I said. The familiar frustration of mystery boiled up inside me. It had been in my hand that night, and then it was just gone. My best guess was it fell on the floor and someone—not Olena or her henchman—had scooped it up and squirreled it away. A crooked FBI agent, the crime scene forensics team, maybe the hotel staff who cleaned the room after it was all said and done. "Do *you* know where it is?" I asked Wallace. "I mean, you'd tell me if you did, right? So I could get out of this whole situation?"

His dark eyes narrowed for the briefest moment, as if I'd insulted him, before his whole face flattened into his customary scowl. "Of course I don't know where it is."

I deflated, although I hadn't expected him to say yes. A big sigh pushed its way out of my lungs, knowing he was right: I was safer under the DSA's protection, even if it meant hopping from job to job with a rotating cast of identities.

Wallace sensed my dismay. He clapped me on the back. "How about a little break, hmm? Maybe we put you up in Hawaii for a few days before the next job."

I grumbled, even though I had to admit it sounded nice. "Make it two weeks and we have a deal."

CHAPTER 20

Present Day

"Sit here and don't touch anything," Bray instructed when he led me back to his desk. His actual desk, not the borrowed office he'd first taken me to. His space was tidy and kempt, and the control freak thoughts I'd had when I first met him, and after seeing his apartment, solidified. A potted succulent sat beside a holder full of pens. His keyboard was free of crumbs, and his monitor was shiny and currently asleep. I noted no picture frames or any personal effects, but what was he going to do, pin up a selfie of him and his mom to remind everyone of his status?

"Where are you going?" I asked when he started walking away.

"I have to see to a few things. I'll be right back."

He left me alone, swiveling in his surprisingly comfy chair (special treatment?), and staring at his keyboard.

He'd told me not to touch anything, but chances were not zero I could guess his password. Knowing him, it was probably *DSA123* or a series of smiley face emoticons. With Bray's computer sitting right in front of me and the need to know more about my own case burning a hole in my sternum, the temptation was too great.

I snapped out a quick hand and hit his enter key.

The screen fizzled to life. Of course a password prompt waited for me. I glanced over my shoulder and made sure no one was looking. Behind me, the aisle leading to offices was empty. Beneath the sound of clacking keyboards and a distant ringing phone, I discreetly typed out *DSA123* and held my breath.

The password box shook in refusal.

"Damn it," I muttered, secretly glad Bray wasn't that foolish, though it would have been to my benefit.

I slid my hands to the keyboard once more and hit a colon and parenthesis to make a smiley face, ready to roll my eyes if I was right, when someone nearby cleared their throat.

"I believe he told you not to touch anything." A male voice floated over from the other side of Bray's screen.

I jerked in surprise and leaned sideways to see who had spoken. A young man in a plaid shirt with square glasses, brown skin, and jet-black, wavy hair sat in the opposite cubicle, staring at his computer screen. His eyes flicked over when he saw me.

"I didn't," I lied and felt my face burn.

"Mm-hmm," he hummed, clearly not believing me. He looked at me with more intention and then slid his chair sideways so we could fully see each other. He looked about Bray's age, a few years older than me, and wore a lanyard around his neck with his photo and name on it.

"Hi, Agent Singh," I said once I read it.

He studied me for a silent moment before his face split into a grin. "Call me Ramesh. You're her, aren't you? The CI who Agent Bray keeps talking about?"

I blinked several times, trying to keep up. He'd gone from scolding me to smiling at me to gossiping like we were besties.

"Um, yes?" I said as my face warmed at the thought that Bray was talking about me. With the way Ramesh had said it, I got the sense Bray was *talking* about me, not that he was sharing updates on the case with his cubicle mate.

Thoughts of my dream crashed into me again, sending a flurry of nerves and heat loose in my belly.

"Nice to meet you," Ramesh said. "I've heard good things."

"Oh?" I said, truly curious. "Like what?"

"Like you're smart and a badass. I think Bray is a little bit afraid of you." He whispered the last part like we were in on a secret.

I flushed again. "I expected you to say he says I'm a pain in the ass."

"Well, yes. That too." He smiled like it was a compliment.

I smiled back. "What do you do here?"

He lifted his hands as if to put his desk on display. "I'm the guy in the chair."

"The what?"

"You know, when the field agents are out on jobs and they need to know something ASAP, like how to get out of a building or the best traffic route to escape or if someone is allergic to peanuts and might have been poisoned, they call me." He proudly grinned.

"I see," I said with a nod. "So, you're basically the brains of any operation."

"Correct. Although the guys and girls out there dodging bullets and punching bad guys don't always see it that way. Bray is one to give credit where it's due though," he said and nodded at where I sat. "He's always been a good guy, but after his recovery and the months he spent in the chair, he knows the job from both sides now."

I thought back to what Bray had said in the stairwell: He'd been at a desk for six months. He must have been a *guy in the chair*, like Ramesh.

"Guy like him doesn't belong at a desk though," Ramesh went on. "It's taking some time to get his legs back, but he's a Goddamn hero, if you ask me."

I casually pinched one of the succulent's thick spears, having a feeling I'd get more information out of a chatty cubicle mate than I ever would from Bray. "He mentioned this is his first case back in the field. What happened?"

Ramesh leaned in and lowered his voice. "He almost died on a job, from multiple gunshot wounds. The doctors were lucky to save him. Had the whole office in a panic, especially his mom—I mean, the director."

Guilt washed over me anew for giving Bray a hard time as Ramesh blushed at his slip. "Was there anyone else, um . . . particularly worried about him?" I asked and pinched the succulent again.

"I mean, we all were," Ramesh said. "But if you're asking if there was a girlfriend, no. No one like that."

A relieved breath whooshed out of me before I could stop it. I flamed in embarrassment again as Ramesh tried to hide a knowing grin. I cleared my throat and changed the subject. "What's the deal with that? Is it weird to have the director's son working here?"

Ramesh shrugged. "Not really. He doesn't take advantage. If anything, she's harder on him." He leaned in again and nearly whispered. "The truth is, I don't know if he ever even wanted this job. I think he'd be in a band somewhere if it paid the bills and he wasn't built for climbing walls and taking bullets."

"Band? What instrument does he play?"

"I guess I shouldn't say *band.* More like an ensemble or an orchestra, or wherever cellos go."

"I knew it!" I blurted. My impression of his elegant hands playing a classy instrument was spot-on.

Ramesh jerked back at my outburst.

"Sorry. I just had a hunch."

His knowing grin came back.

"So," I said, trying to pivot away from my embarrassment. "Are you Bray's guy in the chair for the Del Rio case?"

He gave me a little salute. "Yes. Although, he's had me looking at some classified files these past few days—*your* files, actually."

"And?" I said, nearly climbing onto the desk.

He leaned back and his eyes flicked up over my shoulder. "Agent Bray!" he blurted. "We were just talking about you."

"Oh? All good things, I hope?" Bray said from behind me. He'd returned from wherever he went and was holding a thin folder. "Add this to the Del Rio files, will you?" He handed the folder to Ramesh. "Ms. Daniels, if you'll follow me, please." He nodded for me to join him, and pure curiosity got me out of the chair.

"Nice to meet you, Ramesh," I said, and gave him a wave.

He waved back with a small grin.

"Where are we going?" I asked as I followed Bray down the aisle. His black T-shirt carved out the muscles in his back. I dared not look any lower than that for fear—yep. From behind, his slacks hugged his hips and thighs and everything in between like a glove. I made a mental note to always walk in front of him. "And what's with *Ms. Daniels*? No one calls me that."

He glanced over his shoulder. "What's with *Ramesh*? Did you make a new best friend in the five minutes I was gone?"

"First off, I'm pretty sure Ramesh could make friends with anyone in five minutes, and yes, maybe that's what happened, but more importantly, you've got him working on my case?"

He abruptly stopped walking, and I ran into his back. It was a goddamn brick wall that smelled like fresh mint and soap. I wanted to stay splattered against it like a fly on a windshield. "What did he tell you?"

I took a moment to gather myself. "Nothing. You came back

and interrupted before he could say anything." *Other than you're single, play the cello, are respected at work, and have heroic tendencies.* I kept the latter part to myself and felt the revelations burrow into a dangerously warm pocket of my heart.

The cello? Seriously?

"Well, he doesn't know anything I haven't told you," Bray said.

I gazed up into his gray eyes and looked for any sign he was bluffing.

"I'm serious, Erin. Yes, he's been helping, but I've told you all I know at this point. Which brings me to our next task." He held out his arm, and I only then realized we were standing at an elevator. He reached out to press the call button.

"Are we leaving?" I asked when it arrived with a ding.

"Yes, but we have to make a stop first."

When we stepped in and he hit the button for the basement, I cocked a curious brow at him but decided not to ask.

Our uninterrupted descent into the bowels of the building landed us in a hallway where the telltale scent of gunpowder, hot metal, and rubber curled into my nose. A shooting range.

"What are we doing down here?" I asked.

"Taking matters into our own hands," Bray said as he led me over to one of the stalls. The range was empty, but the ground was littered with shells and the air tinged with smoke as if someone had recently finished taking target practice. In fact, a mangled paper target hung holey and limp at the end of the next stall over.

Bray removed his gun from his holster and released the clip. He set the disassembled pieces on the shooting bench in front of us. "I'll give you a gun if you can show me you know how to use one."

A thrill zipped through me. *Finally*, we were getting somewhere. I glanced at the weapon and arched a brow at him. "I know how to use a gun, Bray."

He stood with one hand on his hip and a stern bend to his brow. He nodded at the gun. "Show me."

Tension strained between us with the chemical bite, the terrifying thrill of live ammunition being nearby. My fingers tingled in anticipation of picking up the firearm. A heat flashed in Bray's eyes, and I couldn't tell if it was fear, doubt, or something darker and more daring.

"Go on," he said with another nod. That authoritative note laced his voice and sizzled down my spine. "You want one, you have to show me you know what you're doing first."

As temptingly as the desire rolled around my mouth, I didn't sass, I didn't smirk. I knew this wasn't something to be taken lightly, but I wasn't about to give him the satisfaction of thinking he knew more than I did. He wanted me to *show* him anyway.

I silently flicked a brow at him and reached for the safety earmuffs hanging on a hook. He mirrored me and grabbed the ones from the next stall over. I turned the knob on the earmuff to drown out the deafening explosions about to happen and reached for the gun. In one fluid motion, I loaded the clip, flicked the safety, and racked the slide.

I spread my feet, locked my elbows, and pulled the trigger twice. *Bang. Bang.* I hit the silhouette target thirty yards away right in the paper eyeballs. The kickback raced up my arms and rattled my skull, but I absorbed it with a well-trained stance.

Bray stood next to me with his arms crossed, watching.

I looked over at him while I moved the gun to only my right hand and pulled the trigger three more times. *Bang. Bang. Bang.* The eyeball holes now had half a smile to go with them. I switched the gun to my left hand and shot three matching holes into the other side of the paper face. *Bang. Bang. Bang.* And then because I knew there were two bullets left in the clip, gave him one in the heart and one an inch from the bottom of the paper, between where the silhouette man's legs would be.

I gave Bray another look while I handily released the empty clip and set the pieces of his gun back on the bench.

I could tell by the bend in his lips and brow he was trying to hide the impressed shock on his face. He cleared his throat. "You missed with that last one."

I held his gaze with a steely defiance. "I promise you, I did not."

His Adam's apple bobbed when he swallowed hard. He hit the button to haul the target forward like a tattered sail. Up close, I was even more impressed with my aim. Ten perfect holes, right where I wanted them to be.

"Satisfied?" I asked with a hand on my hip.

He nodded with his lip pinched between his teeth. "And a little terrified to be honest. What else do you know how to do?" The genuine awe in his voice coupled with sincere curiosity lifted the tension, which had been choking me since we entered the room. Just because I knew how to use guns didn't mean I liked them.

"Ballroom dance." I began the list of unique skills I'd picked up over the years. "Speak conversational French, Spanish, and German. Play chess. Ice-skate pretty decently; that was a weird case. Recite most of the Constitution. Identify sculptors and painters from all the major art movements. Kayak. Change an engine. Hotwire a car. Hold my breath for two minutes. Lie without blinking. And probably knock you on your ass." My mouth flicked up at the corner with the last one, and I couldn't help noticing his do the same.

"Oh?" he said like it was a challenge.

"Yes. I don't suppose you want a demonstration of that too."

"Oh, I *absolutely* want a demonstration." He stepped at me with a cocky smile and reached for my shoulder.

On reflex, I whipped my arm out and blocked it. I moved to

fake punch him with my other arm, but he blocked me. In a split second, both of our arms were locked in battle: him holding one of mine and me holding one of his. The air crackled between us. He gazed down at me with a sly grin, a silent dare as we strained against each other. He was way bigger than me, but I knew how to leverage his size and mine.

"You sure?" I challenged, trying to warn him.

But he only kept grinning.

"Okay then," I said.

I slipped my arm holding his free and slammed my palm into his chest. When he bent over with a gasp, I shoved my elbow into his face, not hard, but hard enough for him to wince. When he stood back up to reach for his watering eyes, I stomped on his foot, which sent him bending forward again. I drove my elbow into the back of his shoulder, and he used his position to grab my legs—which I anticipated. I kicked my feet off the ground and used the leverage of being over his shoulder to hurtle his body backward, hooking my knees under his collarbone and dragging him with me. My hands pressed into the concrete floor, absorbing my fall, while he landed hard on his ass with a grunt. He let go of my legs, and I scrambled back over the top of him so we were face-to-face, me with my hands by his head and knees pressed into the floor on either side of his hips.

"Told you," I said.

We were both breathing hard, our chests nearly pressing together with each inhale. His face was an inch from mine. He looked up at me with wild wonder in his gray eyes. And a heat that made me fully aware of all the places we were touching and especially the ones where we weren't.

"Holy shit, Erin. You're a weapon," he said in awe.

The words hit me with an odd pang. One that cooled the blood flaming through my veins. I climbed off him and wiped the grit from my hands. "I never wanted to be. I learned all that out of necessity."

He sat up and wiped his hands on his pants. He looked at me like he wanted to say something but didn't know how.

I didn't know what to say either. I gazed around with a sigh. "So, if I passed my test, what's next? Back to Del Rio with a Glock in my pocket?"

"Not exactly," Bray said as he stood and held out a hand to help me off the floor.

Chapter 21

By the time Bray had driven us to a tall, angular condo on a hilltop in Larkspur, we'd made most of a full circle around the bay from where we started in Del Rio this morning.

"Is this a continuation of taking matters into our own hands?" I asked as he punched a security code into the driveway's gate.

"Yep."

"Who lives here?"

"You do. For now." He rolled up his window and pulled into the hedge-lined drive where we waited for the garage door to open. "But otherwise, my parents."

My heart dropped. I did not want to be under the same roof as the stern woman who'd refused to provide me with more security when my life was in danger.

"Relax," Bray said, reading it on my face. "They aren't home. They hardly stay here. My mom mainly lives in their house by the station in Oakland, and my dad is there too, when he's not traveling. This place is the most secure building in the Bay, and if she's not going to reassign us, then she has to sacrifice her spare home. Not that I told her about it." His lips turned up into a pleased little grin.

I couldn't help grinning back. "You rebel."

He parked in the garage, and we climbed out into a sterile white space. He used another keypad at the door to access the house, and I could only imagine how secure a DSA director's personal home was. She probably had a panic room and a closet full of guns.

The thought terrified and thrilled me.

"What does your dad do that has him traveling so much?" I asked as we stepped into a glacial-white kitchen with a soaring ceiling. Little pendant lights popped on above a tall bar with stools and spilled a soft gold into the room.

"He's an architect," Bray answered. "Renovated this place himself." His voice echoed up into the vaulted space above us.

I smoothed my hand over an icy granite counter and walked to the room's end. It spilled into a living room with low-profile furniture, also white, and an enormous window taking up a whole wall. I gasped at the view.

The Richmond-San Rafael Bridge spanned the water like a mighty gray bow in the distance. Cargo ships moved slowly toward port. Lights dotted the hills in the distance. And to the north, the ugly stone prison that housed my father snagged my gaze like a tear in an otherwise perfect oil painting.

I immediately turned away from it and back toward Bray. "Hell of a view," I said, and tried to ignore the wound pulsing at the back of my mind. What a terrible coincidence our parents "lived" so close together.

"You haven't seen the best part yet," Bray said and nodded at the back wall, but I didn't turn back around. Behind him, built into the kitchen cabinetry, was an impressive wine collection. I rarely drank, unless the job called for it, but after the day I'd had, a glass didn't sound so bad. Especially if my new living quarters had landed me closer to my father than I'd been in a decade.

"Could I have a drink?" I asked and pointed at the cabinet.

He turned to see what I'd pointed to. "Uh, sure," he said with a moment's hesitation.

"You already broke into their house. You think they're going to care if you raid the liquor cabinet too?" I said with a sly grin.

He smirked back with an irresistible twist of his lips. "It's less that and more drinking on the job."

"I won't tell anyone," I said and made the motion of turning a key in front of my lips.

"You are a vault, after all."

"A vault who likes rich reds." I pointed at the cabinet.

"As you wish," he said, and opened the glass pane. I made no comment when he grabbed two glasses and set them on the counter. The bottle he picked out looked expensive. I watched him twist a corkscrew and work the cork out with a squeaky *pop.* He still wore his T-shirt, so his corded forearms were on full display and putting on a show.

I took a healthy gulp when he handed me a glass. "This is delicious."

"My parents have good taste," he said with a knowing nod. "Come here. I'll show you the best part of this place." He nodded at the back wall again, and I feared his plan involved going outside to gaze at the view.

"Won't it be cold out there?" I tried to protest. With most of the day passed at this point, the sun had sunk behind the hill and left the east-facing side of the condo in the shade.

"I'll grab you a sweater," he said with an enthusiasm suggesting he liked playing host. He set his wine on the island and trotted off toward a sleek hallway. The whole condo was sleek. The marble floor, the white walls and furniture, the minimalist design with splashes of color. Given its location, his parents must have paid a fortune for it.

"Do you have a room here?" I asked in his direction and gulped more wine. It went down like a silk ribbon.

"Not officially, but I keep some stuff in the guest room just in case I stay over." He reappeared with a pair of sweaters: the cream cable knit cardigan he'd pulled over his T-shirt, and its gray twin, which he handed to me.

I froze for a second at the sight of him looking coastal chic. Like he'd walked out of a catalog of gorgeous men wearing thick sweaters and posing in the misty trees. "Thank you." It took me a moment to find my voice. His sweater, of course, swallowed me whole when I put it on, and of course smelled like mint and soap, and of course I wanted to curl up and drown in it.

Instead of me dying in cable-knit man heaven, he led us through a sliding glass door and onto the patio off the living room. A sectional sofa hugged a long, narrow stone fire feature sparkling with blue crystal glass. A line of flame leapt to life when Bray flipped a switch.

"Not bad, huh?" he said and gestured toward the sofa.

I intentionally sat with my back to the prison and sipped my wine. "Not bad at all." Aside from the sofa and the fire feature, the patio held a small barbecue, a café table and pair of chairs, a covered drink cart, and a breathtaking view of sky, water, and hills twinkling with lights.

Bray sat adjacent to me, on the long leg of the L-shape. The setting felt like a date. Though, if we were on a date, I'd have been halfway in his lap by this point. Maybe even inside his sweater for extra warmth.

"Are you warm enough?" Bray asked.

With the fire two feet away and his enormous sweater wrapping me like a blanket, I couldn't have been more content. Minus the part where we were within spitting distance of my father, and the whole reason we were even on the posh patio of a luxury condo in the first place being because a madwoman wanted to kill me.

"I'm good," I said.

We sat in silence, and both stared at the fire. The flickering flames cast the mesmerizing elemental spell that always called to something primitive in my brain. I felt myself melt into a pleasant haze, despite the circumstances.

"Erin," Bray eventually said. "We need to talk about what's next."

"You mean I can't just stay hiding out in your parents' luxury condo drinking expensive wine and staring at the bay forever?"

He quietly chuckled. "For now, yes. But not forever. My dad will eventually notice if all his wine is gone."

"This is really excellent," I said and smacked my lips after another sip.

Bray swirled his glass turned ruby red by the firelight. "I think it's from his last trip to New Zealand."

"How did your parents meet?" I asked. I rarely got the chance to ask someone personal questions without an ulterior motive; I was usually gathering intel to report back to my handler. Sitting out here in the twilight air sipping wine with Bray, I was genuinely curious to know more about him. "A secret government agent and an architect seem like an odd pair. And on that note, does your dad know what your mom does? Does he know what *you* do?" My interest continued to be piqued as the questions spilled from my mouth.

He smiled at my enthusiasm. "Yes, to both—in general terms, at least. And they met in college. They've been married for over thirty years."

I couldn't imagine such a thing. I'd never had a long-term relationship in my life. I silently wondered if my parents would still be married if my mother hadn't died. How would my life have turned out?

"Do you have any siblings?" I asked to avoid falling into a pit of what-ifs.

"I do. An older brother."

"Is he in the family biz too?"

"Yes, but not this one." He gestured at himself. "He actually works for my dad's firm. I think it kind of broke my mom's heart when her firstborn didn't want to join the DSA." He looked into his wineglass and took another sip. The potent juice seemed to be loosening his lips.

I thought about what Ramesh had said about Bray not wanting his career. "So, you followed in her footsteps to make up for it? Are you a mama's boy?"

He smirked at me, but it was halfhearted. "No. But it did set me up for a lot to live up to. I do the best I can, and she still treats me like a child, as you saw."

"She cares about you. Is that such a bad thing?"

"No, but it's hard to be good at this with training wheels on."

I felt the note of annoyance in his voice because I'd been there too. Being bossed around and not allowed to be independent. "But you've kicked those wheels off by going rogue, right?" I said with a sly grin.

He grinned back. "To taking matters into our own hands." He lifted his glass, and I clinked mine against it.

"Do you even like your job?" I asked after a healthy sip.

He paused for a telling beat and then shrugged one shoulder. "It has its moments."

"That was convincing. Would you rather work for your dad's firm?"

At this, he laughed. "No. Johnny was always the one sketching and building things, not the one getting suspended for fighting in school, so our respective parent-pleasing roles make sense."

I gasped in shock. "*You*, Agent Calvin Bray, got *suspended* for fighting in school?"

He held up a hand and half smiled. "It was in defense of a friend who was being bullied, but yes."

"Hmm. So, the hero mentality started young, I see."

"Hero?"

"Yes, Ramesh said he thinks you're a hero."

Color spotted his cheeks. "What else did he say?"

I shifted to tuck my legs up underneath me and pulled his sweater tighter. "Let's see . . ." I trailed off like the list was long and watched his face grow redder. "He said you play the cello."

A laugh bubbled out of him. "Ah, yes. That was my dad's attempt at turning me into something more refined than a kid throwing punches on the playground."

"Did it work?"

He stroked his jaw, and then leaned back with his arm draped over the sofa's back. "I'd say so."

The wine had gone to my head, and I so desperately wanted to crawl to him and tuck myself under his arm. Instead, I did something even more reckless. "Can I get a refill?" I held up my glass before sipping the last drops.

He eyed the dregs of red clinging to the glass like he was considering the right answer. "Sure, but then we have to talk about serious things." He stood from the sofa and reached for my glass.

"I think your musical talents and history with playground violence are *very* serious things."

He snorted a laugh and headed for the door. "Be right back."

I snuck a peek over my shoulder while he was gone. The prison had never left my mind. It perched like a hawk on a high branch, waiting to strike. I somehow knew, deep in my gut, when Wallace sent me here, my path would cross with my father. And here we were. Closer in physical proximity than we'd been in years, and the case that had sent him to prison, and my life into an endless spiral of alternating identities, was stalking me like a hungry wolf.

I closed my eyes and saw his face from that night in the hotel. The last time I'd seen him. The fear. The failure. The realization we'd finally been caught. The pain.

"Here you go." Bray's voice cut into my memory and made me jump. "Sorry," he said when he noticed.

I shook myself and took the wineglass with both hands. "Thank you." I gulped half of it in one go. I noted he had not refilled his glass, but he did sit closer to me when he returned to the couch. He landed where the angled cushions met, close enough his knee almost touched mine.

"It's a shame such a beautiful piece of waterfront property is a prison," he said and nodded in the direction I'd been looking.

"Big shame," I echoed and downed another gulp, wanting to move from the subject, though I knew we were headed toward another unpleasant one. I considered going and getting the wine bottle in preparation.

"So," Bray said, getting to business by his tone. "We've probably only got a few days before someone at the DSA notices we're not in Del Rio. I can buy us some time, but we're going to have to move quick if we're going to do this on our own. In my eyes, solving this case proves to my mom—the director—I'm capable, and sets you free from Olena. It's a win-win."

I figured he'd been thinking something of the sort. "Easier said than done," I said with a frown. "You realize *solving this case* means finding that diamond, right?"

"Yes." He said it so simply. As if I hadn't been unsuccessfully looking for it in back channels during every spare second I had for the past ten years. "We need to find it and officially lock it up in evidence, and then Olena has no choice but to trust you don't have it."

Lock it up, what a shame, a sinister little voice said in the back of my mind. I tried to quiet it by keeping my eyes on Bray's determined face.

"Right. Do you happen to know where it is?" I asked.

"No, but do you?"

I gaped at him. "Are you still on this? *No*, Bray. I don't know where it is. If I did—"

Suddenly, he shifted and removed my glass so he could set it aside. He took both my hands in his. His large palms burned warm against my skin. "Erin, you were the last one to see it that night. Maybe if you try, you can remember what happened." The fire danced in his pleading eyes, setting the gray off into shimmering silver. He looked almost otherworldly.

"I—" My voice caught in my throat. A cocktail of emotion swelled in my chest: shock he was touching me, desire for him to put his hands other places, but most of all, fear at what he was asking me to do. I swallowed against my dry mouth and found my voice. "Bray, you're asking me to remember the worst night of my life."

His hands tightened around mine. "I know, and I'm sorry. But I've been there too. I know what it's like to have shock blank out parts of your memory, believe me." He paused and another emotion swelled in my chest. This one warm and aching at the same time.

Of course he knew. He'd almost died in a traumatic situation. I'd almost been shot that night, and he *had* been shot.

"Calvin . . ." His first name slipped from my trembling lips by accident.

The jolt of intimacy made him curl his fingers around my hands so he was holding each in one of his. His fingertips pressed into my palms. A tiny smile quirked the corners of his mouth. "Please," he whispered. "Just try. I'm right here with you."

My heart had picked up its pace, nearing an uncomfortable

rate. But knowing he was close helped soothe my fear. I nodded with a pained wince, afraid of the memory I was about to dive into, and closed my eyes.

I saw my father again. The hotel room. Olena's furious face. I felt the gun's cold barrel pressed to my temple like the kiss of death. The ghost's fingers curled around my throat.

The diamond. Where is the diamond?

It had been in my hand, frozen like a translucent chunk of ice. I'd had it. I'd *had* it. I needed it now, and I could see it in my teenaged palm, sitting there like the answer to everything. Where did it go? Had I dropped it? Had Olena snatched it back when the money burned the wrong color? Had my father taken it? I looked as hard as I could, but it was all a blur. The smoke, the gun, my father telling me to run.

I jerked my hands out of Bray's and stood. "I'm sorry," I said and threw a palm over my wetting eyes. I turned away from the fire and walked to the railing. The hillside tumbled away from the balcony with nothing but shrubbery and dirt below before the next home clung to the earth a good thirty feet away.

I sensed Bray's warmth behind me before he placed a hand on my shoulder. It was greedy, and maybe selfish, but in that moment, I wanted a hug—a *real* hug. I couldn't even remember the last one I'd had, and I knew he'd give me one.

I turned so his arm wrapped around my shoulders and buried my face in his chest. He threw his other arm around me without hesitation, and I nearly sagged against him. I breathed him in, that minty soap smell like a balm so close, and let him hold me. I could feel his heart under my palm, having sped up like mine but still steady and strong. His breath moved in and out of his lungs and spilled down the gap where his too-large sweater curved against my neck. He felt like a living shield, and despite his mistakes, I knew on a bone-deep level he wasn't going to let anything happen to me.

"I'm sorry," he said quietly into the evening air. "I'm just trying to help."

"I know." I sniffled against his chest, not yet ready to leave his embrace, however inappropriate it might have been. "But I really don't remember."

He leaned back to look down at me, his eyes now liquid gray in the fading light and full of understanding. The flames dancing behind him backlit his face into dramatic shadows. The scar on his chin stood out in stark relief.

I moved my hand up to smooth my thumb over the scar. His breath stuttered. "I'm sorry this happened to you. You must have been terrified."

His arms remained wrapped around my back. He slowly nodded. "I was."

I tried to make something smooth come out of my mouth. Something one of my alter egos would know to say in this situation, but this was too real, and my body was humming too hard with forbidden possibility to focus. "I'm glad you survived."

Bray's mouth twitched at the corner again. "Me too."

We continued staring at each other, and I saw honesty rise to the surface in his eyes. "What you asked me earlier, about liking my job, the truth is, my heart hasn't really been in it since I got shot. I've just been doing it out of a sense of duty. But with you . . . Well, let's just say my heart feels a little different about things now."

My heart hit my ribs hard at the same time it swelled bigger than the moon. "What are you saying?"

He softly laughed as color filled his face. "I don't know. Things I probably shouldn't be. But I guess the point is, you've made me care."

If not for his arms around me, I might have collapsed. *He cared.* About me. And his job, but because of me. I let the feeling fill up the empty chambers of my heart, and then sealed them off to keep it close. I wasn't sure I was allowed to possess something so special.

"Well, I'm glad to be the one to make your Grinch heart grow, Agent Bray," I said with a half smile.

Saying his name seemed to snap the spell. He released his grip and took a step back. He combed a nervous hand through his hair. "Sorry about that. I shouldn't have—" He gestured toward me, and I filled in the awkward silence with *hugged you.*

"It's okay. I needed a hug."

"Well, I've got more if you ever need another." He clumsily chuckled and looked away in embarrassment.

"Noted," I said, thrilled at the prospect he might hold me again.

A sudden wind whipped through, sending the flames dancing, and reminding me we had a problem to solve. I wrapped the sweater tighter and leaned back on the railing. "So, the diamond. I still have no idea where it is."

"Is there anyone else who might?"

As soon as he asked, an idea knocked against my skull like a hammer. *No.* I tried to shoo it away because it wasn't actually viable. *I couldn't.*

"I mean, Olena obviously doesn't know where it is, otherwise she wouldn't be stalking you," Bray went on, oblivious to my silent struggle. "If the Feds had grabbed it that night, it would already be locked up in evidence. We can't ask Agent Wallace, obviously . . ."

His voice faded to a low buzz while my own thoughts overpowered his list of dead ends. There was someone we could ask. The only other person still alive from that night who didn't want to kill me. Well, I assumed he didn't want to kill me.

Bray was pacing the patio now, fingers pinching his lip as he rambled.

"There is someone," I blurted, seeing it as the only option.

He stopped pacing and looked at me with his brows lifted. "Who?"

The words sat on my tongue like a grenade. I couldn't bring myself to pull the pin. Instead, I gestured to my right.

Bray followed my arm with his gaze as if he expected to see someone standing there. "What?"

I huffed in frustration, wanting him to figure it out so I didn't have to say it. I gestured again, this time with both arms like I was showcasing a prize on a game show.

He frowned. "The bay? You think someone threw it in the water?"

"Oh my God," I grumbled and dropped my arms with a slap at my thighs. I grabbed his hand and pulled him to the patio's end. "My father, Bray! He's in that prison!"

"Oh. *Oh!*" he said when it sunk in. "Oh shit, he is?"

"Yes. I thought you read my file."

"Yes, *your* file. That detail isn't in there."

"Well, *he's* in *there*." I pointed with my free hand and realized he was still holding my other. His thumb took a brief journey over my knuckles. It sent a hot zap straight to my chest.

"Do you think he knows where the diamond is?" Bray asked.

"I don't know, but he's the only person left to ask who doesn't want to kill me. I think."

His grip tightened on my hand, and he chewed his lip, thinking.

"There's only one problem though," I said.

"What's that?"

"I'm not going in there to talk to him."

He slipped his grip free and closed the distance to the railing with a few steps. He'd commanded me to do several unpleasant things since we'd met: become a nanny, make friends, go to work with a sprained ankle. But I could tell by his pensive silence he put this task in another category. Relief washed over me when I realized he wasn't going to demand I do it.

When he turned back around, the fire lit the eager look on his face. "What if I could get him to come to you?"

"What? How?" I mentally stumbled in confusion. "Last I checked, they don't give day passes to federal prisoners unless they've got a *really* good reason."

He stepped toward me and looked like he wanted to take my hand again. "Saving your life is good enough reason for me, but don't worry. I still have some strings to pull." He reached in his pocket for his phone and lit up the little rectangle.

A grin tugged at my mouth while I watched him tap at his screen. "Taking matters into your own hands."

"Indeed. I'll have to make some arrangements, but it shouldn't take long. Maybe by tomorrow. Would you be ready?"

The question hit me like a sledgehammer and left me winded. *Would I be ready to see my father tomorrow?* The answer must have been *no* because my brain refused to connect and make anything come out of my mouth.

Bray stepped toward me. "Erin, I know this is asking a lot, but it'll be safe. I'll make sure of it."

I looked up into his big, hopeful eyes and wanted to tell him there was no such thing as *safe* when it came to my father. Even if it was a conversation in a padded room, my father would find a way to scheme, to outmaneuver. To create danger.

But Bray was looking at me like he'd take a bullet for me if it came to it. I may not have trusted my father, but I trusted Bray to make this work.

"Yes, I can do it. But, Bray, you have to know, whatever strings you're going to pull to get to him, he'll be ready with ten strings of his own. He's always conning. Don't forget this is the man who used his own daughter as bait."

Sympathetic pain furrowed his brow, but he nodded. "I know."

I shivered at the thought of what we were going to set in motion. *Tomorrow.* I'd be face-to-face with the man who'd derailed my life. The man who had *given* me life and used it for his own purposes.

Bray nodded toward the door, thinking I was cold from the temperature, not from the chill that had haunted me for years. "Let's go back inside where it's warmer. Agent Simmons will be here soon anyway."

"He will? Why?" I asked and followed him inside.

"Because, as far as anyone at the station knows, he's still on night patrol protecting you in Del Rio, which is only a half lie. But in reality, he's bringing supplies: clothes, toiletries, things you need to stay here for a while. He'll stay the night here with you too. I need to get back to the station."

I stopped short. Any fantasy I'd had of falling asleep on the couch with my feet in his lap, still wrapped in our sweaters—or better yet, the same bed after we'd removed the sweaters and everything else—evaporated like mist. He was back to business. Treating me like an asset. *Handling* me in the unfun operational sense of the word. Despite whatever moment we'd had on the patio, my fantasies were futile anyway. He'd never cross that line. He was too heroic.

I quietly sighed in disappointment and removed my shoes. The condo looked like a please-remove-your-shoes home anyway, and I figured I should get comfortable if I was staying awhile.

"You're bringing me clothes and products and setting me up in this fancy condo like a sugar baby. You're not going to Christian Grey me, are you?"

He looked over his shoulder with a frown. "Who?"

"Never mind. Can I order food, or is the fridge stocked?"

He rounded into the kitchen and opened the fridge's stainless-steel door. "Looks pretty sparse; my parents haven't been here for a while. If you want something ordered, just tell Simmons."

"My own manservant to boot, not bad."

Bray rolled his eyes and nodded toward the hallway. "Come here, I'll give you a tour."

I diligently followed across the dining room complete with a teak dining table and intricate chandelier that could have been displayed in a museum of modern art. "What, no geeky school portraits of the Bray children to line the walls?" I asked as we passed a pair of underlit oil paintings in the hall.

"You'd have to visit my parents' house in Oakland for those. All you'll get is custom art here."

"I can't imagine having two houses. I've never even had *one.*" The words slipped out in wonder before I realized it.

I caught his sympathetic, if not guilty, gaze as we rounded into a bedroom. "You can have the main room; Simmons will take the guest room." He pointed out the doorway back across the hall. I ignored him and instead threw myself on the cloud of a bed. The fluffy white comforter billowed around me like I'd jumped on a tent.

"This is even better than Del Rio." I flipped over to make snow angels in the fluff and heard him laugh.

"Bathroom is through there. There should be plenty of towels. The floors are heated, and there's a soaking tub and shower. Whatever you need."

"I need this bed and a new identity so no one ever finds me here." I hugged a marshmallow pillow, which smelled like lavender and jasmine.

He laughed again. "Come on, I'll show you how the house system works."

"There's a system?" I reluctantly followed him out of the room.

By the time he showed me the alarm; how the touchscreens

in the walls controlled the sound system, the lights, and could raise and lower the window coverings; and demonstrated how to navigate an unreasonable number of streaming options on the TV, I could tell caring for others was his true calling. He thrived in this element. And having him care for *me* was setting my body abuzz with a warmth I'd never known.

Agent Simmons arrived at the end of my tour.

"Ms. Daniels," he greeted me with a curt nod. He'd rolled in a suitcase and carried two bags from Nordstrom before he'd returned out the front door for more supplies.

"It's still creepy you know my size in everything," I said to Bray and pawed through one of the bags Simmons had set on the kitchen island to find a cashmere sweater and two pairs of leggings.

"More like convenient," Bray said.

Simmons returned with another suitcase, presumably his own, and a black case he carried in his hand, this one smaller and with a lock on it.

"Thanks, Mike," Bray said and took it from him. Simmons nodded and headed down the hall toward the guest room, giving away nothing about how breaking rules might be making him feel.

"Is he the type of babysitter to stay up and play boardgames with me all night? Or am I going to be prying words out of him like barnacles from a rock?" I asked with a smirk.

Bray smirked back. He'd set the small case on the island and placed his hand on top of it. "He'll follow your lead, but I don't think he's much for Monopoly. He's more of a chess guy."

"Pity. I was ready to take him for all he's worth."

Bray took a breath, sounding serious once more. "Before I give this to you, I want to ask you something."

I glanced down at the case, realizing it was the gun I'd been promised. *Thank God.* The thought of a weapon nearby *I* could wield so I didn't have to only rely on my protectors fizzed a wave of relief through me. "I promise not to shoot you in the balls with it like I did the poster target in the range," I said and held up a hand like I was taking an oath.

He lost the battle to keep the smile off his face. "Thank you, but that's not what I was going to ask."

"Oh?"

"No." He cleared his throat and looked nervous. "Back at the range, you said you never wanted to be a weapon. What do you want to be?"

The question almost took me to my knees. No one had ever asked me before, save maybe an elementary schoolteacher asking the obligatory *What do you want to be when you grow up?* years ago.

As Bray looked at me with sincere interest in his eyes, the answer came to me easier than I would have thought.

"Free."

My response looked like it nearly took *him* to his knees. It took him a moment to find his voice. "What would you do then?"

I hadn't put a ton of thought into it because I never thought it would happen. But again, the answers came easily. "Go to college. Maybe study literature. Get a dog. Go on a date."

His eyes crinkled at the corners, with sympathy or pity or something else altogether, I couldn't tell. Words waited on his tongue; I could sense them there. I willed him to say them. To tell me I *could* be free. Soon. And maybe even that he'd take me on a date. *Please.* But his lips stayed closed.

I huffed a sad laugh and shook my head. "Pipe dreams."

He gave me a weak smile and slid the gun case to me. "I have to get going. The combo is your birthday."

I picked up the case and poked at the little numbered

wheels lined up and ready to spin. “Is anything about me a mystery to you?” I asked as he turned to go.

He turned back and gave me a coy smile. “Many things, Erin. Many, many things.”

He left me in the kitchen with a gun, a new wardrobe, and the thought of his smile dangerously warming my heart.

Chapter 22

It took me approximately thirty minutes of tossing and turning in Bray's parents' luxury cloud bed to conclude I was never going to sleep. I'd shared Thai takeout with Simmons, coerced him into telling me he had a girlfriend and a dog named Buddy, and watched a baseball game on TV until the last out. Then I'd soft-boiled myself in the tub, used the full line of skincare I'd been provided, brushed my teeth, and climbed into the bed to alternate between staring at the ceiling and at the inky night spotted with hillside lights and ships on the water.

By eleven p.m. I surrendered to temptation and grabbed my phone to text Bray, somehow sensing he was still awake.

Simmons snores.

He responded almost immediately and brought a smile to my face.

Really? There should be some earplugs in the nightstand.

No, not really. And I'm not about to go rooting through your parents' nightstands. I don't want to stumble on any . . . nightstand things.

Ew. Please don't say that.

You brought it up.

Well then let's change the subject.

Okay, why is it so quiet here? I can hear my hair growing.

Because my dad used special sound-blocking insulation in the walls. If it's really bothering you, there's a sound machine in the guest room. I use it when I can't sleep there.

Thanks, but I can't sleep no matter what. Life as a CI doesn't lend itself to deep, sweet dreams.

I'm sorry. Does anything help?

Sleeping pills, but those are dangerous when you might need to wake up on a moment's notice.

What about a hot bath?

Already did it.

Warm milk?

I'm not a cat.

Umm . . . lullaby?

Sure. Wanna sing me one? Oh! Even better, play me one on your cello ☺

I don't have it with me, sorry.

Are you still at the station?

Unfortunately. I might just crash here.

I thought of texting *plenty of room in this bed,* but the half joke would not land on screen like it would in person. And honestly, it wasn't a joke. I would have loved to feel the warmth of his body next to mine. Holding me like he had on the balcony.

I chased the impossible thoughts away with a reminder of what was to come.

Have you made progress for tomorrow?

Yes. Still some work to do, but I'm talking to the right people now.

Does that mean some underground prison network that trades in favors?

That's classified.

Always so noble.

I'm a hero, remember?

Ugh. Don't let it go to your head.

Too late ☺

I'd missed his smiley faces. Things had gotten too dark in the past twenty-four hours. Our conversation paused, and I found myself surprised when my phone began to buzz with an incoming call and his name on the screen.

"Are you really going to sing to me?" I asked when I answered.

"Why are you really up right now?" His voice was bedroom soft. Tender.

"I told you: It's too quiet here to sleep."

"Erin."

The slight admonishment both warmed me that he cared enough to ask, and made me feel guilty for not telling him the truth. I sighed and a wall came down with it.

"Because I'm . . . scared. About tomorrow. The last time I saw my father, things didn't go well. Obviously. And truthfully, when he got arrested, part of me was relieved, and I think that makes me a bad person."

"You're not a bad person."

"Aren't I though? Conflicted feelings toward my father aside, I went from one life of crime to another, except this one gives me permission to lie and steal."

A pause filled the line. His voice came back resolved, as if he'd had an internal argument and succeeded in convincing himself of something. "You didn't have a choice in either case."

"Yeah, but I still did those things—*do* them."

As the words left my mouth, I thought about the truth behind them. I'd have been lying if I didn't admit part of me *liked* doing bad things. Having the DSA's permission to do them only dulled the thrill a tad. Like a drop of cream in very strong coffee. The compulsion was probably tied to my formative years spent being rewarded for such behavior, first by my father and then by Agent Wallace. My value was bound up in doing dirty deeds for others. It was all I knew; ingrained in my self-worth. Given the choice, I couldn't say I would break good.

"I think you'd be disappointed by the choices I'd make on my own, Bray," I said.

Another pause filled the line. This one strained around the edges. I could only imagine what he was thinking.

He cleared his throat and came back with his DSA voice. "Well, for what it's worth, I think you'll do fine tomorrow. This is our only shot at finding the diamond and keeping you safe. A face-to-face with *you* will get us more than if he talked to anyone else."

I silently agreed with him.

"Will he know I'm coming?"

"No."

"Good. Better to catch him off guard. Where will it happen?"

"Somewhere off-grid," he answered. "We can't take him far, but there are plenty of abandoned shipyards and garages nearby to choose from."

"Perfect setup for everything to go wrong."

"I'll be there, don't worry."

"I'm bringing my gun."

"I don't think that would be a good idea."

I huffed. "Then why'd you give it to me?"

"For you to feel safe at the house."

"Bray, this place has a keycode to get into the garage, and I've got an armed babysitter sleeping in the next room over. I'm not worried about being safe here."

"Good. Glad to know my provisions are working."

"They'd work better if you were here too." The words slipped out, and I couldn't take them back. I scrunched into a ball under the impossibly high thread count linens and wanted to disappear. I swore I could feel him blushing over the phone.

"You don't want me there. I *do* snore."

"Really?"

"No, but I am not the most peaceful sleeper."

"You didn't seem to have a problem sleeping on my couch last night."

"I—" He paused and quietly laughed. "You're right. That was a fluke. Ever since my injury, I startle pretty easy."

"*Injury.* What a heroic choice of word."

He quietly laughed again. "Look at us: two trauma insomniacs."

"Yeah, maybe if we slept together, we would cancel each other out."

Oh my God.

I wanted to die.

"I can't believe I just said that. I'm sorry. I didn't mean—"

He chuckled again. "It's okay. You're obviously tired enough to be mashing your words, so maybe you are ready for sleep. Either that, or you raided the wine cabinet, and I'll have to explain to my dad why his best labels are all gone."

"I didn't pop any more bottles, promise."

"Good. I was right to trust you with them."

"Bray?"

"Yeah?"

"Thanks for talking to me. And for keeping me safe."

The pause filling the line this time was warm and gentle and made me wish I was talking to his face and not my phone. "You're welcome. Good night, Erin."

"Good night . . . Cal."

The smile in his voice was apparent. "Get some rest. Everything will be fine tomorrow."

I ended the call and rolled over, convincing myself he was right.

Whatever strings Bray was pulling to get to my father, it took all day to pull them. Long enough that I ran ten miles on his parents' treadmill, binged half a season of *The Office*, convinced Simmons to play chess with me, and considered opening another bottle of wine. The sun had fully set by the time my phone rang.

"We're ready. I'll be there in twenty minutes," Bray said with no preamble or further information.

I dressed in the cashmere sweater, jeans, and a coat because the night had grown chilly, and I assumed our rendezvous would be outdoors, maybe near water. Someplace off the grid, as Bray had said. Having been invisible for a decade, I certainly couldn't walk into a prison for a chat, not even with a really good disguise. The risk was too great. While I waited for him to arrive, I stood at the back window, staring at the prison, and wondering how Bray had made this happen. What reason they'd given my father for an off-site fieldtrip on no notice.

Somewhere in the back of my mind, beneath the nerves and tension roiling through me, I wondered if he already knew. If some network on the inside told him Olena was out, and there was a hit on the girl who supposedly stole from her and got her sent to prison.

"Ms. Daniels," Simmons's voice cut through my thoughts.

I turned to see him in the kitchen, and Bray entering through the garage door. The relief spilling over me at the sight of him was not subtle. He wore slacks and a windbreaker over his dark shirt. His gun was holstered at his hip. A layer of scruff coated his jaw, and I wondered if he truly had spent the night at the station.

"Hey. Ready?" he asked when he saw me.

I nodded even though it wasn't true.

"Great. Simmons will drive. You and I will ride in back. The prison transporter is meeting us in a half hour. We won't have long with him."

I nodded again, unable to speak around my nerves.

"Give us a minute, will you?" he said to Simmons, and crossed the room to where I stood.

Simmons left through the garage door, and it was just the two of us in the stark white kitchen. I could nearly hear my heart pounding.

"Erin, it's going to be fine. He'll be cuffed and monitored. Going anywhere high security would put you on radar you don't want to be on, so it has to be this way."

I nodded and swallowed against my dry throat. "I know."

He placed his warm hands on my shoulders. "You'll be fine."

I nodded once more.

I thought he might pull me into another hug, but he slid his palms down my arms and then gave the coat pockets at my hips a little pat. I arched a brow at him. "Are you checking to see if I have the gun?"

His face flushed but he became more shameless in his work. His palms moved to my jeans' hips and quickly spread against my lower back. "Just making sure you aren't going to do anything that could get you killed," he muttered.

"If you wanted to feel me up, you could at least open another bottle of wine first."

He frowned at me and then squatted to squeeze both my ankles.

"Bray, I don't have it," I said to the top of his head. His hair was mussed, maybe by the wind, and I was tempted to run my fingers through it.

"Good. Thanks for following directions, for once."

"Hey, I've done everything you've said since we left Del Rio."

"Yes, you have. Good job. Now, let's go. We've got a short window to make this happen."

I followed him to the car with my skin on fire from where he'd dragged his palms over my body. Even my ankles tingled.

Simmons drove us down a winding road from the hill, and we headed north. We passed the prison and crossed the Richmond-San Rafael Bridge into the East Bay. By the time we parked in a dark lot crowded with shipping crates near the shoreline, my heart was beating so hard, I had to calm it with several deep breaths.

Bray reached over and squeezed my clammy hand.

"Sorry. I don't usually get this nervous on jobs, but this is—"

"It's okay," he said. "I understand. Simmons, could you give us another minute?"

Simmons nodded and climbed out of the driver's seat, leaving us alone in the car. The dark night crowded in, save for the scant streetlights casting yellow pools on the concrete outside.

"You're going to be fine, Erin," Bray said and leaned down to meet my eyes. I was staring at my lap, still breathing deeply. My hands had started to shake. He squeezed them with both of his.

I took another deep breath right as headlights flashed across us.

"They're here," he announced. He went to reach for the door, but I refused to let go of his hands.

"Could I—?" Nerves shook my voice as he turned back to me.

"Could you what?"

An embarrassed heat curled into my face, but I forced the words out. "Could I cash in on one of those hugs you offered?"

His rigid posture softened, and he gave me a sympathetic smile. "Sure." He wrapped his arms around my shoulders, and I tucked myself to his middle, weaving my arms around his back, inside his windbreaker. His signature scent of minty soap filled my nose where I pressed it to his chest and inhaled. A soft, warm sound escaped his throat and almost undid me on the spot.

I pulled back before we got too carried away, though I wanted nothing more than to stay squeezed against him. When he held on for a second longer, reluctant to let me go, I almost did stay. But we had a job to do.

"Hang back for a second," Bray instructed when he turned for the door.

I did as I was told and straightened my jacket and my hair, which had gotten mussed in our embrace.

Cold air poured in the door when he opened it. I let the night, gritty with fog and salt, wash over my hot skin to clear my mind. My eyes were closed when I heard Bray's foot scrape against the concrete. I heard a van door slide open nearby and the sound of jangling chains.

And then, the voice that still haunted my dreams.

"What the hell is this? If you boys wanted to whack me, you coulda just handed someone a shiv. An *accident*, you know? No need to drag me out into the cold like this."

My father. Always half joking, but always serious at the same time. The deep rumble of his voice hit me like a punch to the gut. I gasped, and then steeled myself against any sway he might still have over me.

"Mr. Daniels," Bray said from outside the partly opened car door. "I'm Agent Bray. We brought you here tonight to ask you a few questions."

Silence filled the air, and I knew my father was sizing Bray up. What kind of threat was he? What were his weaknesses, his tells, his vulnerabilities? How could he be played? Used?

Thought of my father doing anything to Bray filled my veins with courage. And anger. I slid across the back seat and reached for the door.

"Go ahead and ask," my father said, and I could hear the sinister sneer in his voice. The *I'm smarter than you* condescension had been the melody of my childhood. He already thought he'd won the game we'd only just started playing.

But we had a move he didn't know about.

"Not me," Bray said. He pulled open the door at the same time I pushed it from the inside.

I stepped out onto the pavement, both my feet firm, and stared at the man who'd ruined my life.

"Hi, Dad."

His jaw fell open. True shock filled his face hardened by years behind bars. The only other time I'd seen his mask slip was that night in the hotel room. A surge of pride swelled my chest at the thought *I* could have that effect on him. The master of grift.

He wore an orange jumpsuit and had chains linking his ankles and wrists and wrapping around his waist. His dark hair streaked with gray had grown wavy and long, but his beard was cropped short. His blue eyes still shone like constantly scheming torches. Even so, he was truly stunned to see me.

"Erin." The word floated on the air like a ghost. He continued gaping at me, taking in every inch of the woman I'd become. "My God, you're beautiful. What are you doing here?"

My jaw had grown tight with resistance at the same time my traitorous heart tugged toward him. I hadn't known how I'd react when I saw him in the flesh, but I expected it to be painful and complicated. So far, the experience was delivering.

"We're here to ask you some questions," Bray filled in for me when I didn't respond.

My father glanced at him then looked back to me. "*We?* Baby, don't tell me you work for *them* now."

The nickname slid down my spine like ice. Instantly, I was a child again. "You didn't leave me much of a choice," I hissed between my teeth.

He took a step forward but the chains around his ankles, along with the arm one of his guards held out, stopped him. "Baby, I know I made mistakes, and I'm sorry. It's just been so long. I can't believe you're here." He lifted his arms as far as they could go, like he was reaching out to hug me. We still stood some ten feet apart. Bray shifted his weight toward me, and the guards reached for my father once more.

The complex push and pull inside me tipped me over into a decision I hoped I wouldn't regret. "It's okay," I said.

My father's head snapped up; his eyes met mine. I saw a glint in them, a plea, and it tugged on my last resisting heart-string.

"It's okay," I said again. I nodded at Bray and at the guards. "It's been years. Would it be okay if I gave him a hug?"

"Erin—" Bray started to protest, but I shook my head.

"I want to. It's okay."

The guards looked to Bray, because clearly, he was the one in charge.

"Are you sure?" he asked me.

"I'm sure."

Bray released a stiff breath and nodded at the guards. "Just his wrists."

My father shrugged out of their grip. "You heard him, fellas. My baby wants to hug her old man."

One of the guards pulled at the keys connected to his belt by a retractable cord and set about unlocking the cuffs around my father's wrists. The smile on my father's face continued to stretch until it matched the crescent moon in the sky.

I braced myself once more and took a step forward. The primitive part of my brain battled over screaming at me to run away, or to run into my original protector's arms. Each step was a conflicted fight, but soon, I was standing right in front of him.

"Hi, Dad," I said again.

With a deep breath, he softened into the man I once knew. The one who'd give me piggybacks and buy me ice cream and tell me ghost stories in the backyard tent. Not the one who'd served me up as bait, nearly gotten me killed, and stolen my innocence. I let myself believe as I wrapped my arms around his shoulders he was that original man, and he really was happy to see me.

"My sweet girl. I've missed you so much." His voice turned warm and paternal as his arms circled my back. He pulled me close, the chains around his waist digging into my belly, but his upper body otherwise free.

Some sliver of my hardened heart had missed him too. And it felt good to be held in his arms. I lingered and let him give me another squeeze.

"My good girl," he whispered for only me to hear. Then his hand dropped to my waist, and in a practiced flash, grabbed the gun I had stashed in the back of my waistband. Before I could blink, he spun me around and had one arm around my throat and the other holding the gun to my temple.

"Drop it!" Bray shouted and reached for his holster. I saw a full spectrum of emotion play out on his face when he realized his holster was empty because the gun pointed at my head was his, and I'd taken it when we'd hugged in the car. Guilt tore through me, but it had to be done. He gaped at me before his face bent in pained anger. "God damn it, Erin."

Simmons had moved in from where he'd been on standby, gun now aimed at my father. Both of the guards had pulled weapons too. All four of them were aimed in my direction.

"Easy," my father said and pivoted us in a circle. "Everyone just take a breath, now." The barrel pressing into my temple brought me back to that night in the hotel room. The last time I'd been inches from death, except this time, it was at the hands of the man who'd given me life.

I struggled to breathe against his grip and my pounding heart. Bray continued glaring at me, now with his hands up in a plea not to shoot.

"Let her go," he commanded and took a step forward.

My father swung the gun out to aim at him and the others, and then pinned it back against my temple. "I'll let her go, but I'm going with her." He turned his head inward to kiss my cheek. His beard scratched against my face like sandpaper. "Thank you for this gift, baby. Sorry it had to go down this way, but you're my ticket out. Always have been."

"Let her *go!*" Bray commanded again.

My father chuckled a sound darker than the night. "This one seems to like you, baby. Is that true? You got a thing for my daughter, *Agent Bray?*" he taunted with a nod at him.

Bray took another step forward.

"Bray, stop!" I commanded, knowing my father had no qualms over pulling the trigger to get his way.

Bray gave me another anguished look like he wanted to rip the world in half to save me, but he was also really *really* pissed at me at the same time.

"It's okay," I told him.

"How is this okay?" His voice cracked with worry.

I squirmed against my father's grip, getting him to move right where I wanted him. "I just needed to know," I said.

Bray's brow furrowed.

My father turned his head toward me. "What did you need to know, baby?"

I filled my lungs with one last breath before I turned and looked right in his eyes. "What kind of man you really are." Before my words fully landed, I shoved my elbow into his belly. He doubled over with a grunt, and in a practiced move, I spun and wrenched the gun from his grip. I kicked him between the legs, sending him to his knees, and before he knew it, I had the gun pointed in his face.

"Stand down," Bray told the guards, and they lowered their weapons.

Everyone—except Bray, who looked equally relieved and pissed—blinked at me in shock. My father looked up at me with watering eyes, holding his crotch in utter disbelief.

I shook my hair out of my face and kept the gun trained on

him. "Yeah, I've learned a few new things since the last time you saw me, Dad."

Through his shock, he had the gall to let a proud grin twitch his lip.

"Now, like Agent Bray said: We have some questions for you."

His tongue flashed across his lips, and his eyes glinted. "You're in charge, baby."

"Stop calling me that," I commanded and got straight to the point. "Olena Nova is out of prison and knows where I am. She wants to kill me. I need to know where the diamond is from that night."

He blinked once, immediately catching up. "I don't know where it is."

"Bullshit," I hissed and jabbed the gun in his direction. "Someone has to know, and you're the only one left. Where is it?"

A chuckle bounced his shoulders. "Baby—"

I racked the gun's slide to show him I wasn't messing around.

He flinched. "Sorry. *Erin*, you think I'd have spent ten years in prison if I had that rock?"

"I don't know, you tell me. Maybe this is a long-con and part of your plan."

"My plan was to end up with my daughter holding me at gunpoint?"

"Seems pretty on-brand to me. Just hope I don't pull this trigger." My jaw was nearly locked shut while I spoke.

"Erin—" Bray said from behind me.

"I'm fine," I spat over my shoulder.

"You should listen to your boyfriend, sweetheart," my father said. "I don't know what kind of deal you've got going, but I'm not invisible. With a reputation like mine, my death would be hard to make disappear if your finger gets too twitchy there."

"You have no idea what I can make disappear," Bray said. The cold threat in his voice slid down my spine like ice, in the best way.

"Okay, easy, Romeo," my father said. "No need to get defensive, especially if you want anything to do with my daughter—"

"Don't you dare," I warned. "My *life* is *none* of your business." My finger moved closer to the trigger. Angry tears blurred my eyes.

My father flinched. Maybe it was the look on my face. Maybe it was the fact that his life was in my very angry hands. Maybe he'd simply finally run out of deceit. Whatever it was, I saw something in him break. Something previously unbendable finally surrendered to decency. "I don't know where that rock is, and you can trust me on that. But I heard through the grapevine Joseph Wallace died in Houston, so maybe start there."

Hearing him say Wallace's name threw me for a loop. They'd both been there on that critical night, and they were both giant figures in my life, but I'd never seen them in the same room. They were two spheres that never overlapped in my world. But of course my father knew who Wallace was. Maybe they'd even met before.

"You think that's relevant?" I asked, having yet to follow up on this same lead since Bray told me.

My father shrugged. "Houston is the last place they both were—the rock and Wallace. Doesn't seem like a coincidence."

I had to agree he was right. By the look on his face, we weren't going to get anything else out of him, and I wasn't in the mood for more of a reunion than we'd already had.

I lowered the gun and took a step back. "Bye, Dad. Enjoy prison."

"Feel free to visit any time you like!" he called after me.

I ignored him and handed Bray his gun. I climbed in the car

and shut the door, ready to go home. The closed door dulled sounds of them shuffling my father back into the van. Bray and Simmons exchanged a few words outside before they both returned to the car.

The ride back to the condo was silent aside from the smooth jazz satellite station Simmons had the radio tuned to. Bray fumed in the back seat beside me. I assumed he was saving his lecture for privacy. I knew he'd be upset with me, but I also knew my father would take the bait, and I needed to know. I finally had my answer: I was the child of a selfish, cruel man who couldn't be trusted and would always put himself first. That night in the hotel room when he'd shot the ghost and told me to run might have been the only honest moment of care I'd ever receive from him—and he might have only done it because I was still nearly a child then. Now that I was an adult, I was fully on my own.

My heart split a crack, and I hoped Bray wasn't going to go too hard on me, because that one really hurt. I'd assumed, sure. But to see it play out in action shot an incurable pain through my entire body.

When we arrived back at the condo, Simmons marched inside and headed for the guest room, leaving me and Bray alone in the kitchen. The dark night twinkled outside the windows. The soft yellow lights inside cast the room in a warm glow. But still, the air felt frigid and tense.

Bray busied himself at the liquor cabinet, this time skipping a bottle of wine and going straight for scotch. He didn't offer me a glass.

"So, are you gonna yell at me now?" I asked, and watched him pour two fingers' worth of caramel liquid into a crystal tumbler.

He held up a hand. "Don't. Just . . . don't." He set the bottle beside his glass and recorked it.

"I'm sorry, but I knew he'd go for the gun, and I knew I could disarm him. It was no big deal."

He had the glass halfway to his mouth when he stopped and huffed a breath. He shook his head. "No big deal? *No big deal?* Erin, he had a gun to your head! *My* gun! So I couldn't even do anything to help!" His angry voice ballooned into the room.

"Bray, I had it under control. You didn't have to worry."

He scoffed. "If someone has a gun to your head, I'm going to worry, Erin. I don't care what kind of Jason Bourne shit you're capable of." He finally took a swig of his drink.

"Jason Bourne is amateur hour," I said with an arched brow.

"This is not the time for jokes."

"It's not a joke."

He grumbled and tugged a handful of hair. "*Erin*, how am I supposed to trust you? You took my *gun.*"

I winced, at the anguish in his voice. "In fairness, I also took your gun within ten seconds of meeting you for the first time."

"This is not funny!"

"I'm not laughing! I'm just stating a fact. And yes, it was a little unfair of me not to tell you my plan, but you wouldn't have let me do it if I had told you."

"You're damn right I wouldn't have."

I took a breath to calm us both and circled over to his side of the island. "Look, Bray. We can't all have perfect families like yours, with parents who buy them cello lessons and let them crash in their condos." I waved my arms around, and he flinched. "This was likely the only time I was going to see my father, and I wanted to know if he'd changed. If maybe there was something there to start building off of. To start over. Clearly, there isn't. I'm sorry if I upset you, but can you at least try to understand why I did it?"

His jaw worked as he studied my face. The anger in his gray eyes began to cool but didn't fully dissolve. "On some level, yes, I can understand. But you didn't have to be so goddamned reckless about it."

We stood inches apart. Close enough I could smell the fiery liquor on his breath in a way that made me want to take a sip—of him, not it. The tiny flare in his nostrils and the color warming his cheeks said he was still angry, but maybe a little bit something else too. My hand had landed a few inches from his on the island top. The icy granite against my palm was the only thing keeping me grounded.

I looked up into his stone eyes and reminded him of a truth. "I told you that you wouldn't like the choices I'd make on my own."

He stared at me for a heart-pounding second and then blinked, as if something had snapped. In a move even I couldn't anticipate or thwart, he grabbed my hands and walked me the few steps backward until my back hit the wall. There, he sunk his fingers between mine and pinned my hands above my head. Before I could even gasp, his lips were on mine. The kiss was bruising and pent-up and *holy hell*, so good. His whole body pressed me into the wall, his hips deliciously pinning mine and his arms bracketing my head. He was a very welcome and warm cage I wanted to be locked inside forever.

A soft moan escaped my throat, and it only made him kiss me harder. His tongue pushed into my mouth, and I met it with mine. They slid and tangled together, dancing while our lips continued to suck and my heart beat harder than when I'd had a gun to my head. I fought against his grip, wanting to free my hands to touch him in other places, but he only gripped tighter and held me harder.

God, this man could kiss. I'd wondered what his lips felt like the first moment I saw him, and the answer was wickedly divine. Liquid flame raced through my veins, pumping straight to the core of my belly as I wondered what else his mouth could do. My hips bucked against his, wanting more, though they didn't get far with his powerful body crushing me to the wall. I silently begged him to let go, to put his hands on all the places my pulse was pounding in need: my throat, my chest, between my thighs. But he held me firm. I'd knocked him on his ass yesterday, but I had no leverage now. I was at his mercy, and through the haze of his hot mouth devouring mine, I wondered if this was some kind of punishment. A show of dominance and who was really in charge. And God damn it, it did everything for me.

I moaned again and stopped fighting. I let my hands go limp in his and my body sag. Only then did he pull back.

The look on his flushed face said not that he'd been trying to put me in my place, but that he'd lost a battle he'd been waging for a long time. Something had overtaken his willpower, and he'd finally surrendered.

My heart hammered. I could see it pushing my chest out with each thrashing beat. He still held my arms up over my head. We both panted.

"That wasn't very heroic," I managed through inhales. I gave him a grin as wicked as his lips had felt.

He let go of me and regrettably stepped back. My body instantly ached for the heat of his to return. He hung his head in shame and stroked his jaw.

I stood there flushed and feral and ready to do whatever he wanted next. My body was one giant livewire begging to be touched. I didn't care about crossing lines. Not after that.

He eventually lifted his head and gave me a stern look. "Go to bed," he commanded and stepped away.

The cold command stung in contrast to the heat pumping between us moments before.

"Are you coming with me?" I said to his back, hopeful and only half joking, as he walked toward the garage.

He glanced over his shoulder for a split second, as if looking any longer would tempt him to turn around and stay.

"Good night, Erin." He opened the garage door and disappeared through it.

I stood alone in the silent kitchen, hearing only my heartbeat and wondering what the hell had just happened. Temptation to follow him stirred in my blood, but I knew he would only reject me again. His hero mask had slipped for those few perfect moments of sin, but now it was back in place.

I let out a big sigh and helped myself to the rest of the drink he'd left sitting on the island. "Good night, Cal."

CHAPTER 23

I hardly slept that night. And not because of nerves or worry or fear, but because every time I closed my eyes, I saw Bray. I felt him pinning me to the wall, his mouth against mine. My blood looped through my veins in ways that had my hands finding all the places on my body I wanted him to touch.

I checked my phone an embarrassing number of times while dozing off between fantasies and waking with my heart racing, hoping for a text.

I didn't hear from him until he walked in the door carrying to-go coffees and a takeout bag the next morning. He was freshly showered and shaved, smelling like mint and soap. At the sight of him, I half wanted to punch his handsome face and half attack it with kisses for sentencing me to a lonely night dreaming of his mouth.

"Good morning," I said as he set the breakfast offering on the island. Simmons was in the living room watching the morning news, and I was sipping coffee and scrolling a takeout menu on my phone. I still wore my pajamas and had my hair piled on my head in a sloppy bun, but when Bray's eyes raked over me, a flush filled his cheeks.

Good. Even if he was acting aloof and like last night didn't happen, his body couldn't deny that it had.

He opened the takeout bag and slid a wrapped breakfast sandwich at me. "Wheels up in an hour, so hurry up and eat."

I took his offering and peeled the foil back. Scent of egg, bacon, and cheese wafted out and made my mouth water. "Wheels? Where are we going?"

"Houston."

I stopped with the sandwich halfway to my mouth.

Bray unwrapped his own sandwich. "Ramesh was able to track Wallace's last moves before he died. He visited a bank in downtown Houston that same day. Security log shows he accessed a safe-deposit box." He let the words linger with an obvious weight.

My head briefly spun as I kept up. Wallace was murdered in Houston; the diamond was last known to be in Houston; Wallace had visited a bank the day he died. "So, the diamond is in the box? It's right where this whole thing started?"

Bray nodded. "He either put something in the box or took something out of it."

"He couldn't have taken it out. They would have found it when they killed him, and none of this would be happening."

"I agree. So, we need to get to Houston and see what's in that box."

I shoved another bite into my mouth, still sorting it out. "So, to summarize, Wallace finds out Olena is on to us, has me relocated, makes a pitstop in Houston, and never makes it back out. That means they were able to follow him to Houston. They must know he's protecting me, or at least that he knew where I was."

Ice slid through my veins. We didn't know what was in that safe-deposit box, and neither did they. They might not even have known Wallace went to the bank. They were tracking him—they *killed* him—to get to *me.*

"And I led them straight to me." I numbly finished my thought aloud.

"What?" Bray asked and unwedged one of the coffee cups from its tray.

The pieces were crashing together in my mind. "*That's* how they found me, Bray. That day in Del Rio when I thought Wallace was calling me, it was Olena's guy on the other end, and I blabbed my own location to him. He had Wallace's phone because he killed him."

Bray considered with narrowed eyes and then pulled out his own phone and tapped at it. "I'll have Ramesh run Wallace's phone records from after his death. He didn't look further than that, but I bet you are right."

I palmed my face. "It's my own fault they found me."

"You couldn't have known," he justified.

"It was still a stupid mistake," I muttered and let it all sink in. Wallace *was* trying to protect me. He died trying to protect me.

I thought back to that night on the phone with him. The scrape in his voice, the cracking sound. The way he'd called me by my real name. It was a goodbye.

Bray's hand landed on my shoulder. "Erin, I'm sorry about last night. I crossed a line, and it won't happen again."

I startled at the abrupt change in topic, half shocked he was addressing it at all. A coy smile bent my mouth. "Which part, when you yelled at me or when you pinned me to the wall and kissed me to within an inch of my life?"

His lips pressed together. His cheeks turned pink. "You know which part."

I shrugged. "I like it when you cross lines."

"Well it's not going to happen again. I'm sorry."

I held his eyes with a look that said I wasn't sorry. That I'd let him do it again right now.

"We should go," he said, breaking the spell and severing the chance at anything happening.

"I have to get changed." I shoved a big bite of my sandwich in my mouth and slowly turned away from him. I felt his eyes on my back as I walked toward the hall, and wondered if he'd keep his promise.

I hadn't been on a chartered plane in years. Not since Wallace put me on a job tracking art theft in an elite ring of one-percenters. I'd otherwise flown commercial, usually coach, but then, I hadn't been palling around with a DSA director's son.

Simmons stayed behind, leaving the small, sleek bullet of a jet empty except for me and Bray, the pilot, and one flight attendant.

"How long is this trip?" I asked once we were in the air. We'd taken off from Oakland.

"Just under four hours. We should be on the ground by five p.m. local time," Bray answered. He had his laptop balanced on his knees and was clacking away at it.

"Are you talking to your guy in the chair?" I asked, leaning across the narrow aisle to see his screen where he sat opposite me. The plane had room for six passengers, with beige leather seats and wood paneling.

"My what?" he asked, and didn't take his eyes off the screen.

"Ramesh. Your guy in the chair. You know, the agent who stays in the office and tells the agents in the field what to do."

A smile turned up the corners of his mouth. "Yes, I am talking to my guy in the chair. He says Wallace's phone's geotag jumped from Houston to Del Rio after he died, so you're right. They used it to find you."

My heart sunk at the thought I'd made such a foolish mistake. "I wonder what else they found on there," I muttered.

"Hopefully not much. It's been remote deactivated by now."

"Which means they know we know."

"Not necessarily," he said. "It's DSA protocol to deactivate devices when an agent passes. They only had a slight head start because Wallace's death wasn't immediately reported."

I shrunk back into my seat, feeling deflated.

"I'm sorry," Bray said when he noticed. "I know he was . . . important to you."

"Another interesting choice of words," I said and gave him a sad smile.

I thought about what we'd learned in the past several hours. If we were right, if Wallace's dying act was having me moved to protect me, that rewrote everything I thought I knew about our relationship. My real father had held a gun to my head last night, and this man, this stranger who'd draped his coat over my shivering, scared shoulders on the worst night of my life, had sacrificed himself for me. Yes, he'd spent a decade bossing me around and using me for his own gain, but ultimately, he'd saved me.

And I'd undone his work by leading Olena right to me. I couldn't let his death be in vain.

I turned to Bray with resolve. "We have to end this."

We headed straight to the bank when we touched down in Houston. A sporty black sedan was waiting for us at the airport. Bray got behind the wheel and handed me an earpiece to match the one he was wearing.

"Ramesh?" I asked as I buried it in my ear like an invisible bug.

"And me," Bray said. "I'm not a hundred percent sure what we are walking into, so I want open comms."

"You got it, buddy," Ramesh's voice said, crystal clear in my ear.

"Hey, my very own guy in the chair, what a privilege," I said.

"Happy to be of service today, Ms. Daniels," Ramesh said.

"Don't call her that," Bray instructed as he turned the car onto a highway.

"Roger," Ramesh said. "What should I call her?"

"Not Roger," I said. I expected Bray to chime in with some made-up name, but instead, he turned to me.

"You pick. What do you want to be called for this job?"

The question had never been posed to me. Not once in my decade of service. I'd always been handed a folder with an identity already designated. I thought about it for a second and knew right away.

"Katherine. It was my mom's name."

Bray nodded. "Katherine it is, then."

Ramesh helped us navigate downtown, and soon we were parking a few blocks from the bank Wallace had visited. The late spring air was already ripening with signs of summer, but still pleasant enough we weren't sweating in our coats as we walked up the street. The city's skyscrapers towered over us, casting portions of the busy street in long shadows. I hadn't set foot here since that night in the hotel room, yet it somehow felt the same. Like a familiar acquaintance I didn't particularly want to see welcoming me home.

"Take a left," Ramesh said into our ears. He was tracking us through our cell phone pings sending signals to him, and I assumed staring at a map.

"You sure we weren't followed?" I asked with more than a hint of nerves at being on an open street after days sequestered away in the condo.

"From the Bay?" Ramesh asked. "Yes, I'm sure. Your trail has been wiped. Entrance to the bank is half a block up."

I took a breath to try and calm myself. Bray had let me bring my gun this time. I felt its cold presence against my back, near where he'd touched me. My heart rate picked up as we closed in on the bank.

Its glass front walls spanned the bottom floor of a tall, silver building. A security guard patrolled out front, and inside, I could see smiling employees conversing with customers at glossy desks. A row of tellers lined the back wall.

"Fancy place," I muttered.

"I mean, if you're stashing a giant diamond inside, I'd think it would have to be," Bray muttered back. "You're going to get us into this box, right, Ramesh?" he said.

"Roger. Your name has been added to the authorized list for access," Ramesh said into our ears.

"Do I even want to know how you managed that?" I asked.

"I couldn't tell you anyway," Ramesh said. I could hear the grin in his voice.

"Okay, showtime," Bray said when we approached the bank's door. He swung it open and again put his hand on my lower back. It shot a tingle through me, maybe because I missed his touch, maybe because it soothed my nerves. We were moments away from what we'd come for. The keystone of the past ten years was locked inside a small metal box somewhere inside this bank.

We walked inside and the smell of money and high-gloss floors mingled in my nose. No matter how modern and new a bank was, it could never shake the telltale salty, stale aroma of the world's ultimate motivator.

Bray led us to an open teller. My heart was in my throat. "Hello," he said pleasantly. "We need to access my family's safe-deposit box." He pulled a slip of paper out of his coat pocket and slid it across the teller's desk.

The teller, a Black woman who looked to be in her thirties, took the slip and read the number on it. She entered something into her computer and turned back to us with a welcoming smile. "I'd be happy to assist you today. May I see some ID?"

"Of course," Bray said and reached for his wallet. I silently prayed she wasn't going to ask me for ID too, because all I had was Lauren Thomas's, and I doubted she was on any list. "This is my wife," Bray said and nodded at me. "She's been helping me take care of a few things in the wake of my uncle's death."

I was shocked at how smoothly the lie rolled off his tongue.

The teller seemed to buy it. For good measure, I gave her a sad smile with just my lips and then wove my arm through Bray's and leaned against his shoulder.

"I'm sorry for your loss, Mr. Bray," the teller said once she looked at his ID. Her name tag said JASMINE. "I can escort you back to the safe-deposit room when you are ready."

"We are ready right now," Bray said, and I squeezed his arm to stop him from sounding too eager.

"Sure," Jasmine politely said. "I'll meet you at the end of the aisle here." She pointed to her left.

"He's *your* uncle now?" I whispered to Bray once she was out of earshot.

"It was the safest bet with a different last name," he muttered back. "And the lie worked for you, didn't it?"

"Sure, to fool some neighborhood moms about why I was crying, not to break into a vault."

"Well, it worked, so I'll take it."

"This way, please," Jasmine said when we met her at the end of the bank of tellers. She opened a swinging gate to let us onto her side, and then led us to a door that required a keycard to access.

We passed into a sterile hallway with another keyed door at the end, and then into a room lined with hundreds of locked boxes. Each had a combination lock built into its face, made up of five numbered wheels.

Jasmine stood to the side and gestured for us to enter. She watched us with discerning eyes, as if seeing if we'd pass the final test of opening the box.

I silently prayed Bray knew the combination and wasn't about to blow this. Sure, I could have broken into it with the right tools, but that was off the table if we were playing the roles of grieving nephew and spouse.

My heart thumped hard as I followed him to box 237.

"Two-thirty-seven, here we go," he said out loud. "Just need to remember the right five digits," he muttered, and I realized he was talking to Ramesh.

"Five, one, eight, one, six," Ramesh read off.

I sucked in a breath, recognizing the pattern of numbers.

Bray shot a glance at me, and I discreetly shook my head, silently saying I'd tell him later.

When he entered the numbers, the box made a clicking sound and popped out half an inch. Another quiet gasp leapt from my lips.

Bray smiled before he turned around to Jasmine. "Can we have a minute please? There are rather personal effects in here."

"Of course," she said with a polite nod and stepped out. The door shut with a thick thud behind her.

Bray exhaled a breath and slowly pulled the narrow box from its slot like he was defusing a bomb. The top was covered, I assumed to keep any dust from accumulating on its contents. My hands grew tacky at the thought of seeing it again. The most beautiful jewel I'd ever seen. I could already feel its weight in my hand. Bray moved the box to the table in the center of the room and set it down with a slight shake in his hands. I gripped his arms in nerves, excitement, relief.

The solution to my problems was right in front of us.

"You guys have gotten way too quiet," Ramesh said. "What's going on? Do you have it yet?"

Bray grinned at me. "Would you like to do the honors?"

I grinned back, thrilled and nervous in equal measure. With a shake in my own hand, I reached for the lid and lifted it. I held my breath as the velvet interior became visible, and lying on top of it was . . .

Nothing.

"What?" Bray asked and shoved his hand into the empty box. "How is this possible?"

"What happened?" Ramesh asked.

I was too shocked to respond. How had we been wrong?

"It's empty," Bray told Ramesh. "There's nothing in the box."

"What?" Ramesh said. "Are you sure you opened the right box?"

"Box 237," Bray said. "And it would be pretty wild if we somehow got it wrong and that combo happened to work on another box in here." He spun around to look anyway, like the answer to this new mystery would jump out at him.

I was still too numb to say anything. My hope of ending this game of cat and mouse collapsed like a building in front of me. "God damn it, Wallace," were the first words to leave my mouth.

Bray swiped a hand through his hair. "So what does this mean? What do we do now?"

I shrugged in defeat, suddenly very tired and feeling the fact I'd hardly slept in the past few nights. "I don't know," I muttered. "Back to square one."

"Which is what?" Bray asked.

I looked around in dismay. "Getting out of this creepy room of secrets would be a good start."

Bray replaced the box with a sigh and met me at the door. "Look sad," he reminded me.

"That's not hard," I muttered.

Jasmine greeted us with a kind smile on the other side and led us back to the front of the bank.

Soon, we were back outside standing on the street corner, at a total loss. A light wind blew and ruffled Bray's hair. The busy sidewalks teemed with people going about their daily business, none the wiser that our plan had just imploded in our faces.

Bray scuffed his foot against the concrete. "What's the significance of the combination?" he asked me.

"What?"

"Inside, when Ramesh read off the combo, you gasped like it meant something."

"Oh. It was the date of the night my father got arrested. The night I met Wallace. May 18, 2016."

He snorted. "That's either clever or cruel, I can't decide."

"You just described Agent Wallace in one sentence."

He looked up at the evening sky, and I traced the long line of his jaw and throat with my eyes. "What do you think it means?" he asked. "Did he put the diamond in there the night you met? Or was it never in there at all, and none of this is connected?"

"I unfortunately have no idea."

He looked back down at me with a sad half smile right as a man walked up behind him. Bray lurched toward me as if something had been shoved into his back.

"Hand it over, and I won't kill the girl," the man said.

I instantly recognized the accent. One of Olena's ghosts.

My blood froze over. I took a step back and bumped up against a wall. Except it wasn't a wall, it was another man.

Two ghosts.

Maybe we hadn't been followed, but they knew we were coming.

The ghost behind me wrapped his arm around the front of my shoulders like he was hugging me from behind. "Don't even think about reaching for your gun, princess," he said in the same accent the other ghost had.

I looked at Bray, suddenly racked with terror and trying to keep calm. His wide, gray eyes stared back at me as he swallowed hard. He slowly lifted his hands.

"We don't have it," he said.

We weren't making a scene yet. To anyone passing by, I was being hugged and he was being patted on the shoulder, not held at gunpoint.

"Bullshit," the first ghost said in his thick accent. "You don't fly halfway across country to secret bank for no reason. We have been waiting for you. Hand it over."

My ghost gave me a shake and gripped me tighter. I sucked in a hard breath and felt the power of his body behind mine. I couldn't see him, but he was at least as big as the other ghost.

"There's nothing to hand over," Bray said calmly. "Why don't we go somewhere and talk before anyone gets hurt?"

"Oh shit. What's happening?" Ramesh said in our ears. "Erin—I mean Katherine, cough if you guys are in trouble."

I coughed.

"Shit, shit, shit. Okay, I'm working on a satellite feed based on your position so I can see. Hang tight," Ramesh said.

"No time for that," I muttered.

"What's that, princess?" my ghost said and leaned over to see my face. He smelled like thick cologne and cigarettes. I coughed again, both because the scent was choking me and in signal to Ramesh.

"I'm hurrying, I'm hurrying," Ramesh said. "Corner of Walker Street and . . ."

My body hummed with the urge to flee. I knew I could get away; I'd done it many times before out of this exact hold. But I didn't want to leave Bray to fend for himself—or worse, risk him getting shot.

I met his eyes again, conveying as much as I could with mine.

I can take him, I said silently.

It's too risky, he said back with a subtle shake of his head.

I'll go get help.

Erin, no.

The plea in his eyes almost broke my heart. I couldn't let another person sacrifice themselves for me, but Bray was looking at me like it might kill him if they killed me first.

"Ten more seconds or so . . ." Ramesh said, but I could hardly hear him over my own heartbeat and the silent argument I was having with Bray.

I'm going to go for it, I told him with my eyes.

Don't, he scolded back with a glare.

There's no other choice.

Erin!

Just as I made the decision to throw my elbow into the ghost's solar plexus, a screech of tires and loud crash turned everyone's heads toward the street.

A car had flown through the intersection and T-boned another. A second car followed, screeching to a halt, but not in time. Glass exploded everywhere. Metal crunched.

"I got you," Ramesh's voice buzzed in my ear over the honking and shouting. The injuries looked minor, but it was enough to block the intersection and cause everyone on the sidewalks to move toward the scene.

My ghost loosened his grip, caught in the same surprise as everyone else. Bray was halfway bent over, having flinched from the noise of the accident behind him. He met my eyes, realizing he'd been freed from his ghost's grip too. This time, there was no argument between us.

"Run!" he shouted.

Chapter 24

I shoved my elbow back into the ghost's nose and heard it crack. Then I stomped on his toe and ran like hell.

The chaos of the accident was still drawing everyone's attention. Aside from the people I shoved out of the way, no one noticed the woman fleeing through the crowd with blood on her coat's sleeve.

"Was that you, Ramesh?" I asked as I sucked air, preparing my body for escape.

"Yes. I hacked the traffic system and kept that light green to cause an accident. I'll beg for forgiveness later."

"Nice one, guy in the chair," I commended and flew back past the bank. "Now, how the hell do we get out of here?"

"You, turn right at the next intersection. Bray, go left on your street," Ramesh commanded.

"Wait, you're not behind me, Bray?" I asked. I held my finger to my earpiece as I looked over my shoulder and kept running. No sign of Bray, but the ghost was plowing up the sidewalk like a rolling boulder, shoving people out of the way.

"No," Bray huffed. "Better if we split them up."

"Where are you?" I swiveled my head again but only saw a blur of stone buildings, street, sidewalk, and faces. I was already a block from the accident, where people weren't as concerned yet.

"Don't worry about me," Bray said. "Ramesh, where are we meeting?"

"You're both going opposite directions from where you parked, but I don't think we want to turn this into a car chase through the streets of downtown Houston anyway. Let me get you into a building."

I had never stopped running. I was dodging people left and right. Bobbing and weaving in and out of pedestrians and intermittently glancing over my shoulder to see the ghost still chasing me.

"Any of these buildings an option?" I said through a tight breath. "It would be nice to lose this guy."

"Working on it . . ." Ramesh trailed off.

"Oh, shit," Bray hissed.

"What happened?" I asked over my thundering heart.

"Nothing. Don't worry about me."

"I'm always worried about you, Agent Bray," I said.

"Katherine—alley up ahead," Ramesh cut in.

"Is there a fence at the other end of it?" I asked.

"No," Ramesh said.

"Pity, you should see her jump one," Bray said with an audible smile.

"Turn right at the next opportunity," Ramesh instructed.

My feet pounded the pavement. Air moved in and out of my lungs. I saw the gap up ahead: an alley between a law firm and a restaurant. "There better not be anyone waiting down this alley for me, Ramesh," I said, and closed in on it.

"Satellite says it's clear. Turn now," he responded.

"You can see me? You're not just Google Maps-ing this?"

"Live, in living color."

"Damn. I'm going to demand my own guy in a chair from here on out." I flew around the corner and felt the temperature drop in the shade between the buildings. A glance over my shoulder said the ghost had fallen behind. "Oh God, I think this is a seafood restaurant." I nearly gagged with a hand over my mouth as I ran past a dumpster.

"All-you-can-eat shrimp on Tuesdays," Ramesh reported. "Now, on the other side, take a left. Two blocks up, you'll run into the Lancaster Hotel. I'm booking a room for you under Calvin Bray and . . ."

"Lauren Thomas," I filled in for him. "It's the only ID I've got."

"Got it," he said. "Bray? You still with us."

The pause that carried over the line made my heart skip a beat.

"Yeah, I'm here. Lancaster Hotel, got it," Bray said.

"Good. I figure you guys disappear and lay low for tonight, and we'll work on a way out tomorrow," Ramesh said.

"Sounds good to me," I grunted as I broke free of the dim light on the other side of the alley.

"Left," Ramesh reminded me. "Bray, you keep going straight. That garage would be a shortcut, but I don't like the look of it. I'll lose sight of you."

"It'll get me off the street faster," Bray protested.

"I see the hotel," I reported. "It's a block away." I hurried across the street while the WALK sign was on and slowed on the other side. "Any sign of him?" I asked.

"I think you lost him," Ramesh reported.

"Good." It would look less suspicious if I didn't hurtle myself into a hotel, out of breath, and say I was checking in like nothing was amiss.

I forced air in and out of my lungs in a practiced way to help slow my heart rate. I reached the hotel door when I heard a sharp crack in my ear. It stopped me in my tracks.

"What was that?" I asked.

Bray grunted and then there was a muffled sound like his earpiece had fallen out.

"Bray? What's going on?" I demanded.

"Bray, you there?" Ramesh asked with the same concern. "Damn it, I told you not to go into that garage. I can't see you."

My calmed heart picked back up. "Where is he? What happened?"

"I don't know. I can't see," Ramesh said. "Bray? Say something."

"I'm going back for him," I said, and turned around.

"No. Go in the hotel right now," Ramesh commanded. "Your guy is back. He's a block away. Get inside before he sees you."

"Shit," I hissed and yanked the door back open. Cool, floral-scented air greeted me on the other side. The fresh cleanse made me realize I'd broken a sweat in my escape. I walked to the registration counter as casually as I could, all the while wanting to scream into my earpiece. But I needed to get inside behind a locked door as soon as I could.

"Hi, checking in for Thomas?" I said to the smiling clerk.

"Sure thing, Ms. Thomas," she said and tapped her keyboard. "I see we have you with us for one night, and you've already paid in full. Will you need help with your—?" She cut off when she noticed I had no luggage.

"I travel light," I said with a tight smile, telling her not to ask anything more.

"Of course," she said with her pearly teeth still showing. "You'll be in room 1447. Wi-Fi is in the room info packet, and breakfast is served from six thirty to ten. Please call down if you need anything." She slid two keycards across the desk. "All I need is a signature."

"Thank you." I swiped the cards to stash in my pocket and scribbled something remotely resembling Lauren Thomas on the electronic pad.

"Enjoy your stay," the clerk said.

I tightly smiled and quickly turned away. "Fourteenth floor is a long way to run for an escape, Ramesh," I muttered.

"You'll take what I can give you on short notice."

"At least you didn't pick the hotel that started this all. Where's Bray?"

"You're listening to the same channel I am. He's gone dark."

I cursed again and hit the elevator call button. The elegant lobby blurred around me. All I could think of was getting into my room and throwing the dead bolt. Maybe sitting on the bed with my gun pointed at the door. "Bray, answer us, damn it."

"I have eyes on the garage he must have cut through, but he hasn't come out the side he should have," Ramesh said.

The elevator arrived, and I climbed in. My jaw was so tight, I was grinding my teeth to dust. I couldn't bear the thought of him bleeding out in a parking garage because of me. "How far is that from where I am?" I asked.

"Four blocks. At a run, he should be there in five minutes, tops."

"Well, if he's not here in ten, I'm going to look for him."

"I have to advise against that."

"Yeah, well, I'm not the best rule follower."

"He mentioned that about you."

The elevator arrived on my floor, and I stepped out into the hall. "God damn it, Bray. Had to be a hero."

"I'm sure he's fine," Ramesh said.

"He didn't sound fine. That sounded like a gunshot."

"He's taken a few of those before."

"Is that supposed to be comforting?" I gaped at what he'd said while I swiped my keycard at my door.

"Sorry. I'm just saying, he'll pull through."

"He better."

I entered my room to the same smell that had filled the lobby: fresh florals. Curtains at the far end framed a view of the surrounding buildings in the fading light. I immediately walked to the minibar and uncapped the bottle of water sitting there.

"How long has it been?" I asked when I finished gulping.

"Two minutes," Ramesh reported.

"Any sign of him?"

"Not yet."

I paced to the bathroom and splashed my face with cold water at the sink. I pawed at my hair, which had gotten tangled and mussed in my escape. A flush still colored my cheeks. My reflection looked both bursting with life and a hundred years old, and that was exactly how I felt.

I walked back to the bedroom and untucked the gun from my waistband. I set it on the TV stand and then sunk onto the bed. The downy fluff cradled me like a hug. I would have flopped back and relaxed if my entire body wasn't screaming with angst over what was happening to Bray.

"How long now?" I asked Ramesh.

"Six minutes."

"This isn't good."

"It's not bad yet, either. Give him time," Ramesh said.

"He's had plenty of time. Can you see his phone signal?"

"That's dark too."

I swallowed the curse stinging my tongue and lay back on the bed. How did this happen? How did the people chasing *me* end up catching *him*? Behind my closed eyes, all I could see was the ghost pointing a gun at Bray and pulling the trigger.

"No," I said and sat up sharply.

"No?" Ramesh asked. "No what?"

I pushed up from the bed and marched to the window. The city crawled below, a grid of lights and dark spaces. He was down there somewhere, and I was going to find him.

"No, I'm not waiting anymore," I said. "I'm going to find him."

"Erin, you can't. You have to stay where you are. He told me to make sure you're safe above all else." He dispensed with my code name, making this sound much more serious.

"I'm sure he did, but he doesn't get to die for me. No one else does."

"Erin, please—"

"I'm sorry, Ramesh. I'll go dark if you don't want to help, but it will be better if you do." I shoved my gun back in my pants and headed for the door.

"Erin!" Ramesh protested right as I wrenched it open to someone standing on the other side.

Bray, bruised and bloodied, leaned on the doorframe. My heart shot to the moon at the sight of him. He held up a finger like he was going to lecture me. "Don't go trying to be a hero. I've already got that locked down." Then he tumbled through the doorway and nearly collapsed in my arms.

Chapter 25

"He's here," I reported to Ramesh. "He's okay, I think. Are you okay, Bray?" My voice came out shaky with relief and worry at once.

"I'm okay," he said, and stumbled to sit on the bed. "Just a little roughed up."

"Is he in one piece?" Ramesh demanded.

"Yes. I'll take care of him. We'll check in tomorrow," I said and pinched the bug out of my ear. "Bray, what happened?"

He winced when he sat, and I noted his shirt was streaked with dirt. His lip was cut, and his nose rimmed with dried blood. "He caught up to me, but I got away. You should see him," he said and gestured to his bruised face with a small chuckle.

"Here, let me help you." I hurried to the bathroom and ran a washcloth under warm water. His eyes were still wild with adrenaline when I returned and leaned in close to dab at his bloodied nose. He winced.

"It's been a while since I took a few to the face, but it's no big deal," he said.

"It doesn't look like no big deal. Why didn't you listen to Ramesh?"

"I was trying to get to you." He said it like an undeniable and completely logical fact. "I can't stand to see you in danger."

"I can take care of myself, Bray."

"Clearly, but still. *Ouch.*" He winced again when I softly dabbed the cloth at his cut lip.

"Sorry. How did you know what room I was in?"

"They told me at the desk. When I went to check in, they told me my wife was already here. I think they were happy to get rid of me quickly, given the face situation."

I huffed a little laugh and felt my own face warm. "So, Ramesh booked us one room?"

"Seems that way."

"Did you tell him to do that?"

"No, but I can't say I'm sorry he did." He reached up and gently wrapped his hand around my wrist where I was still dabbing his face. His thumb circled over my pulse and sent it leaping into overdrive.

I clocked the hungry look in his eyes and gave him a half smile. "I thought you weren't going to cross any more lines."

He watched my lips through hooded lids while I spoke, and then looked up to meet my gaze. "I lied." He said it with complete surrender. It was an admission that he couldn't fight whatever he was feeling anymore.

I had stopped fighting ages ago.

I let him pull me onto his lap so I was straddling him. I kissed him softly at first, testing out his pain tolerance and tasting a hint of blood on his lip. He squeezed me against himself, deepening the kiss, and telling me all I needed to know. I could feel his heart pounding. Mine echoed its call as adrenaline sped through both of us. We'd just escaped death, and I was feeling profoundly alive.

His wide palms swept over my back, and he pushed my coat from my shoulders. It fell to the floor behind me as I kicked off my shoes. They landed with a *thunk thunk.* With his hands and mouth on me, I was suddenly on fire. I went to peel my shirt off over my head, but Bray stopped me.

"Wait," he gasped and reached around to my lower back. "Let's get rid of this first." He pulled my gun from my waistband and gently tossed it to the floor.

I grinned against his next kiss. "Good idea." I took advantage of sliding my hands down his chest to his abdomen and making a show of unbuckling the belt holding his holster. "Don't want any accidents." I removed the leather with the gun inside it and noticed it was hot. I paused with it in my hands. "Did you shoot him?"

"*At* him," Bray said before he kissed me again. "Unfortunately, I missed." He slipped his hand under my shirt and started pushing it up.

"Unfortunate," I said, lost in the haze of his touch and ignoring the fact that I was holding a recently fired weapon. I dropped the gun and holster to the floor and leaned into him, letting him drag my shirt up over my arms and head. My hair spilled around my shoulders, and he tangled his hands in it, hungrily pulling my mouth back to his. He held me like something precious. Like something that could shatter if he used too much force. At the same time, the power in his grip, his hands, the cage of his arms, felt like an impenetrable forcefield. Nothing could touch me when he was touching me. I was completely safe.

I rocked my hips forward, feeling the bulge in his pants, and moaned at the same time he did. The sounds mingled in perfect harmony, one layered on top of the other, and set my blood aflame.

"I'm probably going to get fired for this, but I can't stop," he growled in the hot air between us.

"I won't tell anyone," I panted as he found the clasp for my bra and undid it. I kissed a trail from his jaw to his shoulder and back.

"You *are* a professional secret keeper."

"I'm a vault," I said and pretended to twist a key in front of my lips while he slid my bra straps down my arms. Once I was freed of it, he hungrily looked at my bare chest. Then in a swift move worthy of a cage fight, he gripped my thigh and shoulder and flipped us over so he was on top. "You'll have to teach me that one," I said as I caught my breath.

He grinned down at me like the devil and then worked his mouth from mine all the way to the top of my jeans. I quivered beneath his hot touch, his tongue tracing the skin below my belly button. When he paused to take his shirt off by grabbing the collar at the back of his neck, I couldn't help but stare. It was a move that specifically showed off his arms. And then his abs. And then he was half naked, standing over me like some sort of Italian Renaissance marble statue.

"Um, how do you look like that if you just spent six months at a desk?" I said, my mouth hanging open.

He softly chuckled. "Getting back in the field was my biggest motivator, and I had to be in shape."

"*Shape* is one word for it," I muttered as he crawled back over me. The dim lamplight glinted off the scars on his shoulder. I met his chest with my palms and greedily spread them over the firm muscle and dusting of dark hair. His heart thundered inside. He pressed his mouth to mine and brought back the memory of when he held me against the wall. The longing, the need, the gentle dominance. *Fuck.* I wanted to drown in it. His tongue possessively dipped into my mouth, and I wondered where he learned to kiss so well. Or maybe I'd just never been kissed by anyone like him. He moved his hands to my throat and my chest, brushing his thumbs over my hardened nipples, touching me in all the ways I'd wanted him to that night. Except for one.

I ground my hips into his and coaxed a groan out of him.

The hard bulge pressing into the hot space between my legs told me he wanted more as much as I did.

"You wouldn't happen to have a condom, would you?" I breathily asked.

He paused kissing the hollow below my ear and gave me a sad pout. "No. Do you?"

"Fresh out," I said and combed my hand through his tousled hair. He dropped his head in dismay.

"But," I said, figuring this would be the case, because why would either of us have condoms on hand while fleeing henchmen? "I am on birth control, and I haven't had any partners since I was last tested like . . . five years ago." I nearly muttered the last part as my face heated.

He looked at me with his head tilted in interest and a hint of surprise.

I shyly shrugged. "This life doesn't really lend itself to intimacy."

The look on his face softened into one of warmth and vulnerability. He shyly twisted his lips. "Well, I am healthy too, and in truth, I haven't, um, been with anyone since before my injury, so." His flushed face grew even pinker, and it pumped my heart full.

I stroked my hands through his messy hair again and smoothed my thumb over the cut on his swollen lip. "Well, then I think we owe it to ourselves to end our respective droughts."

"I couldn't agree more," he said with a little breath saying he'd been waiting for me to take the lead.

And so, we did end our droughts. Twice before showering and ordering room service, and once more before we fell asleep. Having been deprived of physical intimacy for so long, I found myself both ravenous and insatiable. Or maybe it was just him. The way he explored my body with intention and care, as if studying all my seams to know how to unstitch me just so he could put me back together and make me come apart again. The way he held me, during and after, like he wanted to sink his fingers into my soul and feel the very essence of me. The way someone so big and strong could come completely unraveled at my touch.

When I woke in the morning, wrapped in the soft linens and nothing else, he was still asleep next to me. I studied his long lashes fanned over his cheeks, the scar on his chin, the way his already full lip puffed out from being split last night. The scruff on his jaw, which felt positively divine against my throat, my chest, my thighs.

I didn't know where last night left us, but I'd have been content to stay in bed forever.

Bray stirred with a deep breath, and his eyes fluttered open. When he recognized me lying inches away, he softly smiled. "You're awake."

"You're asleep."

He reached out and placed his hand on the curve of my lower back. "I was awake earlier, but you were asleep and looked so peaceful."

"Hmm, thank you for leaving me that way," I hummed and nuzzled into his neck when he pulled me close.

"I actually slept great, which is . . . rare for me." The note of surprise in his voice floated above my head.

"Me too. Told you we'd cancel each other out if we slept together."

A warm laugh rumbled in his chest. He flattened his hand against my lower back and pushed his hips into mine. A small gasp snuck from my lips. "Looks like you were right, but I think I'm ready to move on from that kind of *sleeping* together."

One part of his body was fully awake and the feel of it hotly pressing into my belly had me really, *really* not wanting to leave the bed.

“How long until we have to check in with Ramesh?” I asked as he pulled me over on top of him.

“Hours.” He tucked my spilling hair back and kissed my neck. The promise in his voice had me ready to use every last one of those hours before we returned to reality.

Chapter 26

We flew back to the Bay and headed straight for the station. With our only lead a dead end, and no way of knowing if the ghosts were still following us, Bray both wanted to be someplace safe and to talk to Ramesh in person. We'd shopped for a change of clothes before our return charter so we didn't have to wear what we'd fled the henchmen in. I was back in jeans, a tee, and a hoodie, and he was in a pair of slacks and a button-down. We hadn't said much about our night together once we left the hotel, perhaps because we both knew we were operating under *What happens in Houston* rules. But I caught him glancing at me, and I'd glance back. And when our eyes would meet, suddenly, we were in a sweaty, naked tangle again, and I didn't know how we were going to put it behind us.

"Stay close," he instructed me as we entered the station lobby.

"Gladly," I muttered and shot him a coy grin.

He tried and failed to fight grinning back.

When the elevator dumped us out on his floor, Ramesh popped up from his desk at the sight of us like a prairie dog. He began walking toward us like he was trying to be discreet while flicking his eyes side to side. He gestured at us to hurry closer.

"What? What is it?" Bray asked and glanced around the room like there was a threat.

"You are in deep shit, my friend," Ramesh muttered as we fell into step and walked down the aisle between cubicles.

"What? With whom?" Bray asked.

"Your mother. She found out about . . . everything, and she's pissed. She already handed me my ass for helping, and she's just waiting for you to—"

"Agent Bray?" a stern voice called from the end of the aisle. A woman leaned out from the hallway where I'd sat while Bray had begged for my protection. She didn't have the harsh bob I'd imagined, but rather her brunette hair, the same color as her son's, was pulled up into a tight bun. She stood tall and slender in a smart skirt suit and heels, which made her look like the headmistress of a very fancy and strict boarding school.

"Oh God," Bray whispered. I swore I saw him shrivel. "Um . . . okay. Shit." He turned to me, his face flushed with panic. "Stay here with Ramesh, and I'll—"

"Bring Ms. Daniels with you," the director called. She turned back toward her office without waiting for him to acknowledge.

I shot Bray a look, which was anything but flirtatious. My veins had turned to ice again. This time, not from henchmen chasing me but from having to stand trial in front of my hookup's mother.

"Don't say anything unless she speaks to you," Bray instructed as we approached her office like we were heading for the gallows.

"No problem," I muttered. "Guess they noticed we were gone?"

His jaw tightened in guilt. "They are the DSA after all."

"So much for taking matters into our own hands . . ." I muttered in defeat.

"You wanted to see us, Director?" he asked when we reached the door, forcing his voice to sound steady. I couldn't help but feel like we were teens who'd been caught making out with the bedroom door closed. I'd been reprimanded before; hauled in front of directors and supervisors, but never had I been in bed with one of their offspring some six hours prior.

"Come in and shut the door," the director said in a tone two degrees above frigid.

I shivered.

Bray led the way, and we stood side by side in front of her heavy wooden desk. She remained seated in an unnecessary display of power. Simply being in the same room as her was intimidating enough. I knew in an instant Bray inherited the hard facets of his demeanor from her. His father made up his softer side.

"Agent Bray, it has come to my attention that over the past three days, you have made unauthorized use of DSA resources to conduct unsanctioned activity." She held the painful silence after, waiting for him to confess.

"Yes, ma'am," he said in a quiet voice.

"Not only did you coordinate an off-site visit with a federal prisoner with no justification, you also exposed an asset's identity to said prisoner—"

He tried to interject with a defense. "With all due respect, ma'am, there was—"

"I wasn't finished." She cut him off with an arched brow sharp enough to cut glass. "In addition, you chartered a flight on DSA resources for an unsanctioned trip to and from Houston, where I am told you caused a traffic accident and then engaged in a public foot chase, which resulted in you discharging your weapon."

"No one got hurt," he muttered.

"Oh, I think the three people in the traffic accident Agent Singh orchestrated for your benefit would beg to differ."

Bray shrunk at each accusation. I felt myself doing the same.

The director's jaw tightened the same way Bray's did when he was upset or embarrassed. A hint of color curled into her cheeks. "And then there is the hotel room, where I can only imagine what kind of breach of protocol took place."

My body caught fire. *How could she know?* But of course she knew. She knew every detail of our trip, and it was only fair to assume what went down in that room.

"Ma'am, I assure you, nothing inappropriate occurred," Bray tried to defend.

"Don't lie to me, Calvin," she snapped. "It's unbecoming of you." The director mask dropped from her face, and she was a full-on pissed-off mom. "Don't tell me nothing *inappropriate* happened when I have footage of you and Ms. Daniels *in my house* engaging in highly inappropriate behavior from mere nights ago."

She whipped her computer monitor around to show us a still image of Bray pinning me against the kitchen wall and kissing the air straight out of me.

The air left my lungs all over again. I had never been so embarrassed in my life. Not only was this a professional reprimand, the woman berating us was his mother. *His mother.* In that moment, I felt supremely stupid. *Of course* there would be security cameras in that fortress of a condo. She probably had footage of us all but cuddling on the back patio too.

I glanced at Bray. He seemed to be at a loss for words. His face burned scarlet, and he looked like he wanted to die right alongside me.

"Now, I don't know what part of me telling you to stay on the Del Rio case you interpreted as going rogue in pursuing a classified case and free rein to harbor a DSA asset at my personal address, but this is a gross abuse of power," the director went on. "Engaging in intimate conduct with an asset is a violation of so many policies, I could have you terminated right now." Her face was red to match his.

Her words stung for more reasons than one. *Abuse of power* made me sound helpless. Like I'd been taken advantage of. Like it wasn't me begging for him to put his hands and mouth on me the whole time.

I softly cleared my throat. "Ma'am, I can promise you, it was all consensual."

She shot me a sharp glare, which nearly made me take a step back. "Ms. Daniels," she said coldly. "Consensual or not, an agent is prohibited from having any relationship with an asset outside of a professional one. Agent Bray's behavior is in direct violation of policy, and he should be ashamed of himself." Each word felt like a lash of a whip. I thought I was done flinching until she came back with more. "And also, I would expect more from *you*, having been a valued DSA asset for over a decade. This behavior is reckless and a sign that I was correct in my decision to keep you on the Del Rio case—which you *will* stay on this time."

"You can't!" Bray snapped, suddenly coming back to life.

The director jumped at his outburst and turned her stern gaze to him. "Agent Bray, what I can and can't do is not up to you. You've clearly displayed in recent days that you are incapable of making sound decisions, so as of this moment, I am removing you as Ms. Daniels's handler."

"No, you can't do that," he tried to protest.

"*Yes*, I can, and I just did. She will be formally passed to an alternate handler while she remains on the Del Rio case."

Bray all but leapt forward and placed his hands on her desk. "Mom, they are going to *kill* her. The only reason I did what I did was because you wouldn't listen to me about her being in danger. She needs to be protected, and I was going to solve the case on my own to prove to you that I can handle it."

The director didn't even flinch. "Clearly, you can't, Calvin. And as far as Ms. Daniels's safety, the expendability of assets is inherent to their use. That's a risk that comes with the job."

I was at a total loss, watching my life get tossed back and forth like a beach ball as they argued.

"Let me fix this," Bray protested.

"*No*," she said back.

"Mom, please." The plea in his voice made my own heart ache.

Finally, she stood from her chair. "Calvin, this is not up to you. Now, I don't know what personal feelings might have sprung up between you two, but they cannot be permitted to persist. People already think I give you special treatment, and if word gets out you've been running around taking private flights and staying in fancy hotels with your girlfriend on the DSA's dime, it will be *me* who has to answer for it. I can't have you jeopardizing my position as well as your own. You are no longer her handler, you are off the Del Rio case, don't even think about touching the classified case, and if I catch you within so much as ten feet of her, I will put you back on a desk. Do I make myself clear?" The finality in her voice rang around the room like a cold gong.

Bray looked like he might stage one final attempt to fight back, but he sighed in defeat. My guess was it was the threat of being put back on a desk that did it. "Yes, ma'am."

"Good," she said with a nod and then turned to me. "Ms. Daniels, you will be escorted back to your residence in Del Rio and assigned a new handler. Please stand by for more information on your assignment."

Had I been thinking straight, I might have told her my cover with Melanie Browning was already blown, and there was no way I could continue to penetrate her operation. But I was too stricken by what had just happened. In mere hours, I'd gone from being in bed with Bray to being forbidden to see him. And now I had to go back to the place where the ghost knew to find me. Like a damn sitting duck.

"Yes, ma'am," I muttered.

"You are both excused," the director said and sat back in her chair.

We left the room in a numb silence. I left my body for a moment and floated around in a world where I wasn't an object to be passed around. What a dream to just walk away.

The feel of Bray's hand closing around my elbow brought me back to earth. He glanced over his shoulder and led me back into the stairwell where we'd stood a few days ago when we lived in a different reality.

The concrete shaft felt extra icy today.

"Erin, I'm so sorry. I'll fix this." He looked at me with a pained plea. Ramesh had told me Bray didn't take advantage of his position as the director's son, but clearly, everything he'd done to protect me had involved special treatment. Too bad it led to nothing.

I stood with my arms crossed for warmth and to keep myself from falling apart. "You can't, Bray. You heard her. I'm just an asset. I have no rights here."

"That's not true. You are more than that."

"Am I?" My voice was as cold as the stone walls.

"Yes! To me you are." He stepped forward and placed his hand on my arm.

I looked down at it, thinking of his touch and how it had felt to be wrapped in his arms, to sleep so deeply beside him. I silently wondered if there was a world where we ran away together. Where we just said *to hell with this* and disappeared. But I knew as soon as I thought it there wasn't. No. There was only the world where he was a government agent and I was a criminal indefinitely paying my dues, forever in captivity.

I placed my hand on his to remove it. "Maybe that was all a mistake. There's no way this was ever going to work."

Bray's face folded into a defiant frown, like he was going to protest, but then softened in defeat, knowing I was right. There was no world where we made sense.

"Goodbye, Agent Bray," I said and turned to go.

I made it one step before he gripped my shoulders and spun me around. Before I could take another breath, he had me pinned to the wall. His mouth found mine, and in his kiss, I felt a plea. A deep, longing ache to make me stay. To make this work. To live in a world where he could kiss me like this without worry. Where he could make my heart pound and my blood scream for more, and then give it to me.

For one indulgent moment, I kissed him back, wrapping my arms around his neck and shivering. I was caught in the dichotomy of his hot, hard body and the cold, hard wall. I wanted to exist in the slip of space forever. Caged in his arms, inhaling him as he sucked and nipped and stroked my tongue with his. *God damn it* he could kiss. If I stayed any longer, I would never leave.

I broke away and pressed my hand to my lips, sealing in the memory and knowing it would be the last time I ever felt something so real. I fought to catch my breath, to calm my pounding heart, and looked in his tortured stone eyes.

"Goodbye, Agent Bray."

CHAPTER 27

Del Rio waited for me like a sunny little prison. The lawns were still perfectly mowed, the flower beds popping like confetti. The smell of fresh baked cookies and joy on the air. A new face, not Bray, Ramesh, or Agent Simmons, had driven me back to the apartment and left me without ceremony. And no gun. Of course they'd confiscated the one Bray had given me back at the station. I was unarmed, unless you counted the umbrella and the bat, and right back where I'd started, except now more clueless and with the memory of the best kiss of my life blistering my lips. My best hope was the ghosts were still in Houston trying to find us, but that hope was slim. It was only a matter of time before someone came around to finish the job.

I entered the still silence of my apartment and strained my ears for signs of threat. Maybe they'd rigged the place with explosives while I was gone. Maybe they'd set up their own cameras. Maybe Olena herself was camping out in the closet, just waiting for me to return.

After a quick sweep, I found it was, indeed, empty. Everything was how I'd left it that day I went to work at Melanie's, and then got dragged to the station by Agent Simmons and never came back. A dirty coffee mug still sat in the sink, and my one shoe left over from when the ghost had twisted my ankle sat by the door. It was a sad portrait of a lonely life interrupted. I was alone once more.

Until the doorbell rang. All my senses jumped to high alert. I reached for the gun I no longer had and cursed. Whoever was ringing had to have been watching to see I'd come home. I reminded myself with a deep breath that the ghosts wouldn't ring. They'd bust down the door or slither in through a crack I didn't know about. This could not be them. Still, I approached the door with caution.

When I saw Alisha's smiling face on the other side, I nearly melted into a puddle of relief.

"Hey, neighbor!" she greeted with a bright smile when I opened the door. Jeffrey was bundled in his BuggyBaby luxury stroller, and she held a small stack of envelopes in her hand. She lightly bounced like she always did, even though she wasn't holding the baby, and I found myself smiling back at her.

"Hi there."

"Hi. I saw you just got back home. This letter for you was accidentally put in my slot in the mail room. I figured I'd drop it off since I was on my way out!" I nearly flinched. I didn't even know who had my address to send me mail. The thought sent a chill down my spine, because the answer should have been *no one*.

"I didn't open it, don't worry!" she said with an innocent and genuinely sweet smile.

"Oh, thank you!" I said, still stumbling to keep up, and now with my curiosity truly piqued.

Letter writing seemed too indirect for Olena. The woman had stationed two henchmen in Houston to wait for me to show up. She wasn't about to pen a personal missive and drop it in the mail.

Another candidate popped into my mind. Could it have been from . . . my father? Maybe it was an apology for the other night. Maybe he'd gotten my address through whatever back channel Bray had used to get to him.

"No problem," Alisha said, and handed it to me. "I hope everything is going okay since your uncle passed."

"Oh . . . yes. It is. Thank you," I muttered, having forgotten I was supposed to be mourning a dead relative but mostly wanting to end this conversation so I could find out what this mysterious letter was. "I'm still getting settled from the trip to his funeral. Lots to do." I gave her a polite smile and started to close the door.

"Of course. Glad to see you are back. We are off for a walk. See you around!" she sang, and started pushing the stroller toward the sidewalk.

"Bye!" I sang back, already sucked back into the Del Rio rhythm. I shut the door and locked it. My heart picked up speed as I walked to the dining table and sat. The envelope was addressed to Lauren Thomas from a J. Wallace, with a return address in San Francisco.

"What?" I said under my breath and flipped it over, heart in my throat, to rip the seal. I gasped at the sight of familiar handwriting.

Hey kid,

If you're reading this, it means my plan has been put in motion and I'm probably gone. Sorry I couldn't be straight with you, but it was for your own safety. I've spent ten years trying to keep you safe, and I can only hope this final attempt worked.

The truth is, I've had the diamond this whole time. I intercepted it and put it in a safe-deposit box in Houston as an insurance policy that night we met. The reason I did it is complicated, but I hope you'll hear me out.

See, you were the true gem I stumbled on that night. When the Feds called in they'd caught a teenaged grifter as part of a larger sting, my ears perked up. I'd been working cases for years and had never seen anyone with as much potential as you. I wanted the opportunity to actually do some good, and I knew after looking through your file and talking to you for five minutes, you and I could do great things together. You were the best partner I ever had, kid.

I also knew if I would have handed over the diamond to evidence, Olena would have stopped looking for you, and you'd have been safe, because then they'd have known where it was and not thought you had it. But I kept it hidden to keep you. To make a reason to keep you in the DSA under our protection, because you were so useful to me. You wouldn't have gone to prison for more than a few years if a judge didn't let you off entirely. I made all that up that night. I only said all that to scare you into saying yes to my offer. It was selfish and wrong, and I'm so sorry, kid. I wish I could tell you to your face.

You did a lot of good in the years we were together, you can believe me on that. But it wasn't right of me to keep you locked up for so long. It might be too late, but I'm doing everything in my power now to hand you your freedom.

Just like you, that rock is too beautiful to be locked up. I moved it, and you, for your safety. I have a feeling you'll find a way to get your hands on it.

Yours, JW

I read the letter twice, the first time through a shocked haze, and the second, through a blur of complicated tears. Was it anger? Relief? Sadness? I couldn't pinpoint which emotion had the strongest grip on me.

Bray and I were right: The diamond had been in that safe-deposit box. Wallace really *had* had it the whole time. *The whole goddamned time.* He'd kept it to keep *me*. If Olena had recovered it that night in the hotel, or even knew it was in police custody, she wouldn't have spent the past decade plotting my capture and probably murder. I would have been free. Sure, maybe I would have gotten arrested alongside my father that night, but maybe I would have had a lenient judge who took pity on the con man's poor daughter just weeks into legal adulthood and let me off easy. Maybe I wouldn't have spent the past ten years being Lauren, Vivian, Megan, Shelly, Quinn, Jessica, Noelle, Sloane, Rain, Veronica, Jackie, and all the other women I'd pretended to be. *Maybe*, I would have gone to college, gotten a dog, lived in a cute little apartment I'd decorated myself. Maybe I would have met a man who kissed me and meant it like Bray—maybe I'd even have met Bray.

Memory of that case from five years ago, that day deep in the Oregon woods when I tried to quit, shoved its way to the front of my mind. I'd asked Wallace if he knew where the diamond was, and he'd lied to my face. He'd lied to keep me trapped.

I abruptly stood from the dining chair I'd sunken into, with hot tears in my eyes and hands in fists. Anger raged through me. In that moment, if a ghost walked through my door, I would have broken his neck out of sheer fury. *Come at me, I dare you.* I'd been passed from the arms of one man who used me, my father, straight into another's. I'd known I was a pawn, but I hadn't known *why* all these years. Not the real reason, anyway.

A guttural growl ripped out of me. I was furious at the lies I'd been told, the men who'd controlled me. And this apology from Wallace? This letter from the grave? What was I supposed to do with it? I gripped it between my shaking fists, considering ripping it to shreds. But something stopped me. Something about the way he'd said sorry—the way he'd used his last moves on earth to protect me. My own father had held a gun to my head when given the opportunity to reconcile, and Wallace . . . he'd sacrificed himself.

I sunk back into the chair, fully crying now. "God damn it, Wallace," I sobbed. I wiped my eyes with a sniffle, furious and heartbroken all at once. How dare he make me care. How dare he spend a decade being selfish only to commit the most selfless act in the end. I sniffled again and smoothed the letter on the tabletop. The words swam in a blur.

I'm doing everything in my power now to hand you your freedom. I read the line again. *Just like you, that rock is too beautiful to be locked up. I moved it, and you, for your safety. I have a feeling you'll find a way to get your hands on it.*

"Way to be cryptic, Wallace," I muttered. The diamond *had* been in Houston, but it wasn't anymore. He'd moved it the day he'd died, just like we'd thought, based on Ramesh's records. But where did he send it?

I flipped the letter over to see if there was anything more on the back. It was blank. The envelope had a postmark for five days ago, so he must have put it in the mail the same day he moved the diamond. I sighed when I realized I would have gotten it, had I been home and not hiding out in Bray's parents' condo. It would have saved us a trip to Houston. But if we hadn't gone to Houston, Bray and I never would have had that night together.

My body flushed with heat at the memory. I bit my lip.

The urge to call Bray and ask him for help solving this latest mystery thrummed through me. But his mother had forbidden him from seeing me. She may have even deactivated his phone. And besides, telling him would only lead to him continuing to help find the diamond, and if he found it, I'd still be trapped. We'd turn it in to evidence and get Olena off my back, but I'd still be linked to the DSA. Still under the control of another man. I needed a way to get to it on my own. To free myself from her, from the DSA. From everyone. Then I could finally give Javi that call he'd been waiting ten years for, sell it, and disappear. This had always been the plan. Bray would hate me for it, but it had to be done.

I read Wallace's words once more: *Just like you, that rock is too beautiful to be locked up. I moved it, and you, for your safety. I have a feeling you'll find a way to get your hands on it.*

Wallace knew better than anyone I could find ways to get my hands on things. He'd used me for that exact reason for ten years. So where was this diamond now? *Too beautiful to be locked up* suggested it wasn't hiding. Where did diamonds go when they weren't hiding? Better yet, where did *giant* diamonds go when they weren't hiding?

There was no way he pawned it to a jeweler and had it strung on a necklace. That thing could only have been mounted in a tiara for a queen, unless he pulled a *Titanic* and really did have it created into a monstrously obscene piece of jewelry. Maybe I was looking for the Heart of the Ocean . . .

I shook the thought and dug deeper for a more logical explanation. *Too beautiful to be locked up.* When diamonds weren't jewelry, they were often on display. Where? In a museum, an art gallery, a private collection of a very wealthy individual. Had Wallace somehow passed it off to one of those places? And how in the world was I supposed to know which one?

With a sigh, I flipped the letter over once more. Still blank on the other side. "What the hell, Wallace," I muttered. I picked up the envelope, looking for more clues, and my eyes snagged on the postmark. I hoped I didn't have to make another trip to Houston to solve his little puzzle, but maybe he'd taken it from the safe-deposit box to a museum there. I went to pull out my phone to google *Houston museums with diamonds* to start hunting one by one, when something else on the envelope caught my eye.

The return address in San Francisco.

Wallace had never lived in San Francisco, as far as I knew. He'd been mostly nomadic, like me, with the closest thing to a home base being in Washington, D.C. Why would this letter have a return address for San Francisco—especially if he'd been in Houston when he sent it?

My fingers twitched with intrigue as I pulled out my phone. I entered the address into a search bar and gasped at what the results returned.

The San Francisco Museum of Contemporary Culture.

I clicked the link and was greeted by a polished homepage advertising an annual gala this weekend. I navigated to the *About Us* page and learned the museum opened three years ago with an aim to bring cultural diversity and history to the Bay by showcasing rare and interesting artifacts. I scrolled past the funders and beneficiaries and clicked on the *New Exhibits* link. My breath lodged in my throat as I waited for the next screen to load.

Could this really be it? Did Wallace have the diamond sent to a museum right in my new backyard?

The page finished loading, and I got my answer in the form of the big, shiny jewel staring back at me.

"Oh my God," I said, half laughing, half wildly impressed he'd pulled it off. I quickly read the caption under the photo.

DONATED BY AN ANONYMOUS BENEFACTOR, THIS RARE FIFTY-CARAT DIAMOND WILL BE THE CENTERPIECE OF OUR ANNUAL GALA.

I sat back against my chair with a small chuckle. Of course. Anyone in possession of such a jewel would want to show it off. Maybe Wallace pulled some DSA strings to get it featured as their gala centerpiece, or maybe it was sheer pride that the owners wanted to brag about their new piece. Big, shiny, expensive objects did strange things to people.

No wonder yorkiedork123 hadn't heard anything on the dark web. She was looking in seedy places, not at local museums. The same probably went for Olena. The criminal underworld wouldn't expect stolen jewels to resurface as gala centerpieces. I wouldn't have thought to look for it there either if Wallace hadn't directed me to it.

Which meant I had a head start.

It hit me all at once what I was staring down here. A good old-fashioned heist. The diamond was on display in a museum, and it was the key to my freedom. Wallace had all but drawn a map to it for me, and, in his own words, he knew I'd *figure out how to get my hands on it.*

Well, challenge accepted.

A familiar tingle twitched my fingers. The opportunity to sneak in somewhere—somewhere big—hadn't crossed my path in years, but it was my favorite kind of challenge. The problem was, the job wasn't something to go alone. I needed a team to pull off a jewel heist. And where was I going to get one of those now that I'd been banished from Bray and sequestered back in my suburban prison?

A sharp squeal and giggle pulled my attention out the kitchen window. I looked up to see Sandra Whitley walking down the sidewalk holding her toddling kid's hand, with her other hand stroking her growing belly. She smiled down at her toddler and pretended to tickle him, which only inspired more squeals. She suddenly looked up and across the street, and there was Jana calling to her with a friendly wave, her ever-present stroller out in front of her.

All at once, I knew exactly where I was going to get my team.

CHAPTER 28

I was on the way out my front door the next morning, ready to meet the moms at the park where I knew they would be with the kids, when I nearly bumped into a young woman in a pantsuit standing on my doorstep.

My nerves rocketed to high alert so quickly I almost punched her in the face on pure reflex.

"Whoa! Good morning," she said, and leaned back from my half jab.

I eyed her up and down: sleek low ponytail, pressed shirt, minimal makeup, telltale bulge at her hip beneath her suit. Olena was either getting more direct sending someone to kill me, or I was staring at my new handler.

"Who are you?" I asked, needing to get to the park so I didn't miss my opportunity to approach the moms before naptime.

The woman tugged on her lapels. "I'm Agent Yang. Do you mind if we step inside to talk?"

An ounce of relief seeped out of me. At least she wasn't here to kill me, but I wasn't sure I was ready for another babysitter. She looked about my age. Young. Fresh. Maybe the DSA had assigned a newbie since this case was so *low risk*, as everyone liked to believe.

"Sure, but it has to be quick. I have to be somewhere." I turned inside and let her follow.

"Yes, I've been briefed on your case. I understand you are Mrs. Browning's nanny," she said.

I froze mid-step. Bray must have been keeping the secret in place by not telling anyone my cover was already blown. The DSA didn't know it was blown if they were sending in a new handler for the same case. I slowly turned around and held my face neutral, deciding to test her. "Right. I am about to head to the park up the street to meet her and the kids. I'll be busy for the rest of the day."

"Noted," she said with a nod. She'd folded her hands in front of her pants and stood with a rigid posture. She looked like someone used to taking orders, not giving them.

"And tomorrow, I'll be at the Brownings' house all day," I said, not letting on that would only be true if my plan today worked in my favor.

Agent Yang held up her hands. "I understand. I'm not here to get in your way. I only wanted to introduce myself and let you know you've been passed to me as your new handler."

Passed to me. Once again, I was dehumanized into an object. But at least she didn't know my cover was blown. I'd rather be locked in Bray's parents' condo, or shipped to the middle of nowhere, but if I had to be anywhere, being in the clutch of neighborhood watch and security cameras in Del Rio while I worked on my plan was the best option.

"Great," I said with a stiff smile. "If you're not here to get in my way, then we are already on the same page."

She nodded, and I got the sense I was right about her taking orders. "I understand the importance of keeping cover. I will check in as needed, but please brief me as frequently as you see fit."

I couldn't believe my luck. This newbie was just going to . . . stay out of my hair?

"Will do," I said. "Now, if you'll excuse me, I need to go."

"Of course, but one more thing?" she said when I reached for the door.

I thought she might say *just kidding* and slap an ankle monitor on me, but instead she lifted her phone and wagged it at me. "Let me give you my number."

"Oh, right." She recited it, and I punched the numbers into my phone. Staring at my screen made me long for a text from Bray. It had been less than twenty-four hours, but I missed him.

I shoved the pang of longing back into the box I'd built for it. I couldn't miss him. There was no world where that longing could ever be satisfied, so I had to stop feeling it. I was on my own.

"All set," Agent Yang said with a small smile. "I look forward to working together."

I thought about asking her if she had any experience working with CIs, how she got put on my case, if she knew why my old handler had been given the boot, and if she knew anything about the past seventy-two hours, but all that could be saved for later. Or, if things went well with the moms, we'd never have a chance to have the conversation because I'd be gone. Finally free.

"I look forward to it too," I lied right to her face. It was nothing personal, of course. She seemed fine in the five minutes we'd known each other, maybe even easy. But I could have had the jolliest person alive as my handler, and they'd still be my handler.

"Great. I'll let you go," she said, and moved for the door. I let her leave first and waited for the sound of her car pulling away before I opened the door again and headed out on my mission.

Del Rio Park looked the way it always did: clean, safe, glittering in the morning sun, and full of joyous parents and children frolicking about. I spotted the moms right away. They sat on the same blanket in the same place as they had on the day I had joined them. I wondered if the park worked like high school cafeteria seating. All the cliques had their designated seats, and no one dared cross a social status line.

As I approached, my nerves were anything but at peace. Not only was I on constant lookout for any ghosts or even Olena herself, but I was also walking into a lion's den. I thought back to that day in Melanie's kitchen and the look of terror on her face when I'd mentioned Montrose, but also the way she looked like she wanted to kill me. My hope hinged on the fact that I knew they were in deep, and I had a way for them to get out of trouble. And—this glimmer was fainter—but I hoped I hadn't misread that fleeting connection I'd sensed in Melanie's kitchen when she seemed to understand, and maybe even sympathize with, the fact I was also trapped in a position I didn't choose.

The three women sat on their blanket, Melanie cross-legged with her back to me, Jana with her baby daughter in her lap, and Sandra with her legs stretched out in front of her and a hand on her belly. The older kids were off on the play structure.

"Well well well," Jana said when she saw me. "You've got a lot of nerve showing your face around here." She snapped Melanie's knee with the spit rag she held and nodded up at me.

Melanie slowly turned around, shielding her eyes from the sun with one hand. I saw frown lines immediately fold her brow.

I held up my hands. "I come in peace."

Sandra snorted. "Yeah, right. You've been lying about who you are this whole time."

The sun suddenly felt very hot on the back of my neck. "I'm sorry about that, but I didn't have a choice."

"And you have one now?" Jana said and arched a finely manicured brow.

"Yes. And I'm choosing to help you."

All three of them shifted, suddenly on edge. Clearly, I knew truths about them too.

Melanie continued staring up at me with her hand shielding her eyes. "How could you possibly help us?"

I kneeled onto their blanket so we were all on the same level. I lowered my voice. "I know about Montrose; I know about the seized shipment. I know you are in enough debt to have put a lien on your house." I nodded at Melanie and watched all three of them stiffen once more. "I also know of a job that could fix your problems and mine."

They continued to stare at me, giving nothing away, until Melanie eventually swept her eyes to the other two. They held a silent conversation, Sandra and Jana clearly looking to Melanie for direction. Tension strained between them like a bowstring, but in it, I could also feel the desperation. Something was about to snap.

Finally, Melanie turned her head to me and softly cleared her throat, still with her guard up but letting a hint of vulnerability seep through the cracks. "What kind of job?"

I held her gaze, ignoring the daggers the other two were staring at me. "Stealing a five-million-dollar diamond."

The three of them stared at me, ears perked like a pack of hungry dogs who'd just heard the word *treat.*

As it turned out, all it took to get into Melanie's locked office was offering the chance to commit felony larceny. They'd let me follow them home from the park, and once the kids were down for nap time, we congregated in Melanie's home office.

The space matched the rest of the house in terms of being professionally designed with an imposing and elegant eye. Where I might have expected a dark, high-security surveillance cave, the room was light and bright. The pale jade walls framed a view of the backyard and white, gold-accented furniture sat atop the cream carpet: sofa, armchair, desk, office chair. The wall behind Melanie's queen-sized desk was made up of built-in bookshelves holding neatly placed potted plants, books, and several thick binders. A drink cart sat under the window with a small cityscape of tea boxes and an electric kettle.

The setup looked entirely innocent, much like the three women staring at me from various points in the room.

Melanie sat at her desk, Jana perched on the armchair, and Sandra had sat opposite me on the sofa with one leg stretched out between us.

"So, let me get this straight," Jana said, brow still arched. It hadn't lowered since the park. "Your dad was a con man who used you as bait, and the night he got arrested, you ended up working for some secret government agency in exchange for protection and not going to prison too, and the people from that night are after you."

"Correct." I figured I had to tell them everything, to come fully clean, if I had any shot of getting their help. "I've been working with that agency—the DSA—for the past decade. I got assigned to Del Rio, to your case, because my handler was trying to protect me. This area is so safe, and your case is considered low risk."

Sandra snorted. "I think I might be offended by that."

"Me too," Jana said. "Just because we're women, people think we aren't dangerous? I mean sure, maybe we aren't out there punching and shooting people, but our bottom line is obviously enough to send in the secret agents." She dismissively fluttered her fingers but also glanced at Melanie to make sure she hadn't overstepped.

Melanie gave no indication she had. Her computer, a shiny silver iMac, sat off to the side on her desk, allowing her to see whoever was sitting on her sofa. She leaned back in her chair behind it.

"Well, for what it's worth, I disagree you aren't dangerous," I said. "Clearly, you are in a dangerous situation. What happened with Montrose?" I looked to Melanie for the answer.

She smoothed her hands over her desk and took a deep breath. I sensed she was still weighing the risk of telling me the whole truth. Her face softened, perhaps realizing *I* had just told them my whole truth, and she landed on the side of honesty.

"Long story short, our supplier mixed up shipments and sent us a crate of cocaine instead of strollers. When we said no way were we going to sell it, he said too bad, the product had to be moved like any other. In the time we were arguing, the crate got seized at the port where it had arrived, so then he says we're on the hook and owe him the cost of the loss." Her words bitterly faded out.

The story was run-of-the-mill to me, but for a group of neighborhood moms, I could see how that got out of hand. "So, you really did trust the wrong guy, just like me," I said, calling back to that day in her kitchen.

Her eyes met mine and I saw in them the same connection, the same knowing, I'd seen when standing next to her fruit bowl. "Yes."

"And now you're in trouble, just like me."

"Yes."

A thick silence settled over the room. The tension hanging in it felt less like it was going to snap the air in half, like it had at the park, and more like cautious curiosity.

"Tell us more about this diamond," Sandra said. She stroked her hand over her belly and tucked her leg in closer. She'd kicked off her shoes and had her socks pulled up over her leggings. The scene looked like girlfriends having an afternoon chat, not four criminals plotting a heist.

I nodded. "The night my father got arrested, we were in the middle of an attempted jewel heist. The dealers also got busted that night, long story, but the diamond went missing. Everyone thought I had it because I also went missing that night, but I really went undercover with the DSA. The head dealer—a real nasty criminal, trust me—just got released from prison early, and she's out for revenge because she thinks I have it or I know where it is."

Three pairs of eyes blinked at me in disbelief. As if I'd led them to believe I'd be showing them a PG movie and just turned on something rated R. *I'll see your crate of cocaine and raise you jewel heists and prison.* I could sense the silent conversation they were having. Their eyes darted back and forth. A tiny smile played at Melanie's mouth.

"So, you *do* know where it is," Melanie stated.

I swallowed the lump in my throat. There'd be no turning back after I told them; nothing to stop them from staging their own heist and cutting me out. But I needed them. "Yes. It's on display at the San Francisco Museum of Contemporary Culture. It's the centerpiece of their gala tomorrow night. If we get our hands on it, I have a dealer—the same guy my father and I were going to sell it to that night ten years ago—waiting for my call. I trust him completely. I'll sell it to him and wire you a cut to cover your debt."

The silence that filled the room nearly suffocated me. I had no idea what they were thinking. No idea what they were going to say.

"And what will happen to you?" Jana asked.

"I'll disappear," I said. The words filled me with helium. I was so close to finally being free. I just needed them to say they'd help.

Sandra let out a skeptical groan. "You want us to help you steal a five-million-dollar diamond so you can disappear with it? How do we know you're telling the truth? You just told us how you grew up a grifter, and then worked undercover, basically as a professional liar for a decade. How do we know this isn't just the DSA's new attempt to corner us? We agree to this job, and you walk us right into their waiting arms?"

My throat closed up with a nervous lump. I had nothing to offer them but the truth. "Because I promise you it's not. I have no loyalty to the DSA. I was coerced into working for them, and they've done nothing but exploit me for the past ten years." My voice wobbled with tears as I thought of Wallace's letter. He'd had the diamond the whole damn time. Keeping me trapped for his own benefit and not my protection. "I want nothing more than to be free of them, and this is my only chance. You three are my only chance."

The honest emotion in my voice, the pain, had them all looking at me with sympathy, but Sandra still didn't look convinced.

"How do we know this isn't an act right now?" she asked.

Her doubt snapped something inside me. "Because I would never lie about this. Yes, I've spent most of my life deceiving people, but it was never by choice. I was forced into it, first by my father, and then by the DSA. I'm tired of being used by the men in my life. The woman after me, the trafficker from that night, had her hitman hold a gun to my head. They tried to kill me again three days ago. I want out and the only way to do that is to get the diamond." I hadn't realized genuine tears had filled my eyes until one rolled down my cheek. I dashed it away. "Sorry."

Jana stood and grabbed a tissue from the coffee table. She handed it to me.

"Thanks," I said through a nasally hum.

She nodded at me with a soft smile and went back to her perch on the chair.

Another silence filled the room. The weight of my emotional confession sat heavy on the air, and I worried I'd lost any upper hand I'd had.

Melanie startled me when she moved. She reached for her

trackpad and brought her computer to life. "Tomorrow night is a tight turnaround. We'll have to move quick if we're going to do this." She began tapping her keyboard. "Jana, didn't your PR firm host events at that museum? Do you still know someone who does security there?"

Jana remained frozen for a few seconds, as if she needed time to register Melanie's words. When she finally moved, she reached into the diaper bag she'd carried with her and pulled out a slim laptop. "Yes. I have a contact there."

"Good. Learn what you can about the gala from them and see if you can get a map of the building."

A small smile bent my lips. They were actually going to help. In that moment, I was supremely thankful for Melanie's Queen Bee status, since the other two seemed to be following her lead.

"Are we for real going to do this?" Sandra said, taking one final stand.

"What choice do we have?" Melanie said over the sound of her keyboard. "You know our one-off jobs are not going to cover the debt, and our guy inside Montrose is more pissed off every day. I can't lose my house, and you two can't afford this to drag on either. I see a solution right in front of us, don't you?"

"I thought we weren't in this for the money," Sandra said.

Melanie shot her a glare. "Yeah, well that was before some douchebag overseas mixed up his crates and screwed us over. It may have started as a way to gain some control back in our lives. Between the diapers and doctor's visits and playdates and snotty noses, we got a little bored with the monotony of motherhood. We wanted some adventure, some action, something that was *ours*, where we called all the shots. That *is* where all this came from, and I don't know about you, but I've had enough of this type of adventure for now."

Her words rang out with the power of a speech made for

history books. It broke my arms out in goose bumps. Part of me longed to tell Bray I'd uncovered the truth; he'd been right, and it wasn't about money for them, at least not until they got into trouble. It was so they had something of their own they could control. So they could have some agency in their own lives, which had become so focused on caring for others.

Melanie rounded her desk and pointed to me. "Yes, she may have been dishonest with us, but I see a young woman who, not unlike us, has lost control of her life and is trying to take it back on her own terms. She's trying to break out of the role she's been assigned. I can respect that, and I would think the two of you could too."

Sandra and Jana remained quiet as her words settled. I had an urge to reach out and hug her, but Melanie didn't seem like the hugging type.

"Thank you," I quietly said instead.

"Sure. And if you swear you aren't going to fuck us over, I can get these two on board, and we can get started." She gave me a stare sharper than a razor, and I had no choice but to agree.

"I swear," I said with a nod, trying to hide my nerves and even more thankful I didn't try to hug her.

"Good," she said with her own nod. "Now, let's begin."

Chapter 29

A little over twenty-four hours later, we were pulling up to the gala in Melanie's SUV. The planning had been meticulous but efficient. Having flown solo for so many years, working with a team was both new and refreshing. Everyone had a job; the plan would take all of us to pull off. Perhaps most reassuring, if something went wrong, there'd be someone there to help. I'd never had a safety net before. At least not one in the form of three women who'd take a bullet for one another. I wasn't entirely sure one of them wouldn't use me as a shield from that bullet if it came to it, but at least they had one another's backs, and because their success depended on my success, we were all in it together.

"Ready?" Melanie asked when she put the car in park. We'd slowly rolled along the drop-off line as we got closer and closer to the museum's entrance. Fluttering banners advertising the gala draped the stone and glass building's exterior, and spotlights shone up from the ground on either side of the arched entryway. Melanie had snagged us some last-minute tickets through one of the charity boards she sat on.

"Oh look, they rolled out the red carpet for you," Jana said into the invisible bug in my ear. She'd arrived separately and was parked across the street, watching us from a car decked out with the necessary equipment she'd need to orchestrate the remote parts of the plan. I could hear the eagerness in her voice. The dark thrill at what we were about to embark on. I'd quickly learned the moms were far more complex than their mostly innocent, suburban exteriors would suggest. These women knew what they were doing, and not only were they highly competent, they got off on breaking rules.

"Showtime," Melanie said. She looked over at me like she was giving me one final evaluation. One final check to see if I'd crack.

I was not going to crack. The only thing between me and freedom was that rock. This was just another job to them, but to me, it was the last job. For real this time, because I wasn't going to let anything get in the way. Nothing was going to stop me.

I nodded at Melanie and undid my seat belt. A cool rush of evening air swirled in the door when the valet opened it, fluttering my long skirt. Melanie had let me borrow a sky-blue gown suitable for a gala, since I didn't have one on hand. The one-shouldered bodice hugged my chest and waist and draped loosely around my legs. Glamorous, but also suitable for running, if needed. My heels were strapped securely to my feet and met the same criteria.

Melanie stepped out of her side of the car in a similar outfit, except her gown was black velvet and held up by two elegant cap sleeves. Sandra climbed out of the back seat in a pale pink chiffon dress that specifically showcased her baby bump, an integral part of our plan.

"Good evening, ladies," the valet on my side said. He held out a hand to me but quickly changed tack when he noticed Sandra hoisting herself from the back seat. "Oh, let me help you, ma'am," he said, and hurried to her side.

"Like clockwork," Jana said into our ears. "Everyone loves a pregnant lady."

"Oh, you're too sweet," Sandra cooed and took his hand. She made sure to put her other hand on her belly.

Sandra is our ace in the hole, Melanie had said yesterday while we strategized in her office. *People will bend over backward for a pregnant woman. If she needs any kind of help, no one will be looking at us.* Sandra had fluttered her lashes and dramatically held the back of her hand to her forehead with a sigh, ready to play the part.

I hadn't *not* believed them, but I was happy to see it playing out in person.

"Of course, ma'am. You let any of the staff know tonight if you need anything special," the valet said, and I wondered if he had any sway at all or was just looking for a bigger tip.

"Thank you," Sandra said in a syrupy-sweet voice. In truth, she probably wanted to smack his hand away and tell her she didn't need any help, but her playing the pregnant damsel was key to our plan.

Melanie joined us on the red carpet and the three of us gazed up at the museum entrance.

"Always feels a little like prom, doesn't it?" Sandra said. "Getting dressed up and making a grand entrance."

"I never went to prom," I said. They both looked at me with a hint of pity.

Melanie looped her arm through my elbow. "Well then, let's try to at least have a little fun tonight." Her smile was genuine and laced with that same daring thrill I'd heard in Jana's voice.

I smiled back. "This is my favorite kind of fun."

Sandra looped her arm in my other elbow. "Ours too," she said with a small smile. Her frosty exterior toward me seemed to have thawed, and I was grateful for it.

"Well, don't have too much fun yet," Jana said in our ears. "Security is coming up on the left. Bag check and metal detectors."

We'd planned for as much. Turned out, Jana's old contact

did still work at the museum, and with a little innocent flirting on her part, he was willing to spill on what security would look like for the event.

Getting information out of men was embarrassingly easy sometimes.

We passed through security simply enough. As much as I wished I'd had a gun strapped to my thigh, or even a small dagger in my bra, I was empty-handed. Being unarmed put a jump in my pulse, but I'd dealt with it on enough jobs to know how to improvise. Nearly anything could be turned into a weapon in a pinch: a stem snapped off one of the champagne flutes being passed around, the heels on one of the many stilettos in sight, a necktie if things got really messy.

But there would be no mess tonight. This job was going to be clean, and on the other side of it, my freedom.

Inside, the main hall dripped luxury out of every pore. The string quartet in the corner, the black tie waitstaff circulating with trays of champagne and single-bite appetizers. The glittering baubles on all the wrists and throats just begging to be nicked. I'd been in rooms of such wealth before, and the desire twitching my fingers never faded.

"Not until we get what we came for," Melanie appeared at my side and said.

I turned to her, startled, and saw a knowing glint in her eye. How she could read me so well, I didn't know, but clearly, she knew I was itching to get my hands dirty. She nodded at the front of the room, and when I followed her gaze, there it was.

The diamond.

My breath hitched. Even from across the room, I could see the glittering rainbows shooting off it. The transparent piece of ice I'd held in my hands as a teenager, which set the next decade in motion. It was *right* there.

The desire to sprint to it, punch my fist through the glass case, and hold it in my bloodied hand just out of pure spite thrummed through my body like I'd been hit by lightning. The source of all my problems—literally. The same as when I'd seen my father, I wasn't sure what mix of emotions to expect upon seeing it. The cocktail landed somewhere between hope, rage, and . . . amusement?

A laugh, of all things, burst from my throat.

"What's funny?" Jana said in my ear. Melanie looked at me with the same question lifting her brows.

I didn't have an answer for them. I wasn't sure why I was laughing. Maybe because everything had come full circle. The job that was supposed to set me free ten years ago—stealing this damned stone—was the key once more. And was I any closer? I'd literally had it in my hand ten years ago, and everything fell apart. Even with a team of pros at my side tonight, there was no guarantee it wouldn't fall apart again, despite our best planning.

"I think I need a drink," I said and stepped to the side to grab a champagne flute off a passing tray.

"She's not going rogue on us, is she?" Jana said into our ears.

"No," Melanie said with a certainty like she knew that wouldn't happen.

I wasn't going to go rogue; I had no plans for that. It was more a matter of what plans fate had for us. What wrench might be thrown our way and land me in prison—maybe literally—for another decade.

"Just give her time," Melanie said as I sipped bubbles. They went down like a smooth, golden ribbon.

"Well, we don't have a ton of it," Jana said. "Security shift change is in ten minutes, and you'll need to be in position." An electronic barrier protected the case holding the diamond. With it engaged, the glass was unbreakable, and getting too close would set off an alarm. Jana was going to cut electricity to the whole room, killing the lights and the case so I could grab the diamond. Turned out, behind her stroller-pushing picnic-playdate façade, she was a bona fide hacker. Apparently, she'd double majored in computer sciences, and met someone through a company her husband's firm had invested in who'd showed her the dark side of the web and helped sharpen her skills.

"We will be," Melanie said in a tone that silenced Jana. She stepped in the opposite direction from me and reached for her own champagne flute. Sandra had sat at one of the tables trussed up with towering floral centerpieces and requested a class of sparkling water from a waiter.

Mingling was part of the plan anyway. Jana had the place scoped digitally what with the maps, and had already tapped into the security feed, but we needed to see the room live in person before we made any moves. In case of a change in plans on the museum's part. In case they put the diamond in view of camera B instead of A or rotated security every ten minutes instead of twenty. So far, everything was on track.

Until I felt a warm hand close around my upper arm.

I turned to see the stone-gray eyes of the man I'd accidentally fallen for. If there was any doubt how I felt about him, the hot rush of blood that sent my heart leaping at the sight of him erased it.

"Bray? What are you doing here?" I asked, my voice hardly more than a breath. He wore a tux, which fit like it had been laser-cut for his body. His hair was neatly gelled and, God damn it, he looked like a bona fide secret agent.

"I had to see you," he said and stepped closer. His hand slid down my arm until our palms touched. He gripped my hand, which had broken out in a clammy sweat.

Common sense told me to pull away from him. To resist and keep my head in the game, but he was looking at me with the same bedroom eyes he'd looked at me with in Houston. The plea in them sunk a hook straight into my heart.

"How'd you know I was here?" I managed, feeling like the

rest of the room had disappeared, and only semi-aware the moms could hear everything we were saying.

"Agent Yang," Bray said. "I bribed her to keep tabs on you because I couldn't stand not knowing what was going on. When she told me you were still reporting to your job at Melanie's, I knew you were up to something with the moms, so I followed you."

I huffed a dark laugh, realizing the DSA was corrupt to its core, even if the man in front of me had the noblest of intentions.

"What's happening right now?" Jana said in my ear. "I don't have eyes on her."

"There seems to be an unexpected interference," Melanie said. I'd lost sight of her but assumed she wasn't nearby seeing as she wasn't digging her fingers into my arm and dragging me away from Bray. "That agent is here."

"Huh-uh. Nope. Secret agent accomplice is *not* part of this plan. Get rid of him, Erin," Jana said. "Three minutes until security shift change, and if we miss this one, dinner will start, and it'll be too obvious with people sitting down. *Get. Rid. Of. Him.*"

Jana's harsh hiss in my ear snapped me back to reality. I shook myself from the heady grip of Bray's gaze and slipped my hand from his. "You still didn't tell them my cover was blown."

Guilt shadowed his face. "I know. I don't want them shipping you off to another case if you're not safe. I can't stand the thought of losing you—for any reason." His feelings for me swam in his eyes.

But we couldn't go down that road. Not now. Not here.

"Are you here alone?" I asked, shaking myself from the moment.

"Yes, I wanted to give you the chance to do the right thing."

"You can't be here, Bray," I told him.

He reached for my hand again, a pleading look on his handsome face. "Erin, I know why you're here, and I can't let you do this."

"I'm getting into position," Sandra's voice said into my ear.

"Two minutes," Jana updated. "Do not fuck this up, Erin. We are counting on you."

I winced at her harsh words. I didn't know which way to turn; the path was unclear. Plan A: I could go through with stealing the diamond and surely get us all caught because Bray was right in front of me. Plan B: I could ditch the plan, let down the moms *and* myself, and land back in the DSA's keep for all eternity.

Bray kept staring at me, pleading with me to do the right thing. My heart kept pounding and my mind trying to untangle the knotted threads of each scenario before me.

"One minute until I kill the power," Jana updated. "Mel? What should I do?"

Melanie didn't immediately answer. I glanced sideways to see her and Sandra standing in position a short distance from the diamond case, as planned. Our eyes locked, and hers swam with equal parts hope and threat. If I betrayed them, the consequences might be worse than a life imprisoned with the DSA.

"Erin," she finally said. And in that one word, I knew what I had to do.

I nodded at her and then turned to Bray. "I'm sorry, Calvin," I said, and then gripped his face to kiss him.

His surprise only lasted a second, and then he leaned into it. He leaned into it with so much want, so much need, I nearly lost track of Plan C I'd made up on the spot. While his tongue warmly slid against mine—good God, how was I going to give him up, *again*—I pinched the bug out of my ear and tucked it into his breast pocket. That way, Jana could keep tabs on him and know if he or anyone else from the DSA was coming to get us. It was the only way out.

It was now or never, or this would all be in vain.

I reluctantly broke away from our kiss, leaving Bray flushed and reeling, seconds before a gasp rose up from the other side of the room. It drew Bray's attention, and I slipped from his hold. I was flying solo without the bug in my ear, but I knew I had thirty seconds before Jana cut the house lights. I had to make it to the diamond case in that time.

No one will question a fainting pregnant lady, Melanie had said while we'd planned in her office. *Sandra just needs to pretend to pass out, and everyone will come running. Then Jana cuts the power, you grab the stone in the commotion, and disappear before the lights even come back on.*

It sounded simple enough, but that plan had hinged on having Jana in my ear to navigate.

A second, collective gasp went up when the room turned black. I crashed into a few bodies, stumbling my way across the hall.

"Erin!" I heard Bray shout behind me. I ignored his plea and kept beelining for the case. I'd memorized a floor plan of the room and knew right where to find it. On the way, I snatched a bottle of champagne off a tabletop.

My eyes fought to adjust to the dim light. The only source was the moonlight leaking in from the high windows in the arched ceiling. Otherwise, a few people had pulled out phones to dot the room with tiny flashlights. One of them glinted off the diamond case some five feet in front of me.

It was unguarded.

Perfect.

Part of the reason we'd had Sandra "faint" near the case was to draw the security guard away. If she'd done it across the room, the person charged with guarding the rock wouldn't have been the one to come running.

I stopped at the case, careful not to touch it and leave any fingerprints. The diamond blinked back at me, bigger than I remembered. Even in the dark, it sucked in any available light and shone every shade of the rainbow at once.

"Hello, old friend," I whispered.

I lifted the champagne bottle over my head and turned my face away before I brought it down as hard as I could to a fantastic crash of shattering glass. Shards leapt from every direction, some of them slicing into my arms, but I didn't stop. Surely, it would be mere seconds before I was tackled. I reached into the well of sharp edges and gripped the stone-cold diamond in my fist.

Finally.

I no longer had Jana in my ear to lead me out of the building, so I was relying only on my memory of the floor plan. There was an access door ten feet to the left, behind the case, which would lead to a hallway with a back exit. All the security cameras along the path had been cut with the lights, but we had only minutes before the backup system would turn them back on.

I shoved the diamond into my bra, where it felt like a giant ice cube that would never melt, and turned for the door to make my escape.

It was then another hand gripped my upper arm. This one icy and boney and with no trace of the sympathetic plea Bray's had had.

I whipped around to see who'd grabbed me, somehow already knowing in my gut, and saw the ice-blue eyes that had haunted my dreams for a decade staring back at me, glowing even in the dark.

"Hello, princess," Olena Nova said. "Thanks for doing the hard part."

Chapter 30

Olena dragged me by the arm to the same back door I'd planned to use. Her claw-like grip dug into my flesh the same as it had done when I was a kid. It was as if nothing had changed. The full-circle moment had become even fuller. When Plans A and B weren't options, I'd come up with Plan C, but I had no Plan D. This was never supposed to happen, but I felt instantly foolish for not anticipating it.

"Let go of me!" I cried and struggled against her grip. She was inhumanly strong for someone so birdlike and the shock of seeing her again erased every move I'd ever learned to defend myself from my mind.

She whipped around and slammed me against the hallway wall. Her face moved inches from mine. Close enough I could smell the sour champagne on her breath. She looked the same as she did in my nightmares, only older and hardened. Her eyes still blazed like blue fire. Her beaklike nose had a sharp hook in it now, surely thanks to the elbow I'd thrown in her face years ago. "You stole from me, you little bitch. That diamond was *mine* to sell, and you took it and ruined everything. I spent ten years in prison because of you, and if you think this is going to end any other way than with you at the bottom of the bay and that diamond in my hand, you are *wrong*." She jerked me hard with another shove into the wall. My head banged off the concrete and sent my vision sparkling with stars. "I can't trust anyone to do this job right, so here I am doing it myself. Give it to me."

I was still blinking stars, trying to recover.

"*Give it to me!*" she shouted in a shrill cry, which rang through the empty hallway.

Her voice and her grip and the cruel snarl of her mouth turned me into a frightened teenager. It was suddenly the worst night of my life all over again. I could do nothing but tremble.

"Oh for God's sake, you sniveling little brat," she spat and began roughly patting my body, looking for the diamond. Her cold hand smashed into my chest, my hips, my stomach. Finally, she crudely shoved her hand down my dress and yanked the diamond from my bra. "*Yes*, there you are." She gazed at the jewel with pure reverence. I could have taken the opportunity to punch her in the stomach and make a run for it, but I was still too stunned, reeling in my age-old trauma, to move.

She tucked the diamond into her own gown and yanked me away from the wall. I couldn't help but stumble after her. "Let's go. I need to get rid of you once and for all." She pushed open the hallway door to a dark parking lot where a sleek car with tinted windows waited. "Get in," she said and shoved me at the car's back door.

I obeyed, still nearly frozen with fear. I climbed into the leather back seat, which smelled like expensive perfume and cigarettes. A bulky figure sat behind the wheel, and I knew who it was without even needing to look.

"Hello, princess. Nice to see you again," the ghost from that night purred.

I swallowed the terrified lump in my throat and fully realized, for the first time, I was going to die tonight.

"Go," Olena commanded after she climbed in next to me and slammed the door.

The ghost put the car in drive and flipped around to exit the parking lot. He kept stealing glances at me in the rearview mirror. I could only see his eyes and thick brow, the scar still angry and puckered, but I could tell he was smiling. "What, no prince to save our princess tonight?" he taunted. The reference to Bray made my heart ache. At least I'd gotten a goodbye kiss.

Olena hissed something angry at him in another language, and he stopped smiling.

We drove in silence down Highway 101 for several miles. I could only imagine where they were taking me, what dark shadowy shoreline they planned to dump my body on. Olena would probably end me with a gunshot to the back of the head—or maybe the face, with how much she hated me.

"You were hard to find, you know," she said as we turned east onto one of the many bridges crisscrossing the bay. Maybe they planned to shove me out at the highest point and save a bullet. "I've been looking for you for ten years. No one knew where you were, not even your father." She turned to me with a cruel bend in her lip. "And I believed him because a man like that is always thinking of himself. If he had anything to bargain, he would have used it."

The painful reminder stabbed at me like a knife. Not that I needed it, but it was further confirmation I couldn't trust my father. Olena had given him the chance to give me up, and he hadn't, but only because he couldn't. They would have found me years ago if he'd known where I was.

Olena kept sneering at me like twisting the mean knife was bringing her great pleasure. "That man hiding you, he did a good job," she said. "It was unfortunate we had to kill him." She suddenly leaned in, and I leaned back. The car's window pressed into my bare shoulder; the door handle dug into my arm. I half expected her to try and strangle me again, but instead, she spoke softly but with an edge of certainty. "A man like that, one willing to die to protect, *that* is a father. Why he cared about you so much, I do not know. But you were lucky to have him."

The mention of Wallace made my already aching heart crack. I was mad at him for lying to me, but her reminder he'd died for me—and hearing it in such juxtaposition to my *real* father—put the truth in even sharper perspective. Wallace was right: We *had* done good together, despite all the struggle it put me through, and I couldn't say I regretted it.

Something snapped inside me.

I was not going to die tonight. Not after everything. The frightened teenager vanished, and the woman I'd become—the fighter, the survivor—woke up.

I glanced out the window over Olena's shoulder, not letting on I was scrabbling together a plan in my head. We were out over the water now. A black void waited below us, spotted only by the occasional freighter slowly passing like an enormous, lit-up whale. The East Bay dimly shone in the distance.

"How did you find him?" I casually asked as I discreetly slid my hand down to unbuckle my left shoe.

Olena smugly shrugged and sat back against her seat, facing forward once more. "That man in Florida you targeted, the one selling rare animals, he ran in a circle I knew. Word got to me a pretty young woman matching your description turned him in to the authorities, and that woman had been seen meeting with an older man. It took months to track you down after that, but it was the first trail in years."

Megan Thorpe. That was my identity on that Florida case. It was the last one before I got transferred to New York for the insider trading case as Vivian. Just thinking of the name brought back the feel of the humidity, the smell of swampy wetlands. I'd played the part of a conservationist with one hand in the black-market trade for rare birds, fish, reptiles. Endangered species being shipped around as trophies. The overlap with

Olena's trafficking operation made sense. I'd bet a few tigers had passed through her keep on their way to being illegally caged in someone's home.

"Everette Freeman," I said as I slipped my foot out of my unbuckled shoe. Bless Melanie for lending me such sharp heels.

Olena nodded at the Florida man's name. "His arrest was actually good for my business. Less competition," she said with a snide wink.

"So you kept operating, even from prison," I said, and pressed the sole of my shoe into my palm. Olena was too busy smugly recounting her machinations to notice what I was doing beneath the fluff of my skirt. It didn't take a genius to know she was telling me everything because she planned to kill me.

"Where I could," she said sourly, as if she didn't like the reminder of prison. "I have many hands doing my work, but they cannot fully function without me, the brain."

I had a solid grip on my shoe now, the heel pointed outward like a little couture spear. I knew it was of the highest quality because it belonged to Melanie Browning. I hoped she would forgive me for getting blood on her Jimmy Choo. "You must be happy to be back, then," I said and shifted in my seat. Olena had taken to gazing out her window and didn't see me reach for my seat belt and fasten it. The click drew her attention.

She smiled and a laugh bounced her shoulders. "You think a safety belt is going to help you tonight, princess?"

I calculated the likely outcome of the next sixty seconds and decided it was my best shot. I looked Olena square in the eye and spoke with a determined resolve. "Yeah. I do."

She flinched when I suddenly moved my shoe to my right hand, but she wasn't my target. I sat forward and jammed the sharp heel into the ghost's meaty neck. I shoved as hard as I could, feeling it pierce flesh and twist through tendons until a spurt of blood splattered the windshield.

Olena screamed. The ghost gurgled a startled cry and hit the brakes but swerved into the median as he tried to reach for his neck. My seat belt locked against my shoulder with a hard bite, just as I'd planned, while the car's movement threw Olena into the side window. Her head cracked off it hard enough to splinter the glass and leave her dazed. The car's nose had scraped off the median in a way that left our back end jutting into the middle of the road. Horns blared in brief warning before the car behind us hit the side of our back end. Olena smashed into the window again, her arms flailing like a rag doll and her temple now bleeding. The ghost slumped sideways, still grasping at his neck, and fighting for air. We'd spun and come to a stop, now facing the opposite direction we'd been driving. Oncoming headlights barreled at us as brakes screeched but not in time. Another car hit us head-on, sending the front airbags exploding and the windshield shattering. Olena flew backward and then forward, smashing into the back of the seat in front of her and crumpling into a bloody heap. The seat belt punched me in the shoulder again, but it did its job and held me in place. I could feel a bruise already blooming beneath my skin. My head spun, but we'd finally stopped moving.

I clawed at the buckle on my other shoe and ripped it off, knowing I was going to have to run, and then lunged at Olena. I shoved my hand into her dress, the same as she'd done to me, and grabbed the diamond.

"Thank you for my freedom," I said to her dazed, bloody face and scrambled for my door. The cool night air rushed in, and I had one foot on the pavement when her bird hand clawed into my arm like a talon.

I screamed at her nails digging in and found my other shoe. I held it by the strap and whipped it at her, wishing I could do more damage but needing to get the hell out of the car. The heel cracked off her forehead and sent her reeling back.

"Get back here, you little bitch!" she screamed as I shoved my way out the door.

Outside, the dark night hung thick with misty fog and the grittiness of the air surrounding a busy roadway. Traffic had stopped on our side of the bridge and had only begun to slow on the other as rubberneckers slowed to see what had happened. Cars still whizzed past, sending a rush of air billowing my skirt and my hair flying. The drivers of the two cars that had hit us were out in the roadway, clutching their heads and asking if we were all right.

I didn't have time for pleasantries. I had to go.

By now we were closer to the east side of the bridge than the west, so I took off in that direction. The cold pavement made my bare feet ache, but it didn't take long before they were numb. Nor did it take long for a gunshot to ring out into the night.

I flinched and dove behind one of the stopped cars. I sat on the ground and peeked around its bumper to see Olena limping up the road, gun in hand, looking madder than hell.

"Shit," I hissed. Of course she had a gun. If she hadn't had it stashed in the glove compartment, she probably snatched it off the ghost. "Shit, shit, shit," I muttered. If I took off running, she'd try to shoot me, and someone would get hurt. Traffic had stopped, and more and more cars full of innocent people were in the line of fire.

"Give it back!" Olena screamed, closer now, and fired the gun again.

I flinched and covered my ears. This was not good. I had no weapons—not even a shoe. I was barefoot in a gala gown on a bridge full of cars with a five-million-dollar diamond in my bra and a madwoman shooting at me.

"*Think*," I said, and knocked my head back against the bumper. My car-shield was a minivan, surely with an innocent family inside. If I'd been a better nanny—or a *real* one, even—

I'd probably know a secret button to push to release a hatch, which would let me crawl inside. But then I'd be *with* the innocent family inside their car while a madwoman shot at me, and that wouldn't bode well for anyone.

Still, I was desperate. I stood up from my crouch and peered in through the minivan's back window, looking for anything that might help. My breath caught when I recognized a Buggy-Baby stroller collapsed inside. I saw *X3* stamped onto one of the rods. "No way," I muttered.

You could still break down a door with it, Alisha had told me. *The titanium rods are triple reinforced but light as a feather.*

Break down a door . . . or stop a madwoman from killing me or hurting anyone innocent.

Pressing my luck, I peered around the van again. Olena was five cars away, still charging like a bloody bull.

I frantically looked for a back release latch on the van and found one in the form of a handle I promptly yanked. The hatch slowly rose with a ding. The family was too busy ducking in their seats to notice. A cartoon with a little blue dog played on the screens hanging from the ceiling. I could hear the dad in the front seat, on the phone with a 911 operator, surely. The mom had climbed to the middle seat and thrown her body over the car seat strapped there. The only person who noticed me stealing the stroller was the little girl sitting in the very back seat. She curiously looked at me through her little smudged glasses as she hugged her doll. The last thing I needed was for her to scream and alert her parents I was robbing them of their very expensive stroller.

I gave her my friendliest smile and then held my finger to my lips. "Shhh. I'm a good guy," I whispered. It wasn't entirely true, but I'd learned bending the truth with children was permissible, if not necessary.

She considered me with a tilt of her little head and then mirrored me in pressing her finger to her lips. "Shhh."

"Thank you," I said and pulled the stroller from its keep.

Olena was right around the corner now; I could hear her labored breathing and her footsteps scraping the pavement. "Where did you go, princess?" she called.

The stroller folded up like a beach chair when it was collapsed. I gripped it with both hands and waited until I saw her shadow in the dim yellow light casting pools on the pavement. In the last second before she passed the van, I swung the stroller and smashed it into her upper body.

The shock—and surprising power of the stroller—knocked her to the ground with a yelp.

"Damn, this thing really is a weapon," I said in awe and looked at it still in my hands. It had felt like swinging a Wiffle-ball bat but with the power of a battering ram.

Olena lay on the ground, groaning and holding her chest like I'd cracked a rib. Maybe I had. The good news was the gun had flown from her grip and landed out of her reach. I dropped the stroller and lunged for it.

"Give me that!" she screamed and clawed at my legs. She got a grip on one of them and pulled me to the ground.

I cried out when my knees hit the asphalt. I felt my gown tear and gritty rock dig into my skin. I got one hand on the gun and kicked at her.

"Get off of me!" I landed a kick to her face and managed to scramble away. I was only a few steps away before she dove on me again.

This woman would not quit.

I held the gun out of her reach as she continued to claw and grab at me. I did my best to run, but she was with me every step, punching at me, reaching for the gun, hissing horrible threats in my ear.

"I'm going to kill you and enjoy it. Give me what's mine, you nasty little bitch. I should have killed you when you were a kid."

"Get *off* me!" I roared and shoved her as hard as I could. In the process, the gun flew loose from my hand, but she didn't seem to care. The cold fury in her eyes said she was going to kill me with her bare hands.

She came at me with her talons bared, dress tattered like mine, and blood dripping down her face. We were past the stopped traffic by now. It was just us and the empty road. We were still far out over the water. High enough for a fall to end in certain death. Olena charged and I could do nothing to get out of her way. She shoved me up against the icy railing of the bridge and put one hand around my throat.

"Where is it?" she hissed with pure venom in her voice and rage in her bloodshot eyes. She scratched at my chest, ripping her nails into my skin, and dug the diamond back out of its keep. "Yes! Mine for good this time," she cheered and clutched it in her fist. She was still choking me with her other hand. Her nails drew blood on either side of my throat, I could feel it dripping. I pushed and clawed at her, trying to keep my balance. The bridge's railing hit my midback. All it would take would be a hard shove, and momentum would pull me over the edge to a watery death.

"Goodbye, princess," Olena sang with a laugh worthy of the wickedest witch.

My vision narrowed as my lungs fought for oxygen, which wouldn't come. This was the end. I'd die alone, and no one would mourn me because I had no identity. I was no one. Nothing.

I tilted my head back, searching the night sky for stars or even a plane. Anything more pleasant than the soulless stare of my sworn enemy as she squeezed the life out of me. I thought I saw a star, even through the fog, but that might have been my suffocating brain mustering a twinkle as my vision turned to black.

In the second before I lost consciousness, a gunshot ripped the air apart. And suddenly, I could breathe again. Oxygen filled my lungs. My vision cleared. I was no longer doing a backbend over the railing. I clutched my own throat to feel it free of anyone's grip and sucked in a big breath. My ears rang from the gunshot. I looked down to see Olena Nova dead at my feet with a single bullet wound in her temple and a pool of blood on the pavement.

I was still gasping for breath, gaining my bearings, when I heard my name float out on the air.

"Erin! Erin, you're safe now."

Agent Bray came flying at me out of nowhere and wrapped me in his arms. Through my haze, I returned his hug with one arm. I could see over his shoulder the reason the traffic had stopped: His cruiser sat parked sideways on the bridge with a flashing red siren attached to the top. I could hear more sirens coming up the road from behind it. We'd be swarmed in minutes.

I didn't realize I was trembling until he smoothed my tangled hair and kissed my temple. "Hey, you're okay. I've got you."

I looked up at him in a daze and then down at Olena's body. "Nice shot."

He pivoted us so my back was to her and all I could see were his gray eyes. "I had to. She was going to push you over the edge."

Snark about being well aware of that fact surged up my throat, but my mouth wouldn't form the words. Looking into his face and seeing the biggest emotions I'd ever seen staring back at me, all I could say was, "Thank you."

He softly smiled, like shooting someone to save my life was a given. "She's gone. You're safe now."

She's gone. Olena Nova was gone. The truth of that reality would take a long time to sink in, I knew it, but I could already feel a weight lifting. A glimpse of the freedom I'd been chasing for a decade.

"Erin, she's gone," Bray said again as if I hadn't heard him. He smoothed my hair once more and tilted my chin up with his fingers. "You're safe."

He was right. I was safe. I could let him scoop me up in his strong arms and carry me in my bloodied, tattered dress to the ambulance still blaring up the road. He'd take care of me and maybe take me to his place for the night, screw the rules, and we'd pretend we had a normal life before I went back to working for the DSA.

But that would be it. I would only be safe. And only for now.

"What's wrong?" he asked when I didn't respond. He leaned back to get a better look into my eyes.

I wished I didn't have to do this, but Plan E was already formed in my mind. I looked into his troubled eyes, at the knit in his brow, the pinch of his full lips, and longed to say the words on my tongue, *I think I love you*, but that would only hurt him more than what I was already going to do.

I still had one arm hooked around his back, half embracing him, but I pushed my other arm up between us and slowly opened my hand. "I would be safe, but I wouldn't be free."

He flinched at the sight of the diamond nestled in my dirty palm. I'd wrestled it from Olena's grip without her noticing while she was busy choking the life out of me. She'd died with it in my hand.

Bray's mouth twitched up at the corners. "How'd you—?" he began to ask as I stepped back from him. Realization dawned over his face. My ticket to freedom was right there in my hand. And my escape was about thirty seconds from being in the exact right place for me to hop on board.

When I'd leaned back to gaze at the sky while Olena tried to kill me, I'd clocked a freight barge slowly approaching the bridge. Given its height, it would *just* clear the bottom of the bridge, leaving a short enough distance someone who knew how to take a fall could manage it if they jumped.

I knew how to take a fall, and I had already decided if Olena somehow didn't kill me, I was going to jump.

But I hadn't planned on Bray showing up. Again. He'd been a wrench in all my plans, from the day we met. And now, staring at me with his bottomless gray eyes, begging me to do the right thing, he was a wrench once more.

"Erin . . ." he said as I took another step backward, toward the railing. "Don't."

As much as I wanted it—as much as my heart was screaming for it—a life with him was impossible. A federal agent and a career criminal could never work.

But what *was* possible, what was within reach, was my freedom. Something I'd been chasing my whole life. The thing I wanted more than anything, and the thing I'd sworn to myself in my loneliest moments I'd take if I ever got the chance, no matter what.

"Erin, please," Bray pled again. He stepped closer with his arm out. Pain strained his voice. "You don't have to do this. There's got to be another way."

I glanced over my shoulder to see the barge passing under the bridge. It was a twenty-foot drop at most. I might roll an ankle, but I'd have plenty of time for it to heal while I stowed away on the trip to China, or wherever this ship was headed. And then I'd find my way to Javi, sell this godforsaken diamond, pay the moms, and start a new life. Off anyone's radar. I could be whoever I wanted to be.

The man in front of me was begging me to stay and be me. But I didn't even know who *me* was. Not here, not in this place where I'd been a rotating cast of characters for as long as I could remember. I couldn't do it. I couldn't deny myself the chance to figure out who I really was. Not even if it meant losing the only person who I think ever really loved me.

The boat was as close as it was going to get. It was now or never.

“Erin,” Bray said once more. His heart was breaking, and it was almost more than I could take.

I gave him a half smile, wishing I could give him more. “I told you I’d disappoint you.” Then I tucked the diamond in my dress, turned, and jumped over the rail.

EPILOGUE

One year and six months later

The October afternoon was the slow, lazy kind that felt like summer making a final stand while a hand made of crisper days pulled it toward autumn. Summer tended to linger in Georgia though. It was something I remembered from a job here years ago, and one of the many reasons I'd chosen the state as my new home. Another reason was a university that didn't do a deep dive on my fabricated high school transcripts before accepting me.

I sat in the quad now at a picnic table under a willow tree idly stroking the thick breeze. I had my latest reading assignment spread on the table and was jotting notes in my notebook. My dog Buster's leash hooked around my ankle beneath the table, but he was too loyal to leave my side anyway. The leash was a formality and really just a way to keep the campus security guards off my back. I sipped my sweet tea left over from lunch and turned the page in my book.

I was several weeks into my first official semester—ever—and relishing every moment of it. The routine of going to class, doing homework, visiting office hours. Riding my bike through the quaint college town and not worrying anyone was watching or trying to kill me. Heading home to my cute little apartment off campus with a regular lock on the door and no armed guard babysitting me. I'd even made friends with a few classmates, even though I was nearly a decade older than them.

It was everything I'd ever wanted, and I finally had it. On my own terms.

That night I'd jumped off the bridge, Bray didn't follow me. He apparently didn't try to stop the boat from leaving the bay, and if he did, it hadn't worked. I'd stowed away undetected on board for days, stealing in and out of empty cabins and borrowing a maintenance crew outfit I'd found in a locker. We'd ended up at a port in Panama. From there, I backchanneled my way to Javi, who was equal parts stunned and thrilled to hear from me.

I stayed in South America for a while, trying out different cities, different countries, until an ache for home called me back. I missed hot dogs, and the Fourth of July. And even the stupid Super Bowl. Most of all, I wanted my own place, and a dog, and to take classes at a local university simply because I was interested.

So I reached out to yorkiedork123, who helped forge me a new identity, and returned to the US. I kept my word to the moms and wired their cut of the diamond money into the account Melanie had told me to, though I never set foot in Del Rio again. They cleared their debts and may have carried on misbehaving or maybe not, I couldn't be sure. That part of my life was over. I was a new person. Every day becoming more *me* than I'd ever been and enjoying figuring out who exactly I was.

I turned another page in my book as Buster sat up with a small whine. He'd stretched out in the sun at my feet, exposing his soft white belly, but now he came to my side and nudged my leg with his nose. He was a Border collie mix with a black and white coat and enormous ears. Those ears were the best security system I'd ever had.

"What is it?" I cooed at him and stroked his soft head.

He looked off toward the grassy quad and panted. I thought he'd caught sight of the Frisbee a group of students were throwing around and wanted to go snatch it, but then I noticed someone walking toward our table.

A man with a bulky frame, shiny brown hair, and gray eyes I could see even from a distance.

My heart flipped over, and I couldn't tell if it was fear or straight-up longing. Perhaps a mix of both.

A different air hung about him from the last time I'd seen him. He was looser, calmer, and—to my great relief—void of the telltale weapon bulge at his hip. He wore jeans and a tee with a light windbreaker over it. A slim folder was tucked under his arm.

I watched him approach without saying anything, but that was mostly because my mouth had sealed shut with anxiety.

Bray stopped at the end of the table and held out his hand to let Buster sniff it.

The little traitor sniffed him once before lapping him with his tongue.

"Who's this?" Bray asked with a laugh.

"Buster," I said. "He'll bite you if I tell him to," I lied.

"Oh, I doubt that. You wouldn't bite me, would you, buddy? No, you wouldn't," he cooed, and leaned down to scrub his ears. Buster responded by licking Bray's face and pawing at his legs.

"Some guard dog you are," I muttered and pulled on his leash.

Bray gave him a pat on the head and slid onto the bench across from me. He folded his hands on the table and studied me like I'd been studying my book. "You know, you should have picked a less obvious name if you didn't want me to find you, Katherine Wallace," he said. I could hear the pride in his voice. The triumph that he'd pieced together my new identity and tracked me down, even if it took him over a year. He knew my mother's name was Katherine because I'd told him as much that night in Houston. And through it all, Agent Wallace was more of a father than my own ever was, so taking his name felt right.

I stuck my pen into my book and folded my hands to match his. "Maybe I wanted you to find me." I couldn't fight the upward bend in my lips, despite still not being sure what his intentions were.

In truth, I'd longed for this moment. I'd been looking over my shoulder since that night on the bridge, hoping I'd see him there. Hoping he would find me, and we'd sort out what to make of our messy lives together.

And here he was.

"So, are you here to arrest me?" I asked.

To my relief, he shook his head. "No. I'm here to ask you on a date. Well, I have something to give you first, and depending on how that goes, then I'll ask you out."

The sudden buoyancy in my chest could have floated me off like a balloon. "Consider my interest piqued, Agent Bray."

"You don't have to call me that anymore," he said.

"Oh? Why not?"

"Because I quit."

At this, I reeled. "You quit the DSA?"

A flush curled into his face. "Well, I guess if we want to get technical, I was *relieved of duty.*"

"Oh?"

"Yeah. See, I fell in love with a CI and spent the better part of a year using DSA resources trying to find her when she disappeared. Apparently, that's frowned upon."

I shyly laughed, feeling my heart lift once more. "I can't imagine why, you absolute rebel."

"DSA regulations, what are you gonna do? And I never really liked that job anyway. I just did it out of some warped familial obligation I've been seeing a therapist about," he said, and I could sense the relief in his words, even if he was pretending to be blasé about it. The freedom he felt now that he was on a different path. "But the good news is, I eventually found that CI, and before they gave me the boot, I managed to do one last thing." He pulled the folder from under his arm and placed it on the table. "I know you've built the life you want here. You've got the apartment, the dog." He nodded down at Buster, who'd returned to leaning against my leg. "You're enrolled in classes you like. I can't say much about your dating life, but I'm hoping your calendar is still open?" His voice rose to a comical pitch as he lifted his brows.

"It is," I confirmed with a laugh.

He let out a dramatic sigh of relief and opened the folder. "Good. Then all that's left is your freedom. Officially." He slid it across the table with a smile.

I had no idea what he was handing me, but my heart stilled when I saw my name—real name—inked into an official-looking document. I spun the folder around to read the form right side up.

"Congratulations, you're dead," he said with another grin.

My eyes scanned the document in disbelief.

"Well, Erin Daniels is dead," he added.

As he said it, I realized I was looking at an official death certificate—my own death certificate. According to the dates, I'd died the night of the gala heist.

"Word has it you jumped off a bridge trying to land on a freight barge but fell into the water instead. Recovery efforts never found your body or the diamond," he said with a shrug. "Tragic."

I lifted the certificate and held it up to the sun. The proper watermarks were in place, the stamped seal from the county where I'd *died.*

"I understand why you did what you did that night, and I'm hoping we can have a fresh start. This means no one will ever look for you," he said and nodded down at the table. "Erin Daniels doesn't exist anymore."

I was still struggling to form words. He'd erased my past for me. Even after I'd chosen my future over him the night on the bridge, he'd done everything to find me and hand me my freedom. Officially.

"Bray . . ." I whispered, still unable to fully speak.

He stuck his hand out over the table. "Call me Cal. Please."

I startled at his abrupt movement but caught the smile on his face. It pulled me in like a pair of arms. I smiled back and stuck my hand out to slip my palm in his.

"Call me Katherine."

"Nice to meet you, Katherine."

"It's a pleasure," I said with a bubbly laugh. Joy was shooting out of me like it had burst inside and needed to escape. "So, what do you do now that you're not a secret agent hero anymore?"

"I've been trying out a few things here and there. Might get back into music."

"Playing the cello?"

"Sure, why not. Or maybe I'll take up teaching. I've always liked school, and I want to do something with my heart in it, for once."

"This is a good school," I said, hinting he could stick around.

"It is. Nice town too." He smiled at me.

I smiled back, still unable to fully believe he was here. It seemed too good to be true. "What about your mom? Won't she—?"

He shook his head to cut me off. "Don't worry about her. She has come around to letting me follow my heart. In all ways."

A swell of relief hit me. He'd even removed the obstacle of his mother knowing the truth about me. The woman may never fully approve of me, but at least she couldn't send me to prison anymore.

"So, do you have any plans tonight?" he asked.

I shook my head with a hot burn in my cheeks. "Just some homework I have to finish."

He slid out from his side of the table and joined me on mine. His eyes were glued to me, as if nothing else in the world existed. "Good. And after that?"

"I'm free," I said, and bit my lip.

He used his thumb to pull it from my teeth and watched my mouth as he spoke. "For how long?"

I looked into his gray eyes and knew in my bones all was forgiven, we could have a fresh start, and I was one kiss away from having everything I wanted.

"Forever," I said.

"Good. Me too," he said, and then he kissed me like it was the first of many to come.

ACKNOWLEDGMENTS

It feels surreal to be writing acknowledgments for my sixth book! I am so happy this one came back around. I actually started writing it in 2021, right after selling my debut, but the genre mash-up was too odd at the time. We didn't know what to do with it! It took writing THE BIG FIX to realize this book is the same genre—what I call an action-rom-dramedy—and we ended up with the perfect home for it when THE BIG FIX sold.

Thanks, as always, to my agent, Melissa Edwards, for all the support in this wild business and helping my career grow. Here's to the next one!

My editor, Alexandra Sunshine, thank you for your thoughtful feedback on this story, for helping me make it make sense, and for your impressively prompt responses while we both worked under "baby deadlines." I am so grateful to have you on my team!

The team at Kensington, thank you for giving this book a home and all the effort you put into getting my work on readers' radar!

The online book community: Bookstagrammers, BookTokers, reviewers, thank you for hyping my books, posting creative things that make my day, and for creating a happy corner of the internet for book lovers.

All the booksellers and librarians who stock my books and invite me to events, thank you!

My various writing groups and communities, both online and in person, thanks for the support, the cheering, and for always lending an ear as we navigate this wild journey.

My friends and family, as always, thanks for being genuinely excited when I text you news that I can't tell anyone else for months. Thanks for showing up to my events. Thanks for always cheering. Thanks for everything.

My sister-in-law, Leah, thanks for sharing stories from your days nannying, for always answering my texts when I send them with no context other than "book question," and for sending me a map with pin drops to confirm there are in fact apartments in the same neighborhoods as mansions in Silicon Valley.

My parents, thanks for the continuous support and enthusiasm for my wildest dreams.

My little one who was kicking me from the inside every time I sat down to work on finishing this book, I can't wait to watch the story of your life unfold.

My husband, thank you for the brainstorms, the plot-hole conversations, for always cheering, and for going on this great big adventure with me.

Readers, thank you for picking up another one of my books!